Greatest Works of
RABINDRANATH TAGORE

Greatest works of
Rabindranath Tagore

GREATEST WORKS OF RABINDRANATH TAGORE

ALL RIGHTS RESERVED. No part of this book may be reproduced in a retrieval system or transmitted in any form or by any means electronics, mechanical, photocopying, recording and or without permission of the publisher.

Published by

MAPLE PRESS PRIVATE LIMITED
office: A-63, Sector 58, Noida 201301, U.P., India
phone: +91 120 455 3581, 455 3583
email: info@maplepress.co.in
website: www.maplepress.co.in

Reprinted in 2019

ISBN: 978-93-80005-65-2

Contents

The Home & The World	7 – 202
Chapter One	7
Chapter Two	20
Chapter Three	40
Chapter Four	56
Chapter Five	78
Chapter Six	98
Chapter Seven	110
Chapter Eight	123
Chapter Nine	138
Chapter Ten	156
Chapter Eleven	170
Chapter Twelve	184
The Kabuliwallah	203 – 212
Nationalism	213 – 280
Nationalism in the West	213
Nationalism in Japan	237
Nationalism in India	262
The Sunset Of The Century	281 – 282
The Victory	283 – 290
Gitanjali	291 – 337
The Hungry Stones	338 – 349
My Boyhood Days	350 – 400

The Home & The World

Chapter One

Bimala's Story

I

MOTHER, today there comes back to mind the vermilion mark [1] at the parting of your hair, the *sari* [2] which you used to wear, with its wide red border, and those wonderful eyes of yours, full of depth and peace. They came at the start of my life's journey, like the first streak of dawn, giving me golden provision to carry me on my way.

The sky which gives light is blue, and my mother's face was dark, but she had the radiance of holiness, and her beauty would put to shame all the vanity of the beautiful.

Everyone says that I resemble my mother. In my childhood I used to resent this. It made me angry with my mirror. I thought that it was God's unfairness which was wrapped round my limbs—that my dark features were not my due, but had come to me by some misunderstanding. All that remained for me to ask of my God in reparation was, that I might grow up to be a model of what woman should be, as one reads it in some epic poem.

When the proposal came for my marriage, an astrologer was sent, who consulted my palm and said, "This girl has good signs. She will become an ideal wife."

---

1. The mark of Hindu wifehood and the symbol of all the devotion that it implies.
2. The *sari* is the dress of the Hindu woman.

And all the women who heard it said: "No wonder, for she resembles her mother."

I was married into a Rajah's house. When I was a child, I was quite familiar with the description of the Prince of the fairy story. But my husband's face was not of a kind that one's imagination would place in fairyland. It was dark, even as mine was. The feeling of shrinking, which I had about my own lack of physical beauty, was lifted a little; at the same time a touch of regret was left lingering in my heart.

But when the physical appearance evades the scrutiny of our senses and enters the sanctuary of our hearts, then it can forget itself. I know, from my childhood's experience, how devotion is beauty itself, in its inner aspect. When my mother arranged the different fruits, carefully peeled by her own loving hands, on the white stone plate, and gently waved her fan to drive away the flies while my father sat down to his meals, her service would lose itself in a beauty which passed beyond outward forms. Even in my infancy I could feel its power. It transcended all debates, or doubts, or calculations: it was pure music.

I distinctly remember after my marriage, when, early in the morning, I would cautiously and silently get up and take the dust [3] of my husband's feet without waking him, how at such moments I could feel the vermilion mark upon my forehead shining out like the morning star.

One day, he happened to awake, and smiled as he asked me: "What is that, Bimala? What are you doing?"

I can never forget the shame of being detected by him. He might possibly have thought that I was trying to earn merit secretly. But no, no! That had nothing to do with merit. It was my woman's heart, which must worship in order to love.

My father-in-law's house was old in dignity from the days of the *Badshahs*. Some of its manners were of the Moguls and Pathans, some of its customs of Manu and Parashar. But my husband was absolutely

---

3. Taking the dust of the feet is a formal offering of reverence and is done by lightly touching the feet of the revered one and then one's own head with the same hand. The wife does not ordinarily do this to the husband.

modern. He was the first of the house to go through a college course and take his M.A. degree. His elder brother had died young, of drink, and had left no children. My husband did not drink and was not given to dissipation. So foreign to the family was this abstinence, that to many it hardly seemed decent! Purity, they imagined, was only becoming in those on whom fortune had not smiled. It is the moon which has room for stains, not the stars.

My husband's parents had died long ago, and his old grandmother was mistress of the house. My husband was the apple of her eye, the jewel on her bosom. And so he never met with much difficulty in overstepping any of the ancient usages. When he brought in Miss Gilby, to teach me and be my companion, he stuck to his resolve in spite of the poison secreted by all the wagging tongues at home and outside.

My husband had then just got through his B.A. examination and was reading for his M.A. degree; so he had to stay in Calcutta to attend college. He used to write to me almost every day, a few lines only, and simple words, but his bold, round handwriting would look up into my face, oh, so tenderly! I kept his letters in a sandalwood box and covered them every day with the flowers I gathered in the garden.

At that time the Prince of the fairy tale had faded, like the moon in the morning light. I had the Prince of my real world enthroned in my heart. I was his queen. I had my seat by his side. But my real joy was, that my true place was at his feet.

Since then, I have been educated, and introduced to the modern age in its own language, and therefore these words that I write seem to blush with shame in their prose setting. Except for my acquaintance with this modern standard of life, I should know, quite naturally, that just as my being born a woman was not in my own hands, so the element of devotion in woman's love is not like a hackneyed passage quoted from a romantic poem to be piously written down in round hand in a school-girl's copy-book.

But my husband would not give me any opportunity for worship. That was his greatness. They are cowards who claim absolute devotion from their wives as their right; that is a humiliation for both.

His love for me seemed to overflow my limits by its flood of wealth and service. But my necessity was more for giving than for receiving; for love is a vagabond, who can make his flowers bloom in the wayside dust, better than in the crystal jars kept in the drawing-room.

My husband could not break completely with the old-time traditions which prevailed in our family. It was difficult, therefore, for us to meet at any hour of the day we pleased. [4] I knew exactly the time that he could come to me, and therefore our meeting had all the care of loving preparation. It was like the rhyming of a poem; it had to come through the path of the metre.

After finishing the day's work and taking my afternoon bath, I would do up my hair and renew my vermilion mark and put on my *sari*, carefully crinkled; and then, bringing back my body and mind from all distractions of household duties, I would dedicate it at this special hour, with special ceremonies, to one individual. That time, each day, with him was short; but it was infinite.

My husband used to say, that man and wife are equal in love because of their equal claim on each other. I never argued the point with him, but my heart said that devotion never stands in the way of true equality; it only raises the level of the ground of meeting. Therefore the joy of the higher equality remains permanent; it never slides down to the vulgar level of triviality.

My beloved, it was worthy of you that you never expected worship from me. But if you had accepted it, you would have done me a real service. You showed your love by decorating me, by educating me, by giving me what I asked for, and what I did not. I have seen what depth of love there was in your eyes when you gazed at me. I have known the secret sigh of pain you suppressed in your love for me. You loved my body as if it were a flower of paradise. You loved my whole nature as if it had been given you by some rare providence.

Such lavish devotion made me proud to think that the wealth was all my own which drove you to my gate. But vanity such as this only checks

---

4. It would not be reckoned good form for the husband to be continually going into the zenana, except at particular hours for meals or rest.

the flow of free surrender in a woman's love. When I sit on the queen's throne and claim homage, then the claim only goes on magnifying itself; it is never satisfied. Can there be any real happiness for a woman in merely feeling that she has power over a man? To surrender one's pride in devotion is woman's only salvation.

It comes back to me today how, in the days of our happiness, the fires of envy sprung up all around us. That was only natural, for had I not stepped into my good fortune by a mere chance, and without deserving it? But providence does not allow a run of luck to last for ever, unless its debt of honour be fully paid, day by day, through many a long day, and thus made secure. God may grant us gifts, but the merit of being able to take and hold them must be our own. Alas for the boons that slip through unworthy hands!

My husband's grandmother and mother were both renowned for their beauty. And my widowed sister-in-law was also of a beauty rarely to be seen. When, in turn, fate left them desolate, the grandmother vowed she would not insist on having beauty for her remaining grandson when he married. Only the auspicious marks with which I was endowed gained me an entry into this family otherwise, I had no claim to be here.

In this house of luxury, but few of its ladies had received their meed of respect. They had, however, got used to the ways of the family, and managed to keep their heads above water, buoyed up by their dignity as Ranis of an ancient house, in spite of their daily tears being drowned in the foam of wine, and by the tinkle of the "dancing girls" anklets. Was the credit due to me that my husband did not touch liquor, nor squander his manhood in the markets of woman's flesh? What charm did I know to soothe the wild and wandering mind of men? It was my good luck, nothing else. For fate proved utterly callous to my sister-in-law. Her festivity died out, while yet the evening was early, leaving the light of her beauty shining in vain over empty halls—burning and burning, with no accompanying music!

His sister-in-law affected a contempt for my husband's modern notions. How absurd to keep the family ship, laden with all the weight of its time-honoured glory, sailing under the colours of his slip of a girl-wife alone! Often have I felt the lash of scorn. "A thief who had stolen a husband's love!" "A sham hidden in the shamelessness of her new-fangled finery!" The many-coloured garments of modern fashion with which my husband loved to adorn me roused jealous wrath. "Is not she ashamed to make a show-window of herself—and with her looks, too!"

My husband was aware of all this, but his gentleness knew no bounds. He used to implore me to forgive her.

I remember I once told him: "Women's minds are so petty, so crooked!" "Like the feet of Chinese women," he replied. "Has not the pressure of society cramped them into pettiness and crookedness? They are but pawns of the fate which gambles with them. What responsibility have they of their own?"

My sister-in-law never failed to get from my husband whatever she wanted. He did not stop to consider whether her requests were right or reasonable. But what exasperated me most was that she was not grateful for this. I had promised my husband that I would not talk back at her, but this set me raging all the more, inwardly. I used to feel that goodness has a limit, which, if passed, somehow seems to make men cowardly. Shall I tell the whole truth? I have often wished that my husband had the manliness to be a little less good.

My sister-in-law, the Bara Rani, [5] was still young and had no pretensions to saintliness. Rather, her talk and jest and laugh inclined to be forward. The young maids with whom she surrounded herself were also impudent to a degree. But there was none to gainsay her—for was not this the custom of the house? It seemed to me that my good fortune in having a stainless husband was a special eyesore to her. He, however, felt more the sorrow of her lot than the defects of her character.

---

5. *Bara*= Senior; *Chota*= Junior. In joint families of rank, though the widows remain entitled only to a life-interest in their husbands' share, their rank remains to them according to seniority, and the titles "Senior" and "Junior" continue to distinguish the elder and younger branches, even though the junior branch be the one in power.

II

My husband was very eager to take me out of purdah [6]

One day I said to him: "What do I want with the outside world?"

"The outside world may want you," he replied.

"If the outside world has got on so long without me, it may go on for some time longer. It need not pine to death for want of me."

"Let it perish, for all I care! That is not troubling me. I am thinking about myself."

"Oh, indeed. Tell me what about yourself?"

My husband was silent, with a smile.

I knew his way, and protested at once: "No, no, you are not going to run away from me like that! I want to have this out with you."

"Can one ever finish a subject with words?"

"Do stop speaking in riddles. Tell me…"

"What I want is, that I should have you, and you should have me, more fully in the outside world. That is where we are still in debt to each other."

"Is anything wanting, then, in the love we have here at home?"

"Here you are wrapped up in me. You know neither what you have, nor what you want."

"I cannot bear to hear you talk like this."

"I would have you come into the heart of the outer world and meet reality. Merely going on with your household duties, living all your life in the world of household conventions and the drudgery of household tasks—you were not made for that! If we meet, and recognize each other, in the real world, then only will our love be true."

---

6. The seclusion of the zenana, and all the customs peculiar to it, are designated by the general term "Purdah", which means Screen.

"If there be any drawback here to our full recognition of each other, then I have nothing to say. But as for myself, I feel no want."

"Well, even if the drawback is only on my side, why shouldn't you help to remove it?"

Such discussions repeatedly occurred. One day he said: "The greedy man who is fond of his fish stew has no compunction in cutting up the fish according to his need. But the man who loves the fish wants to enjoy it in the water; and if that is impossible he waits on the bank; and even if he comes back home without a sight of it he has the consolation of knowing that the fish is all right. Perfect gain is the best of all; but if that is impossible, then the next best gain is perfect losing."

I never liked the way my husband had of talking on this subject, but that is not the reason why I refused to leave the zenana. His grandmother was still alive. My husband had filled more than a hundred and twenty per cent of the house with the twentieth century, against her taste; but she had borne it uncomplaining. She would have borne it, likewise, if the daughter-in-law [7] of the Rajah's house had left its seclusion. She was even prepared for this happening. But I did not consider it important enough to give her the pain of it. I have read in books that we are called "caged birds". I cannot speak for others, but I had so much in this cage of mine that there was not room for it in the universe—at least that is what I then felt.

The grandmother, in her old age, was very fond of me. At the bottom of her fondness was the thought that, with the conspiracy of favourable stars which attended me, I had been able to attract my husband's love. Were not men naturally inclined to plunge downwards? None of the others, for all their beauty, had been able to prevent their husbands going headlong into the burning depths which consumed and destroyed them. She believed that I had been the means of extinguishing this fire, so deadly to the men of the family. So she kept me in the shelter of her bosom, and trembled if I was in the least bit unwell.

---

7. The prestige of the daughter-in-law is of the first importance in a Hindu household of rank [Trans.].

His grandmother did not like the dresses and ornaments my husband brought from European shops to deck me with. But she reflected: "Men will have some absurd hobby or other, which is sure to be expensive. It is no use trying to check their extravagance; one is glad enough if they stop short of ruin. If my Nikhil had not been busy dressing up his wife there is no knowing whom else he might have spent his money on!" So whenever any new dress of mine arrived she used to send for my husband and make merry over it.

Thus it came about that it was her taste which changed. The influence of the modern age fell so strongly upon her, that her evenings refused to pass if I did not tell her stories out of English books.

After his grandmother's death, my husband wanted me to go and live with him in Calcutta. But I could not bring myself to do that. Was not this our House, which she had kept under her sheltering care through all her trials and troubles? Would not a curse come upon me if I deserted it and went off to town? This was the thought that kept me back, as her empty seat reproachfully looked up at me. That noble lady had come into this house at the age of eight, and had died in her seventy-ninth year. She had not spent a happy life. Fate had hurled shaft after shaft at her breast, only to draw out more and more the imperishable spirit within. This great house was hallowed with her tears. What should I do in the dust of Calcutta, away from it?

My husband's idea was that this would be a good opportunity for leaving to my sister-in-law the consolation of ruling over the household, giving our life, at the same time, more room to branch out in Calcutta. That is just where my difficulty came in. She had worried my life out, she ill brooked my husband's happiness, and for this she was to be rewarded! And what of the day when we should have to come back here? Should I then get back my seat at the head?

"What do you want with that seat?" my husband would say. "Are there not more precious things in life?"

Men never understand these things. They have their nests in the outside world; they little know the whole of what the household stands for. In these matters they ought to follow womanly guidance. Such were my thoughts at that time.

I felt the real point was, that one ought to stand up for one's rights. To go away, and leave everything in the hands of the enemy, would be nothing short of owning defeat.

But why did not my husband compel me to go with him to Calcutta? I know the reason. He did not use his power, just because he had it.

III

IF one had to fill in, little by little, the gap between day and night, it would take an eternity to do it. But the sun rises and the darkness is dispelled—a moment is sufficient to overcome an infinite distance.

One day there came the new era of *Swadeshi* [8] in Bengal; but as to how it happened, we had no distinct vision. There was no gradual slope connecting the past with the present. For that reason, I imagine, the new epoch came in like a flood, breaking down the dykes and sweeping all our prudence and fear before it. We had no time even to think about, or understand, what had happened, or what was about to happen.

My sight and my mind, my hopes and my desires, became red with the passion of this new age. Though, up to this time, the walls of the home—which was the ultimate world to my mind—remained unbroken, yet I stood looking over into the distance, and I heard a voice from the far horizon, whose meaning was not perfectly clear to me, but whose call went straight to my heart.

From the time my husband had been a college student he had been trying to get the things required by our people produced in our own country. There are plenty of date trees in our district. He tried to invent

---

8. The Nationalist movement, which began more as an economic than a political one, having as its main object the encouragement of indigenous industries [Trans.].

an apparatus for extracting the juice and boiling it into sugar and treacle. I heard that it was a great success, only it extracted more money than juice. After a while he came to the conclusion that our attempts at reviving our industries were not succeeding for want of a bank of our own. He was, at the time, trying to teach me political economy. This alone would not have done much harm, but he also took it into his head to teach his countrymen ideas of thrift, so as to pave the way for a bank; and then he actually started a small bank. Its high rate of interest, which made the villagers flock so enthusiastically to put in their money, ended by swamping the bank altogether.

The old officers of the estate felt troubled and frightened. There was jubilation in the enemy's camp. Of all the family, only my husband's grandmother remained unmoved. She would scold me, saying: "Why are you all plaguing him so? Is it the fate of the estate that is worrying you? How many times have I seen this estate in the hands of the court receiver! Are men like women? Men are born spendthrifts and only know how to waste. Look here, child, count yourself fortunate that your husband is not wasting himself as well!"

My husband's list of charities was a long one. He would assist to the bitter end of utter failure anyone who wanted to invent a new loom or rice-husking machine. But what annoyed me most was the way that Sandip Babu [9] used to fleece him on the pretext of *Swadeshi* work. Whenever he wanted to start a newspaper, or travel about preaching the Cause, or take a change of air by the advice of his doctor, my husband would unquestioningly supply him with the money. This was over and above the regular living allowance which Sandip Babu also received from him. The strangest part of it was that my husband and Sandip Babu did not agree in their opinions.

As soon as the *Swadeshi* storm reached my blood, I said to my husband: "I must burn all my foreign clothes."

---

9. "Babu" is a term of respect, like "Father" or "Mister," but has also meant in colonial days a person who understands some English. [on-line ed.]

"Why burn them?" said he. "You need not wear them as long as you please."

"As long as I please! Not in this life …"

"Very well, do not wear them for the rest of your life, then. But why this bonfire business?"

"Would you thwart me in my resolve?"

"What I want to say is this: Why not try to build up something? You should not waste even a tenth part of your energies in this destructive excitement."

"Such excitement will give us the energy to build."

"That is as much as to say, that you cannot light the house unless you set fire to it."

Then there came another trouble. When Miss Gilby first came to our house there was a great flutter, which afterwards calmed down when they got used to her. Now the whole thing was stirred up afresh. I had never bothered myself before as to whether Miss Gilby was European or Indian, but I began to do so now. I said to my husband: "We must get rid of Miss Gilby."

He kept silent.

I talked to him wildly, and he went away sad at heart.

After a fit of weeping, I felt in a more reasonable mood when we met at night. "I cannot," my husband said, "look upon Miss Gilby through a mist of abstraction, just because she is English. Cannot you get over the barrier of her name after such a long acquaintance? Cannot you realize that she loves you?"

I felt a little ashamed and replied with some sharpness: "Let her remain. I am not over anxious to send her away." And Miss Gilby remained.

But one day I was told that she had been insulted by a young fellow on her way to church. This was a boy whom we were supporting. My husband turned him out of the house. There was not a single soul, that day, who could forgive my husband for that act—not even I. This time Miss Gilby left of her own accord. She shed tears when she came to say good-bye, but my mood would not melt. To slander the poor boy so—and such a fine boy, too, who would forget his daily bath and food in his enthusiasm for __Swadeshi_.

My husband escorted Miss Gilby to the railway station in his own carriage. I was sure he was going too far. When exaggerated accounts of the incident gave rise to a public scandal, which found its way to the newspapers, I felt he had been rightly served.

I had often become anxious at my husband's doings, but had never before been ashamed; yet now I had to blush for him! I did not know exactly, nor did I care, what wrong poor Noren might, or might not, have done to Miss Gilby, but the idea of sitting in judgement on such a matter at such a time! I should have refused to damp the spirit which prompted young Noren to defy the Englishwoman. I could not but look upon it as a sign of cowardice in my husband, that he should fail to understand this simple thing. And so I blushed for him.

And yet it was not that my husband refused to support __Swadeshi__, or was in any way against the Cause. Only he had not been able wholeheartedly to accept the spirit of *Bande Mataram* [10]

"I am willing," he said, "to serve my country; but my worship I reserve for Right which is far greater than my country. To worship my country as a god is to bring a curse upon it."

---

10. Lit.: "Hail Mother"; the opening words of a song by Bankim Chatterjee, the famous Bengali novelist. The song has now become the national anthem, and *Bande Mataram* the national cry, since the days of the *Swadeshi* movement [Trans.].

Chapter Two

Bimala's Story

IV

THIS was the time when Sandip Babu with his followers came to our neighbourhood to preach *Swadeshi*.

There is to be a big meeting in our temple pavilion. We women are sitting there, on one side, behind a screen. Triumphant shouts of *Bande Mataram* come nearer: and to them I am thrilling through and through. Suddenly a stream of barefooted youths in turbans, clad in ascetic ochre, rushes into the quadrangle, like a silt-reddened freshet into a dry river-bed at the first burst of the rains. The whole place is filled with an immense crowd, through which Sandip Babu is borne, seated in a big chair hoisted on the shoulders of ten or twelve of the youths.

Bande Mataram! Bande Mataram! Bande Mataram! It seems as though the skies would be rent and scattered into a thousand fragments.

I had seen Sandip Babu's photograph before. There was something in his features which I did not quite like. Not that he was bad-looking— far from it: he had a splendidly handsome face. Yet, I know not why, it seemed to me, in spite of all its brilliance, that too much of base alloy had gone into its making. The light in his eyes somehow did not shine true. That was why I did not like it when my husband unquestioningly gave in to all his demands. I could bear the waste of money; but it vexed me to think that he was imposing on my husband, taking advantage of friendship. His bearing was not that of an ascetic, nor even of a person of moderate means, but foppish all over. Love of comfort seemed to ... any number of such reflections come back to me today, but let them be.

When, however, Sandip Babu began to speak that afternoon, and the hearts of the crowd swayed and surged to his words, as though they would break all bounds, I saw him wonderfully transformed. Especially when his features were suddenly lit up by a shaft of light from the slowly setting sun, as it sunk below the roof-line of the pavilion, he seemed to me to be marked out by the gods as their messenger to mortal men and women.

From beginning to end of his speech, each one of his utterances was a stormy outburst. There was no limit to the confidence of his assurance. I do not know how it happened, but I found I had impatiently pushed away the screen from before me and had fixed my gaze upon him. Yet there was none in that crowd who paid any heed to my doings. Only once, I noticed, his eyes, like stars in fateful Orion, flashed full on my face.

I was utterly unconscious of myself. I was no longer the lady of the Rajah's house, but the sole representative of Bengal's womanhood. And he was the champion of Bengal. As the sky had shed its light over him, so he must receive the consecration of a woman's benediction ...

It seemed clear to me that, since he had caught sight of me, the fire in his words had flamed up more fiercely. Indra's [11] steed refused to be reined in, and there came the roar of thunder and the flash of lightning. I said within myself that his language had caught fire from my eyes; for we women are not only the deities of the household fire, but the flame of the soul itself.

I returned home that evening radiant with a new pride and joy. The storm within me had shifted my whole being from one centre to another. Like the Greek maidens of old, I fain would cut off my long, resplendent tresses to make a bowstring for my hero. Had my outward ornaments been connected with my inner feelings, then my necklet, my armlets,

---
11. The Jupiter Pluvius of Hindu mythology.

my bracelets, would all have burst their bonds and flung themselves over that assembly like a shower of meteors. Only some personal sacrifice, I felt, could help me to bear the tumult of my exaltation.

When my husband came home later, I was trembling lest he should utter a sound out of tune with the triumphant paean which was still ringing in my ears, lest his fanaticism for truth should lead him to express disapproval of anything that had been said that afternoon. For then I should have openly defied and humiliated him. But he did not say a word … which I did not like either.

He should have said: "Sandip has brought me to my senses. I now realize how mistaken I have been all this time."

I somehow felt that he was spitefully silent, that he obstinately refused to be enthusiastic. I asked how long Sandip Babu was going to be with us.

"He is off to Rangpur early tomorrow morning," said my husband.

"Must it be tomorrow?"

"Yes, he is already engaged to speak there."

I was silent for a while and then asked again: "Could he not possibly stay a day longer?"

"That may hardly be possible, but why?"

"I want to invite him to dinner and attend on him myself."

My husband was surprised. He had often entreated me to be present when he had particular friends to dinner, but I had never let myself be persuaded. He gazed at me curiously, in silence, with a look I did not quite understand.

I was suddenly overcome with a sense of shame. "No, no," I exclaimed, "that would never do!"

"Why not!" said he. "I will ask him myself, and if it is at all possible he will surely stay on for tomorrow."

It turned out to be quite possible.

I will tell the exact truth. That day I reproached my Creator because he had not made me surpassingly beautiful—not to steal any heart away, but because beauty is glory. In this great day the men of the country should realize its goddess in its womanhood. But, alas, the eyes of men fail to discern the goddess, if outward beauty be lacking. Would Sandip Babu find the *Shakti* of the Motherland manifest in me? Or would he simply take me to be an ordinary, domestic woman?

That morning I scented my flowing hair and tied it in a loose knot, bound by a cunningly intertwined red silk ribbon. Dinner, you see, was to be served at midday, and there was no time to dry my hair after my bath and do it up plaited in the ordinary way. I put on a gold-bordered white *sari*, and my short-sleeve muslin jacket was also gold-bordered.

I felt that there was a certain restraint about my costume and that nothing could well have been simpler. But my sister-in-law, who happened to be passing by, stopped dead before me, surveyed me from head to foot and with compressed lips smiled a meaning smile. When I asked her the reason, "I am admiring your get-up!" she said.

"What is there so entertaining about it?" I enquired, considerably annoyed.

"It's superb," she said. "I was only thinking that one of those low-necked English bodices would have made it perfect." Not only her mouth and eyes, but her whole body seemed to ripple with suppressed laughter as she left the room.

I was very, very angry, and wanted to change everything and put on my everyday clothes. But I cannot tell exactly why I could not carry out my impulse. Women are the ornaments of society— thus I reasoned with myself—and my husband would never like it, if I appeared before Sandip Babu unworthily clad.

My idea had been to make my appearance after they had sat down to dinner. In the bustle of looking after the serving the first awkwardness would have passed off. But dinner was not ready in time, and it was getting late. Meanwhile my husband had sent for me to introduce the guest.

I was feeling horribly shy about looking Sandip Babu in the face. However, I managed to recover myself enough to say: "I am so sorry dinner is getting late."

He boldly came and sat right beside me as he replied: "I get a dinner of some kind every day, but the Goddess of Plenty keeps behind the scenes. Now that the goddess herself has appeared, it matters little if the dinner lags behind."

He was just as emphatic in his manners as he was in his public speaking. He had no hesitation and seemed to be accustomed to occupy, unchallenged, his chosen seat. He claimed the right to intimacy so confidently, that the blame would seem to belong to those who should dispute it.

I was in terror lest Sandip Babu should take me for a shrinking, old-fashioned bundle of inanity. But, for the life of me, I could not sparkle in repartees such as might charm or dazzle him. What could have possessed me, I angrily wondered, to appear before him in such an absurd way?

I was about to retire when dinner was over, but Sandip Babu, as bold as ever, placed himself in my way.

"You must not," he said, "think me greedy. It was not the dinner that kept me staying on, it was your invitation. If you were to run away now, that would not be playing fair with your guest."

If he had not said these words with a careless ease, they would have been out of tune. But, after all, he was such a great friend of my husband that I was like his sister.

While I was struggling to climb up this high wave of intimacy, my husband came to the rescue, saying: "Why not come back to us after you have taken your dinner?"

"But you must give your word," said Sandip Babu, "before we let you off."

"I will come," said I, with a slight smile.

"Let me tell you," continued Sandip Babu, "why I cannot trust you.

Nikhil has been married these nine years, and all this while you have eluded me. If you do this again for another nine years, we shall never meet again."

I took up the spirit of his remark as I dropped my voice to reply: "Why even then should we not meet?"

"My horoscope tells me I am to die early. None of my forefathers have survived their thirtieth year. I am now twenty-seven."

He knew this would go home. This time there must have been a shade of concern in my low voice as I said: "The blessings of the whole country are sure to avert the evil influence of the stars."

"Then the blessings of the country must be voiced by its goddess. This is the reason for my anxiety that you should return, so that my talisman may begin to work from today."

Sandip Babu had such a way of taking things by storm that I got no opportunity of resenting what I never should have permitted in another.

"So," he concluded with a laugh, "I am going to hold this husband of yours as a hostage till you come back."

As I was coming away, he exclaimed: "May I trouble you for a trifle?"

I started and turned round.

"Don't be alarmed," he said. "It's merely a glass of water. You might have noticed that I did not drink any water with my dinner. I take it a little later."

Upon this I had to make a show of interest and ask him the reason. He began to give the history of his dyspepsia. I was told how he had been a martyr to it for seven months, and how, after the usual course of nuisances, which included different allopathic and homoeopathic misadventures, he had obtained the most wonderful results by indigenous methods.

"Do you know," he added, with a smile, "God has built even my infirmities in such a manner that they yield only under the bombardment of __Swadeshi__ pills."

My husband, at this, broke his silence. "You must confess," said he, "that you have as immense an attraction for foreign medicine as the earth has for meteors. You have three shelves in your sitting-room full of..."

Sandip Babu broke in: "Do you know what they are? They are the punitive police. They come, not because they are wanted, but because they are imposed on us by the rule of this modern age, exacting fines and-inflicting injuries."

My husband could not bear exaggerations, and I could see he disliked this. But all ornaments are exaggerations. They are not made by God, but by man. Once I remember in defence of some untruth of mine I said to my husband: "Only the trees and beasts and birds tell unmitigated truths, because these poor things have not the power to invent. In this men show their superiority to the lower creatures, and women beat even men. Neither is a profusion of ornament unbecoming for a woman, nor a profusion of untruth."

As I came out into the passage leading to the zenana I found my sister-in-law, standing near a window overlooking the reception rooms, peeping through the venetian shutter.

"You here?" I asked in surprise.

"Eavesdropping!" she replied.

V

When I returned, Sandip Babu was tenderly apologetic. "I am afraid we have spoilt your appetite," he said.

I felt greatly ashamed. Indeed, I had been too indecently quick over my dinner. With a little calculation, it would become quite evident that my non-eating had surpassed the eating. But I had no idea that anyone could have been deliberately calculating.

I suppose Sandip Babu detected my feeling of shame, which only augmented it. "I was sure," he said, "that you had the impulse of the wild deer to run away, but it is a great boon that you took the trouble to keep your promise with me."

I could not think of any suitable reply and so I sat down, blushing and uncomfortable, at one end of the sofa. The vision that I had of myself, as the __Shakti__ of Womanhood, incarnate, crowning Sandip Babu simply with my presence, majestic and unashamed, failed me altogether.

Sandip Babu deliberately started a discussion with my husband. He knew that his keen wit flashed to the best effect in an argument. I have often since observed, that he never lost an opportunity for a passage at arms whenever I happened to be present.

He was familiar with my husband's views on the cult of __Bande Mataram__, and began in a provoking way: "So you do not allow that there is room for an appeal to the imagination in patriotic work?"

"It has its place, Sandip, I admit, but I do not believe in giving it the whole place. I would know my country in its frank reality, and for this I am both afraid and ashamed to make use of hypnotic texts of patriotism."

"What you call hypnotic texts I call truth. I truly believe my country to be my God. I worship Humanity. God manifests Himself both in man and in his country."

"If that is what you really believe, there should be no difference for you between man and man, and so between country and country."

"Quite true. But my powers are limited, so my worship of Humanity is continued in the worship of my country."

"I have nothing against your worship as such, but how is it you propose to conduct your worship of God by hating other countries in which He is equally manifest?"

"Hate is also an adjunct of worship. Arjuna won Mahadeva's favour by wrestling with him. God will be with us in the end, if we are prepared to give Him battle."

"If that be so, then those who are serving and those who are harming the country are both His devotees. Why, then, trouble to preach patriotism?"

"In the case of one's own country, it is different. There the heart clearly demands worship."

"If you push the same argument further you can say that since God is manifested in us, our __self__ has to be worshipped before all else; because our natural instinct claims it."

"Look here, Nikhil, this is all merely dry logic. Can't you recognize that there is such a thing as feeling?"

"I tell you the truth, Sandip," my husband replied. "It is my feelings that are outraged, whenever you try to pass off injustice as a duty, and unrighteousness as a moral ideal. The fact, that I am incapable of stealing, is not due to my possessing logical faculties, but to my having some feeling of respect for myself and love for ideals."

I was raging inwardly. At last I could keep silent no longer.

"Is not the history of every country," I cried, "whether England, France, Germany, or Russia, the history of stealing for the sake of one's own country?"

"They have to answer for these thefts; they are doing so even now; their history is not yet ended."

"At any rate," interposed Sandip Babu, "why should we not follow suit? Let us first fill our country's coffers with stolen goods and then take centuries, like these other countries, to answer for them, if we must. But, I ask you, where do you find this 'answering' in history?"

"When Rome was answering for her sin no one knew it. All that time, there was apparently no limit to her prosperity. But do you not see one thing: how these political bags of theirs are bursting with lies and treacheries, breaking their backs under their weight?"

Never before had I had any opportunity of being present at a discussion between my husband and his men friends. Whenever he argued with me I could feel his reluctance to push me into a corner. This arose out of the very love he bore me. Today for the first time I saw his fencer's skill in debate.

Nevertheless, my heart refused to accept my husband's position.

I was struggling to find some answer, but it would not come.

When the word "righteousness" comes into an argument, it sounds ugly to say that a thing can be too good to be useful.

All of a sudden Sandip Babu turned to me with the question: "What do __you__ say to this?"

"I do not care about fine distinctions," I broke out. "I will tell you broadly what I feel. I am only human. I am covetous. I would have good things for my country. If I am obliged, I would snatch them and filch them. I have anger. I would be angry for my country's sake. If necessary, I would smite and slay to avenge her insults. I have my desire to be fascinated, and fascination must be supplied to me in bodily shape by my country. She must have some visible symbol casting its spell upon my mind. I would make my country a Person, and call her Mother, Goddess, Durga—for whom I would redden the earth with sacrificial offerings. I am human, not divine."

Sandip Babu leapt to his feet with uplifted arms and shouted "Hurrah!"—The next moment he corrected himself and cried: "__ Bande Mataram__."

A shadow of pain passed over the face of my husband. He said to me in a very gentle voice: "Neither am I divine: I am human. And therefore I dare not permit the evil which is in me to be exaggerated into an image of my country—never, never!"

Sandip Babu cried out: "See, Nikhil, how in the heart of a woman Truth takes flesh and blood. Woman knows how to be cruel: her virulence is like a blind storm. It is beautifully fearful. In man it is ugly, because it harbours in its centre the gnawing worms of reason and thought. I tell you, Nikhil, it is our women who will save the country. This is not the time for nice scruples. We must be unswervingly, unreasoningly brutal. We must sin. We must give our women red sandal paste with which to anoint and enthrone our sin. Don't you remember what the poet says:

/*

Come, Sin, O beautiful Sin,

Let thy stinging red kisses pour down fiery red wine into our blood.
Sound the trumpet of imperious evil
And cross our forehead with the wreath of exulting lawlessness,
O Deity of Desecration,
Smear our breasts with the blackest mud of disrepute,
　unashamed.
*/

Down with that righteousness, which cannot smilingly bring rack and ruin."

When Sandip Babu, standing with his head high, insulted at a moment's impulse all that men have cherished as their highest, in all countries and in all times, a shiver went right through my body.

But, with a stamp of his foot, he continued his declamation: "I can see that you are that beautiful spirit of fire, which burns the home to ashes and lights up the larger world with its flame. Give to us the indomitable courage to go to the bottom of Ruin itself. Impart grace to all that is baneful."

It was not clear to whom Sandip Babu addressed his last appeal. It might have been She whom he worshipped with his __Bande Mataram__. It might have been the Womanhood of his country. Or it might have been its representative, the woman before him. He would have gone further in the same strain, but my husband suddenly rose from his seat and touched him lightly on the shoulder saying: "Sandip, Chandranath Babu is here."

I started and turned round, to find an aged gentleman at the door, calm and dignified, in doubt as to whether he should come in or retire. His face was touched with a gentle light like that of the setting sun.

My husband came up to me and whispered: "This is my master, of whom I have so often told you. Make your obeisance to him."

I bent reverently and took the dust of his feet. He gave me his blessing saying: "May God protect you always, my little mother." I was sorely in need of such a blessing at that moment.

Nikhil's Story

I

One day I had the faith to believe that I should be able to bear whatever came from my God. I never had the trial. Now I think it has come.

I used to test my strength of mind by imagining all kinds of evil which might happen to me—poverty, imprisonment, dishonour, death—even Bimala's. And when I said to myself that I should be able to receive these with firmness, I am sure I did not exaggerate. Only I could never even imagine one thing, and today it is that of which I am thinking, and wondering whether I can really bear it. There is a thorn somewhere pricking in my heart, constantly giving me pain while I am about my daily work. It seems to persist even when I am asleep. The very moment I wake up in the morning, I find that the bloom has gone from the face of the sky. What is it? What has happened?

My mind has become so sensitive, that even my past life, which came to me in the disguise of happiness, seems to wring my very heart with its falsehood; and the shame and sorrow which are coming close to me are losing their cover of privacy, all the more because they try to veil their faces. My heart has become all eyes. The things that should not be seen, the things I do not want to see—these I must see.

The day has come at last when my ill-starred life has to reveal its destitution in a long-drawn series of exposures. This penury, all unexpected, has taken its seat in the heart where plenitude seemed to reign. The fees which I paid to delusion for just nine years of my youth have now to be returned with interest to Truth till the end of my days.

What is the use of straining to keep up my pride? What harm if I confess that I have something lacking in me? Possibly it is that unreasoning forcefulness which women love to find in men. But is strength mere display of muscularity? Must strength have no scruples in treading the weak underfoot?

But why all these arguments? Worthiness cannot be earned merely by disputing about it. And I am unworthy, unworthy, unworthy.

What if I am unworthy? The true value of love is this, that it can ever bless the unworthy with its own prodigality. For the worthy there are many rewards on God's earth, but God has specially reserved love for the unworthy.

Up till now Bimala was my home-made Bimala, the product of the confined space and the daily routine of small duties. Did the love which I received from her, I asked myself, come from the deep spring of her heart, or was it merely like the daily provision of pipe water pumped up by the municipal steam-engine of society?

I longed to find Bimala blossoming fully in all her truth and power. But the thing I forgot to calculate was, that one must give up all claims based on conventional rights, if one would find a person freely revealed in truth.

Why did I fail to think of this? Was it because of the husband's pride of possession over his wife? No. It was because I placed the fullest trust upon love. I was vain enough to think that I had the power in me to bear the sight of truth in its awful nakedness. It was tempting Providence, but still I clung to my proud determination to come out victorious in the trial.

Bimala had failed to understand me in one thing. She could not fully realize that I held as weakness all imposition of force. Only the weak dare not be just. They shirk their responsibility of fairness and try quickly to get at results through the short- cuts of injustice. Bimala has no patience with patience. She loves to find in men the turbulent, the angry, the unjust. Her respect must have its element of fear.

I had hoped that when Bimala found herself free in the outer world she would be rescued from her infatuation for tyranny. But now I feel sure that this infatuation is deep down in her nature. Her love is for the boisterous. From the tip of her tongue to the pit of her stomach she must tingle with red pepper in order to enjoy the simple fare of life. But my determination was, never to do my duty with frantic impetuosity, helped on by the fiery liquor of excitement. I know Bimala finds it difficult to respect me for this, taking my scruples for feebleness—and she is quite angry with me because I am not running amuck crying __Bande Mataram__.

For the matter of that, I have become unpopular with all my countrymen because I have not joined them in their carousals. They are certain that either I have a longing for some title, or else that I am afraid of the police. The police on their side suspect me of harbouring some hidden design and protesting too much in my mildness.

What I really feel is this, that those who cannot find food for their enthusiasm in a knowledge of their country as it actually is, or those who cannot love men just because they are men—who needs must shout and deify their country in order to keep up their excitement—these love excitement more than their country.

To try to give our infatuation a higher place than Truth is a sign of inherent slavishness. Where our minds are free we find ourselves lost. Our moribund vitality must have for its rider either some fantasy, or someone in authority, or a sanction from the pundits, in order to make it move. So long as we are impervious to truth and have to be moved by some hypnotic stimulus, we must know that we lack the capacity for self-government. Whatever may be our condition, we shall either need some imaginary ghost or some actual medicine-man to terrorize over us.

The other day when Sandip accused me of lack of imagination, saying that this prevented me from realizing my country in a visible image, Bimala agreed with him. I did not say anything in my defence, because to win in argument does not lead to happiness. Her difference of opinion is not due to any inequality of intelligence, but rather to dissimilarity of nature.

They accuse me of being unimaginative—that is, according to them, I may have oil in my lamp, but no flame. Now this is exactly the accusation which I bring against them. I would say to them: "You are dark, even as the flints are. You must come to violent conflicts and make a noise in order to produce your sparks. But their disconnected flashes merely assist your pride, and not your clear vision."

I have been noticing for some time that there is a gross cupidity about Sandip. His fleshly feelings make him harbour delusions about his religion and impel him into a tyrannical attitude in his patriotism. His intellect is keen, but his nature is coarse, and so he glorifies his selfish lusts under high-sounding names. The cheap consolations of hatred are as urgently necessary for him as the satisfaction of his appetites. Bimala has often warned me, in the old days, of his hankering after money. I understood this, but I could not bring myself to haggle with Sandip. I felt ashamed even to own to myself that he was trying to take advantage of me.

It will, however, be difficult to explain to Bimala today that Sandip's love of country is but a different phase of his covetous self-love. Bimala's hero-worship of Sandip makes me hesitate all the more to talk to her about him, lest some touch of jealousy may lead me unwittingly into exaggeration. It may be that the pain at my heart is already making me see a distorted picture of Sandip. And yet it is better perhaps to speak out than to keep my feelings gnawing within me.

II

I have known my master these thirty years. Neither calumny, nor disaster, nor death itself has any terrors for him. Nothing could have saved me, born as I was into the traditions of this family of ours, but that he has established his own life in the centre of mine, with its peace and truth and spiritual vision, thus making it possible for me to realize goodness in its truth.

My master came to me that day and said: "Is it necessary to detain Sandip here any longer?"

His nature was so sensitive to all omens of evil that he had at once understood. He was not easily moved, but that day he felt the dark shadow of trouble ahead. Do I not know how well he loves me?

At tea-time I said to Sandip: "I have just had a letter from Rangpur. They are complaining that I am selfishly detaining you. When will you be going there?"

Bimala was pouring out the tea. Her face fell at once. She threw just one enquiring glance at Sandip.

"I have been thinking," said Sandip, "that this wandering up and down means a tremendous waste of energy. I feel that if I could work from a centre I could achieve more permanent results."

With this he looked up at Bimala and asked: "Do you not think so too?"

Bimala hesitated for a reply and then said: "Both ways seem good—to do the work from a centre, as well as by travelling about. That in which you find greater satisfaction is the way for you."

"Then let me speak out my mind," said Sandip. "I have never yet found any one source of inspiration suffice me for good. That is why I have been constantly moving about, rousing enthusiasm in the people, from which in turn I draw my own store of energy. Today you have given me the message of my country. Such fire I have never beheld in any man. I shall be able to spread the fire of enthusiasm in my country by borrowing it from you. No, do not be ashamed. You are far above all modesty and diffidence. You are the Queen Bee of our hive, and we the workers shall rally around you. You shall be our centre, our inspiration."

Bimala flushed all over with bashful pride and her hand shook as she went on pouring out the tea.

Another day my master came to me and said: "Why don't you two go up to Darjeeling for a change? You are not looking well. Have you been getting enough sleep?"

I asked Bimala in the evening whether she would care to have a trip to the Hills. I knew she had a great longing to see the Himalayas. But she refused ... The country's Cause, I suppose!

I must not lose my faith: I shall wait. The passage from the narrow to the larger world is stormy. When she is familiar with this freedom, then I shall know where my place is. If I discover that I do not fit in with the arrangement of the outer world, then I shall not quarrel with my fate, but silently take my leave ... Use force? But for what? Can force prevail against Truth?

Sandip's Story

I

The impotent man says: "That which has come to my share is mine." And the weak man assents. But the lesson of the whole world is: "That is really mine which I can snatch away." My country does not become mine simply because it is the country of my birth. It becomes mine on the day when I am able to win it by force.

Every man has a natural right to possess, and therefore greed is natural. It is not in the wisdom of nature that we should be content to be deprived. What my mind covets, my surroundings must supply. This is the only true understanding between our inner and outer nature in this world. Let moral ideals remain merely for those poor anaemic creatures of starved desire whose grasp is weak. Those who can desire with all their soul and enjoy with all their heart, those who have no hesitation or scruple, it is they who are the anointed of Providence. Nature spreads out her riches and loveliest treasures for their benefit. They swim across streams, leap over walls, kick open doors, to help themselves to whatever is worth taking. In such a getting one can rejoice; such wresting as this gives value to the thing taken.

Nature surrenders herself, but only to the robber. For she delights in this forceful desire, this forceful abduction. And so she does not put the garland of her acceptance round the lean, scraggy neck of the ascetic. The music of the wedding march is struck. The time of the wedding I must not let pass. My heart therefore is eager. For, who is the bridegroom? It is I. The bridegroom's place belongs to him who, torch in hand, can come in time. The bridegroom in Nature's wedding hall comes unexpected and uninvited.

Ashamed? No, I am never ashamed! I ask for whatever I want, and I do not always wait to ask before I take it. Those who are deprived by their own diffidence dignify their privation by the name of modesty. The world into which we are born is the world of reality. When a man goes away from the market of real things with empty hands and empty stomach, merely filling his bag with big sounding words, I wonder why he ever came into this hard world at all. Did these men get their appointment from the epicures of the religious world, to play set tunes on sweet, pious texts in that pleasure garden where blossom airy nothings? I neither affect those tunes nor do I find any sustenance in those blossoms.

What I desire, I desire positively, superlatively. I want to knead it with both my hands and both my feet; I want to smear it all over my body; I want to gorge myself with it to the full. The scrannel pipes of those who have worn themselves out by their moral fastings, till they have become flat and pale like starved vermin infesting a long-deserted bed, will never reach my ear.

I would conceal nothing, because that would be cowardly. But if I cannot bring myself to conceal when concealment is needful, that also is cowardly. Because you have your greed, you build your walls. Because I have my greed, I break through them. You use your power: I use my craft. These are the realities of life. On these depend kingdoms and empires and all the great enterprises of men.

As for those __avatars__ who come down from their paradise to talk to us in some holy jargon—their words are not real. Therefore, in spite of all the applause they get, these sayings of theirs only find a place in the hiding corners of the weak.

They are despised by those who are strong, the rulers of the world. Those who have had the courage to see this have won success, while those poor wretches who are dragged one way by nature and the other way by these ava tars, they set one foot in the boat of the real and the other in the boat of the unreal, and thus are in a pitiable plight, able neither to advance nor to keep their place.

There are many men who seem to have been born only with an obsession to die. Possibly there is a beauty, like that of a sunset, in this lingering death in life which seems to fascinate them. Nikhil lives this kind of life, if life it may be called. Years ago, I had a great argument with him on this point.

"It is true," he said, "that you cannot get anything except by force. But then what is this force? And then also, what is this getting? The strength I believe in is the strength of renouncing."

"So you," I exclaimed, "are infatuated with the glory of bankruptcy."

"Just as desperately as the chick is infatuated about the bankruptcy of its shell," he replied. "The shell is real enough, yet it is given up in exchange for intangible light and air. A sorry exchange, I suppose you would call it?"

When once Nikhil gets on to metaphor, there is no hope of making him see that he is merely dealing with words, not with realities. Well, well, let him be happy with his metaphors. We are the flesh-eaters of the world; we have teeth and nails; we pursue and grab and tear. We are not satisfied with chewing in the evening the cud of the grass we have eaten in the morning. Anyhow, we cannot allow your metaphor-mongers to bar the door to our sustenance. In that case we shall simply steal or rob, for we must live.

People will say that I am starting some novel theory just because those who are moving in this world are in the habit of talking differently though they are really acting up to it all the time. Therefore they fail to understand, as I do, that this is the only working moral principle. In point of fact, I know that my idea is not an empty theory at all, for it has been proved in practical life. I have found that my way always wins over the hearts of women, who are creatures of this world of reality and do not roam about in cloud-land, as men do, in idea-filled balloons.

Women find in my features, my manner, my gait, my speech, a masterful passion—not a passion dried thin with the heat of asceticism, not a passion with its face turned back at every step in doubt and debate, but a full-blooded passion. It roars and rolls on, like a flood, with the cry: "I want, I want, I want." Women feel, in their own heart of hearts, that this indomitable passion is the lifeblood of the world, acknowledging no law but itself, and therefore victorious. For this reason they have so often abandoned themselves to be swept away on the flood-tide of my passion, recking naught as to whether it takes them to life or to death. This power which wins these women is the power of mighty men, the power which wins the world of reality.

Those who imagine the greater desirability of another world merely shift their desires from the earth to the skies. It remains to be seen how high their gushing fountain will play, and for how long. But this much is certain: women were not created for these pale creatures—these lotus-eaters of idealism.

"Affinity!" When it suited my need, I have often said that God has created special pairs of men and women, and that the union of such is the only legitimate union, higher than all unions made by law. The reason of it is, that though man wants to follow nature, he can find no pleasure in it unless he screens himself with some phrase—and that is why this world is so overflowing with lies.

"Affinity!" Why should there be only one? There may be affinity with thousands. It was never in my agreement with nature that I should overlook all my innumerable affinities for the sake of only one. I have discovered many in my own life up to now, yet that has not closed the door to one more—and that one is clearly visible to my eyes. She has also discovered her own affinity to me.

And then?

Then, if I do not win I am a coward.

Chapter Three

Bimala's Story

VI

I WONDER what could have happened to my feeling of shame. The fact is, I had no time to think about myself. My days and nights were passing in a whirl, like an eddy with myself in the centre. No gap was left for hesitation or delicacy to enter.

One day my sister-in-law remarked to my husband: "Up to now the women of this house have been kept weeping. Here comes the men's turn.

"We must see that they do not miss it," she continued, turning to me. "I see you are out for the fray, Chota [12] Rani! Hurl your shafts straight at their hearts."

Her keen eyes looked me up and down. Not one of the colours into which my toilet, my dress, my manners, my speech, had blossomed out had escaped her. I am ashamed to speak of it today, but I felt no shame then. Something within me was at work of which I was not even conscious. I used to overdress, it is true, but more like an automaton, with no particular design. No doubt I knew which effort of mine would prove specially pleasing to Sandip Babu, but that required no intuition, for he would discuss it openly before all of them.

---

12. Bimala. the younger brother's wife, was the __Chota__ or Junior Rani.

One day he said to my husband: "Do you know, Nikhil, when I first saw our Queen Bee, she was sitting there so demurely in her gold-bordered _sari_. Her eyes were gazing inquiringly into space, like stars which had lost their way, just as if she had been for ages standing on the edge of some darkness, looking out for something unknown. But when I saw her, I felt a quiver run through me. It seemed to me that the gold border of her _sari_ was her own inner fire flaming out and twining round her. That is the flame we want, visible fire! Look here, Queen Bee, you really must do us the favour of dressing once more as a living flame."

So long I had been like a small river at the border of a village. My rhythm and my language were different from what they are now. But the tide came up from the sea, and my breast heaved; my banks gave way and the great drumbeats of the sea waves echoed in my mad current. I could not understand the meaning of that sound in my blood. Where was that former self of mine? Whence came foaming into me this surging flood of glory? Sandip's hungry eyes burnt like the lamps of worship before my shrine. All his gaze proclaimed that I was a wonder in beauty and power; and the loudness of his praise, spoken and unspoken, drowned all other voices in my world. Had the Creator created me afresh, I wondered? Did he wish to make up now for neglecting me so long? I who before was plain had become suddenly beautiful. I who before had been of no account now felt in myself all the splendour of Bengal itself.

For Sandip Babu was not a mere individual. In him was the confluence of millions of minds of the country. When he called me the Queen Bee of the hive, I was acclaimed with a chorus of praise by all our patriot workers. After that, the loud jests of my sister-in-law could not touch me any longer. My relations with all the world underwent a change. Sandip Babu made it clear how all the country was in need of me. I had no difficulty in believing this at the time, for I felt that I had the power to do everything. Divine strength had come to me. It was something which I had never felt before, which was beyond myself. I had no time to question it to find out what was its nature. It seemed to belong to me, and yet to transcend me. It comprehended the whole of Bengal.

Sandip Babu would consult me about every little thing touching the Cause. At first I felt very awkward and would hang back, but that soon wore off. Whatever I suggested seemed to astonish him. He would go into raptures and say: "Men can only think. You women have a way of understanding without thinking. Woman was created out of God's own fancy. Man, He had to hammer into shape."

Letters used to come to Sandip Babu from all parts of the country which were submitted to me for my opinion. Occasionally he disagreed with me. But I would not argue with him. Then after a day or two—as if a new light had suddenly dawned upon him—he would send for me and say: "It was my mistake. Your suggestion was the correct one." He would often confess to me that wherever he had taken steps contrary to my advice he had gone wrong. Thus I gradually came to be convinced that behind whatever was taking place was Sandip Babu, and behind Sandip Babu was the plain common sense of a woman. The glory of a great responsibility filled my being.

My husband had no place in our counsels. Sandip Babu treated him as a younger brother, of whom personally one may be very fond and yet have no use for his business advice. He would tenderly and smilingly talk about my husband's childlike innocence, saying that his curious doctrine and perversities of mind had a flavour of humour which made them all the more lovable. It was seemingly this very affection for Nikhil which led Sandip Babu to forbear from troubling him with the burden of the country.

Nature has many anodynes in her pharmacy, which she secretly administers when vital relations are being insidiously severed, so that none may know of the operation, till at last one awakes to know what a great rent has been made. When the knife was busy with my life's most intimate tie, my mind was so clouded with fumes of intoxicating gas that I was not in the least aware of what a cruel thing was happening. Possibly this is woman's nature. When her passion is roused she loses her sensibility for all that is outside it. When, like the river, we women keep to our banks, we give nourishment with all that we have: when we overflow them we destroy with all that we are.

Sandip's Story

II

I can see that something has gone wrong. I got an inkling of it the other day.

Ever since my arrival, Nikhil's sitting-room had become a thing amphibious—half women's apartment, half men's: Bimala had access to it from the zenana, it was not barred to me from the outer side. If we had only gone slow, and made use of our privileges with some restraint, we might not have fallen foul of other people. But we went ahead so vehemently that we could not think of the consequences.

Whenever Bee comes into Nikhil's room, I somehow get to know of it from mine. There are the tinkle of bangles and other little sounds; the door is perhaps shut with a shade of unnecessary vehemence; the bookcase is a trifle stiff and creaks if jerked open. When I enter I find Bee, with her back to the door, ever so busy selecting a book from the shelves. And as I offer to assist her in this difficult task she starts and protests; and then we naturally get on to other topics.

The other day, on an inauspicious [13] Thursday afternoon, I sallied forth from my room at the call of these same sounds. There was a man on guard in the passage. I walked on without so much as glancing at him, but as I approached the door he put himself in my way saying: "Not that way, sir."

"Not that way! Why?"

"The Rani Mother is there."

"Oh, very well. Tell your Rani Mother that Sandip Babu wants to see her."

"That cannot be, sir. It is against orders."

I felt highly indignant. "I order you!" I said in a raised voice. "Go and announce me."

---
13. According to the Hindu calendar [Trans.].

The fellow was somewhat taken aback at my attitude. In the meantime I had neared the door. I was on the point of reaching it, when he followed after me and took me by the arm saying: "No, sir, you must not."

What! To be touched by a flunkey! I snatched away my arm and gave the man a sounding blow. At this moment Bee came out of the room to find the man about to insult me.

I shall never forget the picture of her wrath! That Bee is beautiful is a discovery of my own. Most of our people would see nothing in her. Her tall, slim figure these boors would call "lanky". But it is just this lithesomeness of hers that I admire—like an up-leaping fountain of life, coming direct out of the depths of the Creator's heart. Her complexion is dark, but it is the lustrous darkness of a sword-blade, keen and scintillating.

"Nanku!" she commanded, as she stood in the doorway, pointing with her finger, "leave us."

"Do not be angry with him," said I. "If it is against orders, it is I who should retire."

Bee's voice was still trembling as she replied: "You must not go. Come in."

It was not a request, but again a command! I followed her in, and taking a chair fanned myself with a fan which was on the table. Bee scribbled something with a pencil on a sheet of paper and, summoning a servant, handed it to him saying: "Take this to the Maharaja."

"Forgive me," I resumed. "I was unable to control myself, and hit that man of yours."

"You served him right," said Bee.

"But it was not the poor fellow's fault, after all. He was only obeying his orders."

Here Nikhil came in, and as he did so I left my seat with a rapid movement and went and stood near the window with my back to the room.

"Nanku, the guard, has insulted Sandip Babu," said Bee to Nikhil.

Nikhil seemed to be so genuinely surprised that I had to turn round and stare at him. Even an outrageously good man fails in keeping up his pride of truthfulness before his wife—if she be the proper kind of woman.

"He insolently stood in the way when Sandip Babu was coming in here," continued Bee. "He said he had orders ..."

"Whose orders?" asked Nikhil.

"How am I to know?" exclaimed Bee impatiently, her eyes brimming over with mortification.

Nikhil sent for the man and questioned him. "It was not my fault," Nanku repeated sullenly. "I had my orders."

"Who gave you the order?"

"The Bara Rani Mother."

We were all silent for a while. After the man had left, Bee said: "Nanku must go!"

Nikhil remained silent. I could see that his sense of justice would not allow this. There was no end to his qualms. But this time he was up against a tough problem. Bee was not the woman to take things lying down. She would have to get even with her sister-in-law by punishing this fellow. And as Nikhil remained silent, her eyes flashed fire. She knew not how to pour her scorn upon her husband's feebleness of spirit. Nikhil left the room after a while without another word.

The next day Nanku was not to be seen. On inquiry, I learnt that he had been sent off to some other part of the estates, and that his wages had not suffered by such transfer.

I could catch glimpses of the ravages of the storm raging over this, behind the scenes. All I can say is, that Nikhil is a curious creature, quite out of the common.

The upshot was, that after this Bee began to send for me to the sitting-room, for a chat, without any contrivance, or pretence of its being an accident. Thus from bare suggestion we came to broad hint: the implied came to be expressed. The daughter-in- law of a princely house lives in a starry region so remote from the ordinary outsider that there is not even a regular road for his approach. What a triumphal progress of Truth was this which, gradually but persistently, thrust aside veil after veil of obscuring custom, till at length Nature herself was laid bare.

Truth? Of course it was the truth! The attraction of man and woman for each other is fundamental. The whole world of matter, from the speck of dust upwards, is ranged on its side. And yet men would keep it hidden away out of sight, behind a tissue of words; and with home-made sanctions and prohibitions make of it a domestic utensil. Why, it's as absurd as melting down the solar system to make a watch-chain for one's son-in-law! [14]

When, in spite of all, reality awakes at the call of what is but naked truth, what a gnashing of teeth and beating of breasts is there! But can one carry on a quarrel with a storm? It never takes the trouble to reply, it only gives a shaking.

I am enjoying the sight of this truth, as it gradually reveals itself. These tremblings of steps, these turnings of the face, are sweet to me: and sweet are the deceptions which deceive not only others, but also Bee herself. When Reality has to meet the unreal, deception is its principal weapon; for its enemies always try to shame Reality by calling it gross, and so it needs must hide itself, or else put on some disguise. The circumstances are such that it dare not frankly avow: "Yes, I am gross, because I am true. I am flesh. I am passion. I am hunger, unashamed and cruel."

All is now clear to me. The curtain flaps, and through it I can see the preparations for the catastrophe. The little red ribbon, which peeps through the luxuriant masses of her hair, with its flush of secret longing, it is the lolling tongue of the red storm cloud. I feel the warmth of each turn of her __sari__, each suggestion of her raiment, of which even the wearer may not be fully conscious.

---

14. The son-in-law is the pet of a Hindu household.

Bee was not conscious, because she was ashamed of the reality; to which men have given a bad name, calling it Satan; and so it has to steal into the garden of paradise in the guise of a snake, and whisper secrets into the ears of man's chosen consort and make her rebellious; then farewell to all ease; and after that comes death!

My poor little Queen Bee is living in a dream. She knows not which way she is treading. It would not be safe to awaken her before the time. It is best for me to pretend to be equally unconscious.

The other day, at dinner, she was gazing at me in a curious sort of way, little realizing what such glances mean! As my eyes met hers, she turned away with a flush. "You are surprised at my appetite," I remarked. "I can hide everything, except that I am greedy! Anyhow, why trouble to blush for me, since I am shameless?"

This only made her colour more furiously, as she stammered: "No, no, I was only..."

"I know," I interrupted. "Women have a weakness for greedy men; for it is this greed of ours which gives them the upper hand. The indulgence which I have always received at their hands has made me all the more shameless. I do not mind your watching the good things disappear, not one bit. I mean to enjoy every one of them."

The other day I was reading an English book in which sex-problems were treated in an audaciously realistic manner. I had left it lying in the sitting-room. As I went there the next afternoon, for something or other, I found Bee seated with this book in her hand. When she heard my footsteps she hurriedly put it down and placed another book over it—a volume of Mrs. Hemans's poems.

"I have never been able to make out," I began, "why women are so shy about being caught reading poetry. We men—lawyers, mechanics, or what not—may well feel ashamed. If we must read poetry, it should be at dead of night, within closed doors. But you women are so akin to poesy. The Creator Himself is a lyric poet, and Jayadeva [15] must have practised the divine art seated at His feet."

Bee made no reply, but only blushed uncomfortably. She made as if she would leave the room. Whereupon I protested: "No, no, pray read on. I will just take a book I left here, and run away." With which I took up my book from the table. "Lucky you did not think of glancing over its pages," I continued, "or you would have wanted to chastise me."

"Indeed! Why?" asked Bee.

"Because it is not poetry," said I. "Only blunt things, bluntly put, without any finicking niceness. I wish Nikhil would read it."

Bee frowned a little as she murmured: "What makes you wish that?"

"He is a man, you see, one of us. My only quarrel with him is that he delights in a misty vision of this world. Have you not observed how this trait of his makes him look on __Swadeshi__ as if it was some poem of which the metre must be kept correct at every step? We, with the clubs of our prose, are the iconoclasts of metre."

"What has your book to do with __Swadeshi__?"

"You would know if you only read it. Nikhil wants to go by made-up maxims, in __Swadeshi__ as in everything else; so he knocks up against human nature at every turn, and then falls to abusing it. He never will realize that human nature was created long before phrases were, and will survive them too."

Bee was silent for a while and then gravely said: "Is it not a part of human nature to try and rise superior to itself?"

I smiled inwardly. "These are not your words", I thought to myself. "You have learnt them from Nikhil. You are a healthy human being. Your flesh and blood have responded to the call of reality. You are burning in every vein with life-fire—do I not know it? How long should they keep you cool with the wet towel of moral precepts?"

"The weak are in the majority," I said aloud. "They are continually poisoning the ears of men by repeating these shibboleths. Nature has

---

15. A Vaishnava poet (Sanskrit) whose lyrics of the adoration of the Divinity serve as well to express all shades of human passion [Trans.].

denied them strength—it is thus that they try to enfeeble others."

"We women are weak," replied Bimala. "So I suppose we must join in the conspiracy of the weak."

"Women weak!" I exclaimed with a laugh. "Men belaud you as delicate and fragile, so as to delude you into thinking yourselves weak. But it is you women who are strong. Men make a great outward show of their so-called freedom, but those who know their inner minds are aware of their bondage. They have manufactured scriptures with their own hands to bind themselves; with their very idealism they have made golden fetters of women to wind round their body and mind. If men had not that extraordinary faculty of entangling themselves in meshes of their own contriving, nothing could have kept them bound. But as for you women, you have desired to conceive reality with body and soul. You have given birth to reality. You have suckled reality at your breasts."

Bee was well read for a woman, and would not easily give in to my arguments. "If that were true," she objected, "men would not have found women attractive."

"Women realize the danger," I replied. "They know that men love delusions, so they give them full measure by borrowing their own phrases. They know that man, the drunkard, values intoxication more than food, and so they try to pass themselves off as an intoxicant. As a matter of fact, but for the sake of man, woman has no need for any make-believe."

"Why, then, are you troubling to destroy the illusion?"

"For freedom. I want the country to be free. I want human relations to be free."

III

I was aware that it is unsafe suddenly to awake a sleep-walker. But I am so impetuous by nature, a halting gait does not suit me. I knew I was overbold that day. I knew that the first shock of such ideas is apt to be almost intolerable. But with women it is always audacity that wins.

Just as we were getting on nicely, who should walk in but Nikhil's old tutor Chandranath Babu. The world would have been not half a bad place to live in but for these schoolmasters, who make one want to quit in disgust. The Nikhil type wants to keep the world always a school. This incarnation of a school turned up that afternoon at the psychological moment.

We all remain schoolboys in some corner of our hearts, and I, even I, felt somewhat pulled up. As for poor Bee, she at once took her place solemnly, like the topmost girl of the class on the front bench. All of a sudden she seemed to remember that she had to face her examination.

Some people are so like eternal pointsmen lying in wait by the line, to shunt one's train of thought from one rail to another.

Chandranath Babu had no sooner come in than he cast about for some excuse to retire, mumbling: "I beg your pardon, I…"

Before he could finish, Bee went up to him and made a profound obeisance, saying: "Pray do not leave us, sir. Will you not take a seat?" She looked like a drowning person clutching at him for support—the little coward!

But possibly I was mistaken. It is quite likely that there was a touch of womanly wile in it. She wanted, perhaps, to raise her value in my eyes. She might have been pointedly saying to me: "Please don't imagine for a moment that I am entirely overcome by you. My respect for Chandranath Babu is even greater."

Well, indulge in your respect by all means! Schoolmasters thrive on it. But not being one of them, I have no use for that empty compliment.

Chandranath Babu began to talk about __Swadeshi__. I thought I would let him go on with his monologues. There is nothing like letting an old man talk himself out. It makes him feel that he is winding up the world, forgetting all the while how far away the real world is from his wagging tongue.

But even my worst enemy would not accuse me of patience. And when Chandranath Babu went on to say: "If we expect to gather fruit where we have sown no seed, then we …" I had to interrupt him.

"Who wants fruit?" I cried. "We go by the Author of the Gita who says that we are concerned only with the doing, not with the fruit of our deeds."

"What is it then that you do want?" asked Chandranath Babu.

"Thorns!" I exclaimed, "which cost nothing to plant."

"Thorns do not obstruct others only," he replied. "They have a way of hurting one's own feet."

"That is all right for a copy-book," I retorted. "But the real thing is that we have this burning at heart. Now we have only to cultivate thorns for other's soles; afterwards when they hurt us we shall find leisure to repent. But why be frightened even of that? When at last we have to die it will be time enough to get cold. While we are on fire let us seethe and boil."

Chandranath Babu smiled. "Seethe by all means," he said, "but do not mistake it for work, or heroism. Nations which have got on in the world have done so by action, not by ebullition. Those who have always lain in dread of work, when with a start they awake to their sorry plight, they look to short-cuts and scamping for their deliverance."

I was girding up my loins to deliver a crushing reply, when Nikhil came back. Chandranath Babu rose, and looking towards Bee, said: "Let me go now, my little mother, I have some work to attend to."

As he left, I showed Nikhil the book in my hand. "I was telling Queen Bee about this book," I said.

Ninety-nine per cent of people have to be deluded with lies, but it is easier to delude this perpetual pupil of the schoolmaster with the truth. He is best cheated openly. So, in playing with him, the simplest course was to lay my cards on the table.

Nikhil read the title on the cover, but said nothing. "These writers," I continued, "are busy with their brooms, sweeping away the dust of epithets with which men have covered up this world of ours. So, as I was saying, I wish you would read it."

"I have read it," said Nikhil.

"Well, what do you say?"

"It is all very well for those who really care to think, but poison for those who shirk thought."

"What do you mean?"

"Those who preach 'Equal Rights of Property' should not be thieves. For, if they are, they would be preaching lies. When passion is in the ascendant, this kind of book is not rightly understood."

"Passion," I replied, "is the street lamp which guides us. To call it untrue is as hopeless as to expect to see better by plucking out our natural eyes."

Nikhil was visibly growing excited. "I accept the truth of passion," he said, "only when I recognize the truth of restraint. By pressing what we want to see right into our eyes we only injure them: we do not see. So does the violence of passion, which would leave no space between the mind and its object, defeat its purpose."

"It is simply your intellectual foppery," I replied, "which makes you indulge in moral delicacy, ignoring the savage side of truth. This merely helps you to mystify things, and so you fail to do your work with any degree of strength."

"The intrusion of strength," said Nikhil impatiently, "where strength is out of place, does not help you in your work … But why are we arguing about these things? Vain arguments only brush off the fresh bloom of truth."

I wanted Bee to join in the discussion, but she had not said a word up to now. Could I have given her too rude a shock, leaving her assailed with doubts and wanting to learn her lesson afresh from the schoolmaster? Still, a thorough shaking-up is essential. One must begin by realizing that things supposed to be unshakeable can be shaken.

"I am glad I had this talk with you," I said to Nikhil, "for I was on the point of lending this book to Queen Bee to read."

"What harm?" said Nikhil. "If I could read the book, why not Bimala too? All I want to say is, that in Europe people look at everything from the viewpoint of science. But man is neither mere physiology, nor biology, nor psychology, nor even sociology. For God's sake don't forget that. Man is infinitely more than the natural science of himself. You laugh at me, calling me the schoolmaster's pupil, but that is what you are, not I. You want to find the truth of man from your science teachers, and not from your own inner being."

"But why all this excitement?" I mocked.

"Because I see you are bent on insulting man and making him petty."

"Where on earth do you see all that?"

"In the air, in my outraged feelings. You would go on wounding the great, the unselfish, the beautiful in man."

"What mad idea is this of yours?"

Nikhil suddenly stood up. "I tell you plainly, Sandip," he said, "man may be wounded unto death, but he will not die. This is the reason why I am ready to suffer all, knowing all, with eyes open."

With these words he hurriedly left the room.

I was staring blankly at his retreating figure, when the sound of a book, falling from the table, made me turn to find Bee following him with quick, nervous steps, making a detour to avoid passing too near me.

A curious creature, that Nikhil! He feels the danger threatening his home, and yet why does he not turn me out? I know, he is waiting for

Bimal to give him the cue. If Bimal tells him that their mating has been a misfit, he will bow his head and admit that it may have been a blunder! He has not the strength of mind to understand that to acknowledge a mistake is the greatest of all mistakes. He is a typical example of how ideas make for weakness. I have not seen another like him—so whimsical a product of nature! He would hardly do as a character in a novel or drama, to say nothing of real life.

And Bee? I am afraid her dream-life is over from today. She has at length understood the nature of the current which is bearing her along. Now she must either advance or retreat, open-eyed. The chances are she will now advance a step, and then retreat a step. But that does not disturb me. When one is on fire, this rushing to and fro makes the blaze all the fiercer. The fright she has got will only fan her passion.

Perhaps I had better not say much to her, but simply select some modern books for her to read. Let her gradually come to the conviction that to acknowledge and respect passion as the supreme reality, is to be modern—not to be ashamed of it, not to glorify restraint. If she finds shelter in some such word as "modern", she will find strength.

Be that as it may, I must see this out to the end of the Fifth Act. I cannot, unfortunately, boast of being merely a spectator, seated in the royal box, applauding now and again. There is a wrench at my heart, a pang in every nerve. When I have put out the light and am in my bed, little touches, little glances, little words flit about and fill the darkness. When I get up in the morning, I thrill with lively anticipations, my blood seems to course through me to the strains of music ...

There was a double photo-frame on the table with Bee's photograph by the side of Nikhil's. I had taken out hers. Yesterday I showed Bee the empty side and said: "Theft becomes necessary only because of miserliness, so its sin must be divided between the miser and the thief. Do you not think so?"

"It was not a good one," observed Bee simply, with a little smile.

"What is to be done?" said I. "A portrait cannot be better than a portrait. I must be content with it, such as it is."

Bee took up a book and began to turn over the pages. "If you are annoyed," I went on, "I must make a shift to fill up the vacancy."

Today I have filled it up. This photograph of mine was taken in my early youth. My face was then fresher, and so was my mind. Then I still cherished some illusions about this world and the next. Faith deceives men, but it has one great merit: it imparts a radiance to the features.

My portrait now reposes next to Nikhil's, for are not the two of us old friends?

Chapter Four

Nikhil's Story

III

I WAS never self-conscious. But nowadays I often try to take an outside view—to see myself as Bimal sees me. What a dismally solemn picture it makes, my habit of taking things too seriously!

Better, surely, to laugh away the world than flood it with tears. That is, in fact, how the world gets on. We relish our food and rest, only because we can dismiss, as so many empty shadows, the sorrows scattered everywhere, both in the home and in the outer world. If we took them as true, even for a moment, where would be our appetite, our sleep?

But I cannot dismiss myself as one of these shadows, and so the load of my sorrow lies eternally heavy on the heart of my world.

Why not stand out aloof in the highway of the universe, and feel yourself to be part of the all? In the midst of the immense, age-long concourse of humanity, what is Bimal to you? Your wife? What is a wife? A bubble of a name blown big with your own breath, so carefully guarded night and day, yet ready to burst at any pin-prick from outside.

My wife—and so, forsooth, my very own! If she says: "No, I am myself"—am I to reply: "How can that be? Are you not mine?"

"My wife"—Does that amount to an argument, much less the truth? Can one imprison a whole personality within that name?

My wife!—Have I not cherished in this little world all that is purest and sweetest in my life, never for a moment letting it down from my bosom to the dust? What incense of worship, what music of passion, what flowers of my spring and of my autumn, have I not offered up at its shrine? If, like a toy paper-boat, she be swept along into the muddy waters of the gutter—would I not also... ?

There it is again, my incorrigible solemnity! Why "muddy"? What "gutter" names, called in a fit of jealousy, do not change the facts of the world. If Bimal is not mine, she is not; and no fuming, or fretting, or arguing will serve to prove that she is. If my heart is breaking—let it break! That will not make the world bankrupt—nor even me; for man is so much greater than the things he loses in this life. The very ocean of tears has its other shore, else none would have ever wept.

But then there is Society to be considered ... which let Society consider! If I weep it is for myself, not for Society. If Bimala should say she is not mine, what care I where my Society wife may be?

Suffering there must be; but I must save myself, by any means in my power, from one form of self-torture: I must never think that my life loses its value because of any neglect it may suffer. The full value of my life does not all go to buy my narrow domestic world; its great commerce does not stand or fall with some petty success or failure in the bartering of my personal joys and sorrows.

The time has come when I must divest Bimala of all the ideal decorations with which I decked her. It was owing to my own weakness that I indulged in such idolatry. I was too greedy. I created an angel of Bimala, in order to exaggerate my own enjoyment. But Bimala is what she is. It is preposterous to expect that she should assume the rôle of an angel for my pleasure. The Creator is under no obligation to supply me with angels, just because I have an avidity for imaginary perfection.

I must acknowledge that I have merely been an accident in Bimala's life. Her nature, perhaps, can only find true union with one like Sandip. At the same time, I must not, in false modesty, accept my rejection as my desert. Sandip certainly has attractive qualities, which had their sway also upon myself; but yet, I feel sure, he is not a greater man than I. If the wreath of victory falls to his lot today, and I am overlooked, then the dispenser of the wreath will be called to judgement.

I say this in no spirit of boasting. Sheer necessity has driven me to the pass, that to secure myself from utter desolation I must recognize all the value that I truly possess. Therefore, through the, terrible experience of suffering let there come upon me the joy of deliverance—deliverance from self-distrust.

I have come to distinguish what is really in me from what I foolishly imagined to be there. The profit and loss account has been settled, and that which remains is myself—not a crippled self, dressed in rags and tatters, not a sick self to be nursed on invalid diet, but a spirit which has gone through the worst, and has survived.

My master passed through my room a moment ago and said with his hand on my shoulder. "Get away to bed, Nikhil, the night is far advanced."

The fact is, it has become so difficult for me to go to bed till late— till Bimal is fast asleep. In the day-time we meet, and even converse, but what am I to say when we are alone together, in the silence of the night?—so ashamed do I feel in mind and body.

"How is it, sir, you have not yet retired?" I asked in my turn. My master smiled a little, as he left me, saying: "My sleeping days are over. I have now attained the waking age."

I had written thus far, and was about to rise to go off bedwards when, through the window before me, I saw the heavy pall of July cloud suddenly part a little, and a big star shine through. It seemed to say to me: "Dreamland ties are made, and dreamland ties are broken, but I am here for ever—the everlasting lamp of the bridal night."

All at once my heart was full with the thought that my Eternal Love was steadfastly waiting for me through the ages, behind the veil of material things. Through many a life, in many a mirror, have I seen her image—broken mirrors, crooked mirrors, dusty mirrors. Whenever I have sought to make the mirror my very own, and shut it up within my box, I have lost sight of the image. But what of that. What have I to do with the mirror, or even the image?

My beloved, your smile shall never fade, and every dawn there shall appear fresh for me the vermilion mark on your forehead!

"What childish cajolery of self-deception," mocks some devil from his dark corner—"silly prattle to make children quiet!"

That may be. But millions and millions of children, with their million cries, have to be kept quiet. Can it be that all this multitude is quieted with only a lie? No, my Eternal Love cannot deceive me, for she is true!

She is true; that is why I have seen her and shall see her so often, even in my mistakes, even through the thickest mist of tears. I have seen her and lost her in the crowd of life's market-place, and found her again; and I shall find her once more when I have escaped through the loophole of death.

Ah, cruel one, play with me no longer! If I have failed to track you by the marks of your footsteps on the way, by the scent of your tresses lingering in the air, make me not weep for that for ever. The unveiled star tells me not to fear. That which is eternal must always be there.

Now let me go and see my Bimala. She must have spread her tired limbs on the bed, limp after her struggles, and be asleep. I will leave a kiss on her forehead without waking her—that shall be the flower-offering of my worship. I believe I could forget everything after death—all my mistakes, all my sufferings—but some vibration of the memory of that kiss would remain; for the wreath which is being woven out of the kisses of many a successive birth is to crown the Eternal Beloved.

As the gong of the watch rang out, sounding the hour of two, my sister-in-law came into the room. "Whatever are you doing, brother dear?" [16] she cried. "For pity's sake go to bed and stop worrying so. I cannot bear to look on that awful shadow of pain on your face." Tears welled up in her eyes and overflowed as she entreated me thus.

I could not utter a word, but took the dust of her feet, as I went off to bed.

Bimala's Story

VII

At first I suspected nothing, feared nothing; I simply felt dedicated to my country. What a stupendous joy there was in this unquestioning surrender. Verily had I realized how, in thoroughness of self-destruction, man can find supreme bliss.

For aught I know, this frenzy of mine might have come to a gradual, natural end. But Sandip Babu would not have it so, he would insist on revealing himself. The tone of his voice became as intimate as a touch, every look flung itself on its knees in beggary. And, through it all, there burned a passion which in its violence made as though it would tear me up by the roots, and drag me along by the hair.

I will not shirk the truth. This cataclysmal desire drew me by day and by night. It seemed desperately alluring—this making havoc of myself. What a shame it seemed, how terrible, and yet how sweet! Then there was my overpowering curiosity, to which there seemed no limit. He of whom I knew but little, who never could assuredly be mine, whose youth flared so vigorously in a hundred points of flame—oh, the mystery of his seething passions, so immense, so tumultuous!

I began with a feeling of worship, but that soon passed away. I ceased even to respect Sandip; on the contrary, I began to look down upon him. Nevertheless this flesh-and-blood lute of mine, fashioned with my feeling and fancy, found in him a master- player. What though I shrank

---

16. When a relationship is established by marriage, or by mutual understanding arising out of special friendship or affection, the persons so related call each other in terms of such relationship, and not by name. [Trans.].

from his touch, and even came to loathe the lute itself; its music was conjured up all the same.

I must confess there was something in me which ... what shall I say? ... which makes me wish I could have died!

Chandranath Babu, when he finds leisure, comes to me. He has the power to lift my mind up to an eminence from where I can see in a moment the boundary of my life extended on all sides and so realize that the lines, which I took from my bounds, were merely imaginary.

But what is the use of it all? Do I really desire emancipation? Let suffering come to our house; let the best in me shrivel up and become black; but let this infatuation not leave me—such seems to be my prayer.

When, before my marriage, I used to see a brother-in-law of mine, now dead, mad with drink—beating his wife in his frenzy, and then sobbing and howling in maudlin repentance, vowing never to touch liquor again, and yet, the very same evening, sitting down to drink and drink—it would fill me with disgust. But my intoxication today is still more fearful. The stuff has not to be procured or poured out: it springs within my veins, and I know not how to resist it.

Must this continue to the end of my days? Now and again I start and look upon myself, and think my life to be a nightmare which will vanish all of a sudden with all its untruth. It has become so frightfully incongruous. It has no connection with its past. What it is, how it could have come to this pass, I cannot understand.

One day my sister-in-law remarked with a cutting laugh: "What a wonderfully hospitable Chota Rani we have! Her guest absolutely will not budge. In our time there used to be guests, too; but they had not such lavish looking after—we were so absurdly taken up with our husbands. Poor brother Nikhil is paying the penalty of being born too modern. He should have come as a guest if he wanted to stay on. Now it looks as if it were time for him to quit … O you little demon, do your glances never fall, by chance, on his agonized face?"

This sarcasm did not touch me; for I knew that these women had it not in them to understand the nature of the cause of my devotion. I was then wrapped in the protecting armour of the exaltation of sacrifice, through which such shafts were powerless to reach and shame me.

VIII

For some time all talk of the country's cause has been dropped. Our conversation nowadays has become full of modern sex-problems, and various other matters, with a sprinkling of poetry, both old Vaishnava and modern English, accompanied by a running undertone of melody, low down in the bass, such as I have never in my life heard before, which seems to me to sound the true manly note, the note of power.

The day had come when all cover was gone. There was no longer even the pretence of a reason why Sandip Babu should linger on, or why I should have confidential talks with him every now and then. I felt thoroughly vexed with myself, with my sister-in- law, with the ways of the world, and I vowed I would never again go to the outer apartments, not if I were to die for it.

For two whole days I did not stir out. Then, for the first time, I discovered how far I had travelled. My life felt utterly tasteless. Whatever I touched I wanted to thrust away. I felt myself waiting—from the crown of my head to the tips of my toes —waiting for something, somebody; my blood kept tingling with some expectation.

I tried busying myself with extra work. The bedroom floor was clean enough but I insisted on its being scrubbed over again under my eyes. Things were arranged in the cabinets in one kind of order; I pulled them all out and rearranged them in a different way. I found no time that afternoon even to do up my hair; I hurriedly tied it into a loose knot, and went and worried everybody, fussing about the store-room. The stores seemed short, and pilfering must have been going on of late, but I could not muster up the courage to take any particular person to task— for might not the thought have crossed somebody's mind: "Where were your eyes all these days!"

In short, I behaved that day as one possessed. The next day I tried to do some reading. What I read I have no idea, but after a spell of absentmindedness I found I had wandered away, book in hand, along the passage leading towards the outer apartments, and was standing by a window looking out upon the verandah running along the row of rooms on the opposite side of the quadrangle. One of these rooms, I felt, had crossed over to another shore, and the ferry had ceased to ply. I felt like the ghost of myself of two days ago, doomed to remain where I was, and yet not really there, blankly looking out for ever.

As I stood there, I saw Sandip come out of his room into the verandah, a newspaper in his hand. I could see that he looked extraordinarily disturbed. The courtyard, the railings, in front, seemed to rouse his wrath. He flung away his newspaper with a gesture which seemed to want to rend the space before him.

I felt I could no longer keep my vow. I was about to move on towards the sitting-room, when I found my sister-in-law behind me. "O Lord, this beats everything!" she ejaculated, as she glided away. I could not proceed to the outer apartments.

The next morning when my maid came calling, "Rani Mother, it is getting late for giving out the stores," I flung the keys to her, saying, "Tell Harimati to see to it," and went on with some embroidery of English pattern on which I was engaged, seated near the window.

Then came a servant with a letter. "From Sandip Babu," said he. What unbounded boldness! What must the messenger have thought? There was a tremor within my breast as I opened the envelope. There was no address on the letter, only the words: __An urgent matter—touching the Cause. Sandip__.

I flung aside the embroidery. I was up on my feet in a moment, giving a touch or two to my hair by the mirror. I kept the __sari__ I had on, changing only my jacket—for one of my jackets had its associations.

I had to pass through one of the verandahs, where my sister-in-law used to sit in the morning slicing betel-nut. I refused to feel awkward. "Whither away, Chota Rani?" she cried.

"To the sitting-room outside."

"So early! A matinée, eh?"

And, as I passed on without further reply, she hummed after me a flippant song.

IX

When I was about to enter the sitting-room, I saw Sandip immersed in an illustrated catalogue of British Academy pictures, with his back to the door. He has a great notion of himself as an expert in matters of Art.

One day my husband said to him: "If the artists ever want a teacher, they need never lack for one so long as you are there." It had not been my husband's habit to speak cuttingly, but latterly there has been a change and he never spares Sandip.

"What makes you suppose that artists need no teachers?" Sandip retorted.

"Art is a creation," my husband replied. "So we should humbly be content to receive our lessons about Art from the work of the artist."

Sandip laughed at this modesty, saying: "You think that meekness is a kind of capital which increases your wealth the more you use it. It is my conviction that those who lack pride only float about like water reeds which have no roots in the soil."

My mind used to be full of contradictions when they talked thus. On the one hand I was eager that my husband should win in argument and that Sandip's pride should be shamed. Yet, on the other, it was Sandip's unabashed pride which attracted me so. It shone like a precious diamond, which knows no diffidence, and sparkles in the face of the sun itself.

I entered the room. I knew Sandip could hear my footsteps as I went forward, but he pretended not to, and kept his eyes on the book.

I dreaded his Art talks, for I could not overcome my delicacy about the pictures he talked of, and the things he said, and had much ado in putting on an air of overdone insensibility to hide my qualms. So, I was almost on the point of retracing my steps, when, with a deep sigh, Sandip raised his eyes, and affected to be startled at the sight of me. "Ah, you have come!" he said.

In his words, in his tone, in his eyes, there was a world of suppressed reproach, as if the claims he had acquired over me made my absence, even for these two or three days, a grievous wrong. I knew this attitude was an insult to me, but, alas, I had not the power to resent it.

I made no reply, but though I was looking another way, I could not help feeling that Sandip's plaintive gaze had planted itself right on my face, and would take no denial. I did so wish he would say something, so that I could shelter myself behind his words. I cannot tell how long this went on, but at last I could stand it no longer. "What is this matter," I asked, "you are wanting to tell me about?"

Sandip again affected surprise as he said: "Must there always be some matter? Is friendship by itself a crime? Oh, Queen Bee, to think that you should make so light of the greatest thing on earth! Is the heart's worship to be shut out like a stray cur?"

There was again that tremor within me. I could feel the crisis coming, too importunate to be put off. Joy and fear struggled for the mastery. Would my shoulders, I wondered, be broad enough to stand its shock, or would it not leave me overthrown, with my face in the dust?

I was trembling all over. Steadying myself with an effort I repeated: "You summoned me for something touching the Cause, so I have left my household duties to attend to it."

"That is just what I was trying to explain," he said, with a dry laugh. "Do you not know that I come to worship? Have I not told you that, in you, I visualize the __Shakti__ of our country? The Geography of a country is not the whole truth. No one can give up his life for a map! When I see you before me, then only do I realize how lovely my country is. When you have anointed me with your own hands, then shall I know I have the sanction of my country; and if, with that in my heart, I fall fighting, it shall not be on the dust of some map-made land, but on a lovingly spread skirt—do you know what kind of skirt?—like that of the earthen-red _sari_ you wore the other day, with a broad blood-red border. Can I ever forget it? Such are the visions which give vigour to life, and joy to death!"

Sandip's eyes took fire as he went on, but whether it was the fire of worship, or of passion, I could not tell. I was reminded of the day on which I first heard him speak, when I could not be sure whether he was a person, or just a living flame.

I had not the power to utter a word. You cannot take shelter behind the walls of decorum when in a moment the fire leaps up and, with the flash of its sword and the roar of its laughter, destroys all the miser's stores. I was in terror lest he should forget himself and take me by the hand. For he shook like a quivering tongue of fire; his eyes showered scorching sparks on me.

"Are you for ever determined," he cried after a pause, "to make gods of your petty household duties—you who have it in you to send us to life or to death? Is this power of yours to be kept veiled in a zenana? Cast away all false shame, I pray you; snap your fingers at the whispering around. Take your plunge today into the freedom of the outer world."

When, in Sandip's appeals, his worship of the country gets to be subtly interwoven with his worship of me, then does my blood dance, indeed, and the barriers of my hesitation totter. His talks about Art and Sex, his distinctions between Real and Unreal, had but clogged my attempts at response with some revolting nastiness. This, however, now burst again into a glow before which my repugnance faded away. I felt that my resplendent womanhood made me indeed a goddess. Why should not its glory flash from my forehead with visible brilliance? Why does not my voice find a word, some audible cry, which would be like a sacred spell to my country for its fire initiation?

All of a sudden my maid Khema rushed into the room, dishevelled. "Give me my wages and let me go," she screamed. "Never in all my life have I been so ..." The rest of her speech was drowned in sobs.

"What is the matter?"

Thako, the Bara Rani's maid, it appeared, had for no rhyme or reason reviled her in unmeasured terms. She was in such a state, it was no manner of use trying to pacify her by saying I would look into the matter afterwards.

The slime of domestic life that lay beneath the lotus bank of womanhood came to the surface. Rather than allow Sandip a prolonged vision of it, I had to hurry back within.

X

My sister-in-law was absorbed in her betel-nuts, the suspicion of a smile playing about her lips, as if nothing untoward had happened. She was still humming the same song.

"Why has your Thako been calling poor Khema names?" I burst out.

"Indeed? The wretch! I will have her broomed out of the house. What a shame to spoil your morning out like this! As for Khema, where are the hussy's manners to go and disturb you when you are engaged? Anyhow, Chota Rani, don't you worry yourself with these domestic squabbles. Leave them to me, and return to your friend."

How suddenly the wind in the sails of our mind veers round! This going to meet Sandip outside seemed, in the light of the zenana code, such an extraordinarily out-of-the-way thing to do that I went off to my own room, at a loss for a reply. I knew this was my sister-in-law's doing and that she had egged her maid on to contrive this scene. But I had brought myself to such an unstable poise that I dared not have my fling.

Why, it was only the other day that I found I could not keep up to the last the unbending hauteur with which I had demanded from my husband the dismissal of the man Nanku. I felt suddenly abashed when the Bara Rani came up and said: "It is really all my fault, brother dear. We are old-fashioned folk, and I did not quite like the ways of your Sandip Babu, so I only told the guard … but how was I to know that our Chota Rani would take this as an insult?—I thought it would be the other way about! Just my incorrigible silliness!"

The thing which seems so glorious when viewed from the heights of the country's cause, looks so muddy when seen from the bottom. One begins by getting angry, and then feels disgusted.

I shut myself into my room, sitting by the window, thinking how easy life would be if only one could keep in harmony with one's surroundings. How simply the senior Rani sits in her verandah with her betel-nuts and how inaccessible to me has become my natural seat beside my daily duties! Where will it all end, I asked myself? Shall I ever recover, as from a delirium, and forget it all; or am I to be dragged to depths from which there can be no escape in this life? How on earth did I manage to let my good fortune escape me, and spoil my life so? Every wall of this bedroom of mine, which I first entered nine years ago as a bride, stares at me in dismay.

When my husband came home, after his M.A. examination, he brought for me this orchid belonging to some far-away land beyond the seas. From beneath these few little leaves sprang such a cascade of blossoms, it looked as if they were pouring forth from some overturned urn of Beauty. We decided, together, to hang it here, over this window. It flowered only that once, but we have always been in hope of its doing so once more. Curiously enough I have kept on watering it these days, from force of habit, and it is still green.

It is now four years since I framed a photograph of my husband in ivory and put it in the niche over there. If I happen to look that way I have to lower my eyes. Up to last week I used regularly to put there the flowers of my worship, every morning after my bath. My husband has often chided me over this.

"It shames me to see you place me on a height to which I do not belong," he said one day.

"What nonsense!"

"I am not only ashamed, but also jealous!"

"Just hear him! Jealous of whom, pray?"

"Of that false me. It only shows that I am too petty for you, that you want some extraordinary man who can overpower you with his superiority, and so you needs must take refuge in making for yourself another 'me.'"

"This kind of talk only makes me angry," said I.

"What is the use of being angry with me?" he replied. "Blame your fate which allowed you no choice, but made you take me blindfold. This keeps you trying to retrieve its blunder by making me out a paragon."

I felt so hurt at the bare idea that tears started to my eyes that day. And whenever I think of that now, I cannot raise my eyes to the niche.

For now there is another photograph in my jewel case. The other day, when arranging the sitting-room, I brought away that double photo frame, the one in which Sandip's portrait was next to my husband's. To this portrait I have no flowers of worship to offer, but it remains hidden away under my gems. It has all the greater fascination because kept secret. I look at it now and then with doors closed. At night I turn up the lamp, and sit with it in my hand, gazing and gazing. And every night I think of burning it in the flame of the lamp, to be done with it for ever; but every night I heave a sigh and smother it again in my pearls and diamonds.

Ah, wretched woman! What a wealth of love was twined round each one of those jewels! Oh, why am I not dead?

Sandip had impressed it on me that hesitation is not in the nature of woman. For her, neither right nor left has any existence—she only moves forward. When the women of our country wake up, he repeatedly insisted, their voice will be unmistakably confident in its utterance of the cry: "I want."

"I want!" Sandip went on one day—this was the primal word at the root of all creation. It had no maxim to guide it, but it became fire and wrought itself into suns and stars. Its partiality is terrible. Because it had a desire for man, it ruthlessly sacrificed millions of beasts for millions of years to achieve that desire. That terrible word "I want" has taken flesh in woman, and therefore men, who are cowards, try with all their might to keep back this primeval flood With their earthen dykes. They are afraid lest, laughing and dancing as it goes, it should wash away all the hedges and props of their pumpkin field. Men, in every age, flatter themselves that they have secured this force within the bounds of their convenience, but it gathers and grows. Now it is calm and deep like a lake, but gradually its pressure will increase, the dykes will give way, and the force which has so long been dumb will rush forward with the roar: "I want!"

These words of Sandip echo in my heart-beats like a war-drum. They shame into silence all my conflicts with myself. What do I care what people may think of me? Of what value are that orchid and that niche in my bedroom? What power have they to belittle me, to put me to shame? The primal fire of creation burns in me.

I felt a strong desire to snatch down the orchid and fling it out of the window, to denude the niche of its picture, to lay bare and naked the unashamed spirit of destruction that raged within me. My arm was raised to do it, but a sudden pang passed through my breast, tears started to my eyes. I threw myself down and sobbed: "What is the end of all this, what is the end?"

Sandip's Story

IV

When I read these pages of the story of my life I seriously question myself: Is this Sandip? Am I made of words? Am I merely a book with a covering of flesh and blood?

The earth is not a dead thing like the moon. She breathes. Her rivers and oceans send up vapours in which she is clothed. She is covered with a mantle of her own dust which flies about the air. The onlooker, gazing upon the earth from the outside, can see only the light reflected from this vapour and this dust. The tracks of the mighty continents are not distinctly visible.

The man, who is alive as this earth is, is likewise always enveloped in the mist of the ideas which he is breathing out. His real land and water remain hidden, and he appears to be made of only lights and shadows.

It seems to me, in this story of my life, that, like a living plant, I am displaying the picture of an ideal world. But I am not merely what I want, what I think—I am also what I do not love, what I do not wish to be. My creation had begun before I was born. I had no choice in regard to my surroundings and so must make the best of such material as comes to my hand.

My theory of life makes me certain that the Great is cruel To be just is for ordinary men—it is reserved for the great to be unjust. The surface of the earth was even. The volcano butted it with its fiery horn and found its own eminence—its justice was not towards its obstacle, but towards itself. Successful injustice and genuine cruelty have been the only forces by which individual or nation has become millionaire or monarch.

That is why I preach the great discipline of Injustice. I say to everyone: Deliverance is based upon injustice. Injustice is the fire which must keep on burning something in order to save itself from becoming ashes. Whenever an individual or nation becomes incapable of perpetrating injustice it is swept into the dust-bin of the world.

As yet this is only my idea—it is not completely myself. There are rifts in the armour through which something peeps out which is extremely soft and sensitive. Because, as I say, the best part of myself was created before I came to this stage of existence.

From time to time I try my followers in their lesson of cruelty. One day we went on a picnic. A goat was grazing by. I asked them: "Who is there among you that can cut off a leg of that goat, alive, with this knife, and bring it to me?" While they all hesitated, I went myself and did it. One of them fainted at the sight. But when they saw me unmoved they took the dust of my feet, saying that I was above all human weaknesses. That is to say, they saw that day the vaporous envelope which was my idea, but failed to perceive the inner me, which by a curious freak of fate has been created tender and merciful.

In the present chapter of my life, which is growing in interest every day round Bimala and Nikhil, there is also much that remains hidden underneath. This malady of ideas which afflicts me is shaping my life within: nevertheless a great part of my life remains outside its influence; and so there is set up a discrepancy between my outward life and its inner design which I try my best to keep concealed even from myself; otherwise it may wreck not only my plans, but my very life.

Life is indefinite—a bundle of contradictions. We men, with our ideas, strive to give it a particular shape by melting it into a particular mould—into the definiteness of success. All the world-conquerors, from Alexander down to the American millionaires, mould themselves into a sword or a mint, and thus find that distinct image of themselves which is the source of their success.

The chief controversy between Nikhil and myself arises from this: that though I say "know thyself", and Nikhil also says "know thyself", his interpretation makes this "knowing" tantamount to "not knowing".

"Winning your kind of success," Nikhil once objected, "is success gained at the cost of the soul: but the soul is greater than success."

I simply said in answer: "Your words are too vague."

"That I cannot help," Nikhil replied. "A machine is distinct enough, but not so life. If to gain distinctness you try to know life as a machine, then such mere distinctness cannot stand for truth. The soul is not as distinct as success, and so you only lose your soul if you seek it in your success."

"Where, then, is this wonderful soul?"

"Where it knows itself in the infinite and transcends its success."

"But how does all this apply to our work for the country?"

"It is the same thing. Where our country makes itself the final object, it gains success at the cost of the soul. Where it recognizes the Greatest as greater than all, there it may miss success, but gains its soul."

"Is there any example of this in history?"

"Man is so great that he can despise not only the success, but also the example. Possibly example is lacking, just as there is no example of the flower in the seed. But there is the urgence of the flower in the seed all the same."

It is not that I do not at all understand Nikhil's point of view; that is rather where my danger lies. I was born in India and the poison of its spirituality runs in my blood. However loudly I may proclaim the madness of walking in the path of self-abnegation, I cannot avoid it altogether.

This is exactly how such curious anomalies happen nowadays in our country. We must have our religion and also our nationalism; our __Bhagavadgita__ and also our __Bande Mataram__. The result is that both of them suffer. It is like performing with an English military band, side by side with our Indian festive pipes. I must make it the purpose of my life to put an end to this hideous confusion.

I want the western military style to prevail, not the Indian. We shall then not be ashamed of the flag of our passion, which mother Nature has sent with us as our standard into the battlefield of life. Passion is beautiful and pure—pure as the lily that comes out of the slimy soil. It rises superior to its defilement and needs no Pears' soap to wash it clean.

V

A question has been worrying me the last few days. Why am I allowing my life to become entangled with Bimala's? Am I a drifting log to be caught up at any and every obstacle?

Not that I have any false shame at Bimala becoming an object of my desire. It is only too clear how she wants me, and so I look on her as quite legitimately mine. The fruit hangs on the branch by the stem, but that is no reason why the claim of the stem should be eternal. Ripe fruit cannot for ever swear by its slackening stem-hold. All its sweetness has been accumulated for me; to surrender itself to my hand is the reason of its existence, its very nature, its true morality. So I must pluck it, for it becomes me not to make it futile.

But what is teasing me is that I am getting entangled. Am I not born to rule?—to bestride my proper steed, the crowd, and drive it as I will; the reins in my hand, the destination known only to me, and for it the thorns, the mire, on the road? This steed now awaits me at the door, pawing and champing its bit, its neighing filling the skies. But where am I, and what am I about, letting day after day of golden opportunity slip by?

I used to think I was like a storm—that the torn flowers with which I strewed my path would not impede my progress. But I am only wandering round and round a flower like a bee—not a storm. So, as I was saying, the colouring of ideas which man gives himself is only superficial. The inner man remains as ordinary as ever. If someone, who could see right into me, were to write my biography, he would make me out to be no different from that lout of a Panchu, or even from Nikhil!

Last night I was turning over the pages of my old diary ... I had just graduated, and my brain was bursting with philosophy. Even so early I had vowed not to harbour any illusions, whether of my own or other's imagining, but to build my life on a solid basis of reality. But what has since been its actual story? Where is its solidity? It has rather been a network, where, though the thread be continuous, more space is taken up by the holes. Fight as I may, these will not own defeat. Just as I was congratulating myself on steadily following the thread, here I am badly caught in a hole! For I have become susceptible to compunctions.

"I want it; it is here; let me take it"—This is a clear-cut, straightforward policy. Those who can pursue its course with vigour needs must win through in the end. But the gods would not have it that such journey should be easy, so they have deputed the siren Sympathy to distract the wayfarer, to dim his vision with her tearful mist.

I can see that poor Bimala is struggling like a snared deer. What a piteous alarm there is in her eyes! How she is torn with straining at her bonds! This sight, of course, should gladden the heart of a true hunter. And so do I rejoice; but, then, I am also touched; and therefore I dally, and standing on the brink I am hesitating to pull the noose fast.

There have been moments, I know, when I could have bounded up to her, clasped her hands and folded her to my breast, unresisting. Had I done so, she would not have said one word. She was aware that some crisis was impending, which in a moment would change the meaning of the whole world. Standing before that cavern of the incalculable but yet expected, her face went pale and her eyes glowed with a fearful ecstasy. Within that moment, when it arrives, an eternity will take shape, which our destiny awaits, holding its breath.

But I have let this moment slip by. I did not, with uncompromising strength, press the almost certain into the absolutely assured. I now see clearly that some hidden elements in my nature have openly ranged themselves as obstacles in my path.

That is exactly how Ravana, whom I look upon as the real hero of the __Ramayana__, met with his doom. He kept Sita in his Asoka garden, awaiting her pleasure, instead of taking her straight into his harem. This weak spot in his otherwise grand character made the whole of the abduction episode futile. Another such touch of compunction made him disregard, and be lenient to, his traitorous brother Bibhisan, only to get himself killed for his pains.

Thus does the tragic in life come by its own. In the beginning it lies, a little thing, in some dark under-vault, and ends by overthrowing the whole superstructure. The real tragedy is, that man does not know himself for what he really is.

VI

Then again there is Nikhil. Crank though he be, laugh at him as I may, I cannot get rid of the idea that he is my friend. At first I gave no thought to his point of view, but of late it has begun to shame and hurt me. Therefore I have been trying to talk and argue with him in the same enthusiastic way as of old, but it does not ring true. It is even leading me at times into such a length of unnaturalness as to pretend to agree with him. But such hypocrisy is not in my nature, nor in that of Nikhil either. This, at least, is something we have in common. That is why, nowadays, I would rather not come across him, and have taken to fighting shy of his presence.

All these are signs of weakness. No sooner is the possibility of a wrong admitted than it becomes actual, and clutches you by the throat, however you may then try to shake off all belief in it. What I should like to be able to tell Nikhil frankly is, that happenings such as these must be looked in the face—as great Realities—and that which is the Truth should not be allowed to stand between true friends.

There is no denying that I have really weakened. It was not this weakness which won over Bimala; she burnt her wings in the blaze of the full strength of my unhesitating manliness. Whenever smoke obscures its lustre she also becomes confused, and draws back. Then comes a thorough revulsion of feeling, and she fain would take back the garland she has put round my neck, but cannot; and so she only closes her eyes, to shut it out of sight.

But all the same I must not swerve from the path I have chalked out. It would never do to abandon the cause of the country, especially at the present time. I shall simply make Bimala one with my country. The turbulent west wind which has swept away the country's veil of conscience, will sweep away the veil of the wife from Bimala's face, and in that uncovering there will be no shame. The ship will rock as it bears the crowd across the ocean, flying the pennant of _Bande Mataram_, and it will serve as the cradle to my power, as well as to my love.

Bimala will see such a majestic vision of deliverance, that her bonds will slip from about her, without shame, without her even being aware of it. Fascinated by the beauty of this terrible wrecking power, she will not hesitate a moment to be cruel. I have seen in Bimala's nature the cruelty which is the inherent force of existence—the cruelty which with its unrelenting might keeps the world beautiful.

If only women could be set free from the artificial fetters put round them by men, we could see on earth the living image of Kali, the shameless, pitiless goddess. I am a worshipper of Kali, and one day I shall truly worship her, setting Bimala on her altar of Destruction. For this let me get ready.

The way of retreat is absolutely closed for both of us. We shall despoil each other: get to hate each other: but never more be free.

Chapter Five

Nikhil's Story

IV

EVERYTHING is rippling and waving with the flood of August. The young shoots of rice have the sheen of an infant's limbs. The water has invaded the garden next to our house. The morning light, like the love of the blue sky, is lavished upon the earth ... Why cannot I sing? The water of the distant river is shimmering with light; the leaves are glistening; the rice-fields, with their fitful shivers, break into gleams of gold; and in this symphony of Autumn, only I remain voiceless. The sunshine of the world strikes my heart, but is not reflected back.

When I realize the lack of expressiveness in myself, I know why I am deprived. Who could bear my company day and night without a break? Bimala is full of the energy of life, and so she has never become stale to me for a moment, in all these nine years of our wedded life.

My life has only its dumb depths; but no murmuring rush. I can only receive: not impart movement. And therefore my company is like fasting. I recognize clearly today that Bimala has been languishing because of a famine of companionship.

Then whom shall I blame? Like Vidyapati I can only lament:
/*
It is August, the sky breaks into a passionate rain;
Alas, empty is my house.
*/

My house, I now see, was built to remain empty, because its doors cannot open. But I never knew till now that its divinity had been sitting outside. I had fondly believed that she had accepted my sacrifice, and granted in return her boon. But, alas, my house has all along been empty.

Every year, about this time, it was our practice to go in a house-boat over the broads of Samalda. I used to tell Bimala that a song must come back to its refrain over and over again. The original refrain of every song is in Nature, where the rain-laden wind passes over the rippling stream, where the green earth, drawing its shadow-veil over its face, keeps its ear close to the speaking water. There, at the beginning of time, a man and a woman first met—not within walls. And therefore we two must come back to Nature, at least once a year, to tune our love anew to the first pure note of the meeting of hearts.

The first two anniversaries of our married life I spent in Calcutta, where I went through my examinations. But from the next year onwards, for seven years without a break, we have celebrated our union among the blossoming water-lilies. Now begins the next octave of my life.

It was difficult for me to ignore the fact that the same month of August had come round again this year. Does Bimala remember it, I wonder?—she has given me no reminder. Everything is mute about me.

/*

It is August, the sky breaks into a passionate rain;

Alas, empty is my house.

*/

The house which becomes empty through the parting of lovers, still has music left in the heart of its emptiness. But the house that is empty because hearts are asunder, is awful in its silence. Even the cry of pain is out of place there.

This cry of pain must be silenced in me. So long as I continue to suffer, Bimala will never have true freedom. I must free her completely, otherwise I shall never gain my freedom from untruth ...

I think I have come to the verge of understanding one thing. Man has so fanned the flame of the loves of men and women, as to make it overpass its rightful domain, and now, even in the name of humanity itself, he cannot bring it back under control. Man's worship has idolized his passion. But there must be no more human sacrifices at its shrine …

I went into my bedroom this morning, to fetch a book. It is long since I have been there in the day-time. A pang passed through me as I looked round it today, in the morning light. On the clothes rack was hanging a _sari_ of Bimala's, crinkled ready for wear. On the dressing-table were her perfumes, her comb, her hair-pins, and with them, still, her vermilion box! Underneath were her tiny gold-embroidered slippers.

Once, in the old days, when Bimala had not yet overcome her objections to shoes, I had got these out from Lucknow, to tempt her. The first time she was ready to drop for very shame, to go in them even from the room to the verandah. Since then she has worn out many shoes, but has treasured up this pair. When first showing her the slippers, I chaffed her over a curious practice of hers; "I have caught you taking the dust of my feet, thinking me asleep! These are the offerings of my worship to ward the dust off the feet of my wakeful divinity." "You must not say such things," she protested, "or I will never wear your shoes!"

This bedroom of mine—it has a subtle atmosphere which goes straight to my heart. I was never aware, as I am today, how my thirsting heart has been sending out its roots to cling round each and every familiar object. The severing of the main root, I see, is not enough to set life free. Even these little slippers serve to hold one back.

My wandering eyes fall on the niche. My portrait there is looking the same as ever, in spite of the flowers scattered round it having been withered black! Of all the things in the room their greeting strikes me as sincere. They are still here simply because it was not felt worth while even to remove them. Never mind; let me welcome truth, albeit in such sere and sorry garb, and look forward to the time when I shall be able to do so unmoved, as does my photograph.

As I stood there, Bimal came in from behind. I hastily turned my eyes from the niche to the shelves as I muttered: "I came to get Amiel's Journal." What need had I to volunteer an explanation? I felt like a wrong-doer, a trespasser, prying into a secret not meant for me. I could not look Bimal in the face, but hurried away.

V

I had just made the discovery that it was useless to keep up a pretence of reading in my room outside, and also that it was equally beyond me to busy myself attending to anything at all—so that all the days of my future bid fair to congeal into one solid mass and settle heavily on my breast for good—when Panchu, the tenant of a neighbouring _zamindar_, came up to me with a basketful of cocoa-nuts and greeted me with a profound obeisance.

"Well, Panchu," said I. "What is all this for?"

I had got to know Panchu through my master. He was extremely poor, nor was I in a position to do anything for him; so I supposed this present was intended to procure a tip to help the poor fellow to make both ends meet. I took some money from my purse and held it out towards him, but with folded hands he protested: "I cannot take that, sir!"

"Why, what is the matter?"

"Let me make a clean breast of it, sir. Once, when I was hard pressed, I stole some cocoa-nuts from the garden here. I am getting old, and may die any day, so I have come to pay them back."

Amiel's Journal could not have done me any good that day. But these words of Panchu lightened my heart. There are more things in life than the union or separation of man and woman. The great world stretches far beyond, and one can truly measure one's joys and sorrows when standing in its midst.

Panchu was devoted to my master. I know well enough how he manages to eke out a livelihood. He is up before dawn every day, and with a basket of _pan_ leaves, twists of tobacco, coloured cotton yarn, little combs, looking-glasses, and other trinkets beloved of the village women, he wades through the knee- deep water of the marsh and goes over to the Namasudra quarters. There he barters his goods for rice, which fetches him a little more than their price in money. If he can get back soon enough he goes out again, after a hurried meal, to the sweetmeat seller's, where he assists in beating sugar for wafers. As soon as he comes home he sits at his shell-bangle making, plodding on often till midnight. All this cruel toil does not earn, for himself and his family, a bare two meals a day during much more than half the year. His method of eating is to begin with a good filling draught of water, and his staple food is the cheapest kind of seedy banana. And yet the family has to go with only one meal a day for the rest of the year.

At one time I had an idea of making him a charity allowance, "But," said my master, "your gift may destroy the man, it cannot destroy the hardship of his lot. Mother Bengal has not only this one Panchu. If the milk in her breasts has run dry, that cannot be supplied from the outside."

These are thoughts which give one pause, and I decided to devote myself to working it out. That very day I said to Bimal: "Let us dedicate our lives to removing the root of this sorrow in our country."

"You are my Prince Siddharta, [17] I see," she replied with a smile. "But do not let the torrent of your feelings end by sweeping me away also!"

"Siddharta took his vows alone. I want ours to be a joint arrangement."

The idea passed away in talk. The fact is, Bimala is at heart what is called a "lady". Though her own people are not well off, she was born a Rani. She has no doubts in her mind that there is a lower unit of measure for the trials and troubles of the "lower classes". Want is, of course, a permanent feature of their lives, but does not necessarily mean "want"

---

17. The name by which Buddha was known when a Prince, before renouncing the world.

to them. Their very smallness protects them, as the banks protect the pool; by widening bounds only the slime is exposed.

The real fact is that Bimala has only come into my home, not into my life. I had magnified her so, leaving her such a large place, that when I lost her, my whole way of life became narrow and confined. I had thrust aside all other objects into a corner to make room for Bimala—taken up as I was with decorating her and dressing her and educating her and moving round her day and night; forgetting how great is humanity and how nobly precious is man's life. When the actualities of everyday things get the better of the man, then is Truth lost sight of and freedom missed. So painfully important did Bimala make the mere actualities, that the truth remained concealed from me. That is why I find no gap in my misery, and spread this minute point of my emptiness over all the world. And so, for hours on this Autumn morning, the refrain has been humming in my ears:

/*

It is the month of August, and the sky breaks into a passionate rain;

Alas, my house is empty.

*/

Bimala's Story

XI

The change which had, in a moment, come over the mind of Bengal was tremendous. It was as if the Ganges had touched the ashes of the sixty thousand sons of Sagar [18] which no fire could enkindle, no other water knead again into living clay. The ashes of lifeless Bengal suddenly spoke up: "Here am I."

I have read somewhere that in ancient Greece a sculptor had the good fortune to impart life to the image made by his own hand. Even

---

18. The condition of the curse which had reduced them to ashes was such that they could only be restored to life if the stream of the Ganges was brought down to them. [Trans.].

in that miracle, however, there was the process of form preceding life. But where was the unity in this heap of barren ashes? Had they been hard like stone, we might have had hopes of some form emerging, even as Ahalya, though turned to stone, at last won back her humanity. But these scattered ashes must have dropped to the dust through gaps in the Creator's fingers, to be blown hither and thither by the wind. They had become heaped up, but were never before united. Yet in this day which had come to Bengal, even this collection of looseness had taken shape, and proclaimed in a thundering voice, at our very door: "Here I am."

How could we help thinking that it was all supernatural? This moment of our history seemed to have dropped into our hand like a jewel from the crown of some drunken god. It had no resemblance to our past; and so we were led to hope that all our wants and miseries would disappear by the spell of some magic charm, that for us there was no longer any boundary line between the possible and the impossible. Everything seemed to be saying to us: "It is coming; it has come!"

Thus we came to cherish the belief that our history needed no steed, but that like heaven's chariot it would move with its own inherent power—At least no wages would have to be paid to the charioteer; only his wine cup would have to be filled again and again. And then in some impossible paradise the goal of our hopes would be reached.

My husband was not altogether unmoved, but through all our excitement it was the strain of sadness in him which deepened and deepened. He seemed to have a vision of something beyond the surging present.

I remember one day, in the course of the arguments he continually had with Sandip, he said: "Good fortune comes to our gate and announces itself, only to prove that we have not the power to receive it—that we have not kept things ready to be able to invite it into our house."

"No," was Sandip's answer. "You talk like an atheist because you do not believe in our gods. To us it has been made quite visible that the Goddess has come with her boon, yet you distrust the obvious signs of her presence."

"It is because I strongly believe in my God," said my husband, "that I feel so certain that our preparations for his worship are lacking. God has power to give the boon, but we must have power to accept it."

This kind of talk from my husband would only annoy me. I could not keep from joining in: "You think this excitement is only a fire of drunkenness, but does not drunkenness, up to a point, give strength?"

"Yes," my husband replied. "It may give strength, but not weapons."

"But strength is the gift of God," I went on. "Weapons can be supplied by mere mechanics."

My husband smiled. "The mechanics will claim their wages before they deliver their supplies," he said.

Sandip swelled his chest as he retorted: "Don't you trouble about that. Their wages shall be paid."

"I shall bespeak the festive music when the payment has been made, not before," my husband answered.

"You needn't imagine that we are depending on your bounty for the music," said Sandip scornfully. "Our festival is above all money payments."

And in his thick voice he began to sing:

/*
"My lover of the unpriced love, spurning payments,
Plays upon the simple pipe, bought for nothing,
Drawing my heart away."
*/

Then with a smile he turned to me and said: "If I sing, Queen Bee, it is only to prove that when music comes into one's life, the lack of a good voice is no matter. When we sing merely on the strength of our tunefulness, the song is belittled. Now that a full flood of music has swept over our country, let Nikhil practise his scales, while we rouse the land with our cracked voices:

/*

"My house cries to me: Why go out to lose your all?
My life says: All that you have, fling to the winds!
If we must lose our all, let us lose it: what is it worth after all?
If I must court ruin, let me do it smilingly;
For my quest is the death-draught of immortality.
*/

"The truth is, Nikhil, that we have all lost our hearts. None can hold us any longer within the bounds of the easily possible, in our forward rush to the hopelessly impossible.

/*
"Those who would draw us back,
They know not the fearful joy of recklessness.
They know not that we have had our call
From the end of the crooked path.
All that is good and straight and trim—
Let it topple over in the dust."
*/

I thought that my husband was going to continue the discussion, but he rose silently from his seat and left us.

The thing that was agitating me within was merely a variation of the stormy passion outside, which swept the country from one end to the other. The car of the wielder of my destiny was fast approaching, and the sound of its wheels reverberated in my being. I had a constant feeling that something extraordinary might happen any moment, for which, however, the responsibility would not be mine. Was I not removed from the plane in which right and wrong, and the feelings of others, have to be considered? Had I ever wanted this—had I ever been waiting or hoping for any such thing? Look at my whole life and tell me then, if I was in any way accountable.

Through all my past I had been consistent in my devotion—but when at length it came to receiving the boon, a different god appeared! And just as the awakened country, with its __Bande Mataram__, thrills in salutation to the unrealized future before it, so do all my veins and nerves send forth shocks of welcome to the unthought-of, the unknown, the importunate Stranger.

One night I left my bed and slipped out of my room on to the open terrace. Beyond our garden wall are fields of ripening rice. Through the gaps in the village groves to the North, glimpses of the river are seen. The whole scene slept in the darkness like the vague embryo of some future creation.

In that future I saw my country, a woman like myself, standing expectant. She has been drawn forth from her home corner by the sudden call of some Unknown. She has had no time to pause or ponder, or to light herself a torch, as she rushes forward into the darkness ahead. I know well how her very soul responds to the distant flute-strains which call her; how her breast rises and falls; how she feels she nears it, nay it is already hers, so that it matters not even if she run blindfold. She is no mother. There is no call to her of children in their hunger, no home to be lighted of an evening, no household work to be done. So; she hies to her tryst, for this is the land of the Vaishnava Poets. She has left home, forgotten domestic duties; she has nothing but an unfathomable yearning which hurries her on—by what road, to what goal, she recks not.

I, also, am possessed of just such a yearning. I likewise have lost my home and also lost my way. Both the end and the means have become equally shadowy to me. There remain only the yearning and the hurrying on. Ah! wretched wanderer through the night, when the dawn reddens you will see no trace of a way to return. But why return? Death will serve as well. If the Dark which sounded the flute should lead to destruction, why trouble about the hereafter? When I am merged in its blackness, neither I, nor good and bad, nor laughter, nor tears, shall be any more!

XII

In Bengal the machinery of time being thus suddenly run at full pressure, things which were difficult became easy, one following soon after another. Nothing could be held back any more, even in our corner of the country. In the beginning our district was backward, for my husband was unwilling to put any compulsion on the villagers. "Those who make sacrifices for their country's sake are indeed her servants," he would say, "but those who compel others to make them in her name are her enemies. They would cut freedom at the root, to gain it at the top."

But when Sandip came and settled here, and his followers began to move about the country, speaking in towns and market-places, waves of excitement came rolling up to us as well. A band of young fellows of the locality attached themselves to him, some even who had been known as a disgrace to the village. But the glow of their genuine enthusiasm lighted them up, within as well as without. It became quite clear that when the pure breezes of a great joy and hope sweep through the land, all dirt and decay are cleansed away. It is hard, indeed, for men to be frank and straight and healthy, when their country is in the throes of dejection.

Then were all eyes turned on my husband, from whose estates alone foreign sugar and salt and cloths had not been banished. Even the estate officers began to feel awkward and ashamed over it. And yet, some time ago, when my husband began to import country-made articles into our village, he had been secretly and openly twitted for his folly, by old and young alike. When __Swadeshi__ had not yet become a boast, we had despised it with all our hearts.

My husband still sharpens his Indian-made pencils with his Indian-made knife, does his writing with reed pens, drinks his water out of a bell-metal vessel, and works at night in the light of an old-fashioned castor-oil lamp. But this dull, milk-and-water __Swadeshi__ of his never appealed to us. Rather, we had always felt ashamed of the inelegant, unfashionable furniture of his reception-rooms, especially when he had the magistrate, or any other European, as his guest.

My husband used to make light of my protests. "Why allow such trifles to upset you?" he would say with a smile.

"They will think us barbarians, or at all events wanting in refinement."

"If they do, I will pay them back by thinking that their refinement does not go deeper than their white skins."

My husband had an ordinary brass pot on his writing-table which he used as a flower-vase. It has often happened that, when I had news of some European guest, I would steal into his room and put in its place a crystal vase of European make. "Look here, Bimala," he objected at length, "that brass pot is as unconscious of itself as those blossoms are; but this thing protests its purpose so loudly, it is only fit for artificial flowers."

The Bara Rani, alone, pandered to my husband's whims. Once she comes panting to say: "Oh, brother, have you heard? Such lovely Indian soaps have come out! My days of luxury are gone by; still, if they contain no animal fat, I should like to try some."

This sort of thing makes my husband beam all over, and the house is deluged with Indian scents and soaps. Soaps indeed! They are more like lumps of caustic soda. And do I not know that what my sister-in-law uses on herself are the European soaps of old, while these are made over to the maids for washing clothes?

Another time it is: "Oh, brother dear, do get me some of these new Indian pen-holders."

Her "brother" bubbles up as usual, and the Bara Rani's room becomes littered with all kinds of awful sticks that go by the name of __Swadeshi__ pen-holders. Not that it makes any difference to her, for reading and writing are out of her line. Still, in her writing-case, lies the selfsame ivory pen-holder, the only one ever handled.

The fact is, all this was intended as a hit at me, because I would not keep my husband company in his vagaries. It was no good trying to show up my sister-in-law's insincerity; my husband's face would set so hard, if I barely touched on it. One only gets into trouble, trying to save such people from being imposed upon!

The Bara Rani loves sewing. One day I could not help blurting out: "What a humbug you are, sister! When your 'brother' is present, your mouth waters at the very mention of __Swadeshi__ scissors, but it is the English-made article every time when you work."

"What harm?" she replied. "Do you not see what pleasure it gives him? We have grown up together in this house, since he was a boy. I simply cannot bear, as you can, the sight of the smile leaving his face. Poor dear, he has no amusement except this playing at shop-keeping. You are his only dissipation, and you will yet be his ruin!"

"Whatever you may say, it is not right to be double-faced," I retorted.

My sister-in-law laughed out in my face. "Oh, our artless little Chota Rani!—straight as a schoolmaster's rod, eh? But a woman is not built that way. She is soft and supple, so that she may bend without being crooked."

I could not forget those words: "You are his dissipation, and will be his ruin!" Today I feel—if a man needs must have some intoxicant, let it not be a woman.

XIII

Suksar, within our estates, is one of the biggest trade centres in the district. On one side of a stretch of water there is held a daily bazar; on the other, a weekly market. During the rains when this piece of water gets connected with the river, and boats can come through, great quantities of cotton yarns, and woollen stuffs for the coming winter, are brought in for sale.

At the height of our enthusiasm, Sandip laid it down that all foreign articles, together with the demon of foreign influence, must be driven out of our territory.

"Of course!" said I, girding myself up for a fight.

"I have had words with Nikhil about it," said Sandip. "He tells me, he does not mind speechifying, but he will not have coercion."

"I will see to that," I said, with a proud sense of power. I knew how deep was my husband's love for me. Had I been in my senses I should have allowed myself to be torn to pieces rather than assert my claim to that, at such a time. But Sandip had to be impressed with the full strength of my __Shakti__.

Sandip had brought home to me, in his irresistible way, how the cosmic Energy was revealed for each individual in the shape of some special affinity. Vaishnava Philosophy, he said, speaks of the __Shakti__ of Delight that dwells in the heart of creation, ever attracting the heart of her Eternal Lover. Men have a perpetual longing to bring out this __Shakti__ from the hidden depths of their own nature, and those of us who succeed in doing so at once clearly understand the meaning of the music coming to us from the Dark. He broke out singing:

/*
"My flute, that was busy with its song,
Is silent now when we stand face to face.
My call went seeking you from sky to sky
When you lay hidden;
But now all my cry finds its smile
In the face of my beloved."
*/

Listening to his allegories, I had forgotten that I was plain and simple Bimala. I was __Shakti__; also an embodiment of Universal joy. Nothing could fetter me, nothing was impossible for me; whatever I touched would gain new life. The world around me was a fresh creation of mine; for behold, before my heart's response had touched it, there had not been this wealth of gold in the Autumn sky! And this hero, this true servant of the country, this devotee of mine—this flaming intelligence, this burning energy, this shining genius—him also was I creating from moment to moment. Have I not seen how my presence pours fresh life into him time after time?

The other day Sandip begged me to receive a young lad, Amulya, an ardent disciple of his. In a moment I could see a new light flash out from the boy's eyes, and knew that he, too, had a vision of __Shakti__ manifest, that my creative force had begun its work in his blood. "What sorcery is this of yours!" exclaimed Sandip next day. "Amulya is a boy no longer, the wick of his life is all ablaze. Who can hide your fire under your home-roof? Every one of them must be touched up by it, sooner or later, and when every lamp is alight what a grand carnival of a __Dewali__ we shall have in the country!"

Blinded with the brilliance of my own glory I had decided to grant my devotee this boon. I was overweeningly confident that none could baulk me of what I really wanted. When I returned to my room after my talk with Sandip, I loosed my hair and tied it up over again. Miss Gilby had taught me a way of brushing it up from the neck and piling it in a knot over my head. This style was a favourite one with my husband. "It is a pity," he once said, "that Providence should have chosen poor me, instead of poet Kalidas, for revealing all the wonders of a woman's neck. The poet would probably have likened it to a flower-stem; but I feel it to be a torch, holding aloft the black flame of your hair." With which he … but why, oh why, do I go back to all that?

I sent for my husband. In the old days I could contrive a hundred and one excuses, good or bad, to get him to come to me. Now that all this had stopped for days I had lost the art of contriving.

Nikhil's Story

VI

Panchu's wife has just died of a lingering consumption. Panchu must undergo a purification ceremony to cleanse himself of sin and to propitiate his community. The community has calculated and informed him that it will cost one hundred and twenty-three rupees.

"How absurd!" I cried, highly indignant. "Don't submit to this, Panchu. What can they do to you?"

Raising to me his patient eyes like those of a tired-out beast of burden, he said: "There is my eldest girl, sir, she will have to be married. And my poor wife's last rites have to be put through."

"Even if the sin were yours, Panchu," I mused aloud, "you have surely suffered enough for it already."

"That is so, sir," he naïvely assented. "I had to sell part of my land and mortgage the rest to meet the doctor's bills. But there is no escape from the offerings I have to make the Brahmins."

What was the use of arguing? When will come the time, I wondered, for the purification of the Brahmins themselves who can accept such offerings?

After his wife's illness and funeral, Panchu, who had been tottering on the brink of starvation, went altogether beyond his depth. In a desperate attempt to gain consolation of some sort he took to sitting at the feet of a wandering ascetic, and succeeded in acquiring philosophy enough to forget that his children went hungry. He kept himself steeped for a time in the idea that the world is vanity, and if of pleasure it has none, pain also is a delusion. Then, at last, one night he left his little ones in their tumble-down hovel, and started off wandering on his own account.

I knew nothing of this at the time, for just then a veritable ocean-churning by gods and demons was going on in my mind. Nor did my master tell me that he had taken Panchu's deserted children under his own roof and was caring for them, though alone in the house, with his school to attend to the whole day.

After a month Panchu came back, his ascetic fervour considerably worn off. His eldest boy and girl nestled up to him, crying: "Where have you been all this time, father?" His youngest boy filled his lap; his second girl leant over his back with her arms around his neck; and they all wept together. "O sir!" sobbed Panchu, at length, to my master. "I have not the power to give these little ones enough to eat—I am not free to run away from them. What has been my sin that I should be scourged so, bound hand and foot?"

In the meantime the thread of Panchu's little trade connections had snapped and he found he could not resume them. He clung on to the shelter of my master's roof, which had first received him on his return, and said not a word of going back home. "Look here, Panchu," my master was at last driven to say. "If you don't take care of your cottage, it will tumble down altogether. I will lend you some money with which you can do a bit of peddling and return it me little by little."

Panchu was not excessively pleased—was there then no such thing as charity on earth? And when my master asked him to write out a receipt for the money, he felt that this favour, demanding a return, was hardly worth having. My master, however, did not care to make an outward gift which would leave an inward obligation. To destroy self-respect is to destroy caste, was his idea.

After signing the note, Panchu's obeisance to my master fell off considerably in its reverence—the dust-taking was left out. It made my master smile; he asked nothing better than that courtesy should stoop less low. "Respect given and taken truly balances the account between man and man," was the way he put it, "but veneration is overpayment."

Panchu began to buy cloth at the market and peddle it about the village. He did not get much of cash payment, it is true, but what he could realize in kind, in the way of rice, jute, and other field produce, went towards settlement of his account. In two month's time he was able to pay back an instalment of my master's debt, and with it there was a corresponding reduction in the depth of his bow. He must have begun to feel that he had been revering as a saint a mere man, who had not even risen superior to the lure of lucre.

While Panchu was thus engaged, the full shock of the __Swadeshi__ flood fell on him.

VII

It was vacation time, and many youths of our village and its neighbourhood had come home from their schools and colleges. They attached themselves to Sandip's leadership with enthusiasm, and some, in their excess of zeal, gave up their studies altogether. Many of the boys had been free pupils of my school here, and some held college scholarships from me in Calcutta. They came up in a body, and demanded that I should banish foreign goods from my Suksar market.

I told them I could not do it.

They were sarcastic: "Why, Maharaja, will the loss be too much for you?"

I took no notice of the insult in their tone, and was about to reply that the loss would fall on the poor traders and their customers, not on me, when my master, who was present, interposed.

"Yes, the loss will be his—not yours, that is clear enough," he said.

"But for one's country.."

"The country does not mean the soil, but the men on it," interrupted my master again. "Have you yet wasted so much as a glance on what was happening to them? But now you would dictate what salt they shall eat, what clothes they shall wear. Why should they put up with such tyranny, and why should we let them?"

"But we have taken to Indian salt and sugar and cloth ourselves."

"You may do as you please to work off your irritation, to keep up your fanaticism. You are well off, you need not mind the cost. The poor do not want to stand in your way, but you insist on their submitting to your compulsion. As it is, every moment of theirs is a life-and-death struggle for a bare living; you cannot even imagine the difference a few pice means to them—so little have you in common. You have spent your whole past in a superior compartment, and now you come down to use them as tools for the wreaking of your wrath. I call it cowardly."

They were all old pupils of my master, so they did not venture to be disrespectful, though they were quivering with indignation. They turned to me. "Will you then be the only one, Maharaja, to put obstacles in the way of what the country would achieve?"

"Who am I, that I should dare do such a thing? Would I not rather lay down my life to help it?"

The M.A. student smiled a crooked smile, as he asked: "May we enquire what you are actually doing to help?"

"I have imported Indian mill-made yarn and kept it for sale in my Suksar market, and also sent bales of it to markets belonging to neighbouring __zamindars__."

"But we have been to your market, Maharaja," the same student exclaimed, "and found nobody buying this yarn."

"That is neither my fault nor the fault of my market. It only shows the whole country has not taken your vow."

"That is not all," my master went on. "It shows that what you have pledged yourselves to do is only to pester others. You want dealers, who have not taken your vow, to buy that yarn; weavers, who have not taken your vow, to make it up; then their wares eventually to be foisted on to consumers who, also, have not taken your vow. The method? Your clamour, and the __zamindars'__ oppression. The result: all righteousness yours, all privations theirs!"

"And may we venture to ask, further, what your share of the privation has been?" pursued a science student.

"You want to know, do you?" replied my master. "It is Nikhil himself who has to buy up that Indian mill yarn; he has had to start a weaving school to get it woven; and to judge by his past brilliant business exploits, by the time his cotton fabrics leave the loom their cost will be that of cloth-of-gold; so they will only find a use, perhaps, as curtains for his drawing-room, even though their flimsiness may fail to screen him. When you get tired of your vow, you will laugh the loudest at their artistic effect. And if their workmanship is ever truly appreciated at all, it will be by foreigners."

I have known my master all my life, but have never seen him so agitated. I could see that the pain had been silently accumulating in his heart for some time, because of his surpassing love for me, and that his habitual self-possession had become secretly undermined to the breaking point.

"You are our elders," said the medical student. "It is unseemly that we should bandy words with you. But tell us, pray, finally, are you determined not to oust foreign articles from your market?"

"I will not," I said, "because they are not mine."

"Because that will cause you a loss!" smiled the M.A. student.

"Because he, whose is the loss, is the best judge," retorted my master.

With a shout of _Bande Mataram_ they left us.

Chapter Six

Nikhil's Story

VIII

A FEW days later, my master brought Panchu round to me. His __zamindar__, it appeared, had fined him a hundred rupees, and was threatening him with ejectment.

"For what fault?" I enquired.

"Because," I was told, "he has been found selling foreign cloths. He begged and prayed Harish Kundu, his __zamindar__, to let him sell off his stock, bought with borrowed money, promising faithfully never to do it again; but the __zamindar__ would not hear of it, and insisted on his burning the foreign stuff there and then, if he wanted to be let off. Panchu in his desperation blurted out defiantly: "I can't afford it! You are rich; why not buy it up and burn it?" This only made Harish Kundu red in the face as he shouted: "The scoundrel must be taught manners, give him a shoe-beating!" So poor Panchu got insulted as well as fined.

"What happened to the cloth?"

"The whole bale was burnt."

"Who else was there?"

"Any number of people, who all kept shouting __Bande Mataram__. Sandip was also there. He took up some of the ashes, crying: 'Brothers! This is the first funeral pyre lighted by your village in celebration of the last rites of foreign commerce. These are sacred ashes. Smear yourselves with them in token of your __Swadeshi__ vow.'"

"Panchu," said I, turning to him, "you must lodge a complaint."

"No one will bear me witness," he replied.

"None bear witness?—Sandip! Sandip!"

Sandip came out of his room at my call. "What is the matter?" he asked.

"Won't you bear witness to the burning of this man's cloth?"

Sandip smiled. "Of course I shall be a witness in the case," he said. "But I shall be on the opposite side."

"What do you mean," I exclaimed, "by being a witness on this or that side? Will you not bear witness to the truth?"

"Is the thing which happens the only truth?"

"What other truths can there be?"

"The things that ought to happen! The truth we must build up will require a great deal of untruth in the process. Those who have made their way in the world have created truth, not blindly followed it."

"And so—"

"And so I will bear what you people are pleased to call false witness, as they have done who have created empires, built up social systems, founded religious organizations. Those who would rule do not dread untruths; the shackles of truth are reserved for those who will fall under their sway. Have you not read history? Do you not know that in the immense cauldrons, where vast political developments are simmering, untruths are the main ingredients?"

"Political cookery on a large scale is doubtless going on, but—"

"Oh, I know! You, of course, will never do any of the cooking. You prefer to be one of those down whose throats the hotchpotch which is being cooked will be crammed. They will partition Bengal and say it is for your benefit. They will seal the doors of education and call it raising the standard. But you will always remain good boys, snivelling in your corners. We bad men, however, must see whether we cannot erect a defensive fortification of untruth."

"It is no use arguing about these things, Nikhil," my master interposed. "How can they who do not feel the truth within them, realize that to bring it out from its obscurity into the light is man's highest aim—not to keep on heaping material outside?"

Sandip laughed. "Right, sir!" said he. "Quite a correct speech for a schoolmaster. That is the kind of stuff I have read in books; but in the real world I have seen that man's chief business is the accumulation of outside material. Those who are masters in the art, advertise the biggest lies in their business, enter false accounts in their political ledgers with their broadest-pointed pens, launch their newspapers daily laden with untruths, and send preachers abroad to disseminate falsehood like flies carrying pestilential germs. I am a humble follower of these great ones. When I was attached to the Congress party I never hesitated to dilute ten per cent of truth with ninety per cent of untruth. And now, merely because I have ceased to belong to that party, I have not forgotten the basic fact that man's goal is not truth but success."

"True success," corrected my master.

"Maybe," replied Sandip, "but the fruit of true success ripens only by cultivating the field of untruth, after tearing up the soil and pounding it into dust. Truth grows up by itself like weeds and thorns, and only worms can expect to get fruit from it!" With this he flung out of the room.

My master smiled as he looked towards me. "Do you know, Nikhil," he said, "I believe Sandip is not irreligious—his religion is of the obverse side of truth, like the dark moon, which is still a moon, for all that its light has gone over to the wrong side."

"That is why," I assented, "I have always had an affection for him, though we have never been able to agree. I cannot contemn him, even now; though he has hurt me sorely, and may yet hurt me more."

"I have begun to realize that," said my master. "I have long wondered how you could go on putting up with him. I have, at times, even suspected you of weakness. I now see that though you two do not rhyme, your rhythm is the same."

"Fate seems bent on writing __Paradise Lost__ in blank verse, in my case, and so has no use for a rhyming friend!" I remarked, pursuing his conceit.

"But what of Panchu?" resumed my master.

"You say Harish Kundu wants to eject him from his ancestral holding. Supposing I buy it up and then keep him on as my tenant?"

"And his fine?"

"How can the __zamindar__ realize that if he becomes my tenant?"

"His burnt bale of cloth?"

"I will procure him another. I should like to see anyone interfering with a tenant of mine, for trading as he pleases!"

"I am afraid, sir," interposed Panchu despondently, "while you big folk are doing the fighting, the police and the law vultures will merrily gather round, and the crowd will enjoy the fun, but when it comes to getting killed, it will be the turn of only poor me!"

"Why, what harm can come to you?"

"They will burn down my house, sir, children and all!"

"Very well, I will take charge of your children," said my master. "You may go on with any trade you like. They shan't touch you."

That very day I bought up Panchu's holding and entered into formal possession. Then the trouble began.

Panchu had inherited the holding of his grandfather as his sole surviving heir. Everybody knew this. But at this juncture an aunt turned up from somewhere, with her boxes and bundles, her rosary, and a widowed niece. She ensconced herself in Panchu's home and laid claim to a life interest in all he had.

Panchu was dumbfounded. "My aunt died long ago," he protested.

In reply he was told that he was thinking of his uncle's first wife, but that the former had lost no time in taking to himself a second.

"But my uncle died before my aunt," exclaimed Panchu, still more mystified. "Where was the time for him to marry again?"

This was not denied. But Panchu was reminded that it had never been asserted that the second wife had come after the death of the first, but the former had been married by his uncle during the latter's lifetime. Not relishing the idea of living with a co-wife she had remained in her father's house till her husband's death, after which she had got religion and retired to holy Brindaban, whence she was now coming. These facts were well known to the officers of Harish Kundu, as well as to some of his tenants. And if the __zamindar's__ summons should be peremptory enough, even some of those who had partaken of the marriage feast would be forthcoming!

IX

One afternoon, when I happened to be specially busy, word came to my office room that Bimala had sent for me. I was startled.

"Who did you say had sent for me?" I asked the messenger.

"The Rani Mother."

"The Bara Rani?"

"No, sir, the Chota Rani Mother."

The Chota Rani! It seemed a century since I had been sent for by her. I kept them all waiting there, and went off into the inner apartments. When I stepped into our room I had another shock of surprise to find Bimala there with a distinct suggestion of being dressed up. The room, which from persistent neglect had latterly acquired an air of having grown absent-minded, had regained something of its old order this afternoon. I stood there silently, looking enquiringly at Bimala.

She flushed a little and the fingers of her right hand toyed for a time with the bangles on her left arm. Then she abruptly broke the silence. "Look here! Is it right that ours should be the only market in all Bengal which allows foreign goods?"

"What, then, would be the right thing to do?" I asked.

"Order them to be cleared out!"

"But the goods are not mine."

"Is not the market yours?"

"It is much more theirs who use it for trade."

"Let them trade in Indian goods, then."

"Nothing would please me better. But suppose they do not?"

"Nonsense! How dare they be so insolent? Are you not ..."

"I am very busy this afternoon and cannot stop to argue it out. But I must refuse to tyrannize."

"It would not be tyranny for selfish gain, but for the sake of the country."

"To tyrannize for the country is to tyrannize over the country. But that I am afraid you will never understand." With this I came away.

All of a sudden the world shone out for me with a fresh clearness. I seemed to feel it in my blood, that the Earth had lost the weight of its earthiness, and its daily task of sustaining life no longer appeared a burden, as with a wonderful access of power it whirled through space telling its beads of days and nights. What endless work, and withal what illimitable energy of freedom! None shall check it, oh, none can ever check it! From the depths of my being an uprush of joy, like a waterspout, sprang high to storm the skies.

I repeatedly asked myself the meaning of this outburst of feeling. At first there was no intelligible answer. Then it became clear that the bond against which I had been fretting inwardly, night and day, had broken. To my surprise I discovered that my mind was freed from all mistiness. I could see everything relating to Bimala as if vividly pictured on a camera screen. It was palpable that she had specially dressed herself up to coax that order out of me. Till that moment, I had never viewed Bimala's adornment as a thing apart from herself. But today the elaborate manner in which she had done up her hair, in the English fashion, made it appear a mere decoration. That which before had the mystery of her personality about it, and was priceless to me, was now out to sell itself cheap.

As I came away from that broken cage of a bedroom, out into the golden sunlight of the open, there was the avenue of bauhinias, along the gravelled path in front of my verandah, suffusing the sky with a rosy flush. A group of starlings beneath the trees were noisily chattering away. In the distance an empty bullock cart, with its nose on the ground, held up its tail aloft—one of its unharnessed bullocks grazing, the other resting on the grass, its eyes dropping for very comfort, while a crow on its back was pecking away at the insects on its body.

I seemed to have come closer to the heartbeats of the great earth in all the simplicity of its daily life; its warm breath fell on me with the perfume of the bauhinia blossoms; and an anthem, inexpressibly sweet, seemed to peal forth from this world, where I, in my freedom, live in the freedom of all else.

We, men, are knights whose quest is that freedom to which our ideals call us. She who makes for us the banner under which we fare forth is the true Woman for us. We must tear away the disguise of her who weaves our net of enchantment at home, and know her for what she is. We must beware of clothing her in the witchery of our own longings and imaginings, and thus allow her to distract us from our true quest.

Today I feel that I shall win through. I have come to the gateway of the simple; I am now content to see things as they are. I have gained freedom myself; I shall allow freedom to others. In my work will be my salvation.

I know that, time and again, my heart will ache, but now that I understand its pain in all its truth, I can disregard it. Now that I know it concerns only me, what after all can be its value? The suffering which belongs to all mankind shall be my crown.

Save me, Truth! Never again let me hanker after the false paradise of Illusion. If I must walk alone, let me at least tread your path. Let the drum-beats of Truth lead me to Victory.

Sandip's Story

VII

Bimala sent for me that day, but for a time she could not utter a word; her eyes kept brimming up to the verge of overflowing. I could see at once that she had been unsuccessful with Nikhil. She had been so proudly confident that she would have her own way—but I had never shared her confidence. Woman knows man well enough where he is weak, but she is quite unable to fathom him where he is strong. The fact is that man is as much a mystery to woman as woman is to man. If that were not so, the separation of the sexes would only have been a waste of Nature's energy.

Ah pride, pride! The trouble was, not that the necessary thing had failed of accomplishment, but that the entreaty, which had cost her such a struggle to make, should have been refused. What a wealth of colour and movement, suggestion and deception, group themselves round this "me" and "mine" in woman. That is just where her beauty lies—she is ever so much more personal than man. When man was being made, the Creator was a schoolmaster— His bag full of commandments and principles; but when He came to woman, He resigned His headmastership and turned artist, with only His brush and paint-box.

When Bimala stood silently there, flushed and tearful in her broken pride, like a storm-cloud, laden with rain and charged with lightning, lowering over the horizon, she looked so absolutely sweet that I had to go right up to her and take her by the hand. It was trembling, but she did not snatch it away.

"Bee," said I, "we two are colleagues, for our aims are one. Let us sit down and talk it over."

I led her, unresisting, to a seat. But strange! at that very point the rush of my impetuosity suffered an unaccountable check —just as the current of the mighty Padma, roaring on in its irresistible course, all of a sudden gets turned away from the bank it is crumbling by some trifling obstacle beneath the surface. When I pressed Bimala's hand my nerves rang music, like tuned-up strings; but the symphony stopped short at the first movement.

What stood in the way? Nothing singly; it was a tangle of a multitude of things—nothing definitely palpable, but only that unaccountable sense of obstruction. Anyhow, this much has become plain to me, that I cannot swear to what I really am. It is because I am such a mystery to my own mind that my attraction for myself is so strong! If once the whole of myself should become known to me, I would then fling it all away—and reach beatitude!

As she sat down, Bimala went ashy pale. She, too, must have realized what a crisis had come and gone, leaving her unscathed. The comet had passed by, but the brush of its burning tail had overcome her. To help her to recover herself I said: "Obstacles there will be, but let us fight them through, and not be down-hearted. Is not that best, Queen?"

Bimala cleared her throat with a little cough, but simply to murmur: "Yes."

"Let us sketch out our plan of action," I continued, as I drew a piece of paper and a pencil from my pocket.

I began to make a list of the workers who had joined us from Calcutta and to assign their duties to each. Bimala interrupted me before I was through, saying wearily: "Leave it now; I will join you again this evening" and then she hurried out of the room. It was evident she was not in a state to attend to anything. She must be alone with herself for a while—perhaps lie down on her bed and have a good cry!

When she left me, my intoxication began to deepen, as the cloud colours grow richer after the sun is down. I felt I had let the moment of moments slip by. What an awful coward I had been! She must have left me in sheer disgust at my qualms—and she was right!

While I was tingling all over with these reflections, a servant came in and announced Amulya, one of our boys. I felt like sending him away for the time, but he stepped in before I could make up my mind. Then we fell to discussing the news of the fights which were raging in different quarters over cloth and sugar and salt; and the air was soon clear of all fumes of intoxication. I felt as if awakened from a dream. I leapt to my feet feeling quite ready for the fray—Bande Mataram!

The news was various. Most of the traders who were tenants of Harish Kundu had come over to us. Many of Nikhil's officials were also secretly on our side, pulling the wires in our interest. The Marwari shopkeepers were offering to pay a penalty, if only allowed to clear their present stocks. Only some Mahomedan traders were still obdurate.

One of them was taking home some German-made shawls for his family. These were confiscated and burnt by one of our village boys. This had given rise to trouble. We offered to buy him Indian woollen stuffs in their place. But where were cheap Indian woollens to be had? We could not very well indulge him in Cashmere shawls! He came and complained to Nikhil, who advised him to go to law. Of course Nikhil's men saw to it that the trial should come to nothing, even his law-agent being on our side!

The point is, if we have to replace burnt foreign clothes with Indian cloth every time, and on the top of that fight through a law-suit, where is the money to come from? And the beauty of it is that this destruction of foreign goods is increasing their demand and sending up the foreigner's profits—very like what happened to the fortunate shopkeeper whose chandeliers the nabob delighted in smashing, tickled by the tinkle of the breaking glass.

The next problem is—since there is no such thing as cheap and gaudy Indian woollen stuff, should we be rigorous in our boycott of foreign flannels and memos, or make an exception in their favour?

"Look here!" said I at length on the first point, "we are not going to keep on making presents of Indian stuff to those who have got their foreign purchases confiscated. The penalty is intended to fall on them, not on us. If they go to law, we must retaliate by burning down their granaries!—What startles you, Amulya? It is not the prospect of a grand illumination that delights me! You must remember, this is War. If you are afraid of causing suffering, go in for love-making, you will never do for this work!"

The second problem I solved by deciding to allow no compromise with foreign articles, in any circumstance whatever. In the good old days, when these gaily coloured foreign shawls were unknown, our peasantry used to manage well enough with plain cotton quilts—they must learn to do so again. They may not look as gorgeous, but this is not the time to think of looks.

Most of the boatmen had been won over to refuse to carry foreign goods, but the chief of them, Mirjan, was still insubordinate.

"Could you not get his boat sunk?" I asked our manager here.

"Nothing easier, sir," he replied. "But what if afterwards I am held responsible?"

"Why be so clumsy as to leave any loophole for responsibility? However, if there must be any, my shoulders will be there to bear it."

Mirjan's boat was tied near the landing-place after its freight had been taken over to the market-place. There was no one on it, for the manager had arranged for some entertainment to which all had been invited. After dusk the boat, loaded with rubbish, was holed and set adrift. It sank in mid-stream.

Mirjan understood the whole thing. He came to me in tears to beg for mercy. "I was wrong, sir—" he began.

"What makes you realize that all of a sudden?" I sneered.

He made no direct reply. "The boat was worth two thousand rupees," he said. "I now see my mistake, and if excused this time I will never …" with which he threw himself at my feet.

I asked him to come ten days later. If only we could pay him that two thousand rupees at once, we could buy him up body and soul. This is just the sort of man who could render us immense service, if won over. We shall never be able to make any headway unless we can lay our hands on plenty of money.

As soon as Bimala came into the sitting-room, in the evening, I said as I rose up to receive her: "Queen! Everything is ready, success is at hand, but we must have money.

"Money? How much money?"

"Not so very much, but by hook or by crook we must have it!"

"But how much?"

"A mere fifty thousand rupees will do for the present."

Bimala blenched inwardly at the figure, but tried not to show it. How could she again admit defeat?

"Queen!" said I, "you only can make the impossible possible. Indeed you have already done so. Oh, that I could show you the extent of your achievement—then you would know it. But the time for that is not now. Now we want money!"

"You shall have it," she said.

I could see that the thought of selling her jewels had occurred to her. So I said: "Your jewels must remain in reserve. One can never tell when they may be wanted." And then, as Bimala stared blankly at me in silence, I went on: "This money must come from your husband's treasury."

Bimala was still more taken aback. After a long pause she said: "But how am I to get his money?"

"Is not his money yours as well?"

"Ah, no!" she said, her wounded pride hurt afresh.

"If not," I cried, "neither is it his, but his country's, whom he has deprived of it, in her time of need!"

"But how am I to get it?" she repeated.

"Get it you shall and must. You know best how. You must get it for Her to whom it rightfully belongs. _Bande Mataram_! These are the magic words which will open the door of his iron safe, break through the walls of his strong-room, and confound the hearts of those who are disloyal to its call. Say _Bande Mataram_, Bee!"

"_Bande Mataram_!"

Chapter Seven

Sandip's Story

VIII

WE are men, we are kings, we must have our tribute. Ever since we have come upon the Earth we have been plundering her; and the more we claimed, the more she submitted. From primeval days have we men been plucking fruits, cutting down trees, digging up the soil, killing beast, bird and fish. From the bottom of the sea, from underneath the ground, from the very jaws of death, it has all been grabbing and grabbing and grabbing—no strong-box in Nature's store-room has been respected or left unrifled. The one delight of this Earth is to fulfil the claims of those who are men. She has been made fertile and beautiful and complete through her endless sacrifices to them. But for this, she would be lost in the wilderness, not knowing herself, the doors of her heart shut, her diamonds and pearls never seeing the light.

Likewise, by sheer force of our claims, we men have opened up all the latent possibilities of women. In the process of surrendering themselves to us, they have ever gained their true greatness. Because they had to bring all the diamonds of their happiness and the pearls of their sorrow into our royal treasury, they have found their true wealth. So for men to accept is truly to give: for women to give is truly to gain.

The demand I have just made from Bimala, however, is indeed a large one! At first I felt scruples; for is it not the habit of man's mind to be in purposeless conflict with itself? I thought I had imposed too hard a task. My first impulse was to call her back, and tell her I would rather not make her life wretched by dragging her into all these troubles. I forgot, for the moment, that it was the mission of man to be aggressive, to make woman's existence fruitful by stirring up disquiet in the depth of her passivity, to make the whole world blessed by churning up the immeasurable abyss of suffering! This is why man's hands are so strong, his grip so firm. Bimala had been longing with all her heart that I, Sandip, should demand of her some great sacrifice— should call her to her death. How else could she be happy? Had she not waited all these weary years only for an opportunity to weep out her heart—so satiated was she with the monotony of her placid happiness? And therefore, at the very sight of me, her heart's horizon darkened with the rain clouds of her impending days of anguish. If I pity her and save her from her sorrows, what then was the purpose of my being born a man?

The real reason of my qualms is that my demand happens to be for money. That savours of beggary, for money is man's, not woman's. That is why I had to make it a big figure. A thousand or two would have the air of petty theft. Fifty thousand has all the expanse of romantic brigandage. Ah, but riches should really have been mine! So many of my desires have had to halt, again and again, on the road to accomplishment simply for want of money. This does not become me! Had my fate been merely unjust, it could be forgiven—but its bad taste is unpardonable. It is not simply a hardship that a man like me should be at his wit's end to pay his house rent, or should have to carefully count out the coins for an Intermediate Class railway ticket—it is vulgar!

It is equally clear that Nikhil's paternal estates are a superfluity to him. For him it would not have been at all unbecoming to be poor. He would have cheerfully pulled in the double harness of indigent mediocrity with that precious master of his. I should love to have, just for once, the chance to fling about fifty thousand rupees in the service of my country and to the satisfaction of myself. I am a nabob born, and it is a great dream of mine to get rid of this disguise of poverty, though it be for a day only, and to see myself in my true character. I have grave misgivings, however, as to Bimala ever getting that fifty thousand rupees within her reach, and it will probably be only a thousand or two which will actually come to hand. Be it so. The wise man is content with half a loaf, or any fraction for that matter, rather than no bread. I must return to these personal reflections of mine later. News comes that I am wanted at once. Something has gone wrong …

It seems that the police have got a clue to the man who sank Mirjan's boat for us. He was an old offender. They are on his trail, but he should be too practised a hand to be caught blabbing. However, one never knows. Nikhil's back is up, and his manager may not be able to have things his own way.

"If I get into trouble, sir," said the manager when I saw him, "I shall have to drag you in!"

"Where is the noose with which you can catch me?" I asked.

"I have a letter of yours, and several of Amulya Babu's." I could not see that the letter marked "urgent" to which I had been hurried into writing a reply was wanted urgently for this purpose only! I am getting to learn quite a number of things.

The point now is, that the police must be bribed and hush-money paid to Mirjan for his boat. It is also becoming evident that much of the cost of this patriotic venture of ours will find its way as profit into the pockets of Nikhil's manager. However, I must shut my eyes to that for the present, for is he not shouting __Bande Mataram__ as lustily as I am?

This kind of work has always to be carried on with leaky vessels which let as much through as they fetch in. We all have a hidden fund of moral judgement stored away within us, and so I was about to wax indignant with the manager, and enter in my diary a tirade against the unreliability of our countrymen. But, if there be a god, I must acknowledge with gratitude to him that he has given me a clear-seeing mind, which allows nothing inside or outside it to remain vague. I may delude others, but never myself. So I was unable to continue angry.

Whatever is true is neither good nor bad, but simply true, and that is Science. A lake is only the remnant of water which has not been sucked into the ground. Underneath the cult of _Bande Mataram_, as indeed at the bottom of all mundane affairs, there is a region of slime, whose absorbing power must be reckoned with. The manager will take what he wants; I also have my own wants. These lesser wants form a part of the wants of the great Cause—the horse must be fed and the wheels must be oiled if the best progress is to be made.

The long and short of it is that money we must have, and that soon. We must take whatever comes the readiest, for we cannot afford to wait. I know that the immediate often swallows up the ultimate; that the five thousand rupees of today may nip in the bud the fifty thousand rupees of tomorrow. But I must accept the penalty. Have I not often twitted Nikhil that they who walk in the paths of restraint have never known what sacrifice is? It is we greedy folk who have to sacrifice our greed at every step!

Of the cardinal sins of man, Desire is for men who are men—but Delusion, which is only for cowards, hampers them. Because delusion keeps them wrapped up in past and future, but is the very deuce for confounding their footsteps in the present. Those who are always straining their ears for the call of the remote, to the neglect of the call of the imminent, are like Sakuntala [19] absorbed in the memories of her lover. The guest comes unheeded, and the curse descends, depriving them of the very object of their desire.

The other day I pressed Bimala's hand, and that touch still stirs her mind, as it vibrates in mine. Its thrill must not be deadened by repetition, for then what is now music will descend to mere argument. There is at present no room in her mind for the question "why?" So I must not deprive Bimala, who is one of those creatures for whom illusion is necessary, of her full supply of it.

---

19. Sakuntala, after the king, her lover, went back to his kingdom, promising to send for her, was so lost in thoughts of him, that she failed to hear the call of her hermit guest who thereupon cursed her, saying that the object of her love would forget all about her. [Trans.].

As for me, I have so much else to do that I shall have to be content for the present with the foam of the wine cup of passion. O man of desire! Curb your greed, and practise your hand on the harp of illusion till you can bring out all the delicate nuances of suggestion. This is not the time to drain the cup to the dregs.

IX

Our work proceeds apace. But though we have shouted ourselves hoarse, proclaiming the Mussulmans to be our brethren, we have come to realize that we shall never be able to bring them wholly round to our side. So they must be suppressed altogether and made to understand that we are the masters. They are now showing their teeth, but one day they shall dance like tame bears to the tune we play.

"If the idea of a United India is a true one," objects Nikhil, "Mussulmans are a necessary part of it."

"Quite so," said I, "but we must know their place and keep them there, otherwise they will constantly be giving trouble."

"So you want to make trouble to prevent trouble?"

"What, then, is your plan?"

"There is only one well-known way of avoiding quarrels," said Nikhil meaningly.

I know that, like tales written by good people, Nikhil's discourse always ends in a moral. The strange part of it is that with all his familiarity with moral precepts, he still believes in them! He is an incorrigible schoolboy. His only merit is his sincerity. The mischief with people like him is that they will not admit the finality even of death, but keep their eyes always fixed on a hereafter.

I have long been nursing a plan which, if only I could carry it out, would set fire to the whole country. True patriotism will never be roused in our countrymen unless they can visualize the motherland. We must make a goddess of her. My colleagues saw the point at once. "Let us devise an appropriate image!" they exclaimed. "It will not do if you devise it," I admonished them. "We must get one of the current images accepted as representing the country—the worship of the people must flow towards it along the deep-cut grooves of custom."

But Nikhil's needs must argue even about this. "We must not seek the help of illusions," he said to me some time ago, "for what we believe to be the true cause."

"Illusions are necessary for lesser minds," I said, "and to this class the greater portion of the world belongs. That is why divinities are set up in every country to keep up the illusions of the people, for men are only too well aware of their weakness."

"No," he replied. "God is necessary to clear away our illusions. The divinities which keep them alive are false gods."

"What of that? If need be, even false gods must be invoked, rather than let the work suffer. Unfortunately for us, our illusions are alive enough, but we do not know how to make them serve our purpose. Look at the Brahmins. In spite of our treating them as demi-gods, and untiringly taking the dust of their feet, they are a force going to waste.

"There will always be a large class of people, given to grovelling, who can never be made to do anything unless they are bespattered with the dust of somebody's feet, be it on their heads or on their backs! What a pity if after keeping Brahmins saved up in our armoury for all these ages—keen and serviceable —they cannot be utilized to urge on this rabble in the time of our need."

But it is impossible to drive all this into Nikhil's head. He has such a prejudice in favour of truth—as though there exists such an objective reality! How often have I tried to explain to him that where untruth truly exists, there it is indeed the truth. This was understood in our country in the old days, and so they had the courage to declare that for those of little understanding untruth is the truth. For them, who can truly believe their country to be a goddess, her image will do duty for the truth. With our nature and our traditions we are unable to realize our country as she is, but we can easily bring ourselves to believe in her image. Those who want to do real work must not ignore this fact.

Nikhil only got excited. "Because you have lost the power of walking in the path of truth's attainment," he cried, "you keep waiting for some miraculous boon to drop from the skies! That is why when your service to the country has fallen centuries into arrears all you can think of is, to make of it an image and stretch out your hands in expectation of gratuitous favours."

"We want to perform the impossible," I said. "So our country needs must be made into a god."

"You mean you have no heart for possible tasks," replied Nikhil. "Whatever is already there is to be left undisturbed; yet there must be a supernatural result:"

"Look here, Nikhil," I said at length, thoroughly exasperated.

"The things you have been saying are good enough as moral lessons. These ideas have served their purpose, as milk for babes, at one stage of man's evolution, but will no longer do, now that man has cut his teeth.

"Do we not see before our very eyes how things, of which we never even dreamt of sowing the seed, are sprouting up on every side? By what power? That of the deity in our country who is becoming manifest. It is for the genius of the age to give that deity its image. Genius does not argue, it creates. I only give form to what the country imagines.

"I will spread it abroad that the goddess has vouchsafed me a dream. I will tell the Brahmins that they have been appointed her priests, and that their downfall has been due to their dereliction of duty in not seeing to the proper performance of her worship. Do you say I shall be uttering lies? No, say I, it is the truth—nay more, the truth which the country has so long been waiting to learn from my lips. If only I could get the opportunity to deliver my message, you would see the stupendous result."

"What I am afraid of," said Nikhil, "is, that my lifetime is limited and the result you speak of is not the final result. It will have after-effects which may not be immediately apparent."

"I only seek the result," said I, "which belongs to today."

"The result I seek," answered Nikhil, "belongs to all time."

Nikhil may have had his share of Bengal's greatest gift— imagination, but he has allowed it to be overshadowed and nearly killed by an exotic conscientiousness. Just look at the worship of Durga which Bengal has carried to such heights. That is one of her greatest achievements. I can swear that Durga is a political goddess and was conceived as the image of the _Shakti_ of patriotism in the days when Bengal was praying to be delivered from Mussulman domination. What other province of India has succeeded in giving such wonderful visual expression to the ideal of its quest?

Nothing betrayed Nikhil's loss of the divine gift of imagination more conclusively than his reply to me. "During the Mussulman domination," he said, "the Maratha and the Sikh asked for fruit from the arms which they themselves took up. The Bengali contented himself with placing weapons in the hands of his goddess and muttering incantations to her; and as his country did not really happen to be a goddess the only fruit he got was the lopped-off heads of the goats and buffaloes of the sacrifice. The day that we seek the good of the country along the path of righteousness, He who is greater than our country will grant us true fruition."

The unfortunate part of it is that Nikhil's words sound so fine when put down on paper. My words, however, are not meant to be scribbled on paper, but to be scored into the heart of the country. The Pandit records his Treatise on Agriculture in printer's ink; but the cultivator at the point of his plough impresses his endeavour deep in the soil.

X

When I next saw Bimala I pitched my key high without further ado. "Have we been able," I began, "to believe with all our heart in the god for whose worship we have been born all these millions of years, until he actually made himself visible to us?

"How often have I told you," I continued, "that had I not seen you I never would have known all my country as One. I know not yet whether you rightly understand me. The gods are invisible only in their heaven—on earth they show themselves to mortal men."

Bimala looked at me in a strange kind of way as she gravely replied: "Indeed I understand you, Sandip." This was the first time she called me plain Sandip.

"Krishna," I continued, "whom Arjuna ordinarily knew only as the driver of his chariot, had also His universal aspect, of which, too, Arjuna had a vision one day, and that day he saw the Truth. I have seen your Universal Aspect in my country. The Ganges and the Brahmaputra are the chains of gold that wind round and round your neck; in the woodland fringes on the distant banks of the dark waters of the river, I have seen your collyrium-darkened eyelashes; the changeful sheen of your __sari__ moves for me in the play of light and shade amongst the swaying shoots of green corn; and the blazing summer heat, which makes the whole sky lie gasping like a red-tongued lion in the desert, is nothing but your cruel radiance.

"Since the goddess has vouchsafed her presence to her votary in such wonderful guise, it is for me to proclaim her worship throughout our land, and then shall the country gain new life. 'Your image make we in temple after temple.' [20] But this our people have not yet fully realized. So I would call on them in your name and offer for their worship an image from which none shall be able to withhold belief. Oh give me this boon, this power."

---

20. A line from Bankim Chatterjee's national song __Bande Mataram__.

Bimala's eyelids drooped and she became rigid in her seat like a figure of stone. Had I continued she would have gone off into a trance. When I ceased speaking she opened wide her eyes, and murmured with fixed gaze, as though still dazed: "O Traveller in the path of Destruction! Who is there that can stay your progress? Do I not see that none shall stand in the way of your desires? Kings shall lay their crowns at your feet; the wealthy shall hasten to throw open their treasure for your acceptance; those who have nothing else shall beg to be allowed to offer their lives. O my king, my god! What you have seen in me I know not, but I have seen the immensity of your grandeur in my heart. Who am I, what am I, in its presence? Ah, the awful power of Devastation! Never shall I truly live till it kills me utterly! I can bear it no longer, my heart is breaking!"

Bimala slid down from her seat and fell at my feet, which she clasped, and then she sobbed and sobbed and sobbed.

This is hypnotism indeed—the charm which can subdue the world! No materials, no weapons—but just the delusion of irresistible suggestion. Who says "Truth shall Triumph"? [21] Delusion shall win in the end. The Bengali understood this when he conceived the image of the ten-handed goddess astride her lion, and spread her worship in the land. Bengal must now create a new image to enchant and conquer the world. __Bande Mataram__!

I gently lifted Bimala back into her chair, and lest reaction should set in, I began again without losing time: "Queen! The Divine Mother has laid on me the duty of establishing her worship in the land. But, alas, I am poor!"

Bimala was still flushed, her eyes clouded, her accents thick, as she replied: "You poor? Is not all that each one has yours? What are my caskets full of jewellery for? Drag away from me all my gold and gems for your worship. I have no use for them!"

---

21. A quotation from the Upanishads.

Once before Bimala had offered up her ornaments. I am not usually in the habit of drawing lines, but I felt I had to draw the line there. [22] I know why I feel this hesitation. It is for man to give ornaments to woman; to take them from her wounds his manliness.

But I must forget myself. Am I taking them? They are for the Divine Mother, to be poured in worship at her feet. Oh, but it must be a grand ceremony of worship such as the country has never beheld before. It must be a landmark in our history. It shall be my supreme legacy to the Nation. Ignorant men worship gods. I, Sandip, shall create them.

But all this is a far cry. What about the urgent immediate? At least three thousand is indispensably necessary—five thousand would do roundly and nicely. But how on earth am I to mention money after the high flight we have just taken? And yet time is precious!

I crushed all hesitation under foot as I jumped up and made my plunge: "Queen! Our purse is empty, our work about to stop!"

Bimala winced. I could see she was thinking of that impossible fifty thousand rupees. What a load she must have been carrying within her bosom, struggling under it, perhaps, through sleepless nights! What else had she with which to express her loving worship? Debarred from offering her heart at my feet, she hankers to make this sum of money, so hopelessly large for her, the bearer of her imprisoned feelings. The thought of what she must have gone through gives me a twinge of pain;

---

22. There is a world of sentiment attached to the ornaments worn by women in Bengal.

   They are not merely indicative of the love and regard of the giver, but the wearing of them symbolizes all that is held best in wifehood—the constant solicitude for her husband's welfare, the successful performance of the material and spiritual duties of the household entrusted to her care. When the husband dies, and the responsibility for the household changes hands, then are all ornaments cast aside as a sign of the widow's renunciation of worldly concerns. At any other time the giving up of omaments is always a sign of supreme distress and as such appeals acutely to the sense of chivalry of any Bengali who may happen to witness it [Trans.].

for she is now wholly mine. The wrench of plucking up the plant by the roots is over. It is now only careful tending and nurture that is needed.

"Queen!" said I, "that fifty thousand rupees is not particularly wanted just now. I calculate that, for the present, five thousand or even three will serve."

The relief made her heart rebound. "I shall fetch you five thousand," she said in tones which seemed like an outburst of song—the song which Radhika of the Vaishnava lyrics sang:

For my lover will I bind in my hair
The flower which has no equal in the three worlds!

—it is the same tune, the same song: five thousand will I bring! That flower will I bind in my hair!

The narrow restraint of the flute brings out this quality of song. I must not allow the pressure of too much greed to flatten out the reed, for then, as I fear, music will give place to the questions "Why?" "What is the use of so much?" "How am I to get it?"—not a word of which will rhyme with what Radhika sang! So, as I was saying, illusion alone is real—it is the flute itself; while truth is but its empty hollow. Nikhil has of late got a taste of that pure emptiness—one can see it in his face, which pains even me. But it was Nikhil's boast that he wanted the Truth, while mine was that I would never let go illusion from my grasp. Each has been suited to his taste, so why complain?

To keep Bimala's heart in the rarefied air of idealism, I cut short all further discussion over the five thousand rupees. I reverted to the demon-destroying goddess and her worship. When was the ceremony to be held and where? There is a great annual fair at Ruimari, within Nikhil's estates, where hundreds of thousands of pilgrims assemble. That would be a grand place to inaugurate the worship of our goddess!

Bimala waxed intensely enthusiastic. This was not the burning of foreign cloth or the people's granaries, so even Nikhil could have no objection—so thought she. But I smiled inwardly. How little these two persons, who have been together, day and night, for nine whole years, know of each other! They know something perhaps of their home life, but when it comes to outside concerns they are entirely at sea. They had cherished the belief that the harmony of the home with the outside was perfect. Today they realize to their cost that it is too late to repair their neglect of years, and seek to harmonize them now.

What does it matter? Let those who have made the mistake learn their error by knocking against the world. Why need I bother about their plight? For the present I find it wearisome to keep Bimala soaring much longer, like a captive balloon, in regions ethereal. I had better get quite through with the matter in hand.

When Bimala rose to depart and had neared the door I remarked in my most casual manner: "So, about the money ..."

Bimala halted and faced back as she said: "On the expiry of the month, when our personal allowances become due ..."

"That, I am afraid, would be much too late."

"When do you want it then?"

"Tomorrow.

"Tomorrow you shall have it."

Chapter Eight

Nikhil's Story

X

PARAGRAPHS and letters against me have begun to come out in the local papers; cartoons and lampoons are to follow, I am told. Jets of wit and humour are being splashed about, and the lies thus scattered are convulsing the whole country. They know that the monopoly of mud-throwing is theirs, and the innocent passer- by cannot escape unsoiled.

They are saying that the residents in my estates, from the highest to the lowest, are in favour of __Swadeshi__, but they dare not declare themselves, for fear of me. The few who have been brave enough to defy me have felt the full rigour of my persecution. I am in secret league with the police, and in private communication with the magistrate, and these frantic efforts of mine to add a foreign title of my own earning to the one I have inherited, will not, it is opined, go in vain.

On the other hand, the papers are full of praise for those devoted sons of the motherland, the Kundu and the Chakravarti __zamindars__. If only, say they, the country had a few more of such staunch patriots, the mills of Manchester would have, had to sound their own dirge to the tune of __Bande Mataram__.

Then comes a letter in blood-red ink, giving a list of the traitorous __zamindars__ whose treasuries have been burnt down because of their failing to support the Cause. Holy Fire, it goes on to say, has been aroused to its sacred function of purifying the country; and other agencies are also at work to see that those who are not true sons of the motherland do cease to encumber her lap. The signature is an obvious __nom-de- plume__.

I could see that this was the doing of our local students. So I sent for some of them and showed them the letter.

The B.A. student gravely informed me that they also had heard that a band of desperate patriots had been formed who would stick at nothing in order to clear away all obstacles to the success of __Swadeshi__.

"If," said I, "even one of our countrymen succumbs to these overbearing desperadoes, that will indeed be a defeat for the country!"

"We fail to follow you, Maharaja," said the history student. "Our country," I tried to explain, "has been brought to death's door through sheer fear—from fear of the gods down to fear of the police; and if you set up, in the name of freedom, the fear of some other bogey, whatever it may be called; if you would raise your victorious standard on the cowardice of the country by means of downright oppression, then no true lover of the country can bow to your decision."

"Is there any country, sir," pursued the history student, "where submission to Government is not due to fear?"

"The freedom that exists in any country," I replied, "may be measured by the extent of this reign of fear. Where its threat is confined to those who would hurt or plunder, there the Government may claim to have freed man from the violence of man. But if fear is to regulate how people are to dress, where they shall trade, or what they must eat, then is man's freedom of will utterly ignored, and manhood destroyed at the root."

"Is not such coercion of the individual will seen in other countries too?" continued the history student.

"Who denies it?" I exclaimed. "But in every country man has destroyed himself to the extent that he has permitted slavery to flourish."

"Does it not rather show," interposed a Master of Arts, "that trading in slavery is inherent in man—a fundamental fact of his nature?"

"Sandip Babu made the whole thing clear," said a graduate. "He gave us the example of Harish Kundu, your neighbouring __zamindar__. From his estates you cannot ferret out a single ounce of foreign salt. Why? Because he has always ruled with an iron hand. In the case of those who are slaves by nature, the lack of a strong master is the greatest of all calamities."

"Why, sir!" chimed in an undergraduate, "have you not heard of the obstreperous tenant of Chakravarti, the other __zamindar__ close by—how the law was set on him till he was reduced to utter destitution? When at last he was left with nothing to eat, he started out to sell his wife's silver ornaments, but no one dared buy them. Then Chakravarti's manager offered him five rupees for the lot. They were worth over thirty, but he had to accept or starve. After taking over the bundle from him the manager coolly said that those five rupees would be credited towards his rent! We felt like having nothing more to do with Chakravarti or his manager after that, but Sandip Babu told us that if we threw over all the live people, we should have only dead bodies from the burning-grounds to carry on the work with! These live men, he pointed out, know what they want and how to get it—they are born rulers. Those who do not know how to desire for themselves, must live in accordance with, or die by virtue of, the desires of such as these. Sandip Babu contrasted them—Kundu and Chakravarti— with you, Maharaja. You, he said, for all your good intentions, will never succeed in planting __Swadeshi__ within your territory."

"It is my desire," I said, "to plant something greater than __Swadeshi__. I am not after dead logs but living trees—and these will take time to grow."

"I am afraid, sir," sneered the history student, "that you will get neither log nor tree. Sandip Babu rightly teaches that in order to get, you must snatch. This is taking all of us some time to learn, because it runs counter to what we were taught at school. I have seen with my own eyes that when a rent-collector of Harish Kundu's found one of the tenants with nothing which could be sold up to pay his rent, he was made to sell his young wife! Buyers were not wanting, and the __zamindar's__ demand was satisfied. I tell you, sir, the sight of that man's distress prevented my getting sleep for nights together! But, feel it as I did, this much I realized, that the man who knows how to get the money he is out for, even by selling up his debtor's wife, is a better man than I am. I confess it is beyond me—I am a weakling, my eyes fill with tears. If anybody can save our country it is these Kundus and these Chakravartis and their officials!"

I was shocked beyond words. "If what you say be true," I cried, "I clearly see that it must be the one endeavour of my life to save the country from these same Kundus and Chakravartis and officials. The slavery that has entered into our very bones is breaking out, at this opportunity, as ghastly tyranny. You have been so used to submit to domination through fear, you have come to believe that to make others submit is a kind of religion. My fight shall be against this weakness, this atrocious cruelty!" These things, which are so simple to ordinary folk, get so twisted in the minds of our B.A.'s and M.A.'s, the only purpose of whose historical quibbles seems to be to torture the truth!

XI

I am worried over Panchu's sham aunt. It will be difficult to disprove her, for though witnesses of a real event may be few or even wanting, innumerable proofs of a thing that has not happened can always be marshalled. The object of this move is, evidently, to get the sale of Panchu's holding to me set aside. Being unable to find any other way out of it, I was thinking of allowing Panchu to hold a permanent tenure in my estates and building him a cottage on it. But my master would not have it. I should not give in to these nefarious tactics so easily, he objected, and offered to attend to the matter himself.

"You, sir!" I cried, considerably surprised.

"Yes, I," he repeated.

I could not see, at all clearly, what my master could do to counteract these legal machinations. That evening, at the time he usually came to me, he did not turn up. On my making inquiries, his servant said he had left home with a few things packed in a small trunk, and some bedding, saying he would be back in a few days. I thought he might have sallied forth to hunt for witnesses in Panchu's uncle's village. In that case, however, I was sure that his would be a hopeless quest ...

During the day I forget myself in my work. As the late autumn afternoon wears on, the colours of the sky become turbid, and so do the feelings of my mind. There are many in this world whose minds dwell in brick-built houses—they can afford to ignore the thing called the outside. But my mind lives under the trees in the open, directly receives upon itself the messages borne by the free winds, and responds from the bottom of its heart to all the musical cadences of light and darkness.

While the day is bright and the world in the pursuit of its numberless tasks crowds around, then it seems as if my life wants nothing else. But when the colours of the sky fade away and the blinds are drawn down over the windows of heaven, then my heart tells me that evening falls just for the purpose of shutting out the world, to mark the time when the darkness must be filled with the One. This is the end to which earth, sky, and waters conspire, and I cannot harden myself against accepting its meaning. So when the gloaming deepens over the world, like the gaze of the dark eyes of the beloved, then my whole being tells me that work alone cannot be the truth of life, that work is not the be-all and the end-all of man, for man is not simply a serf— even though the serfdom be of the True and the Good.

Alas, Nikhil, have you for ever parted company with that self of yours who used to be set free under the starlight, to plunge into the infinite depths of the night's darkness after the day's work was done? How terribly alone is he, who misses companionship in the midst of the multitudinousness of life.

The other day, when the afternoon had reached the meeting-point of day and night, I had no work, nor the mind for work, nor was my master there to keep me company. With my empty, drifting heart longing to anchor on to something, I traced my steps towards the inner gardens. I was very fond of chrysanthemums and had rows of them, of all varieties, banked up in pots against one of the garden walls. When they were in flower, it looked like a wave of green breaking into iridescent foam. It was some time since I had been to this part of the grounds, and I was beguiled into a cheerful expectancy at the thought of meeting my chrysanthemums after our long separation.

As I went in, the full moon had just peeped over the wall, her slanting rays leaving its foot in deep shadow. It seemed as if she had come a-tiptoe from behind, and clasped the darkness over the eyes, smiling mischievously. When I came near the bank of chrysanthemums, I saw a figure stretched on the grass in front. My heart gave a sudden thud. The figure also sat up with a start at my footsteps.

What was to be done next? I was wondering whether it would do to beat a precipitate retreat. Bimala, also, was doubtless casting about for some way of escape. But it was as awkward to go as to stay! Before I could make up my mind, Bimala rose, pulled the end of her __sari__ over her head, and walked off towards the inner apartments.

This brief pause had been enough to make real to me the cruel load of Bimala's misery. The plaint of my own life vanished from me in a moment. I called out: "Bimala!"

She started and stayed her steps, but did not turn back. I went round and stood before her. Her face was in the shade, the moonlight fell on mine. Her eyes were downcast, her hands clenched.

"Bimala," said I, "why should I seek to keep you fast in this closed cage of mine? Do I not know that thus you cannot but pine and droop?"

She stood still, without raising her eyes or uttering a word.

"I know," I continued, "that if I insist on keeping you shackled my whole life will be reduced to nothing but an iron chain. What pleasure can that be to me?"

She was still silent.

"So," I concluded, "I tell you, truly, Bimala, you are free. Whatever I may or may not have been to you, I refuse to be your fetters." With which I came away towards the outer apartments.

No, no, it was not a generous impulse, nor indifference. I had simply come to understand that never would I be free until I could set free. To try to keep Bimala as a garland round my neck, would have meant keeping a weight hanging over my heart. Have I not been praying with all my strength, that if happiness may not be mine, let it go; if grief needs must be my lot, let it come; but let me not be kept in bondage. To clutch hold of that which is untrue as though it were true, is only to throttle oneself. May I be saved from such self-destruction.

When I entered my room, I found my master waiting there. My agitated feelings were still heaving within me. "Freedom, sir," I began unceremoniously, without greeting or inquiry, "freedom is the biggest thing for man. Nothing can be compared to it— nothing at all!"

Surprised at my outburst, my master looked up at me in silence.

"One can understand nothing from books," I went on. "We read in the scriptures that our desires are bonds, fettering us as well as others. But such words, by themselves, are so empty. It is only when we get to the point of letting the bird out of its cage that we can realize how free the bird has set us. Whatever we cage, shackles us with desire whose bonds are stronger than those of iron chains. I tell you, sir, this is just what the world has failed to understand. They all seek to reform something outside themselves. But reform is wanted only in one's own desires, nowhere else, nowhere else!"

"We think," he said, "that we are our own masters when we get in our hands the object of our desire—but we are really our own masters only when we are able to cast out our desires from our minds."

"When we put all this into words, sir," I went on, "it sounds like some bald-headed injunction, but when we realize even a little of it we find it to be __amrita__—which the gods have drunk and become immortal.

We cannot see Beauty till we let go our hold of it. It was Buddha who conquered the world, not Alexander—this is untrue when stated in dry prose—oh when shall we be able to sing it? When shall all these most intimate truths of the universe overflow the pages of printed books and leap out in a sacred stream like the Ganges from the Gangotrie?"

I was suddenly reminded of my master's absence during the last few days and of my ignorance as to its reason. I felt somewhat foolish as I asked him: "And where have you been all this while, sir?"

"Staying with Panchu," he replied.

"Indeed!" I exclaimed. "Have you been there all these days?"

"Yes. I wanted to come to an understanding with the woman who calls herself his aunt. She could hardly be induced to believe that there could be such an odd character among the gentlefolk as the one who sought their hospitality. When she found I really meant to stay on, she began to feel rather ashamed of herself. 'Mother,' said I, 'you are not going to get rid of me, even if you abuse me! And so long as I stay, Panchu stays also. For you see, do you not, that I cannot stand by and see his motherless little ones sent out into the streets?'

"She listened to my talks in this strain for a couple of days without saying yes or no. This morning I found her tying up her bundles. 'We are going back to Brindaban,' she said. 'Let us have our expenses for the journey.' I knew she was not going to Brindaban, and also that the cost of her journey would be substantial. So I have come to you."

"The required cost shall be paid," I said.

"The old woman is not a bad sort," my master went on musingly. "Panchu was not sure of her caste, and would not let her touch the water-jar, or anything at all of his. So they were continually bickering. When she found I had no objection to her touch, she looked after me devotedly. She is a splendid cook!

"But all remnants of Panchu's respect for me vanished! To the last he had thought that I was at least a simple sort of person. But here was I, risking my caste without a qualm to win over the old woman for my purpose. Had I tried to steal a march on her by tutoring a witness for the trial, that would have been a different matter. Tactics must be met by tactics. But stratagem at the expense of orthodoxy is more than he can tolerate!

"Anyhow, I must stay on a few days at Panchu's even after the woman leaves, for Harish Kundu may be up to any kind of devilry. He has been telling his satellites that he was content to have furnished Panchu with an aunt, but I have gone the length of supplying him with a father. He would like to see, now, how many fathers of his can save him!"

"We may or may not be able to save him," I said; "but if we should perish in the attempt to save the country from the thousand-and-one snares—of religion, custom and selfishness— which these people are busy spreading, we shall at least die happy."

Bimala's Story

XIV

Who could have thought that so much would happen in this one life? I feel as if I have passed through a whole series of births, time has been flying so fast, I did not feel it move at all, till the shock came the other day.

I knew there would be words between us when I made up my mind to ask my husband to banish foreign goods from our market. But it was my firm belief that I had no need to meet argument by argument, for there was magic in the very air about me. Had not so tremendous a man as Sandip fallen helplessly at my feet, like a wave of the mighty sea breaking on the shore? Had I called him? No, it was the summons of that magic spell of mine. And Amulya, poor dear boy, when he first came to me—how the current of his life flushed with colour, like the river at dawn! Truly have I realized how a goddess feels when she looks upon the radiant face of her devotee.

With the confidence begotten of these proofs of my power, I was ready to meet my husband like a lightning-charged cloud. But what was it that happened? Never in all these nine years have I seen such a far-away, distraught look in his eyes—like the desert sky—with no merciful moisture of its own, no colour reflected, even, from what it looked upon. I should have been so relieved if his anger had flashed out! But I could find nothing in him which I could touch. I felt as unreal as a dream—a dream which would leave only the blackness of night when it was over.

In the old days I used to be jealous of my sister-in-law for her beauty. Then I used to feel that Providence had given me no power of my own, that my whole strength lay in the love which my husband had bestowed on me. Now that I had drained to the dregs the cup of power and could not do without its intoxication, I suddenly found it dashed to pieces at my feet, leaving me nothing to live for.

How feverishly I had sat to do my hair that day. Oh, shame, shame on me, the utter shame of it! My sister-in-law, when passing by, had exclaimed: "Aha, Chota Rani! Your hair seems ready to jump off. Don't let it carry your head with it."

And then, the other day in the garden, how easy my husband found it to tell me that he set me free! But can freedom—empty freedom—be given and taken so easily as all that? It is like setting a fish free in the sky—for how can I move or live outside the atmosphere of loving care which has always sustained me?

When I came to my room today, I saw only furniture—only the bedstead, only the looking-glass, only the clothes-rack—not the all-pervading heart which used to be there, over all. Instead of it there was freedom, only freedom, mere emptiness! A dried-up watercourse with all its rocks and pebbles laid bare. No feeling, only furniture!

When I had arrived at a state of utter bewilderment, wondering whether anything true was left in my life, and whereabouts it could be, I happened to meet Sandip again. Then life struck against life, and the sparks flew in the same old way. Here was truth—impetuous truth—which rushed in and overflowed all bounds, truth which was a thousand times truer than the Bara Rani with her maid, Thako and her silly songs, and all the rest of them who talked and laughed and wandered about …

"Fifty thousand!" Sandip had demanded.

"What is fifty thousand?" cried my intoxicated heart. "You shall have it!"

How to get it, where to get it, were minor points not worth troubling over. Look at me. Had I not risen, all in one moment, from my nothingness to a height above everything? So shall all things come at my beck and call. I shall get it, get it, get it —there cannot be any doubt.

Thus had I come away from Sandip the other day. Then as I looked about me, where was it—the tree of plenty? Oh, why does this outer world insult the heart so?

And yet get it I must; how, I do not care; for sin there cannot be. Sin taints only the weak; I with my _Shakti_ am beyond its reach. Only a commoner can be a thief, the king conquers and takes his rightful spoil … I must find out where the treasury is; who takes the money in; who guards it.

I spent half the night standing in the outer verandah peering at the row of office buildings. But how to get that fifty thousand rupees out of the clutches of those iron bars? If by some _mantram_ I could have made all those guards fall dead in their places, I would not have hesitated—so pitiless did I feel!

But while a whole gang of robbers seemed dancing a war-dance within the whirling brain of its Rani, the great house of the Rajas slept in peace. The gong of the watch sounded hour after hour, and the sky overhead placidly looked on.

At last I sent for Amulya.

"Money is wanted for the Cause," I told him. "Can you not get it out of the treasury?"

"Why not?" said he, with his chest thrown out.

Alas! had I not said "Why not?" to Sandip just in the same way? The poor lad's confidence could rouse no hopes in my mind.

"How will you do it?" I asked.

The wild plans he began to unfold would hardly bear repetition outside the pages of a penny dreadful.

"No, Amulya," I said severely, "you must not be childish."

"Very well, then," he said, "let me bribe those watchmen."

"Where is the money to come from?"

"I can loot the bazar," he burst out, without blenching.

"Leave all that alone. I have my ornaments, they will serve.

"But," said Amulya, "it strikes me that the cashier cannot be bribed. Never mind, there is another and simpler way."

"What is that?"

"Why need you hear it? It is quite simple."

"Still, I should like to know."

Amulya fumbled in the pocket of his tunic and pulled out, first a small edition of the __Gita__, which he placed on the table— and then a little pistol, which he showed me, but said nothing further.

Horror! It did not take him a moment to make up his mind to kill our good old cashier! [23] To look at his frank, open face one would not have thought him capable of hurting a fly, but how different were the words which came from his mouth. It was clear that the cashier's place in the world meant nothing real to him; it was a mere vacancy, lifeless, feelingless, with only stock phrases from the __Gita—Who kills the body kills naught!__

---

23. The cashier is the official who is most in touch with the ladies of a __zamindar's__ household, directly taking their requisitions for household stores and doing their shopping for them, and so he becomes more a member of the family than the others. [Trans.].

"Whatever do you mean, Amulya?" I exclaimed at length. "Don't you know that the dear old man has got a wife and children and that he is ..."

"Where are we to find men who have no wives and children?" he interrupted. "Look here, Maharani, the thing we call pity is, at bottom, only pity for ourselves. We cannot bear to wound our own tender instincts, and so we do not strike at all—pity indeed! The height of cowardice!"

To hear Sandip's phrases in the mouth of this mere boy staggered me. So delightfully, lovably immature was he—of that age when the good may still be believed in as good, of that age when one really lives and grows. The Mother in me awoke.

For myself there was no longer good or bad—only death, beautiful alluring death. But to hear this stripling calmly talk of murdering an inoffensive old man as the right thing to do, made me shudder all over. The more clearly I saw that there was no sin in his heart, the more horrible appeared to me the sin of his words. I seemed to see the sin of the parents visited on the innocent child.

The sight of his great big eyes shining with faith and enthusiasm touched me to the quick. He was going, in his fascination, straight to the jaws of the python, from which, once in, there was no return. How was he to be saved? Why does not my country become, for once, a real Mother—clasp him to her bosom and cry out: "Oh, my child, my child, what profits it that you should save me, if so it be that I should fail to save you?"

I know, I know, that all Power on earth waxes great under compact with Satan. But the Mother is there, alone though she be, to contemn and stand against this devil's progress. The Mother cares not for mere success, however great—she wants to give life, to save life. My very soul, today, stretches out its hands in yearning to save this child.

A while ago I suggested robbery to him. Whatever I may now say against it will be put down to a woman's weakness. They only love our weakness when it drags the world in its toils!

"You need do nothing at all, Amulya, I will see to the money," I told him finally. When he had almost reached the door, I called him back.

"Amulya," said I, "I am your elder sister. Today is not the Brothers' Day [24] according to the calendar, but all the days in the year are really Brothers' Days. My blessing be with you: may God keep you always."

These unexpected words from my lips took Amulya by surprise. He stood stock-still for a time. Then, coming to himself, he prostrated himself at my feet in acceptance of the relationship and did me reverence. When he rose his eyes were full of tears … O little brother mine! I am fast going to my death—let me take all your sin away with me. May no taint from me ever tarnish your innocence!

I said to him: "Let your offering of reverence be that pistol!"

"What do you want with it, sister?"

"I will practise death."

"Right, sister. Our women, also, must know how to die, to deal death!" with which Amulya handed me the pistol. The radiance of his youthful countenance seemed to tinge my life with the touch of a new dawn. I put away the pistol within my clothes. May this reverence-offering be the last resource in my extremity …

The door to the mother's chamber in my woman's heart once opened, I thought it would always remain open. But this pathway to the supreme good was closed when the mistress took the place of the mother and

---

24. The daughter of the house occupies a place of specially tender affection in a Bengali household (perhaps in Hindu households all over India) because, by dictate of custom, she must be given away in marriage so early. She thus takes corresponding memories with her to her husband's home, where she has to begin as a stranger before she can get into her place. The resulting feeling, of the mistress of her new home for the one she has left, has taken ceremonial form as the Brothers' Day, on which the brothers are invited to the married sisters' houses. Where the sister is the elder, she offers her blessing and receives the brother's reverence, and vice versa. Presents, called the offerings of reverence (or blessing), are exchanged. [Trans.].

locked it again. The very next day I saw Sandip; and madness, naked and rampant, danced upon my heart.

What was this? Was this, then, my truer self? Never! I had never before known this shameless, this cruel one within me. The snake-charmer had come, pretending to draw this snake from within the fold of my garment—but it was never there, it was his all the time. Some demon has gained possession of me, and what I am doing today is the play of his activity—it has nothing to do with me.

This demon, in the guise of a god, had come with his ruddy torch to call me that day, saying: "I am your Country. I am your Sandip. I am more to you than anything else of yours. _Bande Mataram_!" And with folded hands I had responded: "You are my religion. You are my heaven. Whatever else is mine shall be swept away before my love for you. _Bande Mataram_!"

Five thousand is it? Five thousand it shall be! You want it tomorrow? Tomorrow you shall have it! In this desperate orgy, that gift of five thousand shall be as the foam of wine—and then for the riotous revel! The immovable world shall sway under our feet, fire shall flash from our eyes, a storm shall roar in our ears, what is or is not in front shall become equally dim. And then with tottering footsteps we shall plunge to our death—in a moment all fire will be extinguished, the ashes will be scattered, and nothing will remain behind.

Chapter Nine

Bimala's Story

XV

FOR a time I was utterly at a loss to think of any way of getting that money. Then, the other day, in the light of intense excitement, suddenly the whole picture stood out clear before me.

Every year my husband makes a reverence-offering of six thousand rupees to my sister-in-law at the time of the Durga Puja. Every year it is deposited in her account at the bank in Calcutta. This year the offering was made as usual, but it has not yet been sent to the bank, being kept meanwhile in an iron safe, in a corner of the little dressing-room attached to our bedroom.

Every year my husband takes the money to the bank himself. This year he has not yet had an opportunity of going to town. How could I fail to see the hand of Providence in this? The money has been held up because the country wants it—who could have the power to take it away from her to the bank? And how can I have the power to refuse to take the money? The goddess revelling in destruction holds out her blood-cup crying: "Give me drink. I am thirsty." I will give her my own heart's blood with that five thousand rupees. Mother, the loser of that money will scarcely feel the loss, but me you will utterly ruin!

Many a time, in the old days, have I inwardly called the Senior Rani a thief, for I charged her with wheedling money out of my trusting husband. After her husband's death, she often used to make away with things belonging to the estate for her own use. This I used to point out to my husband, but he remained silent. I would get angry and say: "If you feel generous, make gifts by all means, but why allow yourself to be robbed?" Providence must have smiled, then, at these complaints of mine, for tonight I am on the way to rob my husband's safe of my sister-in-law's money. My husband's custom was to let his keys remain in his pockets when he took off his clothes for the night, leaving them in the dressing-room. I picked out the key of the safe and opened it. The slight sound it made seemed to wake the whole world! A sudden chill turned my hands and feet icy cold, and I shivered all over.

There was a drawer inside the safe. On opening this I found the money, not in currency notes, but in gold rolled up in paper. I had no time to count out what I wanted. There were twenty rolls, all of which I took and tied up in a corner of my __sari__.

What a weight it was. The burden of the theft crushed my heart to the dust. Perhaps notes would have made it seem less like thieving, but this was all gold.

After I had stolen into my room like a thief, it felt like my own room no longer. All the most precious rights which I had over it vanished at the touch of my theft. I began to mutter to myself, as though telling __mantrams__: Bande Mataram, Bande Mataram__, my Country, my golden Country, all this gold is for you, for none else!

But in the night the mind is weak. I came back into the bedroom where my husband was asleep, closing my eyes as I passed through, and went off to the open terrace beyond, on which I lay prone, clasping to my breast the end of the __sari__ tied over the gold. And each one of the rolls gave me a shock of pain.

The silent night stood there with forefinger upraised. I could not think of my house as separate from my country: I had robbed my house, I had robbed my country. For this sin my house had ceased to be mine, my country also was estranged from me. Had I died begging for my country, even unsuccessfully, that would have been worship, acceptable to the gods. But theft is never worship—how then can I offer this gold? Ah me! I am doomed to death myself, must I desecrate my country with my impious touch? The way to put the money back is closed to me. I have not the strength to return to the room, take again that key, open once more that safe—I should swoon on the threshold of my husband's door. The only road left now is the road in front. Neither have I the strength deliberately to sit down and count the coins. Let them remain behind their coverings: I cannot calculate.

There was no mist in the winter sky. The stars were shining brightly. If, thought I to myself, as I lay out there, I had to steal these stars one by one, like golden coins, for my country— these stars so carefully stored up in the bosom of the darkness— then the sky would be blinded, the night widowed for ever, and my theft would rob the whole world. But was not also this very thing I had done a robbing of the whole world— not only of money, but of trust, of righteousness?

I spent the night lying on the terrace. When at last it was morning, and I was sure that my husband had risen and left the room, then only with my shawl pulled over my head, could I retrace my steps towards the bedroom.

My sister-in-law was about, with her brass pot, watering her plants. When she saw me passing in the distance she cried: "Have you heard the news, Chota Rani?"

I stopped in silence, all in a tremor. It seemed to me that the rolls of sovereigns were bulging through the shawl. I feared they would burst and scatter in a ringing shower, exposing to all the servants of the house the thief who had made herself destitute by robbing her own wealth.

"Your band of robbers," she went on, "have sent an anonymous message threatening to loot the treasury."

I remained as silent as a thief.

"I was advising Brother Nikhil to seek your protection," she continued banteringly. "Call off your minions, Robber Queen! We will offer sacrifices to your __Bande Mataram__ if you will but save us. What doings there are these days!—but for the Lord's sake, spare our house at least from burglary."

I hastened into my room without reply. I had put my foot on quicksand, and could not now withdraw it. Struggling would only send me down deeper.

If only the time would arrive when I could hand over the money to Sandip! I could bear it no longer, its weight was breaking through my very ribs.

It was still early when I got word that Sandip was awaiting me. Today I had no thought of adornment. Wrapped as I was in my shawl, I went off to the outer apartments. As I entered the sitting-room I saw Sandip and Amulya there, together. All my dignity, all my honour, seemed to run tingling through my body from head to foot and vanish into the ground. I should have to lay bare a woman's uttermost shame in sight of this boy! Could they have been discussing my deed in their meeting place? Had any vestige of a veil of decency been left for me?

We women shall never understand men. When they are bent on making a road for some achievement, they think nothing of breaking the heart of the world into pieces to pave it for the progress of their chariot. When they are mad with the intoxication of creating, they rejoice in destroying the creation of the Creator. This heart-breaking shame of mine will not attract even a glance from their eyes. They have no feeling for life itself—all their eagerness is for their object. What am I to them but a meadow flower in the path of a torrent in flood?

What good will this extinction of me be to Sandip? Only five thousand rupees? Was not I good for something more than only five thousand rupees? Yes, indeed! Did I not learn that from Sandip himself, and was I not able in the light of this knowledge to despise all else in my world? I was the giver of light, of life, of __Shakti__, of immortality—in that belief, in that joy, I had burst all my bounds and come into the open. Had anyone then fulfilled for me that joy, I should have lived in my death. I should have lost nothing in the loss of my all. Do they want to tell me now that all this was false? The psalm of my praise which was sung so devotedly, did it bring me down from my heaven, not to make heaven of earth, but only to level heaven itself with the dust?

XVI

"The money, Queen?" said Sandip with his keen glance full on my face.

Amulya also fixed his gaze on me. Though not my own mother's child, yet the dear lad is brother to me; for mother is mother all the world over. With his guileless face, his gentle eyes, his innocent youth, he looked at me. And I, a woman—of his mother's sex—how could I hand him poison, just because he asked for it?

"The money, Queen!" Sandip's insolent demand rang in my ears. For very shame and vexation I felt I wanted to fling that gold at Sandip's head. I could hardly undo the knot of my __sari__, my fingers trembled so. At last the paper rolls dropped on the table.

Sandip's face grew black ... He must have thought that the rolls were of silver ... What contempt was in his looks. What utter disgust at incapacity. It was almost as if he could have struck me! He must have suspected that I had come to parley with him, to offer to compound his claim for five thousand rupees with a few hundreds. There was a moment when I thought he would snatch up the rolls and throw them out of the window, declaring that he was no beggar, but a king claiming tribute.

"Is that all?" asked Amulya with such pity welling up in his voice that I wanted to sob out aloud. I kept my heart tightly pressed down, and merely nodded my head. Sandip was speechless. He neither touched the rolls, nor uttered a sound.

My humiliation went straight to the boy's heart. With a sudden, feigned enthusiasm he exclaimed: "It's plenty. It will do splendidly. You have saved us." With which he tore open the covering of one of the rolls.

The sovereigns shone out. And in a moment the black covering seemed to be lifted from Sandip's countenance also. His delight beamed forth from his features. Unable to control his sudden revulsion of feeling, he sprang up from his seat towards me. What he intended I know not. I flashed a lightning glance towards Amulya—the colour had left the boy's face as at the stroke of a whip. Then with all my strength I thrust Sandip from me. As he reeled back his head struck the edge of the marble table and he dropped on the floor. There he lay awhile, motionless. Exhausted with my effort, I sank back on my seat.

Amulya's face lightened with a joyful radiance. He did not even turn towards Sandip, but came straight up, took the dust of my feet, and then remained there, sitting on the floor in front of me. O my little brother, my child! This reverence of yours is the last touch of heaven left in my empty world! I could contain myself no longer, and my tears flowed fast. I covered my eyes with the end of my __sari__, which I pressed to my face with both my hands, and sobbed and sobbed. And every time that I felt on my feet his tender touch trying to comfort me my tears broke out afresh.

After a little, when I had recovered myself and taken my hands from my face, I saw Sandip back at the table, gathering up the sovereigns in his handkerchief, as if nothing had happened. Amulya rose to his seat, from his place near my feet, his wet eyes shining.

Sandip coolly looked up at my face as he remarked: "It is six thousand."

"What do we want with so much, Sandip Babu?" cried Amulya. "Three thousand five hundred is all we need for our work."

"Our wants are not for this one place only," Sandip replied. "We shall want all we can get."

"That may be," said Amulya. "But in future I undertake to get you all you want. Out of this, Sandip Babu, please return the extra two thousand five hundred to the Maharani."

Sandip glanced enquiringly at me.

"No, no," I exclaimed. "I shall never touch that money again. Do with it as you will."

"Can man ever give as woman can?" said Sandip, looking towards Amulya.

"They are goddesses!" agreed Amulya with enthusiasm.

"We men can at best give of our power," continued Sandip. "But women give themselves. Out of their own life they give birth, out of their own life they give sustenance. Such gifts are the only true gifts." Then turning to me, "Queen!" said he, "if what you have given us had been only money I would not have touched it. But you have given that which is more to you than life itself!"

There must be two different persons inside men. One of these in me can understand that Sandip is trying to delude me; the other is content to be deluded. Sandip has power, but no strength of righteousness. The weapon of his which rouses up life smites it again to death. He has the unfailing quiver of the gods, but the shafts in them are of the demons.

Sandip's handkerchief was not large enough to hold all the coins. "Queen," he asked, "can you give me another?" When I gave him mine, he reverently touched his forehead with it, and then suddenly kneeling on the floor he made me an obeisance. "Goddess!" he said, "it was to offer my reverence that I had approached you, but you repulsed me, and rolled me in the dust. Be it so, I accept your repulse as your boon to me, I raise it to my head in salutation!" with which he pointed to the place where he had been hurt.

Had I then misunderstood him? Could it be that his outstretched hands had really been directed towards my feet? Yet, surely, even Amulya had seen the passion that flamed out of his eyes, his face. But Sandip is such an adept in setting music to his chant of praise that I cannot argue; I lose my power of seeing truth; my sight is clouded over like an opium-eater's eyes. And so, after all, he gave me back twice as much in return for the blow I had dealt him—the wound on his head ended by making me bleed at heart. When I had received Sandip's obeisance my theft seemed to gain a dignity, and the gold glittering on the table to smile away all fear of disgrace, all stings of conscience.

Like me Amulya also was won back. His devotion to Sandip, which had suffered a momentary check, blazed up anew. The flower-vase of his mind filled once more with offerings for the worship of Sandip and me. His simple faith shone out of his eyes with the pure light of the morning star at dawn.

After I had offered worship and received worship my sin became radiant. And as Amulya looked on my face he raised his folded hands in salutation and cried __Bande Mataram__! I cannot expect to have this adoration surrounding me for ever; and yet this has come to be the only means of keeping alive my self- respect.

I can no longer enter my bedroom. The bedstead seems to thrust out a forbidding hand, the iron safe frowns at me. I want to get away from this continual insult to myself which is rankling within me. I want to keep running to Sandip to hear him sing my praises. There is just this one little altar of worship which has kept its head above the all-pervading depths of my dishonour, and so I want to cleave to it night and day; for on whichever side I step away from it, there is only emptiness.

Praise, praise, I want unceasing praise. I cannot live if my wine-cup be left empty for a single moment. So, as the very price of my life, I want Sandip of all the world, today.

XVII

When my husband nowadays comes in for his meals I feel I cannot sit before him; and yet it is such a shame not to be near him that I feel I cannot do that either. So I seat myself where we cannot look at each other's face. That was how I was sitting the other day when the Bara Rani came and joined us.

"It is all very well for you, brother," said she, "to laugh away these threatening letters. But they do frighten me so. Have you sent off that money you gave me to the Calcutta bank?"

"No, I have not yet had the time to get it away," my husband replied.

"You are so careless, brother dear, you had better look out..."

"But it is in the iron safe right inside the inner dressing- room," said my husband with a reassuring smile.

"What if they get in there? You can never tell!"

"If they go so far, they might as well carry you off too!"

"Don't you fear, no one will come for poor me. The real attraction is in your room! But joking apart, don't run the risk of keeping money in the room like that."

"They will be taking along the Government revenue to Calcutta in a few days now; I will send this money to the bank under the same escort."

"Very well. But see you don't forget all about it, you are so absent-minded."

"Even if that money gets lost, while in my room, the loss cannot be yours, Sister Rani."

"Now, now, brother, you will make me very angry if you talk in that way. Was I making any difference between yours and mine? What if your money is lost, does not that hurt me? If Providence has thought fit to take away my all, it has not left me insensible to the value of the most devoted brother known since the days of Lakshman." [25]

"Well, Junior Rani, are you turned into a wooden doll? You have not spoken a word yet. Do you know, brother, our Junior Rani thinks I try to flatter you. If things came to that pass I should not hesitate to do so, but I know my dear old brother does not need it!"

Thus the Senior Rani chattered on, not forgetting now and then to draw her brother's attention to this or that special delicacy amongst the dishes that were being served. My head was all the time in a whirl. The crisis was fast coming. Something must be done about replacing that money. And as I kept asking myself what could be done, and how it was

---

25. Of the __Ramayana__. The story of his devotion to his elder brother Rama and his brother's wife Sita, has become a byword.

to be done, the unceasing patter of my sister-in-law's words seemed more and more intolerable.

What made it all the worse was, that nothing could escape my sister-in-law's keen eyes. Every now and then she was casting side glances towards me. What she could read in my face I do not know, but to me it seemed that everything was written there only too plainly.

Then I did an infinitely rash thing. Affecting an easy, amused laugh I said: "All the Senior Rani's suspicions, I see, are reserved for me—her fears of thieves and robbers are only a feint."

The Senior Rani smiled mischievously. "You are right, sister mine. A woman's theft is the most fatal of all thefts. But how can you elude my watchfulness? Am I a man, that you should hoodwink me?"

"If you fear me so," I retorted, "let me keep in your hands all I have, as security. If I cause you loss, you can then repay yourself."

"Just listen to her, our simple little Junior Rani!" she laughed back, turning to my husband. "Does she not know that there are losses which no security can make good, either in this world or in the next?"

My husband did not join in our exchange of words. When he had finished, he went off to the outer apartments, for nowadays he does not take his mid-day rest in our room.

All my more valuable jewels were in deposit in the treasury in charge of the cashier. Still what I kept with me must have been worth thirty or forty thousand. I took my jewel-box to the Bara Rani's room and opened it out before her, saying: "I leave these with you, sister. They will keep you quite safe from all worry."

The Bara Rani made a gesture of mock despair. "You positively astound me, Chota Rani!" she said. "Do you really suppose I spend sleepless nights for fear of being robbed by you?"

"What harm if you did have a wholesome fear of me? Does anybody know anybody else in this world?"

"You want to teach me a lesson by trusting me? No, no! I am bothered enough to know what to do with my own jewels, without keeping watch over yours. Take them away, there's a dear, so many prying servants are about."

I went straight from my sister-in-law's room to the sitting-room outside, and sent for Amulya. With him Sandip came along too. I was in a great hurry, and said to Sandip: "If you don't mind, I want to have a word or two with Amulya. Would you…"

Sandip smiled a wry smile. "So Amulya and I are separate in your eyes? If you have set about to wean him from me, I must confess I have no power to retain him."

I made no reply, but stood waiting.

"Be it so," Sandip went on. "Finish your special talk with Amulya. But then you must give me a special talk all to myself too, or it will mean a defeat for me. I can stand everything, but not defeat. My share must always be the lion's share. This has been my constant quarrel with Providence. I will defeat the Dispenser of my fate, but not take defeat at his hands." With a crushing look at Amulya, Sandip walked out of the room.

"Amulya, my own little brother, you must do one thing for me," I said.

"I will stake my life for whatever duty you may lay on me, sister."

I brought out my jewel-box from the folds of my shawl and placed it before him. "Sell or pawn these," I said, "and get me six thousand rupees as fast as ever you can."

"No, no, Sister Rani," said Amulya, touched to the quick. "Let these jewels be. I will get you six thousand all the same."

"Oh, don't be silly," I said impatiently. "There is no time for any nonsense. Take this box. Get away to Calcutta by the night train. And bring me the money by the day after tomorrow positively."

Amulya took a diamond necklace out of the box, held it up to the light and put it back gloomily.

"I know," I told him, "that you will never get the proper price for these diamonds, so I am giving you jewels worth about thirty thousand. I don't care if they all go, but I must have that six thousand without fail."

"Do you know, Sister Rani," said Amulya, "I have had a quarrel with Sandip Babu over that six thousand rupees he took from you? I cannot tell you how ashamed I felt. But Sandip Babu would have it that we must give up even our shame for the country. That may be so. But this is somehow different. I do not fear to die for the country, to kill for the country—that much __Shakti__ has been given me. But I cannot forget the shame of having taken money from you. There Sandip Babu is ahead of me. He has no regrets or compunctions. He says we must get rid of the idea that the money belongs to the one in whose box it happens to be— if we cannot, where is the magic of __Bande Mataram__?"

Amulya gathered enthusiasm as he talked on. He always warms up when he has me for a listener. "The Gita tells us," he continued, "that no one can kill the soul. Killing is a mere word. So also is the taking away of money. Whose is the money? No one has created it. No one can take it away with him when he departs this life, for it is no part of his soul. Today it is mine, tomorrow my son's, the next day his creditor's. Since, in fact, money belongs to no one, why should any blame attach to our patriots if, instead of leaving it for some worthless son, they take it for their own use?"

When I hear Sandip's words uttered by this boy, I tremble all over. Let those who are snake-charmers play with snakes; if harm comes to them, they are prepared for it. But these boys are so innocent, all the world is ready with its blessing to protect them. They play with a snake not knowing its nature, and when we see them smilingly, trustfully, putting their hands within reach of its fangs, then we understand how terribly dangerous the snake is. Sandip is right when he suspects that though I, for myself, may be ready to die at his hands, this boy I shall wean from him and save.

"So the money is wanted for the use of your patriots?" I questioned with a smile.

"Of course it is!" said Amulya proudly. "Are they not our kings? Poverty takes away from their regal power. Do you know, we always insist on Sandip Babu travelling First Class? He never shirks kingly honours—he accepts them not for himself, but for the glory of us all. The greatest weapon of those who rule the world, Sandip Babu has told us, is the hypnotism of their display. To take the vow of poverty would be for them not merely a penance—it would mean suicide."

At this point Sandip noiselessly entered the room. I threw my shawl over the jewel-case with a rapid movement.

"The special-talk business not yet over?" he asked with a sneer in his tone.

"Yes, we've quite finished," said Amulya apologetically. "It was nothing much."

"No, Amulya," I said, "we have not quite finished."

"So exit Sandip for the second time, I suppose?" said Sandip.

"If you please."

"And as to Sandip's re-entry."

"Not today. I have no time."

"I see!" said Sandip as his eyes flashed. "No time to waste, only for special talks!"

Jealousy! Where the strong man shows weakness, there the weaker sex cannot help beating her drums of victory. So I repeated firmly: "I really have no time."

Sandip went away looking black. Amulya was greatly perturbed.

"Sister Rani," he pleaded, "Sandip Babu is annoyed."

"He has neither cause nor right to be annoyed," I said with some vehemence. "Let me caution you about one thing, Amulya. Say nothing to Sandip Babu about the sale of my jewels—on your life."

"No, I will not."

"Then you had better not delay any more. You must get away by tonight's train."

Amulya and I left the room together. As we came out on the verandah Sandip was standing there. I could see he was waiting to waylay Amulya. To prevent that I had to engage him. "What is it you wanted to tell me, Sandip Babu?" I asked.

"I have nothing special to say—mere small talk. And since you have not the time .. "

"I can give you just a little."

By this time Amulya had left. As we entered the room Sandip asked: "What was that box Amulya carried away?"

The box had not escaped his eyes. I remained firm. "If I could have told you, it would have been made over to him in your presence!"

"So you think Amulya will not tell me?"

"No, he will not."

Sandip could not conceal his anger any longer. "You think you will gain the mastery over me?" he blazed out. "That shall never be. Amulya, there, would die a happy death if I deigned to trample him under foot. I will never, so long as I live, allow you to bring him to your feet!"

Oh, the weak! the weak! At last Sandip has realized that he is weak before me! That is why there is this sudden outburst of anger. He has understood that he cannot meet the power that I wield, with mere strength. With a glance I can crumble his strongest fortifications. So he must needs resort to bluster. I simply smiled in contemptuous silence. At last have I come to a level above him. I must never lose this vantage ground; never descend lower again. Amidst all my degradation this bit of dignity must remain to me!

"I know," said Sandip, after a pause, "it was your jewel-case."

"You may guess as you please," said I, "but you will get nothing out of me.

"So you trust Amulya more than you trust me? Do you know that the boy is the shadow of my shadow, the echo of my echo—that he is nothing if I am not at his side?"

"Where he is not your echo, he is himself, Amulya. And that is where I trust him more than I can trust your echo!"

"You must not forget that you are under a promise to render up all your ornaments to me for the worship of the Divine Mother. In fact your offering has already been made."

"Whatever ornaments the gods leave to me will be offered up to the gods. But how can I offer those which have been stolen away from me?"

"Look here, it is no use your trying to give me the slip in that fashion. Now is the time for grim work. Let that work be finished, then you can make a display of your woman's wiles to your heart's content—and I will help you in your game."

The moment I had stolen my husband's money and paid it to Sandip, the music that was in our relations stopped. Not only did I destroy all my own value by making myself cheap, but Sandip's powers, too, lost scope for their full play. You cannot employ your marksmanship against a thing which is right in your grasp. So Sandip has lost his aspect of the hero; a tone of low quarrelsomeness has come into his words.

Sandip kept his brilliant eyes fixed full on my face till they seemed to blaze with all the thirst of the mid-day sky. Once or twice he fidgeted with his feet, as though to leave his seat, as if to spring right on me. My whole body seemed to swim, my veins throbbed, the hot blood surged up to my ears; I felt that if I remained there, I should never get up at all. With a supreme effort I tore myself off the chair, and hastened towards the door.

From Sandip's dry throat there came a muffled cry: "Whither would you flee, Queen?" The next moment he left his seat with a bound to seize hold of me. At the sound of footsteps outside the door, however, he rapidly retreated and fell back into his chair. I checked my steps near the bookshelf, where I stood staring at the names of the books.

As my husband entered the room, Sandip exclaimed: "I say, Nikhil, don't you keep Browning among your books here? I was just telling Queen Bee of our college club. Do you remember that contest of ours over the translation of those lines from Browning? You don't?

/*
"She should never have looked at me,
If she meant I should not love her,
There are plenty … men you call such,
I suppose … she may discover
All her soul to, if she pleases,
And yet leave much as she found them:
But I'm not so, and she knew it
When she fixed me, glancing round them.
*/

"I managed to get together the words to render it into Bengali, somehow, but the result was hardly likely to be a 'joy forever' to the people of Bengal. I really did think at one time that I was on the verge of becoming a poet, but Providence was kind enough to save me from that disaster. Do you remember old Dakshina? If he had not become a Salt Inspector, he would have been a poet. I remember his rendering to this day …

"No, Queen Bee, it is no use rummaging those bookshelves. Nikhil has ceased to read poetry since his marriage—perhaps he has no further need for it. But I suppose 'the fever fit of poesy', as the Sanskrit has it, is about to attack me again."

"I have come to give you a warning, Sandip," said my husband.

"About the fever fit of poesy?"

My husband took no notice of this attempt at humour. "For some time," he continued, "Mahomedan preachers have been about stirring up the local Mussulmans. They are all wild with you, and may attack you any moment."

"Are you come to advise flight?"

"I have come to give you information, not to offer advice."

"Had these estates been mine, such a warning would have been necessary for the preachers, not for me. If, instead of trying to frighten me, you give them a taste of your intimidation, that would be worthier both of you and me. Do you know that your weakness is weakening your neighbouring __zamindars__ also?"

"I did not offer you my advice, Sandip. I wish you, too, would refrain from giving me yours. Besides, it is useless. And there is another thing I want to tell you. You and your followers have been secretly worrying and oppressing my tenantry. I cannot allow that any longer. So I must ask you to leave my territory."

"For fear of the Mussulmans, or is there any other fear you have to threaten me with?"

"There are fears the want of which is cowardice. In the name of those fears, I tell you, Sandip, you must go. In five days I shall be starting for Calcutta. I want you to accompany me. You may of course stay in my house there—to that there is no objection."

"All right, I have still five day's time then. Meanwhile, Queen Bee, let me hum to you my song of parting from your honey-hive. Ah! you poet of modern Bengal! Throw open your doors and let me plunder your words. The theft is really yours, for it is my song which you have made your own—let the name be yours by all means, but the song is mine." With this Sandip struck up in a deep, husky voice, which threatened to be out of tune, a song in the Bhairavi mode:

/*
"In the springtime of your kingdom, my Queen,
Meetings and partings chase each other in their endless hide
and seek,
And flowers blossom in the wake of those that droop and die in the shade.
In the springtime of your kingdom, my Queen,
My meeting with you had its own songs,
But has not also my leave-taking any gift to offer you?
That gift is my secret hope, which I keep hidden in the shadows of your flower garden,
That the rains of July may sweetly temper your fiery June."
*/

His boldness was immense—boldness which had no veil, but was naked as fire. One finds no time to stop it: it is like trying to resist a thunderbolt: the lightning flashes: it laughs at all resistance.

I left the room. As I was passing along the verandah towards the inner apartments, Amulya suddenly made his appearance and came and stood before me.

"Fear nothing, Sister Rani," he said. "I am off tonight and shall not return unsuccessful."

"Amulya," said I, looking straight into his earnest, youthful face, "I fear nothing for myself, but may I never cease to fear for you."

Amulya turned to go, but before he was out of sight I called him back and asked: "Have you a mother, Amulya?"

"I have."

"A sister?"

"No, I am the only child of my mother. My father died when I was quite little."

"Then go back to your mother, Amulya."

"But, Sister Rani, I have now both mother and sister."

"Then, Amulya, before you leave tonight, come and have your dinner here."

"There won't be time for that. Let me take some food for the journey, consecrated with your touch."

"What do you specially like, Amulya?" "If I had been with my mother I should have had lots of Poush cakes. Make some for me with your own hands, Sister Rani!"

Chapter Ten

Nikhil's Story

XII

I LEARNT from my master that Sandip had joined forces with Harish Kundu, and there was to be a grand celebration of the worship of the demon-destroying Goddess. Harish Kundu was extorting the expenses from his tenantry. Pandits Kaviratna and Vidyavagish had been commissioned to compose a hymn with a double meaning.

My master has just had a passage at arms with Sandip over this. "Evolution is at work amongst the gods as well," says Sandip. "The grandson has to remodel the gods created by the grandfather to suit his own taste, or else he is left an atheist. It is my mission to modernize the ancient deities. I am born the saviour of the gods, to emancipate them from the thraldom of the past."

I have seen from our boyhood what a juggler with ideas is Sandip. He has no interest in discovering truth, but to make a quizzical display of it rejoices his heart. Had he been born in the wilds of Africa he would have spent a glorious time inventing argument after argument to prove that cannibalism is the best means of promoting true communion between man and man. But those who deal in delusion end by deluding themselves, and I fully believe that, each time Sandip creates a new fallacy, he persuades himself that he has found the truth, however contradictory his creations may be to one another.

However, I shall not give a helping hand to establish a liquor distillery in my country. The young men, who are ready to offer their services for their country's cause, must not fall into this habit of getting intoxicated. The people who want to exact work by drugging methods set more value on the excitement than on the minds they intoxicate.

I had to tell Sandip, in Bimala's presence, that he must go. Perhaps both will impute to me the wrong motive. But I must free myself also from all fear of being misunderstood. Let even Bimala misunderstand me ...

A number of Mahomedan preachers are being sent over from Dacca. The Mussulmans in my territory had come to have almost as much of an aversion to the killing of cows as the Hindus. But now cases of cow-killing are cropping up here and there. I had the news first from some of my Mussulman tenants with expressions of their disapproval. Here was a situation which I could see would be difficult to meet. At the bottom was a pretence of fanaticism, which would cease to be a pretence if obstructed. That is just where the ingenuity of the move came in!

I sent for some of my principal Hindu tenants and tried to get them to see the matter in its proper light. "We can be staunch in our own convictions," I said, "but we have no control over those of others. For all that many of us are Vaishnavas, those of us who are Shaktas go on with their animal sacrifices just the same. That cannot be helped. We must, in the same way, let the Mussulmans do as they think best. So please refrain from all disturbance."

"Maharaja," they replied, "these outrages have been unknown for so long."

"That was so," I said, "because such was their spontaneous desire. Let us behave in such a way that the same may become true, over again. But a breach of the peace is not the way to bring this about."

"No, Maharaja," they insisted, "those good old days are gone. This will never stop unless you put it down with a strong hand."

"Oppression," I replied, "will not only not prevent cow-killing, it may lead to the killing of men as well."

One of them had had an English education. He had learnt to repeat the phrases of the day. "It is not only a question of orthodoxy," he argued. "Our country is mainly agricultural, and cows are …"

"Buffaloes in this country," I interrupted, "likewise give milk and are used for ploughing. And therefore, so long as we dance frantic dances on our temple pavements, smeared with their blood, their severed heads carried on our shoulders, religion will only laugh at us if we quarrel with Mussulmans in her name, and nothing but the quarrel itself will remain true. If the cow alone is to be held sacred from slaughter, and not the buffalo, then that is bigotry, not religion."

"But are you not aware, sir, of what is behind all this?" pursued the English-knowing tenant. "This has only become possible because the Mussulman is assured of safety, even if he breaks the law. Have you not heard of the Pachur case?"

"Why is it possible," I asked, "to use the Mussulmans thus, as tools against us? Is it not because we have fashioned them into such with our own intolerance? That is how Providence punishes us. Our accumulated sins are being visited on our own heads."

"Oh, well, if that be so, let them be visited on us. But we shall have our revenge. We have undermined what was the greatest strength of the authorities, their devotion to their own laws. Once they were truly kings, dispensing justice; now they themselves will become law-breakers, and so no better than robbers. This may not go down to history, but we shall carry it in our hearts for all time …"

The evil reports about me which are spreading from paper to paper are making me notorious. News comes that my effigy has been burnt at the river-side burning-ground of the Chakravartis, with due ceremony and enthusiasm; and other insults are in contemplation. The trouble was that they had come to ask me to take shares in a Cotton Mill they wanted to start. I had to tell them that I did not so much mind the loss of my own money, but I would not be a party to causing a loss to so many poor shareholders.

"Are we to understand, Maharaja," said my visitors, "that the prosperity of the country does not interest you?"

"Industry may lead to the country's prosperity," I explained, "but a mere desire for its prosperity will not make for success in industry. Even when our heads were cool, our industries did not flourish. Why should we suppose that they will do so just because we have become frantic?"

"Why not say plainly that you will not risk your money?"

"I will put in my money when I see that it is industry which prompts you. But, because you have lighted a fire, it does not follow that you have the food to cook over it."

XIII

What is this? Our Chakua sub-treasury looted! A remittance of seven thousand five hundred rupees was due from there to headquarters. The local cashier had changed the cash at the Government Treasury into small currency notes for convenience in carrying, and had kept them ready in bundles. In the middle of the night an armed band had raided the room, and wounded Kasim, the man on guard. The curious part of it was that they had taken only six thousand rupees and left the rest scattered on the floor, though it would have been as easy to carry that away also. Anyhow, the raid of the dacoits was over; now the police raid would begin. Peace was out of the question.

When I went inside, I found the news had travelled before me. "What a terrible thing, brother," exclaimed the Bara Rani. "Whatever shall we do?"

I made light of the matter to reassure her. "We still have something left," I said with a smile. "We shall manage to get along somehow."

"Don't joke about it, brother dear. Why are they all so angry with you? Can't you humour them? Why put everybody out?"

"I cannot let the country go to rack and ruin, even if that would please everybody."

"That was a shocking thing they did at the burning-grounds. It's a horrid shame to treat you so. The Chota Rani has got rid of all her fears by dint of the Englishwoman's teaching, but as for me, I had to send for the priest to avert the omen before I could get any peace of mind. For my sake, dear, do get away to Calcutta. I tremble to think what they may do, if you stay on here."

My sister-in-law's genuine anxiety touched me deeply.

"And, brother," she went on, "did I not warn you, it was not well to keep so much money in your room? They might get wind of it any day. It is not the money—but who knows…"

To calm her I promised to remove the money to the treasury at once, and then get it away to Calcutta with the first escort going. We went together to my bedroom. The dressing-room door was shut. When I knocked, Bimala called out: "I am dressing."

"I wonder at the Chota Rani," exclaimed my sister-in-law, "dressing so early in the day! One of their __Bande Mataram__ meetings, I suppose. Robber Queen!" she called out in jest to Bimala. "Are you counting your spoils inside?"

"I will attend to the money a little later," I said, as I came away to my office room outside.

I found the Police Inspector waiting for me. "Any trace of the dacoits?" I asked.

"I have my suspicions."

"On whom?"

"Kasim, the guard."

"Kasim? But was he not wounded?"

"A mere nothing. A flesh wound on the leg. Probably self-inflicted."

"But I cannot bring myself to believe it. He is such a trusted servant."

"You may have trusted him, but that does not prevent his being a thief. Have I not seen men trusted for twenty years together, suddenly developing…"

"Even if it were so, I could not send him to gaol. But why should he have left the rest of the money lying about?"

"To put us off the scent. Whatever you may say, Maharaja, he must be an old hand at the game. He mounts guard during his watch, right enough, but I feel sure he has a finger in all the dacoities going on in the neighbourhood."

With this the Inspector proceeded to recount the various methods by which it was possible to be concerned in a dacoity twenty or thirty miles away, and yet be back in time for duty.

"Have you brought Kasim here?" I asked.

"No," was the reply, "he is in the lock-up. The Magistrate is due for the investigation."

"I want to see him," I said.

When I went to his cell he fell at my feet, weeping. "In God's name," he said, "I swear I did not do this thing."

"I do not doubt you, Kasim," I assured him. "Fear nothing. They can do nothing to you, if you are innocent."

Kasim, however, was unable to give a coherent account of the incident. He was obviously exaggerating. Four or five hundred men, big guns, numberless swords, figured in his narrative. It must have been either his disturbed state of mind or a desire to account for his easy defeat. He would have it that this was Harish Kundu's doing; he was even sure he had heard the voice of Ekram, the head retainer of the Kundus.

"Look here, Kasim," I had to warn him, "don't you be dragging other people in with your stories. You are not called upon to make out a case against Harish Kundu, or anybody else."

XIV

On returning home I asked my master to come over. He shook his head gravely. "I see no good in this," said he—"this setting aside of conscience and putting the country in its place. All the sins of the country will now break out, hideous and unashamed."

"Who do you think could have …"

"Don't ask me. But sin is rampant. Send them all away, right away from here."

"I have given them one more day. They will be leaving the day after tomorrow."

"And another thing. Take Bimala away to Calcutta. She is getting too narrow a view of the outside world from here, she cannot see men and things in their true proportions. Let her see the world—men and their work—give her abroad vision."

"That is exactly what I was thinking."

"Well, don't make any delay about it. I tell you, Nikhil, man's history has to be built by the united effort of all the races in the world, and therefore this selling of conscience for political reasons—this making a fetish of one's country, won't do. I know that Europe does not at heart admit this, but there she has not the right to pose as our teacher. Men who die for the truth become immortal: and, if a whole people can die for the truth, it will also achieve immortality in the history of humanity. Here, in this land of India, amid the mocking laughter of Satan piercing the sky, may the feeling for this truth become real! What a terrible epidemic of sin has been brought into our country from foreign lands…"

The whole day passed in the turmoil of investigation. I was tired out when I retired for the night. I left over sending my sister-in-law's money to the treasury till next morning.

I woke up from my sleep at dead of night. The room was dark. I thought I heard a moaning somewhere. Somebody must have been crying. Sounds of sobbing came heavy with tears like fitful gusts of wind in the rainy night. It seemed to me that the cry rose from the heart of my room itself. I was alone. For some days Bimala had her bed in another room adjoining mine. I rose up and when I went out I found her in the balcony lying prone upon her face on the bare floor.

This is something that cannot be written in words. He only knows it who sits in the bosom of the world and receives all its pangs in His own heart. The sky is dumb, the stars are mute, the night is still, and in the midst of it all that one sleepless cry!

We give these sufferings names, bad or good, according to the classifications of the books, but this agony which is welling up from a torn heart, pouring into the fathomless dark, has it any name? When in that midnight, standing under the silent stars, I looked upon that figure, my mind was struck with awe, and I said to myself: "Who am I to judge her?" O life, O death, O God of the infinite existence, I bow my head in silence to the mystery which is in you.

Once I thought I should turn back. But I could not. I sat down on the ground near Bimala and placed my hand on her head. At the first touch her whole body seemed to stiffen, but the next moment the hardness gave way, and the tears burst out. I gently passed my fingers over her forehead. Suddenly her hands groping for my feet grasped them and drew them to herself, pressing them against her breast with such force that I thought her heart would break.

Bimala's Story

XVIII

Amulya is due to return from Calcutta this morning. I told the servants to let me know as soon as he arrived, but could not keep still. At last I went outside to await him in the sitting-room.

When I sent him off to sell the jewels I must have been thinking only of myself. It never even crossed my mind that so young a boy, trying to sell such valuable jewellery, would at once be suspected. So helpless are we women, we needs must place on others the burden of our danger. When we go to our death we drag down those who are about us.

I had said with pride that I would save Amulya—as if she who was drowning could save others. But instead of saving him, I have sent him to his doom. My little brother, such a sister have I been to you that Death must have smiled on that Brothers' Day when I gave you my blessing—I, who wander distracted with the burden of my own evil-doing.

I feel today that man is at times attacked with evil as with the plague. Some germ finds its way in from somewhere, and then in the space of one night Death stalks in. Why cannot the stricken one be kept far away from the rest of the world? I, at least, have realized how terrible is the contagion—like a fiery torch which burns that it may set the world on fire.

It struck nine. I could not get rid of the idea that Amulya was in trouble, that he had fallen into the clutches of the police. There must be great excitement in the Police Office—whose are the jewels?—where did he get them? And in the end I shall have to furnish the answer, in public, before all the world.

What is that answer to be? Your day has come at last, Bara Rani, you whom I have so long despised. You, in the shape of the public, the world, will have your revenge. O God, save me this time, and I will cast all my pride at my sister-in-law's feet.

I could bear it no longer. I went straight to the Bara Rani. She was in the verandah, spicing her betel leaves, Thako at her side. The sight of Thako made me shrink back for a moment, but I overcame all hesitation, and making a low obeisance I took the dust of my elder sister-in-law's feet.

"Bless my soul, Chota Rani," she exclaimed, "what has come upon you? Why this sudden reverence?"

"It is my birthday, sister," said I. "I have caused you pain. Give me your blessing today that I may never do so again. My mind is so small." I repeated my obeisance and left her hurriedly, but she called me back.

"You never before told me that this was your birthday, Chotie darling! Be sure to come and have lunch with me this afternoon. You positively must."

O God, let it really be my birthday today. Can I not be born over again? Cleanse me, my God, and purify me and give me one more trial!

I went again to the sitting-room to find Sandip there. A feeling of disgust seemed to poison my very blood. The face of his, which I saw in the morning light, had nothing of the magic radiance of genius.

"Will you leave the room," I blurted out.

Sandip smiled. "Since Amulya is not here," he remarked, "I should think my turn had come for a special talk."

My fate was coming back upon me. How was I to take away the right I myself had given. "I would be alone," I repeated.

"Queen," he said, "the presence of another person does not prevent your being alone. Do not mistake me for one of the crowd. I, Sandip, am always alone, even when surrounded by thousands."

"Please come some other time. This morning I am …"

"Waiting for Amulya?"

I turned to leave the room for sheer vexation, when Sandip drew out from the folds of his cloak that jewel-casket of mine and banged it down on the marble table. I was thoroughly startled. "Has not Amulya gone, then?" I exclaimed.

"Gone where?"

"To Calcutta?"

"No," chuckled Sandip.

Ah, then my blessing had come true, in spite of all. He was saved. Let God's punishment fall on me, the thief, if only Amulya be safe.

The change in my countenance roused Sandip's scorn. "So pleased, Queen!" sneered he. "Are these jewels so very precious? How then did you bring yourself to offer them to the Goddess? Your gift was actually made. Would you now take it back?"

Pride dies hard and raises its fangs to the last. It was clear to me I must show Sandip I did not care a rap about these jewels. "If they have excited your greed," I said, "you may have them."

"My greed today embraces the wealth of all Bengal," replied Sandip. "Is there a greater force than greed? It is the steed of the great ones of the earth, as is the elephant, Airauat, the steed of Indra. So then these jewels are mine?"

As Sandip took up and replaced the casket under his cloak, Amulya rushed in. There were dark rings under his eyes, his lips were dry, his hair tumbled: the freshness of his youth seemed to have withered in a single day. Pangs gripped my heart as I looked on him.

"My box!" he cried, as he went straight up to Sandip without a glance at me. "Have you taken that jewel-box from my trunk?"

"Your jewel-box?" mocked Sandip.

"It was my trunk!" Sandip burst out into a laugh. "Your distinctions between mine and yours are getting rather thin, Amulya," he cried. "You will die a religious preacher yet, I see."

Amulya sank on a chair with his face in his hands. I went up to him and placing my hand on his head asked him: "What is your trouble, Amulya?"

He stood straight up as he replied: "I had set my heart, Sister Rani, on returning your jewels to you with my own hand. Sandip Babu knew this, but he forestalled me."

"What do I care for my jewels?" I said. "Let them go. No harm is done.

"Go? Where?" asked the mystified boy.

"The jewels are mine," said Sandip. "Insignia bestowed on me by my Queen!"

"No, no, no," broke out Amulya wildly. "Never, Sister Rani! I brought them back for you. You shall not give them away to anybody else."

"I accept your gift, my little brother," said I. "But let him, who hankers after them, satisfy his greed."

Amulya glared at Sandip like a beast of prey, as he growled: "Look here, Sandip Babu, you know that even hanging has no terrors for me. If you dare take away that box of jewels …"

With an attempt at a sarcastic laugh Sandip said: "You also ought to know by this time, Amulya, that I am not the man to be afraid of you."

"Queen Bee," he went on, turning to me, "I did not come here today to take these jewels, I came to give them to you. You would have done wrong to take my gift at Amulya's hands. In order to prevent it, I had first to make them clearly mine. Now these my jewels are my gift to you. Here they are! Patch up any understanding with this boy you like. I must go. You have been at your special talks all these days together, leaving me out of them. If special happenings now come to pass, don't blame me.

"Amulya," he continued, "I have sent on your trunks and things to your lodgings. Don't you be keeping any belongings of yours in my room any longer." With this parting shot, Sandip flung out of the room.

XIX

"I have had no peace of mind, Amulya," I said to him, "ever since I sent you off to sell my jewels."

"Why, Sister Rani?"

"I was afraid lest you should get into trouble with them, lest they should suspect you for a thief. I would rather go without that six thousand. You must now do another thing for me—go home at once, home to your mother."

Amulya produced a small bundle and said: "But, sister, I have got the six thousand."

"Where from?"

"I tried hard to get gold," he went on, without replying to my question, "but could not. So I had to bring it in notes."

"Tell me truly, Amulya, swear by me, where did you get this money?"

"That I will not tell you."

Everything seemed to grow dark before my eyes. "What terrible thing have you done, Amulya?" I cried. "Is it then …"

"I know you will say I got this money wrongly. Very well, I admit it. But I have paid the full price for my wrong-doing. So now the money is mine."

I no longer had any desire to learn more about it. My very blood-vessels contracted, making my whole body shrink within itself.

"Take it away, Amulya," I implored. "Put it back where you got it from."

"That would be hard indeed!"

"It is not hard, brother dear. It was an evil moment when you first came to me. Even Sandip has not been able to harm you as I have done."

Sandip's name seemed to stab him.

"Sandip!" he cried. "It was you alone who made me come to know that man for what he is. Do you know, sister, he has not spent a pice out of those sovereigns he took from you? He shut himself into his room, after he left you, and gloated over the gold, pouring it out in a heap on the floor. 'This is not money,' he exclaimed, 'but the petals of the divine lotus of power; crystallized strains of music from the pipes that play in the paradise of wealth! I cannot find it in my heart to change them, for they seem longing to fulfil their destiny of adorning the neck of Beauty. Amulya, my boy, don't you look at these with your fleshly eye, they are Lakshmi's smile, the gracious radiance of Indra's queen. No, no, I can't give them up to that boor of a manager. I am sure, Amulya, he was telling us lies. The police haven't traced the man who sank that boat. It's the manager who wants to make something out of it. We must get those letters back from him.'

"I asked him how we were to do this; he told me to use force or threats. I offered to do so if he would return the gold. That, he said, we could consider later. I will not trouble you, sister, with all I did to frighten the man into giving up those letters and burn them—it is a long story. That very night I came to Sandip and said: 'We are now safe. Let me have the sovereigns to return them tomorrow to my sister, the Maharani.' But he cried, 'What infatuation is this of yours? Your precious sister's skirt bids fair to hide the whole country from you. Say __Bande Mataram__ and exorcize the evil spirit.'

"You know, Sister Rani, the power of Sandip's magic. The gold remained with him. And I spent the whole dark night on the bathing-steps of the lake muttering __Bande Mataram__.

"Then when you gave me your jewels to sell, I went again to Sandip. I could see he was angry with me. But he tried not to show it. 'If I still have them hoarded up in any box of mine you may take them,' said he, as he flung me his keys. They were nowhere to be seen. 'Tell me where they are,' I said. 'I will do so,' he replied, 'when I find your infatuation has left you. Not now.'

"When I found I could not move him, I had to employ other methods. Then I tried to get the sovereigns from him in exchange for my currency notes for six thousand rupees. 'You shall have them,' he said, and disappeared into his bedroom, leaving me waiting outside. There he broke open my trunk and came straight to you with your casket through some other passage. He would not let me bring it, and now he dares call it his gift. How can I tell how much he has deprived me of? I shall never forgive him.

"But, oh sister, his power over me has been utterly broken. And it is you who have broken it!"

"Brother dear," said I, "if that is so, then my life is justified. But more remains to be done, Amulya. It is not enough that the spell has been destroyed. Its stains must be washed away. Don't delay any longer, go at once and put back the money where you took it from. Can you not do it, dear?"

"With your blessing everything is possible, Sister Rani."

"Remember, it will not be your expiation alone, but mine also. I am a woman; the outside world is closed to me, else I would have gone myself. My hardest punishment is that I must put on you the burden of my sin."

"Don't say that, sister. The path I was treading was not your path. It attracted me because of its dangers and difficulties. Now that your path calls me, let it be a thousand times more difficult and dangerous, the dust of your feet will help me to win through. Is it then your command that this money be replaced?"

"Not my command, brother mine, but a command from above."

"Of that I know nothing. It is enough for me that this command from above comes from your lips. And, sister, I thought I had an invitation here. I must not lose that. You must give me your __prasad__ [26] before I go. Then, if I can possibly manage it, I will finish my duty in the evening."

Tears came to my eyes when I tried to smile as I said: "So be it."

---

26.   Food consecrated by the touch of a revered person.

Chapter Eleven

Bimala's Story

XX

WITH Amulya's departure my heart sank within me. On what perilous adventure had I sent this only son of his mother? O God, why need my expiation have such pomp and circumstance? Could I not be allowed to suffer alone without inviting all this multitude to share my punishment? Oh, let not this innocent child fall victim to Your wrath.

I called him back—"Amulya!"

My voice sounded so feebly, it failed to reach him.

I went up to the door and called again: "Amulya!"

He had gone.

"Who is there?"

"Rani Mother!"

"Go and tell Amulya Babu that I want him."

What exactly happened I could not make out—the man, perhaps, was not familiar with Amulya's name—but he returned almost at once followed by Sandip.

"The very moment you sent me away," he said as he came in, "I had a presentiment that you would call me back. The attraction of the same moon causes both ebb and flow. I was so sure of being sent for, that I was actually waiting out in the passage. As soon as I caught sight of your man, coming from your room, I said: 'Yes, yes, I am coming, I am coming at once!'—before he could utter a word. That up-country lout was surprised, I can tell you! He stared at me, open-mouthed, as if he thought I knew magic.

"All the fights in the world, Queen Bee," Sandip rambled on, "are really fights between hypnotic forces. Spell cast against spell —noiseless weapons which reach even invisible targets. At last I have met in you my match. Your quiver is full, I know, you artful warrior Queen! You are the only one in the world who has been able to turn Sandip out and call Sandip back, at your sweet will. Well, your quarry is at your feet. What will you do with him now? Will you give him the coup de grâce, or keep him in your cage? Let me warn you beforehand, Queen, you will find the beast as difficult to kill outright as to keep in bondage. Anyway, why lose time in trying your magic weapons?"

Sandip must have felt the shadow of approaching defeat, and this made him try to gain time by chattering away without waiting for a reply. I believe he knew that I had sent the messenger for Amulya, whose name the man must have mentioned. In spite of that he had deliberately played this trick. He was now trying to avoid giving me any opening to tell him that it was Amulya I wanted, not him. But his stratagem was futile, for I could see his weakness through it. I must not yield up a pin's point of the ground I had gained.

"Sandip Babu," I said, "I wonder how you can go on making these endless speeches, without a stop. Do you get them up by heart, beforehand?"

Sandip's face flushed instantly.

"I have heard," I continued, "that our professional reciters keep a book full of all kinds of ready-made discourses, which can be fitted into any subject. Have you also a book?"

Sandip ground out his reply through his teeth. "God has given you women a plentiful supply of coquetry to start with, and on the top of that you have the milliner and the jeweller to help you; but do not think we men are so helpless …"

"You had better go back and look up your book, Sandip Babu. You are getting your words all wrong. That's just the trouble with trying to repeat things by rote."

"You!" shouted Sandip, losing all control over himself. "You to insult me thus! What is there left of you that I do not know to the very bottom? What …" He became speechless.

Sandip, the wielder of magic spells, is reduced to utter powerlessness, whenever his spell refuses to work. From a king he fell to the level of a boor. Oh, the joy of witnessing his weakness! The harsher he became in his rudeness, the more did this joy well up within me. His snaky coils, with which he used to snare me, are exhausted—I am free. I am saved, saved. Be rude to me, insult me, for that shows you in your truth; but spare me your songs of praise, which were false.

My husband came in at this juncture. Sandip had not the elasticity to recover himself in a moment, as he used to do before. My husband looked at him for a while in surprise. Had this happened some days ago I should have felt ashamed. But today I was pleased—whatever my husband might think. I wanted to have it out to the finish with my weakening adversary.

Finding us both silent and constrained, my husband hesitated a little, and then took a chair. "Sandip," he said, "I have been looking for you, and was told you were here."

"I am here," said Sandip with some emphasis. "Queen Bee sent for me early this morning. And I, the humble worker of the hive, left all else to attend her summons."

"I am going to Calcutta tomorrow. You will come with me."

"And why, pray? Do you take me for one of your retinue?"

"Oh, very well, take it that you are going to Calcutta, and that I am your follower."

"I have no business there."

"All the more reason for going. You have too much business here."

"I don't propose to stir."

"Then I propose to shift you."

"Forcibly?"

"Forcibly."

"Very well, then, I will make a move. But the world is not divided between Calcutta and your estates. There are other places on the map."

"From the way you have been going on, one would hardly have thought that there was any other place in the world except my estates."

Sandip stood up. "It does happen at times," he said, "that a man's whole world is reduced to a single spot. I have realized my universe in this sitting-room of yours, that is why I have been a fixture here."

Then he turned to me. "None but you, Queen Bee," he said, "will understand my words—perhaps not even you. I salute you. With worship in my heart I leave you. My watchword has changed since you have come across my vision. It is no longer __Bande Mataram__ (Hail Mother), but Hail Beloved, Hail Enchantress. The mother protects, the mistress leads to destruction—but sweet is that destruction. You have made the anklet sounds of the dance of death tinkle in my heart. You have changed for me, your devotee, the picture I had of this Bengal of ours—'the soft breeze-cooled land of pure water and sweet fruit.' [27] You have no pity, my beloved. You have come to me with your poison cup and I shall drain it, either to die in agony or live triumphing over death.

"Yes," he continued. "The mother's day is past. O love, my love, you have made as naught for me the truth and right and heaven itself. All duties have become as shadows: all rules and restraints have snapped their bonds. O love, my love, I could set fire to all the world outside this land on which you have set your dainty feet, and dance in mad revel over the ashes ... These are mild men. These are good men. They would do good to all—as if this all were a reality! No, no! There is no reality in the world save this one real love of mine. I do you reverence.

---

27. Quotation from the National song—__Bande Mataram__.

My devotion to you has made me cruel; my worship of you has lighted the raging flame of destruction within me. I am not righteous. I have no beliefs, I only believe in her whom, above all else in the world, I have been able to realize."

Wonderful! It was wonderful, indeed. Only a minute ago I had despised this man with all my heart. But what I had thought to be dead ashes now glowed with living fire. The fire in him is true, that is beyond doubt. Oh why has God made man such a mixed creature? Was it only to show his supernatural sleight of hand? Only a few minutes ago I had thought that Sandip, whom I had once taken to be a hero, was only the stage hero of melodrama. But that is not so, not so. Even behind the trappings of the theatre, a true hero may sometimes be lurking.

There is much in Sandip that is coarse, that is sensuous, that is false, much that is overlaid with layer after layer of fleshly covering. Yet—yet it is best to confess that there is a great deal in the depths of him which we do not, cannot understand— much in ourselves too. A wonderful thing is man. What great mysterious purpose he is working out only the Terrible One [28] knows—meanwhile we groan under the brunt of it. Shiva is the Lord of Chaos. He is all Joy. He will destroy our bonds.

I cannot but feel, again and again, that there are two persons in me. One recoils from Sandip in his terrible aspect of Chaos—the other feels that very vision to be sweetly alluring. The sinking ship drags down all who are swimming round it. Sandip is just such a force of destruction. His immense attraction gets hold of one before fear can come to the rescue, and then, in the twinkling of an eye, one is drawn away, irresistibly, from all light, all good, all freedom of the sky, all air that can be breathed—from lifelong accumulations, from everyday cares—right to the bottom of dissolution.

From some realm of calamity has Sandip come as its messenger; and as he stalks the land, muttering unholy incantations, to him flock all the boys and youths. The mother, seated in the lotus- heart of the Country, is wailing her heart out; for they have broken open her store-room,

---

28. Rudra, the Terrible, a name of Shiva. [Trans.].

there to hold their drunken revelry. Her vintage of the draught for the immortals they would pour out on the dust; her time-honoured vessels they would smash to pieces. True, I feel with her; but, at the same time, I cannot help being infected with their excitement.

Truth itself has sent us this temptation to test our trustiness in upholding its commandments. Intoxication masquerades in heavenly garb, and dances before the pilgrims saying: "Fools you are that pursue the fruitless path of renunciation. Its way is long, its time passing slow. So the Wielder of the Thunderbolt has sent me to you. Behold, I the beautiful, the passionate, I will accept you—in my embrace you shall find fulfilment."

After a pause Sandip addressed me again: "Goddess, the time has come for me to leave you. It is well. The work of your nearness has been done. By lingering longer it would only become undone again, little by little. All is lost, if in our greed we try to cheapen that which is the greatest thing on earth. That which is eternal within the moment only becomes shallow if spread out in time. We were about to spoil our infinite moment, when it was your uplifted thunderbolt which came to the rescue. You intervened to save the purity of your own worship—and in so doing you also saved your worshipper. In my leave-taking today your worship stands out the biggest thing. Goddess, I, also, set you free today. My earthen temple could hold you no longer— every moment it was on the point of breaking apart. Today I depart to worship your larger image in a larger temple. I can gain you more truly only at a distance from yourself. Here I had only your favour, there I shall be vouchsafed your boon."

My jewel-casket was lying on the table. I held it up aloft as I said: "I charge you to convey these my jewels to the object of my worship—to whom I have dedicated them through you."

My husband remained silent. Sandip left the room.

XXI

I had just sat down to make some cakes for Amulya when the Bara Rani came upon the scene. "Oh dear," she exclaimed, "has it come to this that you must make cakes for your own birthday?"

"Is there no one else for whom I could be making them?" I asked.

"But this is not the day when you should think of feasting others. It is for us to feast you. I was just thinking of making something up [29] when I heard the staggering news which completely upset me. A gang of five or six hundred men, they say, has raided one of our treasuries and made off with six thousand rupees. Our house will be looted next, they expect."

I felt greatly relieved. So it was our own money after all. I wanted to send for Amulya at once and tell him that he need only hand over those notes to my husband and leave the explanations to me.

"You are a wonderful creature!" my sister-in-law broke out, at the change in my countenance. "Have you then really no such thing as fear?"

"I cannot believe it," I said. "Why should they loot our house?"

"Not believe it, indeed! Who could have believed that they would attack our treasury, either?"

I made no reply, but bent over my cakes, putting in the cocoa-nut stuffing.

"Well, I'm off," said the Bara Rani after a prolonged stare at me. "I must see Brother Nikhil and get something done about sending off my money to Calcutta, before it's too late."

She was no sooner gone than I left the cakes to take care of themselves and rushed to my dressing-room, shutting myself inside. My husband's tunic with the keys in its pocket was still hanging there—so forgetful was he. I took the key of the iron safe off the ring and kept it by me, hidden in the folds of my dress.

---

29. Any dainties to be offered ceremonially should be made by the lady of the house herself. [Trans.].

Then there came a knocking at the door. "I am dressing," I called out. I could hear the Bara Rani saying: "Only a minute ago I saw her making cakes and now she is busy dressing up. What next, I wonder! One of their __Bande Mataram__ meetings is on, I suppose. I say, Robber Queen," she called out to me, "are you taking stock of your loot?"

When they went away I hardly know what made me open the safe. Perhaps there was a lurking hope that it might all be a dream. What if, on pulling out the inside drawer, I should find the rolls of gold there, just as before? ... Alas, everything was empty as the trust which had been betrayed.

I had to go through the farce of dressing. I had to do my hair up all over again, quite unnecessarily. When I came out my sister-in-law railed at me: "How many times are you going to dress today?"

"My birthday!" I said.

"Oh, any pretext seems good enough," she went on. "Many vain people have I seen in my day, but you beat them all hollow."

I was about to summon a servant to send after Amulya, when one of the men came up with a little note, which he handed to me. It was from Amulya. "Sister," he wrote, "you invited me this afternoon, but I thought I should not wait. Let me first execute your bidding and then come for my __prasad__. I may be a little late."

To whom could he be going to return that money? into what fresh entanglement was the poor boy rushing? O miserable woman, you can only send him off like an arrow, but not recall him if you miss your aim.

I should have declared at once that I was at the bottom of this robbery. But women live on the trust of their surroundings—this is their whole world. If once it is out that this trust has been secretly betrayed, their place in their world is lost. They have then to stand upon the fragments of the thing they have broken, and its jagged edges keep on wounding them at every turn. To sin is easy enough, but to make up for it is above all difficult for a woman.

For some time past all easy approaches for communion with my husband have been closed to me. How then could I burst on him with this stupendous news? He was very late in coming for his meal today—nearly two o'clock. He was absent-minded and hardly touched any food. I had lost even the right to press him to take a little more. I had to avert my face to wipe away my tears.

I wanted so badly to say to him: "Do come into our room and rest awhile; you look so tired." I had just cleared my throat with a little cough, when a servant hurried in to say that the Police Inspector had brought Panchu up to the palace. My husband, with the shadow on his face deepened, left his meal unfinished and went out.

A little later the Bara Rani appeared. "Why did you not send me word when Brother Nikhil came in?" she complained. "As he was late I thought I might as well finish my bath in the meantime. However did he manage to get through his meal so soon?"

"Why, did you want him for anything?"

"What is this about both of you going off to Calcutta tomorrow? All I can say is, I am not going to be left here alone. I should get startled out of my life at every sound, with all these dacoits about. Is it quite settled about your going tomorrow?"

"Yes," said I, though I had only just now heard it; and though, moreover, I was not at all sure that before tomorrow our history might not take such a turn as to make it all one whether we went or stayed. After that, what our home, our life would be like, was utterly beyond my ken—it seemed so misty and phantom-like.

In a very few hours now my unseen fate would become visible. Was there no one who could keep on postponing the flight of these hours, from day to day, and so make them long enough for me to set things right, so far as lay in my power? The time during which the seed lies underground is long—so long indeed that one forgets that there is any danger of its sprouting. But once its shoot shows up above the surface, it grows and grows so fast, there is no time to cover it up, neither with skirt, nor body, nor even life itself.

I will try to think of it no more, but sit quiet—passive and callous—let the crash come when it may. By the day after tomorrow all will be over—publicity, laughter, bewailing, questions, explanations—everything.

But I cannot forget the face of Amulya—beautiful, radiant with devotion. He did not wait, despairing, for the blow of fate to fall, but rushed into the thick of danger. In my misery I do him reverence. He is my boy-god. Under the pretext of his playfulness he took from me the weight of my burden. He would save me by taking the punishment meant for me on his own head. But how am I to bear this terrible mercy of my God?

Oh, my child, my child, I do you reverence. Little brother mine, I do you reverence. Pure are you, beautiful are you, I do you reverence. May you come to my arms, in the next birth, as my own child—that is my prayer.

XXII

Rumour became busy on every side. The police were continually in and out. The servants of the house were in a great flurry.

Khema, my maid, came up to me and said: "Oh, Rani Mother! for goodness" sake put away my gold necklace and armlets in your iron safe." To whom was I to explain that the Rani herself had been weaving all this network of trouble, and had got caught in it, too? I had to play the benign protector and take charge of Khema's ornaments and Thako's savings. The milk-woman, in her turn, brought along and kept in my room a box in which were a Benares __sari__ and some other of her valued possessions. "I got these at your wedding," she told me.

When, tomorrow, my iron safe will be opened in the presence of these—Khema, Thako, the milk-woman and all the rest ... Let me not think of it! Let me rather try to think what it will be like when this third day of Magh comes round again after a year has passed. Will all the wounds of my home life then be still as fresh as ever? ...

Amulya writes that he will come later in the evening. I cannot remain alone with my thoughts, doing nothing. So I sit down again to make cakes for him. I have finished making quite a quantity, but still I must go on. Who will eat them? I shall distribute them amongst the servants. I must do so this very night. Tonight is my limit. Tomorrow will not be in my hands.

I went on untiringly, frying cake after cake. Every now and then it seemed to me that there was some noise in the direction of my rooms, upstairs. Could it be that my husband had missed the key of the safe, and the Bara Rani had assembled all the servants to help him to hunt for it? No, I must not pay heed to these sounds. Let me shut the door.

I rose to do so, when Thako came panting in: "Rani Mother, oh, Rani Mother!"

"Oh get away!" I snapped out, cutting her short. "Don't come bothering me."

"The Bara Rani Mother wants you," she went on. "Her nephew has brought such a wonderful machine from Calcutta. It talks like a man. Do come and hear it!"

I did not know whether to laugh or to cry. So, of all things, a gramophone needs must come on the scene at such a time, repeating at every winding the nasal twang of its theatrical songs! What a fearsome thing results when a machine apes a man.

The shades of evening began to fall. I knew that Amulya would not delay to announce himself—yet I could not wait. I summoned a servant and said: "Go and tell Amulya Babu to come straight in here." The man came back after a while to say that Amulya was not in—he had not come back since he had gone.

"Gone!" The last word struck my ears like a wail in the gathering darkness. Amulya gone! Had he then come like a streak of light from the setting sun, only to be gone for ever? All kinds of possible and impossible dangers flitted through my mind. It was I who had sent him to his death. What if he was fearless? That only showed his own greatness of heart. But after this how was I to go on living all by myself?

I had no memento of Amulya save that pistol—his reverence-offering. It seemed to me that this was a sign given by Providence. This guilt which had contaminated my life at its very root—my God in the form of a child had left with me the means of wiping it away, and then vanished. Oh the loving gift— the saving grave that lay hidden within it!

I opened my box and took out the pistol, lifting it reverently to my forehead. At that moment the gongs clanged out from the temple attached to our house. I prostrated myself in salutation.

In the evening I feasted the whole household with my cakes. "You have managed a wonderful birthday feast—and all by yourself too!" exclaimed my sister-in-law. "But you must leave something for us to do." With this she turned on her gramophone and let loose the shrill treble of the Calcutta actresses all over the place. It seemed like a stable full of neighing fillies.

It got quite late before the feasting was over. I had a sudden longing to end my birthday celebration by taking the dust of my husband's feet. I went up to the bedroom and found him fast asleep. He had had such a worrying, trying day. I raised the edge of the mosquito curtain very very gently, and laid my head near his feet. My hair must have touched him, for he moved his legs in his sleep and pushed my head away.

I then went out and sat in the west verandah. A silk-cotton tree, which had shed all its leaves, stood there in the distance, like a skeleton. Behind it the crescent moon was setting. All of a sudden I had the feeling that the very stars in the sky were afraid of me—that the whole of the night world was looking askance at me. Why? Because I was alone.

There is nothing so strange in creation as the man who is alone. Even he whose near ones have all died, one by one, is not alone—companionship comes for him from behind the screen of death. But he, whose kin are there, yet no longer near, who has dropped out of all the varied companionship of a full home—the starry universe itself seems to bristle to look on him in his darkness.

Where I am, I am not. I am far away from those who are around me. I live and move upon a world-wide chasm of separation, unstable as the dew-drop upon the lotus leaf.

Why do not men change wholly when they change? When I look into my heart, I find everything that was there, still there—only they are topsy-turvy. Things that were well-ordered have become jumbled up. The gems that were strung into a necklace are now rolling in the dust. And so my heart is breaking.

I feel I want to die. Yet in my heart everything still lives— nor even in death can I see the end of it all: rather, in death there seems to be ever so much more of repining. What is to be ended must be ended in this life—there is no other way out.

Oh forgive me just once, only this time, Lord! All that you gave into my hands as the wealth of my life, I have made into my burden. I can neither bear it longer, nor give it up. O Lord, sound once again those flute strains which you played for me, long ago, standing at the rosy edge of my morning sky—and let all my complexities become simple and easy. Nothing save the music of your flute can make whole that which has been broken, and pure that which has been sullied. Create my home anew with your music. No other way can I see.

I threw myself prone on the ground and sobbed aloud. It was for mercy that I prayed—some little mercy from somewhere, some shelter, some sign of forgiveness, some hope that might bring about the end. "Lord," I vowed to myself, "I will lie here, waiting and waiting, touching neither food nor drink, so long as your blessing does not reach me."

I heard the sound of footsteps. Who says that the gods do not show themselves to mortal men? I did not raise my face to look up, lest the sight of it should break the spell. Come, oh come, come and let your feet touch my head. Come, Lord, and set your foot upon my throbbing heart, and at that moment let me die.

He came and sat near my head. Who? My husband! At the first touch of his presence I felt that I should swoon. And then the pain at my heart burst its way out in an overwhelming flood of tears, tearing through all my obstructing veins and nerves. I strained his feet to my bosom—oh, why could not their impress remain there for ever?

He tenderly stroked my head. I received his blessing. Now I shall be able to take up the penalty of public humiliation which will be mine tomorrow, and offer it, in all sincerity, at the feet of my God.

But what keeps crushing my heart is the thought that the festive flutes which were played at my wedding, nine years ago, welcoming me to this house, will never sound for me again in this life. What rigour of penance is there which can serve to bring me once more, as a bride adorned for her husband, to my place upon that same bridal seat? How many years, how many ages, aeons, must pass before I can find my way back to that day of nine years ago?

God can create new things, but has even He the power to create afresh that which has been destroyed?

Chapter Twelve

Nikhil's Story

XV

TODAY we are going to Calcutta. Our joys and sorrows lie heavy on us if we merely go on accumulating them. Keeping them and accumulating them alike are false. As master of the house I am in an artificial position—in reality I am a wayfarer on the path of life. That is why the true Master of the House gets hurt at every step and at last there comes the supreme hurt of death.

My union with you, my love, was only of the wayside; it was well enough so long as we followed the same road; it will only hamper us if we try to preserve it further. We are now leaving its bonds behind. We are started on our journey beyond, and it will be enough if we can throw each other a glance, or feel the touch of each other's hands in passing. After that? After that there is the larger world-path, the endless current of universal life.

How little can you deprive me of, my love, after all? Whenever I set my ear to it, I can hear the flute which is playing, its fountain of melody gushing forth from the flute-stops of separation. The immortal draught of the goddess is never exhausted. She sometimes breaks the bowl from which we drink it, only to smile at seeing us so disconsolate over the trifling loss. I will not stop to pick up my broken bowl. I will march forward, albeit with unsatisfied heart.

The Bara Rani came and asked me: "What is the meaning, brother, of all these books being packed up and sent off in box-loads?"

"It only means," I replied, "that I have not yet been able to get over my fondness for them."

"I only wish you would keep your fondness for some other things as well! Do you mean you are never coming back home?"

"I shall be coming and going, but shall not immure myself here any more."

"Oh indeed! Then just come along to my room and see how many things __I__ have been unable to shake off __my__ fondness for." With this she took me by the hand and marched me off.

In my sister-in-law's rooms I found numberless boxes and bundles ready packed. She opened one of the boxes and said: "See, brother, look at all my __pan__-making things. In this bottle I have catechu powder scented with the pollen of screw-pine blossoms. These little tin boxes are all for different kinds of spices. I have not forgotten my playing cards and draught-board either. If you two are over-busy, I shall manage to make other friends there, who will give me a game. Do you remember this comb? It was one of the __Swadeshi__ combs you brought for me..."

"But what is all this for, Sister Rani? Why have you been packing up all these things?"

"Do you think I am not going with you?"

"What an extraordinary idea!"

"Don't you be afraid! I am not going there to flirt with you, nor to quarrel with the Chota Rani! One must die sooner or later, and it is just as well to be on the bank of the holy Ganges before it is too late. It is too horrible to think of being cremated in your wretched burning-ground here, under that stumpy banian tree—that is why I have been refusing to die, and have plagued you all this time."

At last I could hear the true voice of home. The Bara Rani came into our house as its bride, when I was only six years old. We have played together, through the drowsy afternoons, in a corner of the roof-terrace. I have thrown down to her green amras from the tree-top, to be made into deliciously indigestible chutnies by slicing them up with mustard, salt and fragrant herbs. It was my part to gather for her all the forbidden things from the store-room to be used in the marriage celebration of her doll; for, in the penal code of my grandmother, I alone was exempt from punishment. And I used to be appointed her messenger to my brother, whenever she wanted to coax something special out of him, because he could not resist my importunity. I also remember how, when I suffered under the rigorous régime of the doctors of those days—who would not allow anything except warm water and sugared cardamom seeds during feverish attacks—my sister-in-law could not bear my privation and used to bring me delicacies on the sly. What a scolding she got one day when she was caught!

And then, as we grew up, our mutual joys and sorrows took on deeper tones of intimacy. How we quarrelled! Sometimes conflicts of worldly interests roused suspicions and jealousies, making breaches in our love; and when the Chota Rani came in between us, these breaches seemed as if they would never be mended, but it always turned out that the healing forces at bottom proved more powerful than the wounds on the surface.

So has a true relationship grown up between us, from our childhood up till now, and its branching foliage has spread and broadened over every room and verandah and terrace of this great house. When I saw the Bara Rani make ready, with all her belongings, to depart from this house of ours, all the ties that bound us, to their wide-spreading ends, felt the shock.

The reason was clear to me, why she had made up her mind to drift away towards the unknown, cutting asunder all her lifelong bonds of daily habit, and of the house itself, which she had never left for a day since she first entered it at the age of nine. And yet it was this real reason which she could not allow to escape her lips, preferring rather to put forward any other paltry excuse.

She had only this one relationship left in all the world, and the poor, unfortunate, widowed and childless woman had cherished it with all the tenderness hoarded in her heart. How deeply she had felt our proposed separation I never realized so keenly as when I stood amongst her scattered boxes and bundles.

I could see at once that the little differences she used to have with Bimala, about money matters, did not proceed from any sordid worldliness, but because she felt that her claims in regard to this one relationship of her life had been overridden and its ties weakened for her by the coming in between of this other woman from goodness knows where! She had been hurt at every turn and yet had not the right to complain.

And Bimala? She also had felt that the Senior Rani's claim over me was not based merely on our social connection, but went much deeper; and she was jealous of these ties between us, reaching back to our childhood.

Today my heart knocked heavily against the doors of my breast. I sank down upon one of the boxes as I said: "How I should love, Sister Rani, to go back to the days when we first met in this old house of ours."

"No, brother dear," she replied with a sigh, "I would not live my life again—not as a woman! Let what I have had to bear end with this one birth. I could not bear it over again."

I said to her: "The freedom to which we pass through sorrow is greater than the sorrow."

"That may be so for you men. Freedom is for you. But we women would keep others bound. We would rather be put into bondage ourselves. No, no, brother, you will never get free from our toils. If you needs must spread your wings, you will have to take us with you; we refuse to be left behind. That is why I have gathered together all this weight of luggage. It would never do to allow men to run too light."

"I can feel the weight of your words," I said laughing, "and if we men do not complain of your burdens, it is because women pay us so handsomely for what they make us carry."

"You carry it," she said, "because it is made up of many small things. Whichever one you think of rejecting pleads that it is so light. And so with much lightness we weigh you down … When do we start?"

"The train leaves at half past eleven tonight. There will be lots of time."

"Look here, do be good for once and listen to just one word of mine. Take a good nap this afternoon. You know you never get any sleep in the train. You look so pulled down, you might go to pieces any moment. Come along, get through your bath first."

As we went towards my room, Khema, the maid, came up and with an ultra-modest pull at her veil told us, in deprecatingly low tones, that the Police Inspector had arrived with a prisoner and wanted to see the Maharaja.

"Is the Maharaja a thief, or a robber," the Bara Rani flared up, "that he should be set upon so by the police? Go and tell the Inspector that the Maharaja is at his bath."

"Let me just go and see what is the matter," I pleaded. "It may be something urgent."

"No, no," my sister-in-law insisted. "Our Chota Rani was making a heap of cakes last night. I'll send some to the Inspector, to keep him quiet till you're ready." With this she pushed me into my room and shut the door on me.

I had not the power to resist such tyranny—so rare is it in this world. Let the Inspector while away the time eating cakes. What if business is a bit neglected?

The police had been in great form these last few days arresting now this one, now that. Each day some innocent person or other would be brought along to enliven the assembly in my office-room. One more such unfortunate, I supposed, must have been brought in that day. But why should the Inspector alone be regaled with cakes? That would not do at all. I thumped vigorously on the door.

"If you are going mad, be quick and pour some water over your head—that will keep you cool," said my sister-in-law from the passage.

"Send down cakes for two," I shouted. "The person who has been brought in as the thief probably deserves them better. Tell the man to give him a good big helping."

I hurried through my bath. When I came out, I found Bimal sitting on the floor outside. [30] Could this be my Bimal of old, my proud, sensitive Bimal?

What favour could she be wanting to beg, seated like this at my door?

As I stopped short, she stood up and said gently with downcast eyes: "I would have a word with you."

"Come inside then," I said.

"But are you going out on any particular business?"

"I was, but let that be. I want to hear …"

"No, finish your business first. We will have our talk after you have had your dinner."

I went off to my sitting-room, to find the Police Inspector's plate quite empty. The person he had brought with him, however, was still busy eating.

"Hullo!" I ejaculated in surprise. "You, Amulya?"

"It is I, sir," said Amulya with his mouth full of cake. "I've had quite a feast. And if you don't mind, I'll take the rest with me." With this he proceeded to tie up the remaining cakes in his handkerchief.

"What does this mean?" I asked, staring at the Inspector.

---

30. Sitting on the bare floor is a sign of mourning, and so, by association of ideas, of an abject attitude of mind. [Trans.].

The man laughed. "We are no nearer, sir," he said, "to solving the problem of the thief: meanwhile the mystery of the theft deepens." He then produced something tied up in a rag, which when untied disclosed a bundle of currency notes. "This, Maharaja," said the Inspector, "is your six thousand rupees!"

"Where was it found?"

"In Amulya Babu's hands. He went last evening to the manager of your Chakna sub-office to tell him that the money had been found. The manager seemed to be in a greater state of trepidation at the recovery than he had been at the robbery. He was afraid he would be suspected of having made away with the notes and of now making up a cock-and-bull story for fear of being found out. He asked Amulya to wait, on the pretext of getting him some refreshment, and came straight over to the Police Office. I rode off at once, kept Amulya with me, and have been busy with him the whole morning. He refuses to tell us where he got the money from. I warned him he would be kept under restraint till he did so. In that case, he informed me he would have to lie. Very well, I said, he might do so if he pleased. Then he stated that he had found the money under a bush. I pointed out to him that it was not quite so easy to lie as all that. Under what bush? Where was the place? Why was he there?—All this would have to be stated as well. 'Don't you worry,' he said, 'there is plenty of time to invent all that.'"

"But, Inspector," I said, "why are you badgering a respectable young gentleman like Amulya Babu?"

"I have no desire to harass him," said the Inspector. "He is not only a gentleman, but the son of Nibaran Babu, my school-fellow. Let me tell you, Maharaja, exactly what must have happened. Amulya knows the thief, but wants to shield him by drawing suspicion on himself. That is just the sort of bravado he loves to indulge in." The Inspector turned to Amulya. "Look here, young man," he continued, "I also was eighteen once upon a time, and a student in the Ripon College. I nearly got into gaol trying to rescue a hack driver from a police constable. It was a near shave." Then he turned again to me and said: "Maharaja, the real thief will now probably escape, but I think I can tell you who is at the bottom of it all."

"Who is it, then?" I asked.

"The manager, in collusion with the guard, Kasim."

When the Inspector, having argued out his theory to his own satisfaction, at last departed, I said to Amulya: "If you will tell me who took the money, I promise you no one shall be hurt."

"I did," said he.

"But how can that be? What about the gang of armed men?…"

"It was I, by myself, alone!"

What Amulya then told me was indeed extraordinary. The manager had just finished his supper and was on the verandah rinsing out his mouth. The place was somewhat dark. Amulya had a revolver in each pocket, one loaded with blank cartridges, the other with ball. He had a mask over his face. He flashed a bull's-eye lantern in the manager's face and fired a blank shot. The man swooned away. Some of the guards, who were off duty, came running up, but when Amulya fired another blank shot at them they lost no time in taking cover. Then Kasim, who was on duty, came up whirling a quarterstaff. This time Amulya aimed a bullet at his legs, and finding himself hit, Kasim collapsed on the floor. Amulya then made the trembling manager, who had come to his senses, open the safe and deliver up six thousand rupees. Finally, he took one of the estate horses and galloped off a few miles, there let the animal loose, and quietly walked up here, to our place.

"What made you do all this, Amulya?" I asked.

"There was a grave reason, Maharaja," he replied.

"But why, then, did you try to return the money?"

"Let her come, at whose command I did so. In her presence I shall make a clean breast of it."

"And who may 'she' be?"

"My sister, the Chota Rani!"

I sent for Bimala. She came hesitatingly, barefoot, with a white shawl over her head. I had never seen my Bimal like this before. She seemed to have wrapped herself in a morning light.

Amulya prostrated himself in salutation and took the dust of her feet. Then, as he rose, he said: "Your command has been executed, sister. The money is returned."

"You have saved me, my little brother," said Bimal.

"With your image in my mind, I have not uttered a single lie," Amulya continued. "My watchword __Bande Mataram__ has been cast away at your feet for good. I have also received my reward, your __prasad__, as soon as I came to the palace."

Bimal looked at him blankly, unable to follow his last words. Amulya brought out his handkerchief, and untying it showed her the cakes put away inside. "I did not eat them all," he said. "I have kept these to eat after you have helped me with your own hands."

I could see that I was not wanted here. I went out of the room. I could only preach and preach, so I mused, and get my effigy burnt for my pains. I had not yet been able to bring back a single soul from the path of death. They who have the power, can do so by a mere sign. My words have not that ineffable meaning. I am not a flame, only a black coal, which has gone out. I can light no lamp. That is what the story of my life shows—my row of lamps has remained unlit.

XVI

I returned slowly towards the inner apartments. The Bara Rani's room must have been drawing me again. It had become an absolute necessity for me, that day, to feel that this life of mine had been able to strike some real, some responsive chord in some other harp of life. One cannot realize one's own existence by remaining within oneself—it has to be sought outside.

As I passed in front of my sister-in-law's room, she came out saying: "I was afraid you would be late again this afternoon. However, I ordered your dinner as soon as I heard you coming. It will be served in a minute."

"Meanwhile," I said; "let me take out that money of yours and have it kept ready to take with us."

As we walked on towards my room she asked me if the Police Inspector had made any report about the robbery. I somehow did not feel inclined to tell her all the details of how that six thousand had come back. "That's just what all the fuss is about," I said evasively.

When I went into my dressing-room and took out my bunch of keys, I did not find the key of the iron safe on the ring. What an absurdly absent-minded fellow I was, to be sure! Only this morning I had been opening so many boxes and things, and never noticed that this key was not there.

"What has happened to your key?" she asked me.

I went on fumbling in this pocket and that, but could give her no answer. I hunted in the same place over and over again. It dawned on both of us that it could not be a case of the key being mislaid. Someone must have taken it off the ring. Who could it be? Who else could have come into this room?

"Don't you worry about it," she said to me. "Get through your dinner first. The Chota Rani must have kept it herself, seeing how absent-minded you are getting."

I was, however, greatly disturbed. It was never Bimal's habit to take any key of mine without telling me about it. Bimal was not present at my meal-time that day: she was busy feasting Amulya in her own room. My sister-in-law wanted to send for her, but I asked her not to do so.

I had just finished my dinner when Bimal came in. I would have preferred not to discuss the matter of the key in the Bara Rani's presence, but as soon as she saw Bimal, she asked her: "Do you know, dear, where the key of the safe is?"

"I have it," was the reply.

"Didn't I say so!" exclaimed my sister-in-law triumphantly. "Our Chota Rani pretends not to care about these robberies, but she takes precautions on the sly, all the same."

The look on Bimal's face made my mind misgive me. "Let the key be, now," I said. "I will take out that money in the evening."

"There you go again, putting it off," said the Bara Rani. "Why not take it out and send it to the treasury while you have it in mind?"

"I have taken it out already," said Bimal.

I was startled.

"Where have you kept it, then?" asked my sister-in-law.

"I have spent it."

"Just listen to her! Whatever did you spend all that money on?"

Bimal made no reply. I asked her nothing further. The Bara Rani seemed about to make some further remark to Bimala, but checked herself. "Well, that is all right, anyway," she said at length, as she looked towards me. "Just what I used to do with my husband's loose cash. I knew it was no use leaving it with him— his hundred and one hangers-on would be sure to get hold of it. You are much the same, dear! What a number of ways you men know of getting through money. We can only save it from you by stealing it ourselves! Come along now. Off with you to bed."

The Bara Rani led me to my room, but I hardly knew where I was going. She sat by my bed after I was stretched on it, and smiled at Bimal as she said: "Give me one of your pans, Chotie darling— what? You have none! You have become a regular mem-sahib. Then send for some from my room."

"But have you had your dinner yet?" I anxiously enquired.

"Oh long ago," she replied—clearly a fib.

She kept on chattering away there at my bedside, on all manner of things. The maid came and told Bimal that her dinner had been served and was getting cold, but she gave no sign of having heard it. "Not had your dinner yet? What nonsense! It's fearfully late." With this the Bara Rani took Bimal away with her.

I could divine that there was some connection between the taking out of this six thousand and the robbing of the other. But I have no curiosity to learn the nature of it. I shall never ask.

Providence leaves our life moulded in the rough—its object being that we ourselves should put the finishing touches, shaping it into its final form to our taste. There has always been the hankering within me to express some great idea in the process of giving shape to my life on the lines suggested by the Creator. In this endeavour I have spent all my days. How severely I have curbed my desires, repressed myself at every step, only the Searcher of the Heart knows.

But the difficulty is, that one's life is not solely one's own. He who would create it must do so with the help of his surroundings, or he will fail. So it was my constant dream to draw Bimal to join me in this work of creating myself. I loved her with all my soul; on the strength of that, I could not but succeed in winning her to my purpose—that was my firm belief.

Then I discovered that those who could simply and naturally draw their environment into the process of their self-creation belonged to one species of the genus "man",—and I to another. I had received the vital spark, but could not impart it. Those to whom I have surrendered my all have taken my all, but not myself with it.

My trial is hard indeed. Just when I want a helpmate most, I am thrown back on myself alone. Nevertheless, I record my vow that even in this trial I shall win through. Alone, then, shall I tread my thorny path to the end of this life's journey …

I have begun to suspect that there has all along been a vein of tyranny in me. There was a despotism in my desire to mould my relations with Bimala in a hard, clear-cut, perfect form. But man's life was not meant to be cast in a mould. And if we try to shape the good, as so much mere material, it takes a terrible revenge by losing its life.

I did not realize all this while that it must have been this unconscious tyranny of mine which made us gradually drift apart. Bimala's life, not finding its true level by reason of my pressure from above, has had to find an outlet by undermining its banks at the bottom. She has had to steal this six thousand rupees because she could not be open with me, because she felt that, in certain things, I despotically differed from her.

Men, such as I, possessed with one idea, are indeed at one with those who can manage to agree with us; but those who do not, can only get on with us by cheating us. It is our unyielding obstinacy, which drives even the simplest to tortuous ways. In trying to manufacture a helpmate, we spoil a wife.

Could I not go back to the beginning? Then, indeed, I should follow the path of the simple. I should not try to fetter my life's companion with my ideas, but play the joyous pipes of my love and say: "Do you love me? Then may you grow true to yourself in the light of your love. Let my suggestions be suppressed, let God's design, which is in you, triumph, and my ideas retire abashed."

But can even Nature's nursing heal the open wound, into which our accumulated differences have broken out? The covering veil, beneath the privacy of which Nature's silent forces alone can work, has been torn asunder. Wounds must be bandaged—can we not bandage our wound with our love, so that the day may come when its scar will no longer be visible? It is not too late? So much time has been lost in misunderstanding; it has taken right up to now to come to an understanding; how much more time will it take for the correcting? What if the wound does eventually heal?—can the devastation it has wrought ever be made good?

There was a slight sound near the door. As I turned over I saw Bimala's retreating figure through the open doorway. She must have been waiting by the door, hesitating whether to come in or not, and at last have decided to go back. I jumped up and bounded to the door, calling: "Bimal."

She stopped on her way. She had her back to me. I went and took her by the hand and led her into our room. She threw herself face downwards on a pillow, and sobbed and sobbed. I said nothing, but held her hand as I sat by her head.

When her storm of grief had abated she sat up. I tried to draw her to my breast, but she pushed my arms away and knelt at my feet, touching them repeatedly with her head, in obeisance. I hastily drew my feet back, but she clasped them in her arms, saying in a choking voice: "No, no, no, you must not take away your feet. Let me do my worship."

I kept still. Who was I to stop her? Was I the god of her worship that I should have any qualms?

Bimala's Story

XXIII

Come, come! Now is the time to set sail towards that great confluence, where the river of love meets the sea of worship. In that pure blue all the weight of its muddiness sinks and disappears.

I now fear nothing—neither myself, nor anybody else. I have passed through fire. What was inflammable has been burnt to ashes; what is left is deathless. I have dedicated myself to the feet of him, who has received all my sin into the depths of his own pain.

Tonight we go to Calcutta. My inward troubles have so long prevented my looking after my things. Now let me arrange and pack them.

After a while I found my husband had come in and was taking a hand in the packing.

"This won't do," I said. "Did you not promise me you would have a sleep?"

"I might have made the promise," he replied, "but my sleep did not, and it was nowhere to be found."

"No, no," I repeated, "this will never do. Lie down for a while, at least."

"But how can you get through all this alone?"

"Of course I can."

"Well, you may boast of being able to do without me. But frankly I can't do without you. Even sleep refused to come to me, alone, in that room." Then he set to work again.

But there was an interruption, in the shape of a servant, who came and said that Sandip Babu had called and had asked to be announced. I did not dare to ask whom he wanted. The light of the sky seemed suddenly to be shut down, like the leaves of a sensitive plant.

"Come, Bimal," said my husband. "Let us go and hear what Sandip has to tell us. Since he has come back again, after taking his leave, he must have something special to say."

I went, simply because it would have been still more embarrassing to stay. Sandip was staring at a picture on the wall. As we entered he said: "You must be wondering why the fellow has returned. But you know the ghost is never laid till all the rites are complete." With these words he brought out of his pocket something tied in his handkerchief, and laying it on the table, undid the knot. It was those sovereigns.

"Don't you mistake me, Nikhil," he said. "You must not imagine that the contagion of your company has suddenly turned me honest; I am not the man to come back in slobbering repentance to return ill-gotten money. But…"

He left his speech unfinished. After a pause he turned towards Nikhil, but said to me: "After all these days, Queen Bee, the ghost of compunction has found an entry into my hitherto untroubled conscience. As I have to wrestle with it every night, after my first sleep is over, I cannot call it a phantom of my imagination. There is no escape even for me till its debt is paid. Into the hands of that spirit, therefore, let me make restitution. Goddess! From you, alone, of all the world, I shall not be able to take away anything. I shall not be rid of you till I am destitute. Take these back!"

He took out at the same time the jewel-casket from under his tunic and put it down, and then left us with hasty steps.

"Listen to me, Sandip," my husband called after him.

"I have not the time, Nikhil," said Sandip as he paused near the door. "The Mussulmans, I am told, have taken me for an invaluable gem, and are conspiring to loot me and hide me away in their graveyard. But I feel that it is necessary that I should live. I have just twenty-five minutes to catch the North-bound train. So, for the present, I must be gone. We shall have our talk out at the next convenient opportunity. If you take my advice, don't you delay in getting away either. I salute you, Queen Bee, Queen of the bleeding hearts, Queen of desolation!"

Sandip then left almost at a run. I stood stock-still; I had never realized in such a manner before, how trivial, how paltry, this gold and these jewels were. Only a short while ago I was so busy thinking what I should take with me, and how I should pack it. Now I felt that there was no need to take anything at all. To set out and go forth was the important thing.

My husband left his seat and came up and took me by the hand. "It is getting late," he said. "There is not much time left to complete our preparations for the journey."

At this point Chandranath Babu suddenly came in. Finding us both together, he fell back for a moment. Then he said, "Forgive me, my little mother, if I intrude. Nikhil, the Mussulmans are out of hand. They are looting Harish Kundu's treasury. That does not so much matter. But what is intolerable is the violence that is being done to the women of their house."

"I am off," said my husband.

"What can you do there?" I pleaded, as I held him by the hand. "Oh, sir," I appealed to his master. "Will you not tell him not to go?"

"My little mother," he replied, "there is no time to do anything else."

"Don't be alarmed, Bimal," said my husband, as he left us.

When I went to the window I saw my husband galloping away on horseback, with not a weapon in his hands.

In another minute the Bara Rani came running in. "What have you done, Chotie darling," she cried. "How could you let him go?"

"Call the Dewan at once," she said, turning to a servant.

The Ranis never appeared before the Dewan, but the Bara Rani had no thought that day for appearances.

"Send a mounted man to bring back the Maharaja at once," she said, as soon as the Dewan came up.

"We have all entreated him to stay, Rani Mother," said the Dewan, "but he refused to turn back."

"Send word to him that the Bara Rani is ill, that she is on her death-bed," cried my sister-in-law wildly.

When the Dewan had left she turned on me with a furious outburst. "Oh, you witch, you ogress, you could not die yourself, but needs must send him to his death! …"

The light of the day began to fade. The sun set behind the feathery foliage of the blossoming __Sajna__ tree. I can see every different shade of that sunset even today. Two masses of cloud on either side of the sinking orb made it look like a great bird with fiery-feathered wings outspread. It seemed to me that this fateful day was taking its flight, to cross the ocean of night.

It became darker and darker. Like the flames of a distant village on fire, leaping up every now and then above the horizon, a distant din swelled up in recurring waves into the darkness.

The bells of the evening worship rang out from our temple. I knew the Bara Rani was sitting there, with palms joined in silent prayer. But I could not move a step from the window.

The roads, the village beyond, and the still more distant fringe of trees, grew more and more vague. The lake in our grounds looked up into the sky with a dull lustre, like a blind man's eye. On the left the tower seemed to be craning its neck to catch sight of something that was happening.

The sounds of night take on all manner of disguises. A twig snaps, and one thinks that somebody is running for his life. A door slams, and one feels it to be the sudden heart-thump of a startled world.

Lights would suddenly flicker under the shade of the distant trees, and then go out again. Horses' hoofs would clatter, now and again, only to turn out to be riders leaving the palace gates.

I continually had the feeling that, if only I could die, all this turmoil would come to an end. So long as I was alive my sins would remain rampant, scattering destruction on every side. I remembered the pistol in my box. But my feet refused to leave the window in quest of it. Was I not awaiting my fate?

The gong of the watch solemnly struck ten. A little later, groups of lights appeared in the distance and a great crowd wound its way, like some great serpent, along the roads in the darkness, towards the palace gates.

The Dewan rushed to the gate at the sound. Just then a rider came galloping in. "What's the news, Jata?" asked the Dewan.

"Not good," was the reply.

I could hear these words distinctly from my window. But something was next whispered which I could not catch.

Then came a palanquin, followed by a litter. The doctor was walking alongside the palanquin.

"What do you think, doctor?" asked the Dewan.

"Can't say yet," the doctor replied. "The wound in the head is a serious one."

"And Amulya Babu?"

"He has a bullet through the heart. He is done for."

THE KABULIWALLAH

My five years' old daughter Mini cannot live without chattering. I really believe that in all her life she has not wasted a minute in silence. Her mother is often vexed at this, and would stop her prattle, but I would not. To see Mini quiet is unnatural, and I cannot bear it long. And so my own talk with her is always lively.

One morning, for instance, when I was in the midst of the seventeenth chapter of my new novel, my little Mini stole into the room, and putting her hand into mine, said: "Father! Ramdayal the door-keeper calls a crow a krow! He doesn't know anything, does he?"

Before I could explain to her the differences of language in this world, she was embarked on the full tide of another subject. "What do you think, Father? Bhola says there is an elephant in the clouds, blowing water out of his trunk, and that is why it rains!"

And then, darting off anew, while I sat still making ready some reply to this last saying, "Father! what relation is Mother to you?"

"My dear little sister in the law!" I murmured involuntarily to myself, but with a grave face contrived to answer: "Go and play with Bhola, Mini! I am busy!"

The window of my room overlooks the road. The child had seated herself at my feet near my table, and was playing softly, drumming on her knees. I was hard at work on my seventeenth chapter, where Protrap Singh, the hero, had just caught Kanchanlata, the heroine, in his arms, and was about to escape with her by the third story window of the castle, when all of a sudden Mini left her play, and ran to the window, crying, "A Kabuliwallah! a Kabuliwallah!" Sure enough in the street below was a Kabuliwallah, passing slowly along. He wore the loose soiled clothing of his people, with a tall turban; there was a bag on his back, and he carried boxes of grapes in his hand.

I cannot tell what were my daughter's feelings at the sight of this man, but she began to call him loudly. "Ah!" I thought, "he will come in, and my seventeenth chapter will never be finished!" At which exact moment the Kabuliwallah turned, and looked up at the child. When she saw this, overcome by terror, she fled to her mother's protection, and disappeared. She had a blind belief that inside the bag, which the big man carried, there were perhaps two or three other children like herself. The pedlar meanwhile entered my doorway, and greeted me with a smiling face.

So precarious was the position of my hero and my heroine, that my first impulse was to stop and buy something, since the man had been called. I made some small purchases, and a conversation began about Abdurrahman, the Russians, she English, and the Frontier Policy.

As he was about to leave, he asked: "And where is the little girl, sir?"

And I, thinking that Mini must get rid of her false fear, had her brought out.

She stood by my chair, and looked at the Kabuliwallah and his bag. He offered her nuts and raisins, but she would not be tempted, and only clung the closer to me, with all her doubts increased.

This was their first meeting.

One morning, however, not many days later, as I was leaving the house, I was startled to find Mini, seated on a bench near the door, laughing and talking, with the great Kabuliwallah at her feet. In all her life, it appeared; my small daughter had never found so patient a listener, save her father. And already the corner of her little sari was stuffed with almonds and raisins, the gift of her visitor, "Why did you give her those?" I said, and taking out an eight-anna bit, I handed it to him. The man accepted the money without demur, and slipped it into his pocket.

Alas, on my return an hour later, I found the unfortunate coin had made twice its own worth of trouble! For the Kabuliwallah had given it to Mini, and her mother catching sight of the bright round object, had pounced on the child with: "Where did you get that eight-anna bit?"

"The Kabuliwallah gave it me," said Mini cheerfully.

"The Kabuliwallah gave it you!" cried her mother much shocked. "Oh, Mini! how could you take it from him?"

I, entering at the moment, saved her from impending disaster, and proceeded to make my own inquiries.

It was not the first or second time, I found, that the two had met. The Kabuliwallah had overcome the child's first terror by a judicious bribery of nuts and almonds, and the two were now great friends.

They had many quaint jokes, which afforded them much amusement. Seated in front of him, looking down on his gigantic frame in all her tiny dignity, Mini would ripple her face with laughter, and begin: "O Kabuliwallah, Kabuliwallah, what have you got in your bag?"

And he would reply, in the nasal accents of the mountaineer: "An elephant!" Not much cause for merriment, perhaps; but how they both enjoyed the witticism! And for me, this child's talk with a grown-up man had always in it something strangely fascinating.

Then the Kabuliwallah, not to be behind hand, would take his turn: "Well, little one, and when are you going to the father-in-law's house?"

Now most small Bengali maidens have heard long ago about the father-in-law's house; but we, being a little new-fangled, had kept these things from our child, and Mini at this question must have been a trifle bewildered. But she would not show it, and with ready tact replied: "Are you going there?"

Amongst men of the Kabuliwallah's class, however, it is well known that the words father-in-law's house have a double meaning. It is a euphemism for jail, the place where we are well cared for, at no expense to ourselves. In this sense would the sturdy pedlar take my daughter's question. "Ah," he would say, shaking his fist at an invisible policeman, "I will thrash my father-in-law!" Hearing this, and picturing the poor discomfited relative, Mini would go off into peals of laughter, in which her formidable friend would join.

These were autumn mornings, the very time of year when kings of old went forth to conquest; and I, never stirring from my little corner in Calcutta, would let my mind wander over the whole world. At the very name of another country, my heart would go out to it, and at the sight of a foreigner in the streets, I would fall to weaving a network of dreams,--the mountains, the glens, and the forests of his distant home, with his cottage in its setting, and the free and independent life of far-away wilds. Perhaps the scenes of travel conjure themselves up before me, and pass and repass in my imagination all the more vividly, because I lead such a vegetable existence, that a call to travel would fall upon me like a thunderbolt. In the presence of this Kabuliwallah, I was immediately transported to the foot of arid mountain peaks, with narrow little defiles twisting in and out amongst their towering heights. I could see the string of camels bearing the merchandise, and the company of turbaned merchants, carrying some of their queer old firearms, and some of their spears, journeying downward towards the plains. I could see--but at some such point Mini's mother would intervene, imploring me to "beware of that man."

Mini's mother is unfortunately a very timid lady. Whenever she hears a noise in the street, or sees people coming towards the house, she always jumps to the conclusion that they are either thieves, or drunkards, or snakes, or tigers, or malaria or cockroaches, or caterpillars, or an English sailor. Even after all these years of experience, she is not able to overcome her terror. So she was full of doubts about the Kabuliwallah, and used to beg me to keep a watchful eye on him.

I tried to laugh her fear gently away, but then she would turn round on me seriously, and ask me solemn questions.

Were children never kidnapped?

Was it, then, not true that there was slavery in Kabul?

Was it so very absurd that this big man should be able to carry off a tiny child?

I urged that, though not impossible, it was highly improbable. But this was not enough, and her dread persisted. As it was indefinite, however, it did not seem right to forbid the man the house, and the intimacy went on unchecked.

Once a year in the middle of January Rahmun, the Kabuliwallah, was in the habit of returning to his country, and as the time approached he would be very busy, going from house to house collecting his debts. This year, however, he could always find time to come and see Mini. It would have seemed to an outsider that there was some conspiracy between the two, for when he could not come in the morning, he would appear in the evening.

Even to me it was a little startling now and then, in the corner of a dark room, suddenly to surprise this tall, loose-garmented, much bebagged man; but when Mini would run in smiling, with her, "O! Kabuliwallah! Kabuliwallah!" and the two friends, so far apart in age, would subside into their old laughter and their old jokes, I felt reassured.

One morning, a few days before he had made up his mind to go, I was correcting my proof sheets in my study. It was chilly weather. Through the window the rays of the sun touched my feet, and the slight warmth was very welcome. It was almost eight o'clock, and the early pedestrians were returning home, with their heads covered. All at once, I heard an uproar in the street, and, looking out, saw Rahmun being led away bound between two policemen, and behind them a crowd of curious boys. There were bloodstains on the clothes of the Kabuliwallah, and one of the policemen carried a knife. Hurrying out, I stopped them, and enquired what it all meant. Partly from one, partly from another, I gathered that a certain neighbour had owed the pedlar something for a Rampuri shawl, but had falsely denied having bought it, and that in the course of the quarrel, Rahmun had struck him. Now in the heat of his excitement, the prisoner began calling his enemy all sorts of names, when suddenly in a verandah of my house appeared my little Mini, with her usual exclamation: "O Kabuliwallah! Kabuliwallah!" Rahmun's face lighted up as he turned to her. He had no bag under his arm today, so she could not discuss the elephant with him. She at once therefore proceeded to the next question: "Are you going to the father-in-law's house?" Rahmun laughed and said: "Just where I am going, little one!" Then seeing that the reply did not amuse the child, he held up his fettered hands. "Ali," he said, "I would have thrashed that old father-in-law, but my hands are bound!"

On a charge of murderous assault, Rahmun was sentenced to some years' imprisonment.

Time passed away, and he was not remembered. The accustomed work in the accustomed place was ours, and the thought of the once-free mountaineer spending his years in prison seldom or never occurred to us. Even my light-hearted Mini, I am ashamed to say, forgot her old friend. New companions filled her life. As she grew older, she spent more of her time with girls. So much time indeed did she spend with them that she came no more, as she used to do, to her father's room. I was scarcely on speaking terms with her.

Years had passed away. It was once more autumn and we had made arrangements for our Mini's marriage. It was to take place during the Puja Holidays. With Durga returning to Kailas, the light of our home also was to depart to her husband's house, and leave her father's in the shadow.

The morning was bright. After the rains, there was a sense of ablution in the air, and the sun-rays looked like pure gold. So bright were they that they gave a beautiful radiance even to the sordid brick walls of our Calcutta lanes. Since early dawn to-day the wedding-pipes had been sounding, and at each beat my own heart throbbed. The wail of the tune, Bhairavi, seemed to intensify my pain at the approaching separation. My Mini was to be married to-night.

From early morning noise and bustle had pervaded the house. In the courtyard the canopy had to be slung on its bamboo poles; the chandeliers with their tinkling sound must be hung in each room and verandah. There was no end of hurry and excitement. I was sitting in my study, looking through the accounts, when some one entered, saluting respectfully, and stood before me. It was Rahmun the Kabuliwallah. At first I did not recognise him. He had no bag, nor the long hair, nor the same vigour that he used to have. But he smiled, and I knew him again.

"When did you come, Rahmun?" I asked him.

"Last evening," he said, "I was released from jail."

The words struck harsh upon my ears. I had never before talked with one who had wounded his fellow, and my heart shrank within itself, when I realised this, for I felt that the day would have been better-omened had he not turned up.

"There are ceremonies going on," I said, "and I am busy. Could you perhaps come another day?"

At once he turned to go; but as he reached the door he hesitated, and said: "May I not see the little one, sir, for a moment?" It was his belief that Mini was still the same. He had pictured her running to him as she used, calling "O Kabuliwallah! Kabuliwallah!" He had imagined too that they would laugh and talk together, just as of old. In fact, in memory of former days he had brought, carefully wrapped up in paper, a few almonds and raisins and grapes, obtained somehow from a countryman, for his own little fund was dispersed.

I said again: "There is a ceremony in the house, and you will not be able to see any one to-day."

The man's face fell. He looked wistfully at me for a moment, said "Good morning," and went out. I felt a little sorry, and would have called him back, but I found he was returning of his own accord. He came close up to me holding out his offerings and said: "I brought these few things, sir, for the little one. Will you give them to her?"

I took them and was going to pay him, but he caught my hand and said: "You are very kind, sir! Keep me in your recollection. Do not offer me money!--You have a little girl, I too have one like her in my own home. I think of her, and bring fruits to your child, not to make a profit for myself."

Saying this, he put his hand inside his big loose robe, and brought out a small and dirty piece of paper. With great care he unfolded this, and smoothed it out with both hands on my table. It bore the impression of a little band. Not a photograph. Not a drawing. The impression of an ink-smeared hand laid flat on the paper. This touch of his own little daughter had been always on his heart, as he had come year after year to Calcutta, to sell his wares in the streets.

Tears came to my eyes. I forgot that he was a poor Kabuli fruit-seller, while I was--but no, what was I more than he? He also was a father. That impression of the hand of his little Parbati in her distant mountain home reminded me of my own little Mini.

I sent for Mini immediately from the inner apartment. Many difficulties were raised, but I would not listen. Clad in the red silk of her wedding-day, with the sandal paste on her forehead, and adorned as a young bride, Mini came, and stood bashfully before me.

The Kabuliwallah looked a little staggered at the apparition. He could not revive their old friendship. At last he smiled and said: "Little one, are you going to your father-in-law's house?"

But Mini now understood the meaning of the word "father-in-law," and she could not reply to him as of old. She flushed up at the question, and stood before him with her bride-like face turned down.

I remembered the day when the Kabuliwallah and my Mini had first met, and I felt sad. When she had gone, Rahmun heaved a deep sigh, and sat down on the floor. The idea had suddenly come to him that his daughter too must have grown in this long time, and that he would have to make friends with her anew. Assuredly he would not find her, as he used to know her. And besides, what might not have happened to her in these eight years?

The marriage-pipes sounded, and the mild autumn sun streamed round us. But Rahmun sat in the little Calcutta lane, and saw before him the barren mountains of Afghanistan.

I took out a bank-note, and gave it to him, saying: "Go back to your own daughter, Rahmun, in your own country, and may the happiness of your meeting bring good fortune to my child!"

Having made this present, I had to curtail some of the festivities. I could not have the electric lights I had intended, nor the military band, and the ladies of the house were despondent at it. But to me the wedding feast was all the brighter for the thought that in a distant land a long-lost father met again with his only child.

NATIONALISM

NATIONALISM IN THE WEST

Man's history is being shaped according to the difficulties it encounters. These have offered us problems and claimed their solutions from us, the penalty of non-fulfilment being death or degradation.

These difficulties have been different in different peoples of the earth, and in the manner of our overcoming them lies our distinction.

The Scythians of the earlier period of Asiatic history had to struggle with the scarcity of their natural resources. The easiest solution that they could think of was to organize their whole population, men, women, and children, into bands of robbers. And they were irresistible to those who were chiefly engaged in the constructive work of social co-operation.

But fortunately for man the easiest path is not his truest path. If his nature were not as complex as it is, if it were as simple as that of a pack of hungry wolves, then, by this time, those hordes of marauders would have overrun the whole earth. But man, when confronted with difficulties, has to acknowledge that he is man, that he has his responsibilities to the higher faculties of his nature, by ignoring which he may achieve success that is immediate, perhaps, but that will become a death-trap to him. For what are obstacles to the lower creatures are opportunities to the higher life of man.

To India has been given her problem from the beginning of history—it is the race problem. Races ethnologically different have in this country come into close contact. This fact has been and still continues to be the most important one in our history. It is our mission to face it and prove our humanity by dealing with it in the fullest truth. Until we fulfil our mission all other benefits will be denied us.

There are other peoples in the world who have to overcome obstacles in their physical surroundings, or the menace of their powerful neighbours. They have organized their power till they are not only reasonably free from the tyranny of Nature and human neighbours, but have a surplus of it left in their hands to employ against others. But in India, our difficulties being internal, our history has been the history of continual social adjustment and not that of organized power for defence and aggression.

Neither the colourless vagueness of cosmopolitanism, nor the fierce self-idolatry of nation-worship, is the goal of human history. And India has been trying to accomplish her task through social regulation of differences, on the one hand, and the spiritual recognition of unity on the other. She has made grave errors in setting up the boundary walls too rigidly between races, in perpetuating in her classifications the results of inferiority; often she has crippled her children's minds and narrowed their lives in order to fit them into her social forms; but for centuries new experiments have been made and adjustments carried out.

Her mission has been like that of a hostess who has to provide proper accommodation for numerous guests, whose habits and requirements are different from one another. This gives rise to infinite complexities whose solution depends not merely upon tactfulness but upon sympathy and true realization of the unity of man. Towards this realization have worked, from the early time of the Upanishads up to the present moment, a series of great spiritual teachers, whose one object has been to set at naught all differences of man by the overflow of our consciousness of God. In fact, our history has not been of the rise and fall of kingdoms, of fights for political supremacy. In our country records of these days have been despised and forgotten, for they in no way represent the true history of our people. Our history is that of our social life and attainment of spiritual ideals.

But we feel that our task is not yet done. The world-flood has swept over our country, new elements have been introduced, and wider adjustments are waiting to be made.

We feel this all the more, because the teaching and example of the West have entirely run counter to what we think was given to India to accomplish. In the West the national machinery of commerce and politics turns out neatly compressed bales of humanity which have their use and high market value; but they are bound in iron hoops, labelled and separated off with scientific care and precision. Obviously God made man to be human; but this modern product has such marvellous square-cut finish, savouring of gigantic manufacture, that the Creator will find it difficult to recognize it as a thing of spirit and a creature made in His own divine image.

But I am anticipating. What I was about to say is this. Take it in whatever spirit you like, here is India, of about fifty centuries at least, who tried to live peacefully and think deeply, the India devoid of all politics, the India of no nations, whose one ambition has been to know this world as of soul, to live here every moment of her life in the meek spirit of adoration, in the glad consciousness of an eternal and personal relationship with it. It was upon this remote portion of humanity, childlike in its manner, with the wisdom of the old, upon which burst the Nation of the west.

Through all the fights and intrigues and deceptions of her earlier history India had remained aloof. Because her homes, her fields, her temples of worship, her schools, where her teachers and students lived together in the atmosphere of simplicity and devotion and learning, her village self-government with its simple laws and peaceful administration—all these truly belonged to her. But her thrones were not her concern. They passed over her head like clouds, now tinged with purple gorgeousness, now black with the threat of thunder. Often they brought devastations in their wake, but they were like catastrophes of nature whose traces are soon forgotten.

But this time it was different. It was not a mere drift over her surface of life,—drift of cavalry and foot soldiers, richly caparisoned elephants, white tents and canopies, strings of patient camels bearing the loads of royalty, bands of kettle-drums and flutes, marble domes of mosques, palaces and tombs, like the bubbles of the foaming wine of extravagance; stories of treachery and loyal devotion, of changes of fortune, of dramatic surprises of fate. This time it was the Nation of the West driving its tentacles of machinery deep down into the soil.

Therefore I say to you, it is we who are called as witnesses to give evidence as to what our Nation has been to humanity. We had known the hordes of Moghals and Pathans who invaded India, but we had known them as human races, with their own religions and customs, likes and dislikes,—we had never known them as a nation. We loved and hated them as occasions arose; we fought for them and against them, talked with them in a language which was theirs as well as our own, and guided the destiny of the Empire in which we had our active share. But this time we had to deal, not with kings, not with human races, but with a nation—we, who are no nation ourselves.

Now let us from our own experience answer the question, What is this Nation?

A nation, in the sense of the political and economic union of a people, is that aspect which a whole population assumes when organized for a mechanical purpose. Society as such has no ulterior purpose. It is an end in itself. It is a spontaneous self-expression of man as a social being. It is a natural regulation of human relationships, so that men can develop ideals of life in co-operation with one another. It has also a political side, but this is only for a special purpose. It is for self-preservation. It is merely the side of power, not of human ideals. And in the early days it had its separate place in society, restricted to the professionals. But when with the help of science and the perfecting of organization this power begins to grow and brings in harvests of wealth, then it crosses its boundaries with amazing rapidity. For then it goads all its neighbouring societies with greed of material prosperity, and consequent mutual jealousy, and by the fear of each other's growth into powerfulness. The time comes when it can stop no longer, for the competition grows keener, organization grows vaster, and selfishness attains supremacy. Trading upon the greed and fear of man, it occupies more and more space in society, and at last becomes its ruling force.

It is just possible that you have lost through habit consciousness that the living bonds of society are breaking up, and giving place to merely mechanical organization. But you see signs of it everywhere. It is owing to this that war has been declared between man and woman, because the natural thread is snapping which holds them together in harmony; because man is driven to professionalism, producing wealth for himself and others, continually turning the wheel of power for his own sake or for the sake of the universal officialdom, leaving woman alone to wither and to die or to fight her own battle unaided. And thus there where co-operation is natural has intruded competition. The very psychology of men and women about their mutual relation is changing and becoming the psychology of the primitive fighting elements, rather than of humanity seeking its completeness through the union based upon mutual self-surrender. For the elements which have lost their living bond of reality have lost the meaning of their existence. Like gaseous particles forced into a too narrow space, they come in continual conflict with each other till they burst the very arrangement which holds them in bondage.

Then look at those who call themselves anarchists, who resent the imposition of power, in any form whatever, upon the individual. The only reason for this is that power has become too abstract—it is a scientific product made in the political laboratory of the Nation, through the dissolution of personal humanity.

And what is the meaning of these strikes in the economic world, which like the prickly shrubs in a barren soil shoot up with renewed vigour each time they are cut down? What, but that the wealth-producing mechanism is incessantly growing into vast stature, out of proportion to all other needs of society,—and the full reality of man is more and more crushed under its weight? This state of things inevitably gives rise to eternal feuds among the elements freed from the wholeness and wholesomeness of human ideals, and interminable economic war is waged between capital and labour. For greed of wealth and power can never have a limit, and compromise of self-interest can never attain the final spirit of reconciliation. They must go on breeding jealousy and suspicion to the end—the end which only comes through some sudden catastrophe or a spiritual re-birth.

When this organization of politics and commerce, whose other name is the Nation, becomes all-powerful at the cost of the harmony of the higher social life, then it is an evil day for humanity. When a father becomes a gambler and his obligations to his family take the secondary place in his mind, then he is no longer a man, but an automaton led by the power of greed. Then he can do things which, in his normal state of mind, he would be ashamed to do. It is the same thing with society. When it allows itself to be turned into a perfect organization of power, then there are few crimes which it is unable to perpetrate. Because success is the object and justification of a machine, while goodness only is the end and purpose of man. When this engine of organization begins to attain a vast size, and those who are mechanics are made into parts of the machine, then the personal man is eliminated to a phantom, everything becomes a revolution of policy carried out by the human parts of the machine, with no twinge of pity or moral responsibility. It may happen that even through this apparatus the moral nature of man tries to assert itself, but the whole series of ropes and pullies creak and cry, the forces of the human heart become entangled among the forces of the human automaton, and only with difficulty can the moral purpose transmit itself into some tortured shape of result.

This abstract being, the Nation, is ruling India. We have seen in our country some brand of tinned food advertised as entirely made and packed without being touched by hand. This description applies to the governing of India, which is as little touched by the human hand as possible. The governors need not know our language, need not come into personal touch with us except as officials; they can aid or hinder our aspirations from a disdainful distance, they can lead us on a certain path of policy and then pull us back again with the manipulation of office red tape; the newspapers of England, in whose columns London street accidents are recorded with some decency of pathos, need but take the scantiest notice of calamities which happen in India over areas of land sometimes larger than the British Isles.

But we, who are governed, are not a mere abstraction. We, on our side, are individuals with living sensibilities. What comes to us in the shape of a mere bloodless policy may pierce into the very core of our life, may threaten the whole future of our people with a perpetual helplessness of emasculation, and yet may never touch the chord of humanity on the other side, or touch it in the most inadequately feeble manner. Such wholesale and universal acts of fearful responsibility man can never perform, with such a degree of systematic unawareness, where he is an individual human being. These only become possible, where the man is represented by an octopus of abstractions, sending out its wriggling arms in all directions of space, and fixing its innumerable suckers even into the far-away future. In this reign of the nation, the governed are pursued by suspicions; and these are the suspicions of a tremendous mass of organized brain and muscle. Punishments are meted out, which leave a trail of miseries across a large bleeding tract of the human heart; but these punishments are dealt by a mere abstract force, in which a whole population of a distant country has lost its human personality.

I have not come here, however, to discuss the question as it affects my own country, but as it affects the future of all humanity. It is not a question of the British Government, but of government by the Nation—

the Nation which is the organized self-interest of a whole people, where it is least human and least spiritual. Our only intimate experience of the Nation is with the British Nation, and as far as the government by the Nation goes there are reasons to believe that it is one of the best. Then, again, we have to consider that the West is necessary to the East. We are complementary to each other because of our different outlooks upon life which have given us different aspects of truth. Therefore if it be true that the spirit of the West has come upon our fields in the guise of a storm it is nevertheless scattering living seeds that are immortal. And when in India we become able to assimilate in our life what is permanent in Western civilization we shall be in the position to bring about a reconciliation of these two great worlds. Then will come to an end the one-sided dominance which is galling. What is more, we have to recognize that the history of India does not belong to one particular race but to a process of creation to which various races of the world contributed—the Dravidians and the Aryans, the ancient Greeks and the Persians, the Mohammedans of the West and those of central Asia. Now at last has come the turn of the English to become true to this history and bring to it the tribute of their life, and we neither have the right nor the power to exclude this people from the building of the destiny of India. Therefore what I say about the Nation has more to do with the history of Man than specially with that of India.

This history has come to a stage when the moral man, the complete man, is more and more giving way, almost without knowing it, to make room for the political and the commercial man, the man of the limited purpose. This process, aided by the wonderful progress in science, is assuming gigantic proportion and power, causing the upset of man's moral balance, obscuring his human side under the shadow of soul-less organization. We have felt its iron grip at the root of our life, and for the sake of humanity we must stand up and give warning to all, that this nationalism is a cruel epidemic of evil that is sweeping over the human world of the present age, and eating into its moral vitality.

I have a deep love and a great respect for the British race as human beings. It has produced great-hearted men, thinkers of great thoughts, doers of great deeds. It has given rise to a great literature. I know that these people love justice and freedom, and hate lies. They are clean in their minds, frank in their manners, true in their friendships; in their behaviour they are honest and reliable. The personal experience which I have had of their literary men has roused my admiration not merely for their power of thought or expression but for their chivalrous humanity. We have felt the greatness of this people as we feel the sun; but as for the Nation, it is for us a thick mist of a stifling nature covering the sun itself.

This government by the Nation is neither British nor anything else; it is an applied science and therefore more or less similar in its principles wherever it is used. It is like a hydraulic press, whose pressure is impersonal, and on that account completely effective. The amount of its power may vary in different engines. Some may even be driven by hand, thus leaving a margin of comfortable looseness in their tension, but in spirit and in method their differences are small. Our government might have been Dutch, or French, or Portuguese, and its essential features would have remained much the same as they are now. Only perhaps, in some cases, the organization might not have been so densely perfect, and, therefore, some shreds of the human might still have been clinging to the wreck, allowing us to deal with something which resembles our own throbbing heart.

Before the Nation came to rule over us we had other governments which were foreign, and these, like all governments, had some element of the machine in them. But the difference between them and the government by the Nation is like the difference between the hand-loom and the power-loom. In the products of the hand-loom the magic of man's living fingers finds its expression, and its hum harmonizes with the music of life. But the power-loom is relentlessly lifeless and accurate and monotonous in its production.

We must admit that during the personal government of the former days there have been instances of tyranny, injustice and extortion. They caused sufferings and unrest from which we are glad to be rescued. The protection of law is not only a boon, but it is a valuable lesson to us. It is teaching us the discipline which is necessary for the stability of civilization and for continuity of progress. We are realizing through it that there is a universal standard of justice to which all men, irrespective of their caste and colour, have their equal claim.

This reign of law in our present Government in India has established order in this vast land inhabited by peoples different in their races and customs. It has made it possible for these peoples to come in closer touch with one another and cultivate a communion of aspiration.

But this desire for a common bond of comradeship among the different races of India has been the work of the spirit of the West, not that of the Nation of the West. Wherever in Asia the people have received the true lesson of the West it is in spite of the Western Nation. Only because Japan had been able to resist the dominance of this Western Nation could she acquire the benefit of the Western Civilization in fullest measure. Though China has been poisoned at the very spring of her moral and physical life by this Nation, her struggle to receive the best lessons of the West may yet be successful if not hindered by the Nation. It was only the other day that Persia woke up from her age-long sleep at the call of the West to be instantly trampled into stillness by the Nation. The same phenomenon prevails in this country also, where the people are hospitable, but the Nation has proved itself to be otherwise, making an Eastern guest feel humiliated to stand before you as a member of the humanity of his own motherland.

In India we are suffering from this conflict between the spirit of the West and the Nation of the West. The benefit of the Western civilization is doled out to us in a miserly measure by the Nation, which tries to regulate the degree of nutrition as near the zero-point of vitality as possible. The portion of education allotted to us is so raggedly insufficient that it ought to outrage the sense of decency of a Western humanity. We have seen in these countries how the people are encouraged and trained and given every facility to fit themselves for the great movements of commerce and industry spreading over the world, while in India the only assistance we get is merely to be jeered at by the Nation for lagging behind. While depriving us of our opportunities and reducing our education to the minimum required for conducting a foreign government, this Nation pacifies its conscience by calling us names, by sedulously giving currency to the arrogant cynicism that the East is east and the West is west and never the twain shall meet. If we must believe our schoolmaster in his taunt that, after nearly two centuries of his tutelage, India not only remains unfit for self-government but unable to display originality in her intellectual attainments, must we ascribe it to something in the nature of Western culture and our inherent incapacity to receive it or to the judicious niggardliness of the Nation that has taken upon itself the white man's burden of civilizing the East? That Japanese people have some qualities which we lack we may admit, but that our intellect is naturally unproductive compared to theirs we cannot accept even from them whom it is dangerous for us to contradict.

The truth is that the spirit of conflict and conquest is at the origin and in the centre of Western nationalism; its basis is not social co-operation. It has evolved a perfect organization of power, but not spiritual idealism. It is like the pack of predatory creatures that must have its victims. With all its heart it cannot bear to see its hunting-grounds converted into cultivated fields. In fact, these nations are fighting among themselves for the extension of their victims and their reserve forests. Therefore the Western Nation acts like a dam to check the free flow of Western civilization into the country of the No-Nation. Because this civilization is the civilization of power, therefore it is exclusive, it is naturally unwilling to open its sources of power to those whom it has selected for its purposes of exploitation.

But all the same moral law is the law of humanity, and the exclusive civilization which thrives upon others who are barred from its benefit carries its own death-sentence in its moral limitations. The slavery that it gives rise to unconsciously drains its own love of freedom dry. The helplessness with which it weighs down its world of victims exerts its force of gravitation every moment upon the power that creates it. And the greater part of the world which is being denuded of its self-sustaining life by the Nation will one day become the most terrible of all its burdens, ready to drag it down into the bottom of destruction. Whenever Power removes all checks from its path to make its career easy, it triumphantly rides into its ultimate crash of death. Its moral brake becomes slacker every day without its knowing it, and its slippery path of ease becomes its path of doom.

Of all things in Western civilization, those which this Western Nation has given us in a most generous measure are law and order. While the small feeding-bottle of our education is nearly dry, and sanitation sucks its own thumb in despair, the military organization, the magisterial offices, the police, the Criminal Investigation Department, the secret spy system, attain to an abnormal girth in their waists, occupying every inch of our country. This is to maintain order. But is not this order merely a negative good? Is it not for giving people's life greater opportunities for the freedom of development? Its perfection is the perfection of an egg-shell, whose true value lies in the security it affords to the chick and its nourishment and not in the convenience it offers to the person at the breakfast table. Mere administration is unproductive, it is not creative, not being a living thing. It is a steam-roller, formidable in its weight and power, having its uses, but it does not help the soil to become fertile. When after its enormous toil it comes to offer us its boon of peace we can but murmur under our breath that "peace is good, but not more so than life, which is God's own great boon."

On the other hand, our former governments were woefully lacking in many of the advantages of the modern government. But because those were not the governments by the Nation, their texture was loosely woven, leaving big gaps through which our own life sent its threads and imposed its designs. I am quite sure in those days we had things that were extremely distasteful to us. But we know that when we walk barefooted upon ground strewn with gravel, our feet come gradually to adjust themselves to the caprices of the inhospitable earth; while if the tiniest particle of gravel finds its lodgment inside our shoes we can never forget and forgive its intrusion. And these shoes are the government by the Nation,—it is tight, it regulates our steps with a closed-up system, within which our feet have only the slightest liberty to make their own adjustments. Therefore, when you produce your statistics to compare the number of gravels which our feet had to encounter in former days with the paucity in the present régime, they hardly touch the real points. It is not a question of the number of outside obstacles but the comparative powerlessness of the individual to cope with them. This narrowness of freedom is an evil which is more radical, not because of its quantity but because of its nature. And we cannot but acknowledge this paradox, that while the spirit of the West marches under its banner of freedom, the Nation of the West forges its iron chains of organization which are the most relentless and unbreakable that have ever been manufactured in the whole history of man.

When the humanity of India was not under the government of the Organization, the elasticity of change was great enough to encourage men of power and spirit to feel that they had their destinies in their own hands. The hope of the unexpected was never absent, and a freer play of imagination, on the part both of the governor and the governed, had its effect in the making of history. We were not confronted with a future, which was a dead white wall of granite blocks eternally guarding against the expression and extension of our own powers, the hopelessness of which lies in the reason that these powers are becoming atrophied at their very roots by the scientific process of paralysis. For every single individual in the country of the No-Nation is completely in the grip of a whole nation,—whose tireless vigilance, being the vigilance of a machine, has not the human power to overlook or to discriminate. At the least pressing of its button the monster organization becomes all eyes, whose ugly stare of inquisitiveness cannot be avoided by a single person amongst the immense multitude of the ruled. At the least turn of its screw, by the fraction of an inch, the grip is tightened to the point of suffocation around every man, woman and child of a vast population, for whom no escape is imaginable in their own country, or even in any country outside their own.

It is the continual and stupendous dead pressure of this inhuman upon the living human under which the modern world is groaning. Not merely the subject races, but you who live under the delusion that you are free, are every day sacrificing your freedom and humanity to this fetich of nationalism, living in the dense poisonous atmosphere of world-wide suspicion and greed and panic.

I have seen in Japan the voluntary submission of the whole people to the trimming of their minds and clipping of their freedom by their government, which through various educational agencies regulates their thoughts, manufactures their feelings, becomes suspiciously watchful when they show signs of inclining toward the spiritual, leading them through a narrow path not toward what is true but what is necessary for the complete welding of them into one uniform mass according to its own recipe. The people accept this all-pervading mental slavery with cheerfulness and pride because of their nervous desire to turn themselves into a machine of power, called the Nation, and emulate other machines in their collective worldliness.

When questioned as to the wisdom of its course the newly converted fanatic of nationalism answers that "so long as nations are rampant in this world we have not the option freely to develop our higher humanity. We must utilize every faculty that we possess to resist the evil by assuming it ourselves in the fullest degree. For the only brotherhood possible in the modern world is the brotherhood of hooliganism." The recognition of the fraternal bond of love between Japan and Russia, which has lately been celebrated with an immense display of rejoicing in Japan, was not owing to any sudden recrudescence of the spirit of Christianity or of Buddhism, but it was a bond established according to the modern faith in a surer relationship of mutual menace of bloodshedding. Yes, one cannot but acknowledge that these facts are the facts of the world of the Nation, and the only moral of it is that all the peoples of the earth should strain their physical, moral and intellectual resources to the utmost to defeat one another in the wrestling match of powerfulness. In the ancient days Sparta paid all her attention to becoming powerful; she did become so by crippling her humanity, and died of the amputation.

But it is no consolation to us to know that the weakening of humanity from which the present age is suffering is not limited to the subject races, and that its ravages are even more radical because insidious and voluntary in peoples who are hypnotized into believing that they are free. This bartering of your higher aspirations of life for profit and power has been your own free choice, and I leave you there, at the wreckage of your soul, contemplating your protuberant prosperity. But will you never be called to answer for organizing the instincts of self-aggrandizement of whole peoples into perfection and calling it good? I ask you what disaster has there ever been in the history of man, in its darkest period, like this terrible disaster of the Nation fixing its fangs deep into the naked flesh of the world, taking permanent precautions against its natural relaxation?

You, the people of the West, who have manufactured this abnormality, can you imagine the desolating despair of this haunted world of suffering man possessed by the ghastly abstraction of the organizing man? Can you put yourself into the position of the peoples, who seem to have been doomed to an eternal damnation of their own humanity, who not only must suffer continual curtailment of their manhood, but even raise their voices in pæans of praise for the benignity of a mechanical apparatus in its interminable parody of providence?

Have you not seen, since the commencement of the existence of the Nation, that the dread of it has been the one goblin-dread with which the whole world has been trembling? Wherever there is a dark corner, there is the suspicion of its secret malevolence; and people live in a perpetual distrust of its back where it has no eyes. Every sound of a footstep, every rustle of movement in the neighbourhood, sends a thrill of terror all around. And this terror is the parent of all that is base in man's nature. It makes one almost openly unashamed of inhumanity. Clever lies become matters of self-congratulation. Solemn pledges become a farce,—laughable for their very solemnity. The Nation, with all its paraphernalia of power and prosperity, its flags and pious hymns, its blasphemous prayers in the churches, and the literary mock thunders of its patriotic bragging, cannot hide the fact that the Nation is the greatest evil for the Nation, that all its precautions are against it, and any new birth of its fellow in the world is always followed in its mind by the dread of a new peril. Its one wish is to trade on the feebleness of the rest of the world, like some insects that are bred in the paralysed flesh of victims kept just enough alive to make them toothsome and nutritious. Therefore it is ready to send its poisonous fluid into the vitals of the other living peoples, who, not being nations, are harmless. For this the Nation has had and still has its richest pasture in Asia. Great China, rich with her ancient wisdom and social ethics, her discipline of industry and self-control, is like a whale awakening the lust of spoil in the heart of the Nation. She is already carrying in her quivering flesh harpoons sent by the unerring aim of the Nation, the creature of science and selfishness. Her pitiful attempt to shake off her traditions of humanity, her social ideals, and spend her last exhausted resources in drilling herself into modern efficiency, is thwarted at every step by the Nation. It is tightening its financial ropes round her, trying to drag her up on the shore and cut her into pieces, and then go and offer public thanksgiving to God for supporting the one existing evil and shattering the possibility of a new one. And for all this the Nation has been claiming the gratitude of history, and all eternity for its exploitation; ordering its band of praise to be struck up from end to end of the world, declaring itself to be the salt of the earth, the flower of humanity, the blessing of God hurled with all His force upon the naked skulls of the world of No-Nations.

I know what your advice will be. You will say, form yourselves into a nation, and resist this encroachment of the Nation. But is this the true advice? that of a man to a man? Why should this be a necessity? I could well believe you if you had said, Be more good, more just, more true in your relation to man, control your greed, make your life wholesome in its simplicity and let your consciousness of the divine in humanity be more perfect in its expression. But must you say that it is not the soul, but the machine, which is of the utmost value to ourselves, and that man's salvation depends upon his disciplining himself into a perfection of the dead rhythm of wheels and counterwheels? that machine must be pitted against machine, and nation against nation, in an endless bull-fight of politics?

You say, these machines will come into an agreement, for their mutual protection, based upon a conspiracy of fear. But will this federation of steam-boilers supply you with a soul, a soul which has her conscience and her God? What is to happen to that larger part of the world where fear will have no hand in restraining you? Whatever safety they now enjoy, those countries of No-Nation, from the unbridled license of forge and hammer and turn-screw, results from the mutual jealousy of the powers. But when, instead of being numerous separate machines, they become riveted into one organized gregariousness of gluttony, commercial and political, what remotest chance of hope will remain for those others, who have lived and suffered, have loved and worshipped, have thought deeply and worked with meekness, but whose only crime has been that they have not organized?

But, you say, "That does not matter, the unfit must go to the wall—they shall *die*, and this is science."

No, for the sake of your own salvation, I say, they shall *live*, and this is truth. It is extremely bold of me to say so, but I assert that man's world is a moral world, not because we blindly agree to believe it, but because it is so in truth which would be dangerous for us to ignore. And this moral nature of man cannot be divided into convenient compartments for its preservation. You cannot secure it for your home consumption with protective tariff walls, while in foreign parts making it enormously accommodating in its free trade of license.

Has not this truth already come home to you now, when this cruel war has driven its claws into the vitals of Europe? when her hoard of wealth is bursting into smoke and her humanity is shattered into bits on her battlefields? You ask in amazement what has she done to deserve this? The answer is, that the West has been systematically petrifying her moral nature in order to lay a solid foundation for her gigantic abstractions of efficiency. She has all along been starving the life of the personal man into that of the professional.

In your medieval age in Europe, the simple and the natural man, with all his violent passions and desires, was engaged in trying to find out a reconciliation in the conflict between the flesh and the spirit. All through the turbulent career of her vigorous youth the temporal and the spiritual forces both acted strongly upon her nature, and were moulding it into completeness of moral personality. Europe owes all her greatness in humanity to that period of discipline,—the discipline of the man in his human integrity.

Then came the age of intellect, of science. We all know that intellect is impersonal. Our life, and our heart, are one with us, but our mind can be detached from the personal man and then only can it freely move in its world of thoughts. Our intellect is an ascetic who wears no clothes, takes no food, knows no sleep, has no wishes, feels no love or hatred or pity for human limitations, who only reasons, unmoved, through the vicissitudes of life. It burrows to the roots of things, because it has no personal concern with the thing itself. The grammarian walks straight through all poetry and goes to the root of words without obstruction, because he is not seeking reality, but law. When he finds the law, he is able to teach people how to master words. This is a power,—the power which fulfils some special usefulness, some particular need of man.

Reality is the harmony which gives to the component parts of a thing the equilibrium of the whole. You break it, and have in your hands the nomadic atoms fighting against one another, therefore unmeaning. Those who covet power try to get mastery of these aboriginal fighting elements, and through some narrow channels force them into some violent service for some particular needs of man.

This satisfaction of man's needs is a great thing. It gives him freedom in the material world. It confers on him the benefit of a greater range of time and space. He can do things in a shorter time and occupies a larger space with more thoroughness of advantage. Therefore he can easily outstrip those who live in a world of a slower time and of space less fully occupied.

This progress of power attains more and more rapidity of pace. And, for the reason that it is a detached part of man, it soon outruns the complete humanity. The moral man remains behind, because it has to deal with the whole reality, not merely with the law of things, which is impersonal and therefore abstract.

Thus, man with his mental and material power far outgrowing his moral strength, is like an exaggerated giraffe whose head has suddenly shot up miles away from the rest of him, making normal communication difficult to establish. This greedy head, with its huge dental organization, has been munching all the topmost foliage of the world, but the nourishment is too late in reaching his digestive organs, and his heart is suffering from want of blood. Of this present disharmony in man's nature the West seems to have been blissfully unconscious. The enormity of its material success has diverted all its attention toward self-congratulation on its bulk. The optimism of its logic goes on basing the calculations of its good fortune upon the indefinite prolongation of its railway lines toward eternity. It is superficial enough to think that all to-morrows are merely to-days, with the repeated additions of twenty-four hours. It has no fear of the chasm, which is opening wider every day, between man's ever-growing storehouses and the emptiness of his hungry humanity. Logic does not know that, under the lowest bed of endless strata of wealth and comforts, earthquakes are being hatched to restore the balance of the moral world, and one day the gaping gulf of spiritual vacuity will draw into its bottom the store of things that have their eternal love for the dust.

Man in his fulness is not powerful, but perfect. Therefore, to turn him into mere power, you have to curtail his soul as much as possible.

When we are fully human, we cannot fly at one another's throats; our instincts of social life, our traditions of moral ideals stand in the way. If you want me to take to butchering human beings, you must break up that wholeness of my humanity through some discipline which makes my will dead, my thoughts numb, my movements automatic, and then from the dissolution of the complex personal man will come out that abstraction, that destructive force, which has no relation to human truth, and therefore can be easily brutal or mechanical. Take away man from his natural surroundings, from the fulness of his communal life, with all its living associations of beauty and love and social obligations, and you will be able to turn him into so many fragments of a machine for the production of wealth on a gigantic scale. Turn a tree into a log and it will burn for you, but it will never bear living flowers and fruit.

This process of dehumanizing has been going on in commerce and politics. And out of the long birth-throes of mechanical energy has been born this fully developed apparatus of magnificent power and surprising appetite which has been christened in the West as the Nation. As I have hinted before, because of its quality of abstraction it has, with the greatest ease, gone far ahead of the complete moral man. And having the conscience of a ghost and the callous perfection of an automaton, it is causing disasters of which the volcanic dissipations of the youthful moon would be ashamed to be brought into comparison. As a result, the suspicion of man for man stings all the limbs of this civilization like the hairs of the nettle. Each country is casting its net of espionage into the slimy bottom of the others, fishing for their secrets, the treacherous secrets which brew in the oozy depths of diplomacy. And what is their secret service but the nation's underground trade in kidnapping, murder and treachery and all the ugly crimes bred in the depth of rottenness? Because each nation has its own history of thieving and lies and broken faith, therefore there can only flourish international suspicion and jealousy, and international moral shame becomes anaemic to a degree of ludicrousness. The nation's bagpipe of righteous indignation has so often changed its tune according to the variation of time and to the altered groupings of the alliances of diplomacy, that it can be enjoyed with amusement as the variety performance of the political music hall.

I am just coming from my visit to Japan, where I exhorted this young nation to take its stand upon the higher ideals of humanity and never to follow the West in its acceptance of the organized selfishness of Nationalism as its religion, never to gloat upon the feebleness of its neighbours, never to be unscrupulous in its behaviour to the weak, where it can be gloriously mean with impunity, while turning its right cheek of brighter humanity for the kiss of admiration to those who have the power to deal it a blow. Some of the newspapers praised my utterances for their poetical qualities, while adding with a leer that it was the poetry of a defeated people. I felt they were right. Japan had been taught in a modern school the lesson how to become powerful. The schooling is done and she must enjoy the fruits of her lessons. The West in the voice of her thundering cannon had said at the door of Japan, Let there be a nation—and there was a Nation. And now that it *has* come into existence, why do you not feel in your heart of hearts a pure feeling of gladness and say that it is good? Why is it that I saw in an English paper an expression of bitterness at Japan's boasting of her superiority of civilization—the thing that the British, along with other nations, has been carrying on for ages without blushing? Because the idealism of selfishness must keep itself drunk with a continual dose of self-laudation. But the same vices which seem so natural and innocuous in its own life make it surprised and angry at their unpleasantness when seen in other nations. Therefore, when you see the Japanese nation, created in your own image, launched in its career of national boastfulness you shake your head and say, it is not good. Has it not been one of the causes that raise the cry on these shores for preparedness to meet one more power of evil with a greater power of injury? Japan protests that she has her *bushido*, that she can never be treacherous to America, to whom she owes her gratitude. But you find it difficult to believe her,—for the wisdom of the Nation is not in its faith in humanity but in its complete distrust. You say to yourself that it is not with Japan of the *bushido*, the Japan of the moral ideals, that you have to deal—it is with the abstraction of the popular selfishness, it is with the Nation; and Nation can only trust Nation where their interests coalesce, or at least do not conflict. In fact your instinct tells you that the advent of another people into the arena of nationality makes another addition to the evil which contradicts all that is highest in Man and proves by its success that unscrupulousness is the way to prosperity,—and goodness is good for the weak and God is the only remaining consolation of the defeated.

Yes, this is the logic of the Nation. And it will never heed the voice of truth and goodness. It will go on in its ring-dance of moral corruption, linking steel unto steel, and machine unto machine; trampling under its tread all the sweet flowers of simple faith and the living ideals of man.

But we delude ourselves into thinking that humanity in the modern days is more to the front than ever before. The reason of this self-delusion is because man is served with the necessaries of life in greater profusion, and his physical ills are being alleviated with more efficacy. But the chief part of this is done, not by moral sacrifice, but by intellectual power. In quantity it is great, but it springs from the surface and spreads over the surface. Knowledge and efficiency are powerful in their outward effect, but they are the servants of man, not the man himself. Their service is like the service in a hotel, where it is elaborate, but the host is absent; it is more convenient than hospitable.

Therefore we must not forget that the scientific organizations vastly spreading in all directions are strengthening our power, but not our humanity. With the growth of power the cult of the self-worship of the Nation grows in ascendancy; and the individual willingly allows the Nation to take donkey-rides upon his back; and there happens the anomaly which must have such disastrous effects, that the individual worships with all sacrifices a god which is morally much inferior to himself. This could never have been possible if the god had been as real as the individual.

Let me give an illustration of this in point. In some parts of India it has been enjoined as an act of great piety for a widow to go without food and water on a particular day every fortnight. This often leads to cruelty, unmeaning and inhuman. And yet men are not by nature cruel to such a degree. But this piety being a mere unreal abstraction completely deadens the moral sense of the individual, just as the man, who would not hurt an animal unnecessarily, would cause horrible suffering to a large number of innocent creatures when he drugs his feelings with the abstract idea of "sport." Because these ideas are the creations of our intellect, because they are logical classifications, therefore they can so easily hide in their mist the personal man.

And the idea of the Nation is one of the most powerful anæsthetics that man has invented. Under the influence of its fumes the whole people can carry out its systematic programme of the most virulent self-seeking without being in the least aware of its moral perversion,—in fact feeling dangerously resentful if it is pointed out.

But can this go on indefinitely? continually producing barrenness of moral insensibility upon a large tract of our living nature? Can it escape its nemesis for ever? Has this giant power of mechanical organization no limit in this world against which it may shatter itself all the more completely because of its terrible strength and velocity? Do you believe that evil can be permanently kept in check by competition with evil, and that conference of prudence can keep the devil chained in its makeshift cage of mutual agreement?

This European war of Nations is the war of retribution. Man, the person, must protest for his very life against the heaping up of things where there should be the heart, and systems and policies where there should flow living human relationship. The time has come when, for the sake of the whole outraged world, Europe should fully know in her own person the terrible absurdity of the thing called the Nation.

The Nation has thriven long upon mutilated humanity. Men, the fairest creations of God, came out of the National manufactory in huge numbers as war-making and money-making puppets, ludicrously vain of their pitiful perfection of mechanism. Human society grew more and more into a marionette show of politicians, soldiers, manufacturers and bureaucrats, pulled by wire arrangements of wonderful efficiency.

But the apotheosis of selfishness can never make its interminable breed of hatred and greed, fear and hypocrisy, suspicion and tyranny, an end in themselves. These monsters grow into huge shapes but never into harmony. And this Nation may grow on to an unimaginable corpulence, not of a living body, but of steel and steam and office buildings, till its deformity can contain no longer its ugly voluminousness,—till it begins to crack and gape, breathe gas and fire in gasps, and its death-rattles sound in cannon roars. In this war the death-throes of the Nation have commenced. Suddenly, all its mechanism going mad, it has begun the dance of the Furies, shattering its own limbs, scattering them into the dust. It is the fifth act of the tragedy of the unreal.

Those who have any faith in Man cannot but fervently hope that the tyranny of the Nation will not be restored to all its former teeth and claws, to its far-reaching iron arms and its immense inner cavity, all stomach and no heart; that man will have his new birth, in the freedom of his individuality, from the enveloping vagueness of abstraction.

The veil has been raised, and in this frightful war the West has stood face to face with her own creation, to which she had offered her soul. She must know what it truly is.

She had never let herself suspect what slow decay and decomposition were secretly going on in her moral nature, which often broke out in doctrines of scepticism, but still oftener and in still more dangerously subtle manner showed itself in her unconsciousness of the mutilation and insult that she had been inflicting upon a vast part of the world. Now she must know the truth nearer home.

And then there will come from her own children those who will break themselves free from the slavery of this illusion, this perversion of brotherhood founded upon self-seeking, those who will own themselves as God's children and as no bond-slaves of machinery, which turns souls into commodities and life into compartments, which, with its iron claws, scratches out the heart of the world and knows not what it has done.

And we of no nations of the world, whose heads have been bowed to the dust, will know that this dust is more sacred than the bricks which build the pride of power. For this dust is fertile of life, and of beauty and worship. We shall thank God that we were made to wait in silence through the night of despair, had to bear the insult of the proud and the strong man's burden, yet all through it, though our hearts quaked with doubt and fear, never could we blindly believe in the salvation which machinery offered to man, but we held fast to our trust in God and the truth of the human soul. And we can still cherish the hope that, when power becomes ashamed to occupy its throne and is ready to make way for love, when the morning comes for cleansing the blood-stained steps of the Nation along the highroad of humanity, we shall be called upon to bring our own vessel of sacred water—the water of worship—to sweeten the history of man into purity, and with its sprinkling make the trampled dust of the centuries blessed with fruitfulness.

NATIONALISM IN JAPAN

The worst form of bondage is the bondage of dejection, which keeps men hopelessly chained in loss of faith in themselves. We have been repeatedly told, with some justification, that Asia lives in the past,—it is like a rich mausoleum which displays all its magnificence in trying to immortalize the dead. It was said of Asia that it could never move in the path of progress, its face was so inevitably turned backwards. We accepted this accusation, and came to believe it. In India, I know, a large section of our educated community, grown tired of feeling the humiliation of this charge against us, is trying all its resources of self-deception to turn it into a matter of boasting. But boasting is only a masked shame, it does not truly believe in itself.

When things stood still like this, and we in Asia hypnotized ourselves into the belief that it could never by any possibility be otherwise, Japan rose from her dreams, and in giant strides left centuries of inaction behind, overtaking the present time in its foremost achievement. This has broken the spell under which we lay in torpor for ages, taking it to be the normal condition of certain races living in certain geographical limits. We forgot that in Asia great kingdoms were founded, philosophy, science, arts and literatures flourished, and all the great religions of the world had their cradles. Therefore it cannot be said that there is anything inherent in the soil and climate of Asia to produce mental inactivity and to atrophy the faculties which impel men to go forward. For centuries we did hold torches of civilization in the East when the West slumbered in darkness, and that could never be the sign of sluggish mind or narrowness of vision.

Then fell the darkness of night upon all the lands of the East. The current of time seemed to stop at once, and Asia ceased to take any new food, feeding upon its own past, which is really feeding upon itself. The stillness seemed like death, and the great voice was silenced which sent forth messages of eternal truth that have saved man's life from pollution for generations, like the ocean of air that keeps the earth sweet, ever cleansing its impurities.

But life has its sleep, its periods of inactivity, when it loses its movements, takes no new food, living upon its past storage. Then it grows helpless, its muscles relaxed, and it easily lends itself to be jeered at for its stupor. In the rhythm of life, pauses there must be for the renewal of life. Life in its activity is ever spending itself, burning all its fuel. This extravagance cannot go on indefinitely, but is always followed by a passive stage, when all expenditure is stopped and all adventures abandoned in favour of rest and slow recuperation.

The tendency of mind is economical, it loves to form habits and move in grooves which save it the trouble of thinking anew at each of its steps. Ideals once formed make the mind lazy. It becomes afraid to risk its acquisitions in fresh endeavours. It tries to enjoy complete security by shutting up its belongings behind fortifications of habits. But this is really shutting oneself up from the fullest enjoyment of one's own possessions. It is miserliness. The living ideals must not lose their touch with the growing and changing life. Their real freedom is not within the boundaries of security, but in the highroad of adventures, full of the risk of new experiences.

One morning the whole world looked up in surprise when Japan broke through her walls of old habits in a night and came out triumphant. It was done in such an incredibly short time that it seemed like a change of dress and not like the building up of a new structure. She showed the confident strength of maturity, and the freshness and infinite potentiality of new life at the same moment. The fear was entertained that it was a mere freak of history, a child's game of Time, the blowing up of a soap-bubble, perfect in its rondure and colouring, hollow in its heart and without substance. But Japan has proved conclusively that this sudden revealment of her power is not a short-lived wonder, a chance product of time and tide, thrown up from the depth of obscurity to be swept away the next moment into the sea of oblivion.

The truth is that Japan is old and new at the same time. She has her legacy of ancient culture from the East,—the culture that enjoins man to look for his true wealth and power in his inner soul, the culture that gives self-possession in the face of loss and danger, self-sacrifice without counting the cost or hoping for gain, defiance of death, acceptance of countless social obligations that we owe to men as social beings. In a word, modern Japan has come out of the immemorial East like a lotus blossoming in easy grace, all the while keeping its firm hold upon the profound depth from which it has sprung.

And Japan, the child of the Ancient East, has also fearlessly claimed all the gifts of the modern age for herself. She has shown her bold spirit in breaking through the confinements of habits, useless accumulations of the lazy mind, which seeks safety in its thrift and its locks and keys. Thus she has come in contact with the living time and has accepted with eagerness and aptitude the responsibilities of modern civilization.

This it is which has given heart to the rest of Asia. We have seen that the life and the strength are there in us, only the dead crust has to be removed. We have seen that taking shelter in the dead is death itself, and only taking all the risk of life to the fullest extent is living.

I, for myself, cannot believe that Japan has become what she is by imitating the West. We cannot imitate life, we cannot simulate strength for long, nay, what is more, a mere imitation is a source of weakness. For it hampers our true nature, it is always in our way. It is like dressing our skeleton with another man's skin, giving rise to eternal feuds between the skin and the bones at every movement.

The real truth is that science is not man's nature, it is mere knowledge and training. By knowing the laws of the material universe you do not change your deeper humanity. You can borrow knowledge from others, but you cannot borrow temperament.

But at the imitative stage of our schooling we cannot distinguish between the essential and the non-essential, between what is transferable and what is not. It is something like the faith of the primitive mind in the magical properties of the accidents of outward forms which accompany some real truth. We are afraid of leaving out something valuable and efficacious by not swallowing the husk with the kernel. But while our greed delights in wholesale appropriation, it is the function of our vital nature to assimilate, which is the only true appropriation for a living organism. Where there is life it is sure to assert itself by its choice of acceptance and refusal according to its constitutional necessity. The living organism does not allow itself to grow into its food, it changes its food into its own body. And only thus can it grow strong and not by mere accumulation, or by giving up its personal identity.

Japan has imported her food from the West, but not her vital nature. Japan cannot altogether lose and merge herself in the scientific paraphernalia she has acquired from the West and be turned into a mere borrowed machine. She has her own soul, which must assert itself over all her requirements. That she is capable of doing so, and that the process of assimilation is going on, have been amply proved by the signs of vigorous health that she exhibits. And I earnestly hope that Japan may never lose her faith in her own soul, in the mere pride of her foreign acquisition. For that pride itself is a humiliation, ultimately leading to poverty and weakness. It is the pride of the fop who sets more store on his new headdress than on his head itself.

The whole world waits to see what this great Eastern nation is going to do with the opportunities and responsibilities she has accepted from the hands of the modern time. If it be a mere reproduction of the West, then the great expectation she has raised will remain unfulfilled. For there are grave questions that the Western civilization has presented before the world but not completely answered. The conflict between the individual and the state, labour and capital, the man and the woman; the conflict between the greed of material gain and the spiritual life of man, the organized selfishness of nations and the higher ideals of humanity; the conflict between all the ugly complexities inseparable from giant organizations of commerce and state and the natural instincts of man crying for simplicity and beauty and fulness of leisure,—all these have to be brought to a harmony in a manner not yet dreamt of.

We have seen this great stream of civilization choking itself from débris carried by its innumerable channels. We have seen that with all its vaunted love of humanity it has proved itself the greatest menace to Man, far worse than the sudden outbursts of nomadic barbarism from which men suffered in the early ages of history. We have seen that, in spite of its boasted love of freedom, it has produced worse forms of slavery than ever were current in earlier societies,—slavery whose chains are unbreakable, either because they are unseen, or because they assume the names and appearance of freedom. We have seen, under the spell of its gigantic sordidness, man losing faith in all the heroic ideals of life which have made him great.

Therefore you cannot with a light heart accept the modern civilization with all its tendencies, methods and structures, and dream that they are inevitable. You must apply your Eastern mind, your spiritual strength, your love of simplicity, your recognition of social obligation, in order to cut out a new path for this great unwieldy car of progress, shrieking out its loud discords as it runs. You must minimize the immense sacrifice of man's life and freedom that it claims in its every movement. For generations you have felt and thought and worked, have enjoyed and worshipped in your own special manner; and this cannot be cast off like old clothes. It is in your blood, in the marrow of your bones, in the texture of your flesh, in the tissue of your brains; and it must modify everything you lay your hands upon, without your knowing, even against your wishes. Once you did solve the problems of man to your own satisfaction, you had your philosophy of life and evolved your own art of living. All this you must apply to the present situation, and out of it will arise a new creation and not a mere repetition, a creation which the soul of your people will own for itself and proudly offer to the world as its tribute to the welfare of man. Of all countries in Asia, here in Japan you have the freedom to use the materials you have gathered from the West according to your genius and your need. Therefore your responsibility is all the greater, for in your voice Asia shall answer the questions that Europe has submitted to the conference of Man. In your land the experiments will be carried on by which the East will change the aspects of modern civilization, infusing life in it where it is a machine, substituting the human heart for cold expediency, not caring so much for power and success as for harmonious and living growth, for truth and beauty.

I cannot but bring to your mind those days when the whole of Eastern Asia from Burma to Japan was united with India in the closest tie of friendship, the only natural tie which can exist between nations. There was a living communication of hearts, a nervous system evolved through which messages ran between us about the deepest needs of humanity. We did not stand in fear of each other, we had not to arm ourselves to keep each other in check; our relation was not that of self-interest, of exploration and spoliation of each other's pockets; ideas and ideals were exchanged, gifts of the highest love were offered and taken; no difference of languages and customs hindered us in approaching each other heart to heart; no pride of race or insolent consciousness of superiority, physical or mental, marred our relation; our arts and literatures put forth new leaves and flowers under the influence of this sunlight of united hearts; and races belonging to different lands and languages and histories acknowledged the highest unity of man and the deepest bond of love. May we not also remember that in those days of peace and goodwill, of men uniting for those supreme ends of life, your nature laid by for itself the balm of immortality which has helped your people to be born again in a new age, to be able to survive its old outworn structures and take on a new young body, to come out unscathed from the shock of the most wonderful revolution that the world has ever seen?

The political civilization which has sprung up from the soil of Europe and is overrunning the whole world, like some prolific weed, is based upon exclusiveness. It is always watchful to keep the aliens at bay or to exterminate them. It is carnivorous and cannibalistic in its tendencies, it feeds upon the resources of other peoples and tries to swallow their whole future. It is always afraid of other races achieving eminence, naming it as a peril, and tries to thwart all symptoms of greatness outside its own boundaries, forcing down races of men who are weaker, to be eternally fixed in their weakness. Before this political civilization came to its power and opened its hungry jaws wide enough to gulp down great continents of the earth, we had wars, pillages, changes of monarchy and consequent miseries, but never such a sight of fearful and hopeless voracity, such wholesale feeding of nation upon nation, such huge machines for turning great portions of the earth into mincemeat, never such terrible jealousies with all their ugly teeth and claws ready for tearing open each other's vitals. This political civilization is scientific, not human. It is powerful because it concentrates all its forces upon one purpose, like a millionaire acquiring money at the cost of his soul. It betrays its trust, it weaves its meshes of lies without shame, it enshrines gigantic idols of greed in its temples, taking great pride in the costly ceremonials of its worship, calling this patriotism. And it can be safely prophesied that this cannot go on, for there is a moral law in this world which has its application both to individuals and to organized bodies of men. You cannot go on violating these laws in the name of your nation, yet enjoy their advantage as individuals. This public sapping of ethical ideals slowly reacts upon each member of society, gradually breeding weakness, where it is not seen, and causing that cynical distrust of all things sacred in human nature, which is the true symptom of senility. You must keep in mind that this political civilization, this creed of national patriotism, has not been given a long trial. The lamp of ancient Greece is extinct in the land where it was first lighted, the power of Rome lies dead and buried under the ruins of its vast empire. But the civilization, whose basis is society and the spiritual ideal of man, is still a living thing in China and in India. Though it may look feeble and small, judged by the standard of the mechanical power of modern days, yet like small seeds it still contains life and will sprout and grow, and spread its beneficent branches, producing flowers and fruits when its time comes and showers of grace descend upon it from heaven. But ruins of sky-scrapers of power and broken machinery of greed, even God's rain is powerless to raise up again; for they were not of life, but went against life as a whole,—they are relics of the rebellion that shattered itself to pieces against the eternal.

But the charge is brought against us that the ideals we cherish in the East are static, that they have not the impetus in them to move, to open out new vistas of knowledge and power, that the systems of philosophy which are the mainstays of the time-worn civilizations of the East despise all outward proofs, remaining stolidly satisfied in their subjective certainty. This proves that when our knowledge is vague we are apt to accuse of vagueness our object of knowledge itself. To a Western observer our civilization appears as all metaphysics, as to a deaf man piano-playing appears to be mere movements of fingers and no music. He cannot think that we have found some deep basis of reality upon which we have built our institutions.

Unfortunately all proofs of reality are in realization. The reality of the scene before you depends only upon the fact that you can see, and it is difficult for us to prove to an unbeliever that our civilization is not a nebulous system of abstract speculations, that it has achieved something which is a positive truth,—a truth that can give man's heart its shelter and sustenance. It has evolved an inner sense,—a sense of vision, the vision of the infinite reality in all finite things.

But he says, "You do not make any progress, there is no movement in you." I ask him, "How do you know it? You have to judge progress according to its aim. A railway train makes its progress towards the terminus station,—it is movement. But a full-grown tree has no definite movement of that kind, its progress is the inward progress of life. It lives, with its aspiration towards light tingling in its leaves and creeping in its silent sap."

We also have lived for centuries, we still live, and we have our aspiration for a reality that has no end to its realization,—a reality that goes beyond death, giving it a meaning, that rises above all evils of life, bringing its peace and purity, its cheerful renunciation of self. The product of this inner life is a living product. It will be needed when the youth returns home weary and dust-laden, when the soldier is wounded, when the wealth is squandered away and pride is humbled, when man's heart cries for truth in the immensity of facts and harmony in the contradiction of tendencies. Its value is not in its multiplication of materials, but in its spiritual fulfilment.

There are things that cannot wait. You have to rush and run and march if you must fight or take the best place in the market. You strain your nerves and are on the alert when you chase opportunities that are always on the wing. But there are ideals which do not play hide-and-seek with our life; they slowly grow from seed to flower, from flower to fruit; they require infinite space and heaven's light to mature, and the fruits that they produce can survive years of insult and neglect. The East with her ideals, in whose bosom are stored the ages of sunlight and silence of stars, can patiently wait till the West, hurrying after the expedient, loses breath and stops. Europe, while busily speeding to her engagements, disdainfully casts her glance from her carriage window at the reaper reaping his harvest in the field, and in her intoxication of speed cannot but think him as slow and ever receding backwards. But the speed comes to its end, the engagement loses its meaning and the hungry heart clamours for food, till at last she comes to the lowly reaper reaping his harvest in the sun. For if the office cannot wait, or the buying and selling, or the craving for excitement, love waits and beauty and the wisdom of suffering and the fruits of patient devotion and reverent meekness of simple faith. And thus shall wait the East till her time comes.

I must not hesitate to acknowledge where Europe is great, for great she is without doubt. We cannot help loving her with all our heart, and paying her the best homage of our admiration,—the Europe who, in her literature and art, pours out an inexhaustible cascade of beauty and truth fertilizing all countries and all time; the Europe who, with a mind which is titanic in its untiring power, is sweeping the height and the depth of the universe, winning her homage of knowledge from the infinitely great and the infinitely small, applying all the resources of her great intellect and heart in healing the sick and alleviating those miseries of man which up till now we were contented to accept in a spirit of hopeless resignation; the Europe who is making the earth yield more fruit than seemed possible, coaxing and compelling the great forces of nature into man's service. Such true greatness must have its motive power in spiritual strength. For only the spirit of man can defy all limitations, have faith in its ultimate success, throw its search-light beyond the immediate and the apparent, gladly suffer martyrdom for ends which cannot be achieved in its lifetime and accept failure without acknowledging defeat. In the heart of Europe runs the purest stream of human love, of love of justice, of spirit of self-sacrifice for higher ideals. The Christian culture of centuries has sunk deep in her life's core. In Europe we have seen noble minds who have ever stood up for the rights of man irrespective of colour and creed; who have braved calumny and insult from their own people in fighting for humanity's cause and raising their voices against the mad orgies of militarism, against the rage for brutal retaliation or rapacity that sometimes takes possession of a whole people; who are always ready to make reparation for wrongs done in the past by their own nations and vainly attempt to stem the tide of cowardly injustice that flows unchecked because the resistance is weak and innocuous on the part of the injured. There are these knight-errants of modern Europe who have not lost their faith in the disinterested love of freedom, in the ideals which own no geographical boundaries or national self-seeking. These are there to prove that the fountainhead of the water of everlasting life has not run dry in Europe, and from thence she will have her rebirth time after time. Only there, where Europe is too consciously busy in building up her power, defying her deeper nature and mocking it, she is heaping up her iniquities to the sky, crying for God's vengeance and spreading the infection of ugliness, physical and moral, over the face of the earth with her heartless commerce heedlessly outraging man's sense of the beautiful and the good. Europe is supremely good in her beneficence where her face is turned to all humanity; and Europe is supremely evil in her maleficent aspect where her face is turned only upon her own interest, using all her power of greatness for ends which are against the infinite and the eternal in Man.

Eastern Asia has been pursuing its own path, evolving its own civilization, which was not political but social, not predatory and mechanically efficient but spiritual and based upon all the varied and deeper relations of humanity. The solutions of the life problems of peoples were thought out in seclusion and carried out behind the security of aloofness, where all the dynastic changes and foreign invasions hardly touched them. But now we are overtaken by the outside world, our seclusion is lost for ever. Yet this we must not regret, as a plant should never regret when the obscurity of its seed-time is broken. Now the time has come when we must make the world problem our own problem; we must bring the spirit of our civilization into harmony with the history of all nations of the earth; we must not, in foolish pride, still keep ourselves fast within the shell of the seed and the crust of the earth which protected and nourished our ideals; for these, the shell and the crust, were meant to be broken, so that life may spring up in all its vigour and beauty, bringing its offerings to the world in open light.

In this task of breaking the barrier and facing the world Japan has come out the first in the East. She has infused hope in the heart of all Asia. This hope provides the hidden fire which is needed for all works of creation. Asia now feels that she must prove her life by producing living work, she must not lie passively dormant, or feebly imitate the West, in the infatuation of fear or flattery. For this we offer our thanks to this Land of the Rising Sun and solemnly ask her to remember that she has the mission of the East to fulfil. She must infuse the sap of a fuller humanity into the heart of modern civilization. She must never allow it to get choked with the noxious undergrowth, but lead it up towards light and freedom, towards the pure air and broad space, where it can receive, in the dawn of its day and the darkness of its night, heaven's inspiration. Let the greatness of her ideals become visible to all men like her snow-crowned Fuji rising from the heart of the country into the region of the infinite, supremely distinct from its surroundings, beautiful like a maiden in its magnificent sweep of curve, yet firm and strong and serenely majestic.

II

I have travelled in many countries and have met with men of all classes, but never in my travels did I feel the presence of the human so distinctly as in this land. In other great countries signs of man's power loomed large, and I saw vast organizations which showed efficiency in all their features. There, display and extravagance, in dress, in furniture, in costly entertainments, are startling. They seem to push you back into a corner, like a poor intruder at a feast; they are apt to make you envious, or take your breath away with amazement. There, you do not feel man as supreme; you are hurled against a stupendousness of things that alienates. But in Japan it is not the display of power, or wealth, that is the predominating element. You see everywhere emblems of love and admiration, and not mostly of ambition and greed. You see a people whose heart has come out and scattered itself in profusion in its commonest utensils of everyday life, in its social institutions, in its manners, which are carefully perfect, and in its dealings with things which are not only deft but graceful in every movement.

What has impressed me most in this country is the conviction that you have realized nature's secrets, not by methods of analytical knowledge, but by sympathy. You have known her language of lines, and music of colours, the symmetry in her irregularities, and the cadence in her freedom of movements; you have seen how she leads her immense crowds of things yet avoids all frictions; how the very conflicts in her creations break out in dance and music; how her exuberance has the aspect of the fulness of self-abandonment, and not a mere dissipation of display. You have discovered that nature reserves her power in forms of beauty; and it is this beauty which, like a mother, nourishes all the giant forces at her breast, keeping them in active vigour, yet in repose. You have known that energies of nature save themselves from wearing out by the rhythm of a perfect grace, and that she with the tenderness of her curved lines takes away fatigue from the world's muscles. I have felt that you have been able to assimilate these secrets into your life, and the truth which lies in the beauty of all things has passed into your souls. A mere knowledge of things can be had in a short enough time, but their spirit can only be acquired by centuries of training and self-control. Dominating nature from outside is a much simpler thing than making her your own in love's delight, which is a work of true genius. Your race has shown that genius, not by acquirement, but by creation; not by display of things, but by manifestation of its own inner being. This creative power there is in all nations, and it is ever active in getting hold of men's natures and giving them a form according to its ideals. But here, in Japan, it seems to have achieved its success, and deeply sunk into the minds of all men, and permeated their muscles and nerves. Your instincts have become true, your senses keen, and your hands have acquired natural skill. The genius of Europe has given her people the power of organization, which has specially made itself manifest in politics and commerce and in co-ordinating scientific knowledge. The genius of Japan has given you the vision of beauty in nature and the power of realizing it in your life.

All particular civilization is the interpretation of particular human experience. Europe seems to have felt emphatically the conflict of things in the universe, which can only be brought under control by conquest. Therefore she is ever ready for fight, and the best portion of her attention is occupied in organizing forces. But Japan has felt, in her world, the touch of some presence, which has evoked in her soul a feeling of reverent adoration. She does not boast of her mastery of nature, but to her she brings, with infinite care and joy, her offerings of love. Her relationship with the world is the deeper relationship of heart. This spiritual bond of love she has established with the hills of her country, with the sea and the streams, with the forests in all their flowery moods and varied physiognomy of branches; she has taken into her heart all the rustling whispers and sighing of the woodlands and sobbing of the waves; the sun and the moon she has studied in all the modulations of their lights and shades, and she is glad to close her shops to greet the seasons in her orchards and gardens and cornfields. This opening of the heart to the soul of the world is not confined to a section of your privileged classes, it is not the forced product of exotic culture, but it belongs to all your men and women of all conditions. This experience of your soul, in meeting a personality in the heart of the world, has been embodied in your civilization. It is a civilization of human relationship. Your duty towards your state has naturally assumed the character of filial duty, your nation becoming one family with your Emperor as its head. Your national unity has not been evolved from the comradeship of arms for defensive and offensive purpose, or from partnership in raiding adventures, dividing among each member the danger and spoils of robbery. It is not an outcome of the necessity of organization for some ulterior purpose, but it is an extension of the family and the obligations of the heart in a wide field of space and time.

The ideal of "maitri" is at the bottom of your culture,—"maitri" with men and "maitri" with Nature. And the true expression of this love is in the language of beauty, which is so abundantly universal in this land. This is the reason why a stranger, like myself, instead of feeling envy or humiliation before these manifestations of beauty, these creations of love, feels a readiness to participate in the joy and glory of such revealment of the human heart.

And this has made me all the more apprehensive of the change which threatens Japanese civilization, as something like a menace to one's own person. For the huge heterogeneity of the modern age, whose only common bond is usefulness, is nowhere so pitifully exposed against the dignity and hidden power of reticent beauty as in Japan.

But the danger lies in this, that organized ugliness storms the mind and carries the day by its mass, by its aggressive persistence, by its power of mockery directed against the deeper sentiments of heart. Its harsh obtrusiveness makes it forcibly visible to us, overcoming our senses,— and we bring sacrifices to its altar, as does a savage to the fetich which appears powerful because of its hideousness. Therefore its rivalry with things that are modest and profound and have the subtle delicacy of life is to be dreaded.

I am quite sure that there are men in your country who are not in sympathy with your inherited ideals; whose object is to gain, and not to grow. They are loud in their boast that they have modernized Japan. While I agree with them so far as to say that the spirit of the race should harmonize with the spirit of the time, I must warn them that modernizing is a mere affectation of modernism, just as affectation of poesy is poetizing. It is nothing but mimicry, only affectation is louder than the original, and it is too literal. One must bear in mind that those who have the true modern spirit need not modernize, just as those who are truly brave are not braggarts. Modernism is not in the dress of the Europeans; or in the hideous structures, where their children are interned when they take their lessons; or in the square houses with flat, straight wall-surfaces, pierced with parallel lines of windows, where these people are caged in their lifetime; certainly modernism is not in their ladies' bonnets, carrying on them loads of incongruities. These are not modern, but merely European. True modernism is freedom of mind, not slavery of taste. It is independence of thought and action, not tutelage under European schoolmasters. It is science, but not its wrong application in life,—a mere imitation of our science teachers who reduce it into a superstition, absurdly invoking its aid for all impossible purposes.

Life based upon mere science is attractive to some men, because it has all the characteristics of sport; it feigns seriousness, but is not profound. When you go a-hunting, the less pity you have the better; for your one object is to chase the game and kill it, to feel that you are the greater animal, that your method of destruction is thorough and scientific. And the life of science is that superficial life. It pursues success with skill and thoroughness, and takes no account of the higher nature of man. But those whose minds are crude enough to plan their lives upon the supposition that man is merely a hunter and his paradise the paradise of sportsmen will be rudely awakened in the midst of their trophies of skeletons and skulls.

I do not for a moment suggest that Japan should be unmindful of acquiring modern weapons of self-protection. But this should never be allowed to go beyond her instinct of self-preservation. She must know that the real power is not in the weapons themselves, but in the man who wields those weapons; and when he, in his eagerness for power, multiplies his weapons at the cost of his own soul, then it is he who is in even greater danger than his enemies.

Things that are living are so easily hurt; therefore they require protection. In nature, life protects itself within its coverings, which are built with life's own material. Therefore they are in harmony with life's growth, or else when the time comes they easily give way and are forgotten. The living man has his true protection in his spiritual ideals, which have their vital connection with his life and grow with his growth. But, unfortunately, all his armour is not living,—some of it is made of steel, inert and mechanical. Therefore, while making use of it, man has to be careful to protect himself from its tyranny. If he is weak enough to grow smaller to fit himself to his covering, then it becomes a process of gradual suicide by shrinkage of the soul. And Japan must have a firm faith in the moral law of existence to be able to assert to herself that the Western nations are following that path of suicide, where they are smothering their humanity under the immense weight of organizations in order to keep themselves in power and hold others in subjection.

What is dangerous for Japan is, not the imitation of the outer features of the West, but the acceptance of the motive force of the Western nationalism as her own. Her social ideals are already showing signs of defeat at the hands of politics. I can see her motto, taken from science, "Survival of the Fittest," writ large at the entrance of her present-day history—the motto whose meaning is, "Help yourself, and never heed what it costs to others"; the motto of the blind man who only believes in what he can touch, because he cannot see. But those who can see know that men are so closely knit that when you strike others the blow comes back to yourself. The moral law, which is the greatest discovery of man, is the discovery of this wonderful truth, that man becomes all the truer the more he realizes himself in others. This truth has not only a subjective value, but is manifested in every department of our life. And nations who sedulously cultivate moral blindness as the cult of patriotism will end their existence in a sudden and violent death. In past ages we had foreign invasions, but they never touched the soul of the people deeply. They were merely the outcome of individual ambitions. The people themselves, being free from the responsibilities of the baser and more heinous side of those adventures, had all the advantage of the heroic and the human disciplines derived from them. This developed their unflinching loyalty, their single-minded devotion to the obligations of honour, their power of complete self-surrender and fearless acceptance of death and danger. Therefore the ideals, whose seats were in the hearts of the people, would not undergo any serious change owing to the policies adopted by the kings or generals. But now, where the spirit of the Western nationalism prevails, the whole people is being taught from boyhood to foster hatreds and ambitions by all kinds of means—by the manufacture of half-truths and untruths in history, by persistent misrepresentation of other races and the culture of unfavourable sentiments towards them, by setting up memorials of events, very often false, which for the sake of humanity should be speedily forgotten, thus continually brewing evil menace towards neighbours and nations other than their own. This is poisoning the very fountainhead of humanity. It is discrediting the ideals, which were born of the lives of men who were our greatest and best. It is holding up gigantic selfishness as the one universal religion for all nations of the world. We can take anything else from the hands of science, but not this elixir of moral death. Never think for a moment that the hurts you inflict upon other races will not infect you, or that the enmities you sow around your homes will be a wall of protection to you for all time to come. To imbue the minds of a whole people with an abnormal vanity of its own superiority, to teach it to take pride in its moral callousness and ill-begotten wealth, to perpetuate humiliation of defeated nations by exhibiting trophies won from war, and using these in schools in order to breed in children's minds contempt for others, is imitating the West where she has a festering sore, whose swelling is a swelling of disease eating into its vitality.

Our food crops, which are necessary for our sustenance, are products of centuries of selection and care. But the vegetation, which we have not to transform into our lives, does not require the patient thoughts of generations. It is not easy to get rid of weeds; but it is easy, by process of neglect, to ruin your food crops and let them revert to their primitive state of wildness. Likewise the culture, which has so kindly adapted itself to your soil—so intimate with life, so human—not only needed tilling and weeding in past ages, but still needs anxious work and watching. What is merely modern—as science and methods of organization—can be transplanted; but what is vitally human has fibres so delicate, and roots so numerous and far-reaching, that it dies when moved from its soil. Therefore I am afraid of the rude pressure of the political ideals of the West upon your own. In political civilization, the state is an abstraction and relationship of men utilitarian. Because it has no root in sentiments, it is so dangerously easy to handle. Half a century has been enough for you to master this machine; and there are men among you whose fondness for it exceeds their love for the living ideals, which were born with the birth of your nation and nursed in your centuries. It is like a child who, in the excitement of his play, imagines he likes his playthings better than his mother.

Where man is at his greatest, he is unconscious. Your civilization, whose mainspring is the bond of human relationship, has been nourished in the depth of a healthy life beyond reach of prying self-analysis. But a mere political relationship is all-conscious; it is an eruptive inflammation of aggressiveness. It has forcibly burst upon your notice. And the time has come when you have to be roused into full consciousness of the truth by which you live, so that you may not be taken unawares. The past has been God's gift to you; about the present, you must make your own choice.

So the questions you have to put to yourselves are these—"Have we read the world wrong, and based our relation to it upon an ignorance of human nature? Is the instinct of the West right, where she builds her national welfare behind the barricade of a universal distrust of humanity?"

You must have detected a strong accent of fear whenever the West has discussed the possibility of the rise of an Eastern race. The reason of it is this, that the power by whose help she thrives is an evil power; so long as it is held on her own side she can be safe, while the rest of the world trembles. The vital ambition of the present civilization of Europe is to have the exclusive possession of the devil. All her armaments and diplomacy are directed upon this one object. But these costly rituals for invocation of the evil spirit lead through a path of prosperity to the brink of cataclysm. The furies of terror, which the West has let loose upon God's world, come back to threaten herself and goad her into preparations of more and more frightfulness; this gives her no rest, and makes her forget all else but the perils that she causes to others and incurs herself. To the worship of this devil of politics she sacrifices other countries as victims. She feeds upon their dead flesh and grows fat upon it, so long as the carcasses remain fresh,—but they are sure to rot at last, and the dead will take their revenge, by spreading pollution far and wide and poisoning the vitality of the feeder. Japan had all her wealth of humanity, her harmony of heroism and beauty, her depth of self-control and richness of self-expression; yet the Western nations felt no respect for her till she proved that the bloodhounds of Satan are not only bred in the kennels of Europe but can also be domesticated in Japan and fed with man's miseries. They admit Japan's equality with themselves, only when they know that Japan also possesses the key to open the floodgate of hell-fire upon the fair earth whenever she chooses, and can dance, in their own measure, the devil dance of pillage, murder and ravishment of innocent women, while the world goes to ruin. We know that, in the early stage of man's moral immaturity, he only feels reverence for the god whose malevolence he dreads. But is this the ideal of man which we can look up to with pride? After centuries of civilization nations fearing each other like the prowling wild beasts of the night-time; shutting their doors of hospitality; combining only for purpose of aggression or defence; hiding in their holes their trade secrets, state secrets, secrets of their armaments; making peace-offerings to each other's barking dogs with the meat which does not belong to them; holding down fallen races which struggle to stand upon their feet; with their right hands dispensing religion to weaker peoples, while robbing them with their left,—is there anything in this to make us envious? Are we to bend our knees to the spirit of this nationalism, which is sowing broadcast over all the world seeds of fear, greed, suspicion, unashamed lies of its diplomacy, and unctuous lies of its profession of peace and good-will and universal brotherhood of Man? Can our minds be free from doubt when we rush to the Western market to buy this foreign product in exchange for our own inheritance? I am aware how difficult it is to know one's self; and the man who is intoxicated furiously denies his drunkenness; yet the West herself is anxiously thinking of her problems and trying experiments. But she is like a glutton, who has not the heart to give up his intemperance in eating, and fondly clings to the hope that he can cure his nightmares of indigestion by medicine. Europe is not ready to give up her political inhumanity, with all the baser passions of man attendant upon it; she believes only in modification of systems, and not in change of heart.

We are willing to buy their machine-made systems, not with our hearts, but with our brains. We shall try them and build sheds for them, but not enshrine them in our homes or temples. There are races who worship the animals they kill; we can buy meat from them when we are hungry, but not the worship which goes with the killing. We must not vitiate our children's minds with the superstition that business is business, war is war, politics is politics. We must know that man's business has to be more than mere business, and so should be his war and politics. You had your own industry in Japan; how scrupulously honest and true it was, you can see by its products,—by their grace and strength, their conscientiousness in details, where they can hardly be observed. But the tidal wave of falsehood has swept over your land from that part of the world where business is business, and honesty is followed merely as the best policy. Have you never felt shame when you see the trade advertisements, not only plastering the whole town with lies and exaggerations, but invading the green fields, where the peasants do their honest labour, and the hill-tops, which greet the first pure light of the morning? It is so easy to dull our sense of honour and delicacy of mind with constant abrasion, while falsehoods stalk abroad with proud steps in the name of trade, politics and patriotism, that any protest against their perpetual intrusion into our lives is considered to be sentimentalism, unworthy of true manliness.

And it has come to pass that the children of those heroes who would keep their word at the point of death, who would disdain to cheat men for vulgar profit, who even in their fight would much rather court defeat than be dishonourable, have become energetic in dealing with falsehoods and do not feel humiliated by gaining advantage from them. And this has been effected by the charm of the word "modern." But if undiluted utility be modern, beauty is of all ages; if mean selfishness be modern, the human ideals are no new inventions. And we must know for certain that however modern may be the proficiency which cripples man for the sake of methods and machines, it will never live to be old.

But while trying to free our minds from the arrogant claims of Europe and to help ourselves out of the quicksands of our infatuation, we may go to the other extreme and blind ourselves with a wholesale suspicion of the West. The reaction of disillusionment is just as unreal as the first shock of illusion. We must try to come to that normal state of mind by which we can clearly discern our own danger and avoid it without being unjust towards the source of that danger. There is always the natural temptation in us of wishing to pay back Europe in her own coin, and return contempt for contempt and evil for evil. But that again would be to imitate Europe in one of her worst features, which comes out in her behaviour to people whom she describes as yellow or red, brown or black. And this is a point on which we in the East have to acknowledge our guilt and own that our sin has been as great, if not greater, when we insulted humanity by treating with utter disdain and cruelty men who belonged to a particular creed, colour or caste. It is really because we are afraid of our own weakness, which allows itself to be overcome by the sight of power, that we try to substitute for it another weakness which makes itself blind to the glories of the West. When we truly know the Europe which is great and good, we can effectively save ourselves from the Europe which is mean and grasping. It is easy to be unfair in one's judgment when one is faced with human miseries,—and pessimism is the result of building theories while the mind is suffering. To despair of humanity is only possible if we lose faith in truth which brings to it strength, when its defeat is greatest, and calls out new life from the depth of its destruction. We must admit that there is a living soul in the West which is struggling unobserved against the hugeness of the organizations under which men, women and children are being crushed, and whose mechanical necessities are ignoring laws that are spiritual and human,—the soul whose sensibilities refuse to be dulled completely by dangerous habits of heedlessness in dealings with races for whom it lacks natural sympathy. The West could never have risen to the eminence she has reached if her strength were merely the strength of the brute or of the machine. The divine in her heart is suffering from the injuries inflicted by her hands upon the world,—and from this pain of her higher nature flows the secret balm which will bring healing to those injuries. Time after time she has fought against herself and has undone the chains which with her own hands she had fastened round helpless limbs; and though she forced poison down the throat of a great nation at the point of the sword for gain of money, she herself woke up to withdraw from it, to wash her hands clean again. This shows hidden springs of humanity in spots which look dead and barren. It proves that the deeper truth in her nature, which can survive such a career of cruel cowardliness, is not greed, but reverence for unselfish ideals. It would be altogether unjust, both to us and to Europe, to say that she has fascinated the modern Eastern mind by the mere exhibition of her power. Through the smoke of cannons and dust of markets the light of her moral nature has shone bright, and she has brought to us the ideal of ethical freedom, whose foundation lies deeper than social conventions and whose province of activity is world-wide.

The East has instinctively felt, even through her aversion, that she has a great deal to learn from Europe, not merely about the materials of power, but about its inner source, which is of mind and of the moral nature of man. Europe has been teaching us the higher obligations of public good above those of the family and the clan, and the sacredness of law, which makes society independent of individual caprice, secures for it continuity of progress, and guarantees justice to all men of all positions in life. Above all things Europe has held high before our minds the banner of liberty, through centuries of martyrdom and achievement,—liberty of conscience, liberty of thought and action, liberty in the ideals of art and literature. And because Europe has won our deep respect, she has become so dangerous for us where she is turbulently weak and false,—dangerous like poison when it is served along with our best food. There is one safety for us upon which we hope we may count, and that is, that we can claim Europe herself as our ally in our resistance to her temptations and to her violent encroachments; for she has ever carried her own standard of perfection, by which we can measure her falls and gauge her degrees of failure, by which we can call her before her own tribunal and put her to shame,—the shame which is the sign of the true pride of nobleness.

But our fear is, that the poison may be more powerful than the food, and what is strength in her to-day may not be the sign of health, but the contrary; for it may be temporarily caused by the upsetting of the balance of life. Our fear is that evil has a fateful fascination when it assumes dimensions which are colossal,—and though at last it is sure to lose its centre of gravity by its abnormal disproportion, the mischief which it creates before its fall may be beyond reparation.

Therefore I ask you to have the strength of faith and clarity of mind to know for certain that the lumbering structure of modern progress, riveted by the iron bolts of efficiency, which runs upon the wheels of ambition, cannot hold together for long. Collisions are certain to occur; for it has to travel upon organized lines, it is too heavy to choose its own course freely; and once it is off the rails, its endless train of vehicles is dislocated. A day will come when it will fall in a heap of ruin and cause serious obstruction to the traffic of the world. Do we not see signs of this even now? Does not the voice come to us, through the din of war, the shrieks of hatred, the wailings of despair, through the churning up of the unspeakable filth which has been accumulating for ages in the bottom of this nationalism,—the voice which cries to our soul that the tower of national selfishness, which goes by the name of patriotism, which has raised its banner of treason against heaven, must totter and fall with a crash, weighed down by its own bulk, its flag kissing the dust, its light extinguished? My brothers, when the red light of conflagration sends up its crackle of laughter to the stars, keep your faith upon those stars and not upon the fire of destruction. For when this conflagration consumes itself and dies down, leaving its memorial in ashes, the eternal light will again shine in the East,—the East which has been the birthplace of the morning sun of man's history. And who knows if that day has not already dawned, and the sun not risen, in the Easternmost horizon of Asia? And I offer, as did my ancestor rishis, my salutation to that sunrise of the East, which is destined once again to illumine the whole world.

I know my voice is too feeble to raise itself above the uproar of this bustling time, and it is easy for any street urchin to fling against me the epithet of "unpractical." It will stick to my coat-tail, never to be washed away, effectively excluding me from the consideration of all respectable persons. I know what a risk one runs from the vigorously athletic crowds in being styled an idealist in these days, when thrones have lost their dignity and prophets have become an anachronism, when the sound that drowns all voices is the noise of the market-place. Yet when, one day, standing on the outskirts of Yokohama town, bristling with its display of modern miscellanies, I watched the sunset in your southern sea, and saw its peace and majesty among your pine-clad hills,—with the great Fujiyama growing faint against the golden horizon, like a god overcome with his own radiance,—the music of eternity welled up through the evening silence, and I felt that the sky and the earth and the lyrics of the dawn and the dayfall are with the poets and idealists, and not with the marketmen robustly contemptuous of all sentiment,—that, after the forgetfulness of his own divinity, man will remember again that heaven is always in touch with his world, which can never be abandoned for good to the hounding wolves of the modern era, scenting human blood and howling to the skies.

NATIONALISM IN INDIA

Our real problem in India is not political. It is social. This is a condition not only prevailing in India, but among all nations. I do not believe in an exclusive political interest. Politics in the West have dominated Western ideals, and we in India are trying to imitate you. We have to remember that in Europe, where peoples had their racial unity from the beginning, and where natural resources were insufficient for the inhabitants, the civilization has naturally taken the character of political and commercial aggressiveness. For on the one hand they had no internal complications, and on the other they had to deal with neighbours who were strong and rapacious. To have perfect combination among themselves and a watchful attitude of animosity against others was taken as the solution of their problems. In former days they organized and plundered, in the present age the same spirit continues—and they organize and exploit the whole world.

But from the earliest beginnings of history India has had her own problem constantly before her—it is the race problem. Each nation must be conscious of its mission, and we, in India, must realize that we cut a poor figure when we are trying to be political, simply because we have not yet been finally able to accomplish what was set before us by our providence.

This problem of race unity which we have been trying to solve for so many years has likewise to be faced by you here in America. Many people in this country ask me what is happening as to the caste distinctions in India. But when this question is asked me, it is usually done with a superior air. And I feel tempted to put the same question to our American critics with a slight modification, "What have you done with the Red Indian and the Negro?" For you have not got over your attitude of caste toward them. You have used violent methods to keep aloof from other races, but until you have solved the question here in America, you have no right to question India.

In spite of our great difficulty, however, India has done something. She has tried to make an adjustment of races, to acknowledge the real differences between them where these exist, and yet seek for some basis of unity. This basis has come through our saints, like Nanak, Kabir, Chaitnaya and others, preaching one God to all races of India.

In finding the solution of our problem we shall have helped to solve the world problem as well. What India has been, the whole world is now. The whole world is becoming one country through scientific facility. And the moment is arriving when you also must find a basis of unity which is not political. If India can offer to the world her solution, it will be a contribution to humanity. There is only one history—the history of man. All national histories are merely chapters in the larger one. And we are content in India to suffer for such a great cause.

Each individual has his self-love. Therefore his brute instinct leads him to fight with others in the sole pursuit of his self-interest. But man has also his higher instincts of sympathy and mutual help. The people who are lacking in this higher moral power and who therefore cannot combine in fellowship with one another must perish or live in a state of degradation. Only those peoples have survived and achieved civilization who have this spirit of co-operation strong in them. So we find that from the beginning of history men had to choose between fighting with one another and combining, between serving their own interest or the common interest of all.

In our early history, when the geographical limits of each country and also the facilities of communication were small, this problem was comparatively small in dimension. It was sufficient for men to develop their sense of unity within their area of segregation. In those days they combined among themselves and fought against others. But it was this moral spirit of combination which was the true basis of their greatness, and this fostered their art, science and religion. At that early time the most important fact that man had to take count of was the fact of the members of one particular race of men coming in close contact with one another. Those who truly grasped this fact through their higher nature made their mark in history.

The most important fact of the present age is that all the different races of men have come close together. And again we are confronted with two alternatives. The problem is whether the different groups of peoples shall go on fighting with one another or find out some true basis of reconciliation and mutual help; whether it will be interminable competition or co-operation.

I have no hesitation in saying that those who are gifted with the moral power of love and vision of spiritual unity, who have the least feeling of enmity against aliens, and the sympathetic insight to place themselves in the position of others, will be the fittest to take their permanent place in the age that is lying before us, and those who are constantly developing their instinct of fight and intolerance of aliens will be eliminated. For this is the problem before us, and we have to prove our humanity by solving it through the help of our higher nature. The gigantic organizations for hurting others and warding off their blows, for making money by dragging others back, will not help us. On the contrary, by their crushing weight, their enormous cost and their deadening effect upon living humanity, they will seriously impede our freedom in the larger life of a higher civilization.

During the evolution of the Nation the moral culture of brotherhood was limited by geographical boundaries, because at that time those boundaries were true. Now they have become imaginary lines of tradition divested of the qualities of real obstacles. So the time has come when man's moral nature must deal with this great fact with all seriousness or perish. The first impulse of this change of circumstance has been the churning up of man's baser passions of greed and cruel hatred. If this persists indefinitely, and armaments go on exaggerating themselves to unimaginable absurdities, and machines and storehouses envelop this fair earth with their dirt and smoke and ugliness, then it will end in a conflagration of suicide. Therefore man will have to exert all his power of love and clarity of vision to make another great moral adjustment which will comprehend the whole world of men and not merely the fractional groups of nationality. The call has come to every individual in the present age to prepare himself and his surroundings for this dawn of a new era, when man shall discover his soul in the spiritual unity of all human beings.

If it is given at all to the West to struggle out of these tangles of the lower slopes to the spiritual summit of humanity then I cannot but think that it is the special mission of America to fulfil this hope of God and man. You are the country of expectation, desiring something else than what is. Europe has her subtle habits of mind and her conventions. But America, as yet, has come to no conclusions. I realize how much America is untrammeled by the traditions of the past, and I can appreciate that experimentalism is a sign of America's youth. The foundation of her glory is in the future, rather than in the past; and if one is gifted with the power of clairvoyance, one will be able to love the America that is to be.

America is destined to justify Western civilization to the East. Europe has lost faith in humanity, and has become distrustful and sickly. America, on the other hand, is not pessimistic or blasé. You know, as a people, that there is such a thing as a better and a best; and that knowledge drives you on. There are habits that are not merely passive but aggressively arrogant. They are not like mere walls, but are like hedges of stinging nettles. Europe has been cultivating these hedges of habits for long years, till they have grown round her dense and strong and high. The pride of her traditions has sent its roots deep into her heart. I do not wish to contend that it is unreasonable. But pride in every form breeds blindness at the end. Like all artificial stimulants its first effect is a heightening of consciousness, and then with the increasing dose it muddles it and brings an exultation that is misleading. Europe has gradually grown hardened in her pride in all her outer and inner habits. She not only cannot forget that she is Western, but she takes every opportunity to hurl this fact against others to humiliate them. This is why she is growing incapable of imparting to the East what is best in herself, and of accepting in a right spirit the wisdom that the East has stored for centuries.

In America national habits and traditions have not had time to spread their clutching roots round your hearts. You have constantly felt and complained of your disadvantages when you compared your nomadic restlessness with the settled traditions of Europe—the Europe which can show her picture of greatness to the best advantage because she can fix it against the background of the Past. But in this present age of transition, when a new era of civilization is sending its trumpet-call to all peoples of the world across an unlimited future, this very freedom of detachment will enable you to accept its invitation and to achieve the goal for which Europe began her journey but lost herself midway. For she was tempted out of her path by her pride of power and greed of possession.

Not merely your freedom from habits of mind in individuals, but also the freedom of your history from all unclean entanglements, fits you in your career of holding the banner of civilization of the future. All the great nations of Europe have their victims in other parts of the world. This not only deadens their moral sympathy but also their intellectual sympathy, which is so necessary for the understanding of races which are different from one's own. Englishmen can never truly understand India, because their minds are not disinterested with regard to that country. If you compare England with Germany or France you will find she has produced the smallest number of scholars who have studied Indian literature and philosophy with any amount of sympathetic insight or thoroughness. This attitude of apathy and contempt is natural where the relationship is abnormal and founded upon national selfishness and pride. But your history has been disinterested, and that is why you have been able to help Japan in her lessons in Western civilization, and that is why China can look upon you with her best confidence in this her darkest period of danger. In fact you are carrying all the responsibility of a great future because you are untrammelled by the grasping miserliness of a past. Therefore of all countries of the earth America has to be fully conscious of this future, her vision must not be obscured and her faith in humanity must be strong with the strength of youth.

A parallelism exists between America and India—the parallelism of welding together into one body various races.

In my country we have been seeking to find out something common to all races, which will prove their real unity. No nation looking for a mere political or commercial basis of unity will find such a solution sufficient. Men of thought and power will discover the spiritual unity, will realize it, and preach it.

India has never had a real sense of nationalism. Even though from childhood I had been taught that idolatry of the Nation is almost better than reverence for God and humanity, I believe I have outgrown that teaching, and it is my conviction that my countrymen will truly gain their India by fighting against the education which teaches them that a country is greater than the ideals of humanity.

The educated Indian at present is trying to absorb some lessons from history contrary to the lessons of our ancestors. The East, in fact, is attempting to take unto itself a history which is not the outcome of its own living. Japan, for example, thinks she is getting powerful through adopting Western methods, but, after she has exhausted her inheritance, only the borrowed weapons of civilization will remain to her. She will not have developed herself from within.

Europe has her past. Europe's strength therefore lies in her history. We, in India, must make up our minds that we cannot borrow other people's history, and that if we stifle our own we are committing suicide. When you borrow things that do not belong to your life, they only serve to crush your life.

And therefore I believe that it does India no good to compete with Western civilization in its own field. But we shall be more than compensated if, in spite of the insults heaped upon us, we follow our own destiny.

There are lessons which impart information or train our minds for intellectual pursuits. These are simple and can be acquired and used with advantage. But there are others which affect our deeper nature and change our direction of life. Before we accept them and pay their value by selling our own inheritance, we must pause and think deeply. In man's history there come ages of fireworks which dazzle us by their force and movement. They laugh not only at our modest household lamps but also at the eternal stars. But let us not for that provocation be precipitate in our desire to dismiss our lamps. Let us patiently bear our present insult and realize that these fireworks have splendour but not permanence, because of the extreme explosiveness which is the cause of their power, and also of their exhaustion. They are spending a fatal quantity of energy and substance compared to their gain and production.

Anyhow, our ideals have been evolved through our own history, and even if we wished we could only make poor fireworks of them, because their materials are different from yours, as is also their moral purpose. If we cherish the desire of paying our all to buy a political nationality it will be as absurd as if Switzerland had staked her existence on her ambition to build up a navy powerful enough to compete with that of England. The mistake that we make is in thinking that man's channel of greatness is only one—the one which has made itself painfully evident for the time being by its depth of insolence.

We must know for certain that there is a future before us and that future is waiting for those who are rich in moral ideals and not in mere things. And it is the privilege of man to work for fruits that are beyond his immediate reach, and to adjust his life not in slavish conformity to the examples of some present success or even to his own prudent past, limited in its aspiration, but to an infinite future bearing in its heart the ideals of our highest expectations.

We must recognize that it is providential that the West has come to India. And yet some one must show the East to the West, and convince the West that the East has her contribution to make to the history of civilization. India is no beggar of the West. And yet even though the West may think she is, I am not for thrusting off Western civilization and becoming segregated in our independence. Let us have a deep association. If Providence wants England to be the channel of that communication, of that deeper association, I am willing to accept it with all humility. I have great faith in human nature, and I think the West will find its true mission. I speak bitterly of Western civilization when I am conscious that it is betraying its trust and thwarting its own purpose. The West must not make herself a curse to the world by using her power for her own selfish needs, but, by teaching the ignorant and helping the weak, she should save herself from the worst danger that the strong is liable to incur by making the feeble acquire power enough to resist her intrusion. And also she must not make her materialism to be the final thing, but must realize that she is doing a service in freeing the spiritual being from the tyranny of matter.

I am not against one nation in particular, but against the general idea of all nations. What is the Nation?

It is the aspect of a whole people as an organized power. This organization incessantly keeps up the insistence of the population on becoming strong and efficient. But this strenuous effort after strength and efficiency drains man's energy from his higher nature where he is self-sacrificing and creative. For thereby man's power of sacrifice is diverted from his ultimate object, which is moral, to the maintenance of this organization, which is mechanical. Yet in this he feels all the satisfaction of moral exaltation and therefore becomes supremely dangerous to humanity. He feels relieved of the urging of his conscience when he can transfer his responsibility to this machine which is the creation of his intellect and not of his complete moral personality. By this device the people which loves freedom perpetuates slavery in a large portion of the world with the comfortable feeling of pride of having done its duty; men who are naturally just can be cruelly unjust both in their act and their thought, accompanied by a feeling that they are helping the world to receive its deserts; men who are honest can blindly go on robbing others of their human rights for self-aggrandizement, all the while abusing the deprived for not deserving better treatment. We have seen in our everyday life even small organizations of business and profession produce callousness of feeling in men who are not naturally bad, and we can well imagine what a moral havoc it is causing in a world where whole peoples are furiously organizing themselves for gaining wealth and power.

Nationalism is a great menace. It is the particular thing which for years has been at the bottom of India's troubles. And in as much as we have been ruled and dominated by a nation that is strictly political in its attitude, we have tried to develop within ourselves, despite our inheritance from the past, a belief in our eventual political destiny.

There are different parties in India, with different ideals. Some are struggling for political independence. Others think that the time has not arrived for that, and yet believe that India should have the rights that the English colonies have. They wish to gain autonomy as far as possible.

In the beginning of the history of political agitation in India there was not the conflict between parties which there is to-day. At that time there was a party known as the Indian Congress; it had no real programme. They had a few grievances for redress by the authorities. They wanted larger representation in the Council House, and more freedom in Municipal government. They wanted scraps of things, but they had no constructive ideal. Therefore I was lacking in enthusiasm for their methods. It was my conviction that what India most needed was constructive work coming from within herself. In this work we must take all risks and go on doing the duties which by right are ours, though in the teeth of persecution; winning moral victory at every step, by our failure and suffering. We must show those who are over us that we have in ourselves the strength of moral power, the power to suffer for truth. Where we have nothing to show, we have only to beg. It would be mischievous if the gifts we wish for were granted to us at once, and I have told my countrymen, time and again, to combine for the work of creating opportunities to give vent to our spirit of self-sacrifice, and not for the purpose of begging.

The party, however, lost power because the people soon came to realize how futile was the half policy adopted by them. The party split, and there arrived the Extremists, who advocated independence of action, and discarded the begging method,—the easiest method of relieving one's mind from his responsibility towards his country. Their ideals were based on Western history. They had no sympathy with the special problems of India. They did not recognize the patent fact that there were causes in our social organization which made the Indian incapable of coping with the alien. What should we do if, for any reason, England was driven away? We should simply be victims for other nations. The same social weaknesses would prevail. The thing we in India have to think of is this—to remove those social customs and ideals which have generated a want of self-respect and a complete dependence on those above us,—a state of affairs which has been brought about entirely by the domination in India of the caste system, and the blind and lazy habit of relying upon the authority of traditions that are incongruous anachronisms in the present age.

Once again I draw your attention to the difficulties India has had to encounter and her struggle to overcome them. Her problem was the problem of the world in miniature. India is too vast in its area and too diverse in its races. It is many countries packed in one geographical receptacle. It is just the opposite of what Europe truly is, namely, one country made into many. Thus Europe in its culture and growth has had the advantage of the strength of the many as well as the strength of the one. India, on the contrary, being naturally many, yet adventitiously one, has all along suffered from the looseness of its diversity and the feebleness of its unity. A true unity is like a round globe, it rolls on, carrying its burden easily; but diversity is a many-cornered thing which has to be dragged and pushed with all force. Be it said to the credit of India that this diversity was not her own creation; she has had to accept it as a fact from the beginning of her history. In America and Australia, Europe has simplified her problem by almost exterminating the original population. Even in the present age this spirit of extermination is making itself manifest, in the inhospitable shutting out of aliens, by those who themselves were aliens in the lands they now occupy. But India tolerated difference of races from the first, and that spirit of toleration has acted all through her history.

Her caste system is the outcome of this spirit of toleration. For India has all along been trying experiments in evolving a social unity within which all the different peoples could be held together, while fully enjoying the freedom of maintaining their own differences. The tie has been as loose as possible, yet as close as the circumstances permitted. This has produced something like a United States of a social federation, whose common name is Hinduism.

India had felt that diversity of races there must be and should be, whatever may be its drawback, and you can never coerce nature into your narrow limits of convenience without paying one day very dearly for it. In this India was right; but what she failed to realize was that in human beings differences are not like the physical barriers of mountains, fixed for ever—they are fluid with life's flow, they are changing their courses and their shapes and volume.

Therefore in her caste regulations India recognized differences, but not the mutability which is the law of life. In trying to avoid collisions she set up boundaries of immovable walls, thus giving to her numerous races the negative benefit of peace and order but not the positive opportunity of expansion and movement. She accepted nature where it produces diversity, but ignored it where it uses that diversity for its world-game of infinite permutations and combinations. She treated life in all truth where it is manifold, but insulted it where it is ever moving. Therefore Life departed from her social system and in its place she is worshipping with all ceremony the magnificent cage of countless compartments that she has manufactured.

The same thing happened where she tried to ward off the collisions of trade interests. She associated different trades and professions with different castes. This had the effect of allaying for good the interminable jealousy and hatred of competition—the competition which breeds cruelty and makes the atmosphere thick with lies and deception. In this also India laid all her emphasis upon the law of heredity, ignoring the law of mutation, and thus gradually reduced arts into crafts and genius into skill.

However, what Western observers fail to discern is that in her caste system India in all seriousness accepted her responsibility to solve the race problem in such a manner as to avoid all friction, and yet to afford each race freedom within its boundaries. Let us admit India has not in this achieved a full measure of success. But this you must also concede, that the West, being more favourably situated as to homogeneity of races, has never given her attention to this problem, and whenever confronted with it she has tried to make it easy by ignoring it altogether. And this is the source of her anti-Asiatic agitations for depriving aliens of their right to earn their honest living on these shores. In most of your colonies you only admit them on condition of their accepting the menial position of hewers of wood and drawers of water. Either you shut your doors against the aliens or reduce them into slavery. And this is your solution of the problem of race-conflict. Whatever may be its merits you will have to admit that it does not spring from the higher impulses of civilization, but from the lower passions of greed and hatred. You say this is human nature—and India also thought she knew human nature when she strongly barricaded her race distinctions by the fixed barriers of social gradations. But we have found out to our cost that human nature is not what it seems, but what it is in truth; which is in its infinite possibilities. And when we in our blindness insult humanity for its ragged appearance it sheds its disguise to disclose to us that we have insulted our God. The degradation which we cast upon others in our pride or self-interest degrades our own humanity—and this is the punishment which is most terrible, because we do not detect it till it is too late.

Not only in your relation with aliens but with the different sections of your own society you have not achieved harmony of reconciliation. The spirit of conflict and competition is allowed the full freedom of its reckless career. And because its genesis is the greed of wealth and power it can never come to any other end but to a violent death. In India the production of commodities was brought under the law of social adjustments. Its basis was co-operation, having for its object the perfect satisfaction of social needs. But in the West it is guided by the impulse of competition, whose end is the gain of wealth for individuals. But the individual is like the geometrical line; it is length without breadth. It has not got the depth to be able to hold anything permanently. Therefore its greed or gain can never come to finality. In its lengthening process of growth it can cross other lines and cause entanglements, but will ever go on missing the ideal of completeness in its thinness of isolation.

In all our physical appetites we recognize a limit. We know that to exceed that limit is to exceed the limit of health. But has this lust for wealth and power no bounds beyond which is death's dominion? In these national carnivals of materialism are not the Western peoples spending most of their vital energy in merely producing things and neglecting the creation of ideals? And can a civilization ignore the law of moral health and go on in its endless process of inflation by gorging upon material things? Man in his social ideals naturally tries to regulate his appetites, subordinating them to the higher purpose of his nature. But in the economic world our appetites follow no other restrictions but those of supply and demand which can be artificially fostered, affording individuals opportunities for indulgence in an endless feast of grossness. In India our social instincts imposed restrictions upon our appetites,—maybe it went to the extreme of repression,—but in the West the spirit of economic organization with no moral purpose goads the people into the perpetual pursuit of wealth; but has this no wholesome limit?

The ideals that strive to take form in social institutions have two objects. One is to regulate our passions and appetites for the harmonious development of man, and the other is to help him to cultivate disinterested love for his fellow-creatures. Therefore society is the expression of those moral and spiritual aspirations of man which belong to his higher nature.

Our food is creative, it builds our body; but not so wine, which stimulates. Our social ideals create the human world, but when our mind is diverted from them to greed of power then in that state of intoxication we live in a world of abnormality where our strength is not health and our liberty is not freedom. Therefore political freedom does not give us freedom when our mind is not free. An automobile does not create freedom of movement, because it is a mere machine. When I myself am free I can use the automobile for the purpose of my freedom.

We must never forget in the present day that those people who have got their political freedom are not necessarily free, they are merely powerful. The passions which are unbridled in them are creating huge organizations of slavery in the disguise of freedom. Those who have made the gain of money their highest end are unconsciously selling their life and soul to rich persons or to the combinations that represent money. Those who are enamoured of their political power and gloat over their extension of dominion over foreign races gradually surrender their own freedom and humanity to the organizations necessary for holding other peoples in slavery. In the so-called free countries the majority of the people are not free, they are driven by the minority to a goal which is not even known to them. This becomes possible only because people do not acknowledge moral and spiritual freedom as their object. They create huge eddies with their passions, and they feel dizzily inebriated with the mere velocity of their whirling movement, taking that to be freedom. But the doom which is waiting to overtake them is as certain as death—for man's truth is moral truth and his emancipation is in the spiritual life.

The general opinion of the majority of the present-day nationalists in India is that we have come to a final completeness in our social and spiritual ideals, the task of the constructive work of society having been done several thousand years before we were born, and that now we are free to employ all our activities in the political direction. We never dream of blaming our social inadequacy as the origin of our present helplessness, for we have accepted as the creed of our nationalism that this social system has been perfected for all time to come by our ancestors, who had the superhuman vision of all eternity and supernatural power for making infinite provision for future ages. Therefore, for all our miseries and shortcomings, we hold responsible the historical surprises that burst upon us from outside. This is the reason why we think that our one task is to build a political miracle of freedom upon the quicksand of social slavery. In fact we want to dam up the true course of our own historical stream, and only borrow power from the sources of other peoples' history.

Those of us in India who have come under the delusion that mere political freedom will make us free have accepted their lessons from the West as the gospel truth and lost their faith in humanity. We must remember whatever weakness we cherish in our society will become the source of danger in politics. The same inertia which leads us to our idolatry of dead forms in social institutions will create in our politics prison-houses with immovable walls. The narrowness of sympathy which makes it possible for us to impose upon a considerable portion of humanity the galling yoke of inferiority will assert itself in our politics in creating the tyranny of injustice.

When our nationalists talk about ideals they forget that the basis of nationalism is wanting. The very people who are upholding these ideals are themselves the most conservative in their social practice. Nationalists say, for example, look at Switzerland where, in spite of race differences, the peoples have solidified into a nation. Yet, remember that in Switzerland the races can mingle, they can intermarry, because they are of the same blood. In India there is no common birthright. And when we talk of Western Nationality we forget that the nations there do not have that physical repulsion, one for the other, that we have between different castes. Have we an instance in the whole world where a people who are not allowed to mingle their blood shed their blood for one another except by coercion or for mercenary purposes? And can we ever hope that these moral barriers against our race amalgamation will not stand in the way of our political unity?

Then again we must give full recognition to this fact that our social restrictions are still tyrannical, so much so as to make men cowards. If a man tells me he has heterodox ideas, but that he cannot follow them because he would be socially ostracized, I excuse him for having to live a life of untruth, in order to live at all. The social habit of mind which impels us to make the life of our fellow-beings a burden to them where they differ from us even in such a thing as their choice of food, is sure to persist in our political organization and result in creating engines of coercion to crush every rational difference which is the sign of life. And tyranny will only add to the inevitable lies and hypocrisy in our political life. Is the mere name of freedom so valuable that we should be willing to sacrifice for its sake our moral freedom?

The intemperance of our habits does not immediately show its effects when we are in the vigour of our youth. But it gradually consumes that vigour, and when the period of decline sets in then we have to settle accounts and pay off our debts, which leads us to insolvency. In the West you are still able to carry your head high, though your humanity is suffering every moment from its dipsomania of organizing power. India also in the heyday of her youth could carry in her vital organs the dead weight of her social organizations stiffened to rigid perfection, but it has been fatal to her, and has produced a gradual paralysis of her living nature.

And this is the reason why the educated community of India has become insensible of her social needs. They are taking the very immobility of our social structures as the sign of their perfection,—and because the healthy feeling of pain is dead in the limbs of our social organism they delude themselves into thinking that it needs no ministration. Therefore they think that all their energies need their only scope in the political field. It is like a man whose legs have become shrivelled and useless, trying to delude himself that these limbs have grown still because they have attained their ultimate salvation, and all that is wrong about him is the shortness of his sticks.

So much for the social and the political regeneration of India. Now we come to her industries, and I am very often asked whether there is in India any industrial regeneration since the advent of the British Government. It must be remembered that at the beginning of the British rule in India our industries were suppressed, and since then we have not met with any real help or encouragement to enable us to make a stand against the monster commercial organizations of the world. The nations have decreed that we must remain purely an agricultural people, even forgetting the use of arms for all time to come. Thus India is being turned into so many predigested morsels of food ready to be swallowed at any moment by any nation which has even the most rudimentary set of teeth in its head.

India therefore has very little outlet for her industrial originality. I personally do not believe in the unwieldy organizations of the present day. The very fact that they are ugly shows that they are in discordance with the whole creation. The vast powers of nature do not reveal their truth in hideousness, but in beauty. Beauty is the signature which the Creator stamps upon His works when He is satisfied with them. All our products that insolently ignore the laws of perfection and are unashamed in their display of ungainliness bear the perpetual weight of God's displeasure. So far as your commerce lacks the dignity of grace it is untrue. Beauty and her twin brother Truth require leisure and self-control for their growth. But the greed of gain has no time or limit to its capaciousness. Its one object is to produce and consume. It has pity neither for beautiful nature nor for living human beings. It is ruthlessly ready without a moment's hesitation to crush beauty and life out of them, moulding them into money. It is this ugly vulgarity of commerce which brought upon it the censure of contempt in our earlier days, when men had leisure to have an unclouded vision of perfection in humanity. Men in those times were rightly ashamed of the instinct of mere money-making. But in this scientific age money, by its very abnormal bulk, has won its throne. And when from its eminence of piled-up things it insults the higher instincts of man, banishing beauty and noble sentiments from its surroundings, we submit. For we in our meanness have accepted bribes from its hands and our imagination has grovelled in the dust before its immensity of flesh.

But its very unwieldiness and its endless complexities are its true signs of failure. The swimmer who is an expert does not exhibit his muscular force by violent movements, but exhibits some power which is invisible and which shows itself in perfect grace and reposefulness. The true distinction of man from animals is in his power and worth which are inner and invisible. But the present-day commercial civilization of man is not only taking too much time and space but killing time and space. Its movements are violent, its noise is discordantly loud. It is carrying its own damnation because it is trampling into distortion the humanity upon which it stands. It is strenuously turning out money at the cost of happiness. Man is reducing himself to his minimum in order to be able to make amplest room for his organizations. He is deriding his human sentiments into shame because they are apt to stand in the way of his machines.

In our mythology we have the legend that the man who performs penances for attaining immortality has to meet with temptations sent by Indra, the Lord of the immortals. If he is lured by them he is lost. The West has been striving for centuries after its goal of immortality. Indra has sent her the temptation to try her. It is the gorgeous temptation of wealth. She has accepted it, and her civilization of humanity has lost its path in the wilderness of machinery.

This commercialism with its barbarity of ugly decorations is a terrible menace to all humanity, because it is setting up the ideal of power over that of perfection. It is making the cult of self-seeking exult in its naked shamelessness. Our nerves are more delicate than our muscles. Things that are the most precious in us are helpless as babes when we take away from them the careful protection which they claim from us for their very preciousness. Therefore, when the callous rudeness of power runs amuck in the broad-way of humanity it scares away by its grossness the ideals which we have cherished with the martyrdom of centuries.

The temptation which is fatal for the strong is still more so for the weak. And I do not welcome it in our Indian life, even though it be sent by the lord of the Immortals. Let our life be simple in its outer aspect and rich in its inner gain. Let our civilization take its firm stand upon its basis of social co-operation and not upon that of economic exploitation and conflict. How to do it in the teeth of the drainage of our life-blood by the economic dragons is the task set before the thinkers of all oriental nations who have faith in the human soul. It is a sign of laziness and impotency to accept conditions imposed upon us by others who have other ideals than ours. We should actively try to adapt the world powers to guide our history to its own perfect end.

From the above you will know that I am not an economist. I am willing to acknowledge that there is a law of demand and supply and an infatuation of man for more things than are good for him. And yet I will persist in believing that there is such a thing as the harmony of completeness in humanity, where poverty does not take away his riches, where defeat may lead him to victory, death to immortality, and where in the compensation of Eternal Justice those who are the last may yet have their insult transmuted into a golden triumph.

THE SUNSET OF THE CENTURY

(Written in the Bengali on the last day of last century)

1

The last sun of the century sets amidst the blood-red clouds of the West and the whirlwind of hatred.

The naked passion of self-love of Nations, in its drunken delirium of greed, is dancing to the clash of steel and the howling verses of vengeance.

2

The hungry self of the Nation shall burst in a violence of fury from its own shameless feeding.

For it has made the world its food,

And licking it, crunching it and swallowing it in big morsels,

It swells and swells

Till in the midst of its unholy feast descends the sudden shaft of heaven piercing its heart of grossness.

3

The crimson glow of light on the horizon is not the light of thy dawn of peace, my Motherland.

It is the glimmer of the funeral pyre burning to ashes the vast flesh,—the self-love of the Nation—dead under its own excess.

Thy morning waits behind the patient dark of the East,

Meek and silent.

4

Keep watch, India.

Bring your offerings of worship for that sacred sunrise.

Let the first hymn of its welcome sound in your voice and sing

"Come, Peace, thou daughter of God's own great suffering

Come with thy treasure of contentment, the sword of fortitude,

And meekness crowning thy forehead."

5

Be not ashamed, my brothers, to stand before the proud and the powerful

With your white robe of simpleness.

Let your crown be of humility, your freedom the freedom of the soul.

Build God's throne daily upon the ample bareness of your poverty

And know that what is huge is not great and pride is not everlasting.

THE END

THE VICTORY

She was the Princess Ajita. And the court poet of King Narayan had never seen her. On the day he recited a new poem to the king he would raise his voice just to that pitch which could be heard by unseen hearers in the screened balcony high above the hall. He sent up his song towards the star-land out of his reach, where, circled with light, the planet who ruled his destiny shone unknown and out of ken.

He would espy some shadow moving behind the veil. A tinkling sound would come to his ear from afar, and would set him dreaming of the ankles whose tiny golden bells sang at each step. Ah, the rosy red tender feet that walked the dust of the earth like God's mercy on the fallen! The poet had placed them on the altar of his heart, where he wove his songs to the tune of those golden bells. Doubt never arose in his mind as to whose shadow it was that moved behind the screen, and whose anklets they were that sang to the time of his beating heart.

Manjari, the maid of the princess, passed by the poet's house on her way to the river, and she never missed a day to have a few words with him on the sly. When she found the road deserted, and the shadow of dusk on the land, she would boldly enter his room, and sit at the corner of his carpet. There was a suspicion of an added care in the choice of the colour of her veil, in the setting of the flower in her hair.

People smiled and whispered at this, and they were not to blame. For Shekhar the poet never took the trouble to hide the fact that these meetings were a pure joy to him.

The meaning of her name was the spray of flowers. One must confess that for an ordinary mortal it was sufficient in its sweetness. But Shekhar made his own addition to this name, and called her the Spray of Spring Flowers. And ordinary mortals shook their heads and said, Ah, me!

In the spring songs that the poet sang the praise of the spray of spring flowers was conspicuously reiterated; and the king winked and smiled at him when he heard it, and the poet smiled in answer.

The king would put him the question; "Is it the business of the bee merely to hum in the court of the spring?"

The poet would answer; "No, but also to sip the honey of the spray of spring flowers."

And they all laughed in the king's hall. And it was rumoured that the Princess Akita also laughed at her maid's accepting the poet's name for her, and Manjari felt glad in her heart.

Thus truth and falsehood mingle in life--and to what God builds man adds his own decoration.

Only those were pure truths which were sung by the poet. The theme was Krishna, the lover god, and Radha, the beloved, the Eternal Man and the Eternal Woman, the sorrow that comes from the beginning of time, and the joy without end. The truth of these songs was tested in his inmost heart by everybody from the beggar to the king himself. The poet's songs were on the lips of all. At the merest glimmer of the moon and the faintest whisper of the summer breeze his songs would break forth in the land from windows and courtyards, from sailing-boats, from shadows of the wayside trees, in numberless voices.

Thus passed the days happily. The poet recited, the king listened, the hearers applauded, Manjari passed and repassed by the poet's room on her way to the river--the shadow flitted behind the screened balcony, and the tiny golden bells tinkled from afar.

Just then set forth from his home in the south a poet on his path of conquest. He came to King Narayan, in the kingdom of Amarapur. He stood before the throne, and uttered a verse in praise of the king. He had challenged all the court poets on his way, and his career of victory had been unbroken.

The king received him with honour, and said: "Poet, I offer you welcome."

Pundarik, the poet, proudly replied: "Sire, I ask for war."

Shekhar, the court poet of the king did not know how the battle of the muse was to be waged. He had no sleep at night. The mighty figure of the famous Pundarik, his sharp nose curved like a scimitar, and his proud head tilted on one side, haunted the poet's vision in the dark.

With a trembling heart Shekhar entered the arena in the morning. The theatre was filled with the crowd.

The poet greeted his rival with a smile and a bow. Pundarik returned it with a slight toss of his head, and turned his face towards his circle of adoring followers with a meaning smile. Shekhar cast his glance towards the screened balcony high above, and saluted his lady in his mind, saying! "If I am the winner at the combat to-day, my lady, thy victorious name shall be glorified."

The trumpet sounded. The great crowd stood up, shouting victory to the king. The king, dressed in an ample robe of white, slowly came into the hall like a floating cloud of autumn, and sat on his throne.

Pundarik stood up, and the vast hall became still. With his head raised high and chest expanded, he began in his thundering voice to recite the praise of King Narayan. His words burst upon the walls of the hall like breakers of the sea, and seemed to rattle against the ribs of the listening crowd. The skill with which he gave varied meanings to the name Narayan, and wove each letter of it through the web of his verses in all mariner of combinations, took away the breath of his amazed hearers.

For some minutes after he took his seat his voice continued to vibrate among the numberless pillars of the king's court and in thousands of speechless hearts. The learned professors who had come from distant lands raised their right hands, and cried, Bravo!

The king threw a glance on Shekhar's face, and Shekhar in answer raised for a moment his eyes full of pain towards his master, and then stood up like a stricken deer at bay. His face was pale, his bashfulness was almost that of a woman, his slight youthful figure, delicate in its outline, seemed like a tensely strung vina ready to break out in music at the least touch.

His head was bent, his voice was low, when he began. The first few verses were almost inaudible. Then he slowly raised his head, and his clear sweet voice rose into the sky like a quivering flame of fire. He began with the ancient legend of the kingly line lost in the haze of the past, and brought it down through its long course of heroism and matchless generosity to the present age. He fixed his gaze on the king's face, and all the vast and unexpressed love of the people for the royal house rose like incense in his song, and enwreathed the throne on all sides. These were his last words when, trembling, he took his seat: "My master, I may be beaten in play of words, but not in my love for thee."

Tears filled the eyes of the hearers, and the stone walls shook with cries of victory.

Mocking this popular outburst of feeling, with an august shake of his head and a contemptuous sneer, Pundarik stood up, and flung this question to the assembly; "What is there superior to words?" In a moment the hall lapsed into silence again.

Then with a marvellous display of learning, he proved that the Word was in the beginning, that the Word was God. He piled up quotations from scriptures, and built a high altar for the Word to be seated above all that there is in heaven and in earth. He repeated that question in his mighty voice: "What is there superior to words?"

Proudly he looked around him. None dared to accept his challenge, and he slowly took his seat like a lion who had just made a full meal of its victim. The pandits shouted, Bravo! The king remained silent with wonder, and the poet Shekhar felt himself of no account by the side of this stupendous learning. The assembly broke up for that day.

Next day Shekhar began his song. It was of that day when the pipings of love's flute startled for the first time the hushed air of the Vrinda forest. The shepherd women did not know who was the player or whence came the music. Sometimes it seemed to come from the heart of the south wind, and sometimes from the straying clouds of the hilltops. It came with a message of tryst from the land of the sunrise, and it floated from the verge of sunset with its sigh of sorrow. The stars seemed to be the stops of the instrument that flooded the dreams of the night with melody. The music seemed to burst all at once from all sides, from fields and groves, from the shady lanes and lonely roads, from the melting blue of the sky, from the shimmering green of the grass. They neither knew its meaning nor could they find words to give utterance to the desire of their hearts. Tears filled their eyes, and their life seemed to long for a death that would be its consummation.

Shekhar forgot his audience, forgot the trial of his strength with a rival. He stood alone amid his thoughts that rustled and quivered round him like leaves in a summer breeze, and sang the Song of the Flute. He had in his mind the vision of an image that had taken its shape from a shadow, and the echo of a faint tinkling sound of a distant footstep.

He took his seat. His hearers trembled with the sadness of an indefinable delight, immense and vague, and they forgot to applaud him. As this feeling died away Pundarik stood up before the throne and challenged his rival to define who was this Lover and who was the Beloved. He arrogantly looked around him, he smiled at his followers and then put the question again: "Who is Krishna, the lover, and who is Radha, the beloved?"

Then he began to analyse the roots of those names,--and various interpretations of their meanings. He brought before the bewildered audience all the intricacies of the different schools of metaphysics with consummate skill. Each letter of those names he divided from its fellow, and then pursued them with a relentless logic till they fell to the dust in confusion, to be caught up again and restored to a meaning never before imagined by the subtlest of word-mongers.

The pandits were in ecstasy; they applauded vociferously; and the crowd followed them, deluded into the certainty that they had witnessed, that day, the last shred of the curtains of Truth torn to pieces before their eyes by a prodigy of intellect. The performance of his tremendous feat so delighted them that they forgot to ask themselves if there was any truth behind it after all.

The king's mind was overwhelmed with wonder. The atmosphere was completely cleared of all illusion of music, and the vision of the world around seemed to be changed from its freshness of tender green to the solidity of a high road levelled and made hard with crushed stones.

To the people assembled their own poet appeared a mere boy in comparison with this giant, who walked with such case, knocking down difficulties at each step in the world of words and thoughts. It became evident to them for the first time that the poems Shekhar wrote were absurdly simple, and it must be a mere accident that they did not write them themselves. They were neither new, nor difficult, nor instructive, nor necessary.

The king tried to goad his poet with keen glances, silently inciting him to make a final effort. But Shekhar took no notice, and remained fixed to his seat.

The king in anger came down from his throne--took off his pearl chain and put it on Pundarik's head. Everybody in the hall cheered. From the upper balcony came a slight sound of the movements of rustling robes and waist-chains hung with golden bells. Shekhar rose from his seat and left the hall.

It was a dark night of waning moon. The poet Shekhar took down his MSS. from his shelves and heaped them on the floor. Some of them contained his earliest writings, which he had almost forgotten. He turned over the pages, reading passages here and there. They all seemed to him poor and trivial--mere words and childish rhymes!

One by one he tore his books to fragments, and threw them into a vessel containing fire, and said: "To thee, to thee, O my beauty, my fire! Thou hast been burning in my heart all these futile years. If my life were a piece of gold it would come out of its trial brighter, but it is a trodden turf of grass, and nothing remains of it but this handful of ashes."

The night wore on. Shekhar opened wide his windows. He spread upon his bed the white flowers that he loved, the jasmines, tuberoses and chrysanthemums, and brought into his bedroom all the lamps he had in his house and lighted them. Then mixing with honey the juice of some poisonous root he drank it and lay down on his bed.

Golden anklets tinkled in the passage outside the door, and a subtle perfume came into the room with the breeze.

The poet, with his eyes shut, said; "My lady, have you taken pity upon your servant at last and come to see him?"

The answer came in a sweet voice "My poet, I have come."

Shekhar opened his eyes--and saw before his bed the figure of a woman.

His sight was dim and blurred. And it seemed to him that the image made of a shadow that he had ever kept throned in the secret shrine of his heart had come into the outer world in his last moment to gaze upon his face.

The woman said; "I am the Princess Ajita."

The poet with a great effort sat up on his bed.

The princess whispered into his car: "The king has not done you justice. It was you who won at the combat, my poet, and I have come to crown you with the crown of victory."

She took the garland of flowers from her own neck, and put it on his hair, and the poet fell down upon his bed stricken by death.

GITANJALI

Song Offerings

A collection of prose translations made by the author from the original Bengali With an introduction by W. B. YEATS to WILLIAM ROTHENSTEIN

Introduction

A few days ago I said to a distinguished Bengali doctor of medicine, 'I know no German, yet if a translation of a German poet had moved me, I would go to the British Museum and find books in English that would tell me something of his life, and of the history of his thought. But though these prose translations from Rabindranath Tagore have stirred my blood as nothing has for years, I shall not know anything of his life, and of the movements of thought that have made them possible, if some Indian traveller will not tell me.' It seemed to him natural that I should be moved, for he said, "I read Rabindranath every day, to read one line of his is to forget all the troubles of the world." I said, "An Englishman living in London in the reign of Richard the Second had he been shown translations from Petrarch or from Dante, would have found no books to answer his questions, but would have questioned some Florentine banker or Lombard merchant as I question you. For all I know, so abundant and simple is this poetry, the new renaissance has been born in your country and I shall never know of it except by hearsay." He answered, "We have other poets, but none that are his equal; we call this the epoch of Rabindranath. No poet seems to me as famous in Europe as he is among us. He is as great in music as in poetry, and his songs are sung from the west of India into Burma wherever Bengali is spoken. He was already famous at nineteen when he wrote his first novel; and plays when he was but little older, are still played in

Calcutta. I so much admire the completeness of his life; when he was very young he wrote much of natural objects, he would sit all day in his garden; from his twenty-fifth year or so to his thirty-fifth perhaps, when he had a great sorrow, he wrote the most beautiful love poetry in our language'; and then he said with deep emotion, 'words can never express what I owed at seventeen to his love poetry. After that his art grew deeper, it became religious and philosophical; all the inspiration of mankind are in his hymns. He is the first among our saints who has not refused to live, but has spoken out of Life itself, and that is why we give him our love." I may have changed his well-chosen words in my memory but not his thought. "A little while ago he was to read divine service in one of our churches—we of the Brahma Samaj use your word 'church' in English—it was the largest in Calcutta and not only was it crowded, but the streets were all but impassable because of the people."

Other Indians came to see me and their reverence for this man sounded strange in our world, where we hide great and little things under the same veil of obvious comedy and half-serious depreciation. When we were making the cathedrals had we a like reverence for our great men? "Every morning at three—I know, for I have seen it"—one said to me, "he sits immovable in contemplation, and for two hours does not awake from his reverie upon the nature of God. His father, the Maha Rishi, would sometimes sit there all through the next day; once, upon a river, he fell into contemplation because of the beauty of the landscape, and the rowers waited for eight hours before they could continue their journey." He then told me of Mr. Tagore's family and how for generations great men have come out of its cradles. "Today," he said, "there are Gogonendranath and Abanindranath Tagore, who are artists; and Dwijendranath, Rabindranath's brother, who is a great philosopher. The squirrels come from the boughs and climb on to his knees and the birds alight upon his hands." I notice in these men's thought a sense of visible beauty and meaning as though they held that doctrine of Nietzsche that we must not believe in the moral or intellectual beauty which does not sooner or later impress itself upon physical things. I said, "In the East you know how to keep a family illustrious. The other day the curator of a museum pointed out to me a little dark-skinned man who was arranging their Chinese prints and said, 'That is the hereditary connoisseur of the Mikado, he is the fourteenth of his family to hold the post.'

He answered, "When Rabindranath was a boy he had all round him in his home literature and music.' I thought of the abundance, of the simplicity of the poems, and said, 'In your country is there much propagandist writing, much criticism? We have to do so much, especially in my own country, that our minds gradually cease to be creative, and yet we cannot help it. If our life was not a continual warfare, we would not have taste, we would not know what is good, we would not find hearers and readers. Four-fifths of our energy is spent in the quarrel with bad taste, whether in our own minds or in the minds of others." "I understand," he replied, "we too have our propagandist writing. In the villages they recite long mythological poems adapted from the Sanskrit in the Middle Ages, and they often insert passages telling the people that they must do their duties."

I have carried the manuscript of these translations about with me for days, reading it in railway trains, or on the top of omnibuses and in restaurants, and I have often had to close it lest some stranger would see how much it moved me. These lyrics— which are in the original, my Indians tell me, full of subtlety of rhythm, of untranslatable delicacies of colour, of metrical invention—display in their thought a world I have dreamed of all my live long. The work of a supreme culture, they yet appear as much the growth of the common soil as the grass and the rushes.

A tradition, where poetry and religion are the same thing, has passed through the centuries, gathering from learned and unlearned metaphor and emotion, and carried back again to the multitude the thought of the scholar and of the noble. If the civilization of Bengal remains unbroken, if that common mind which—as one divines—runs through all, is not, as with us, broken into a dozen minds that know nothing of each other, something even of what is most subtle in these verses will have come, in a few generations, to the beggar on the roads. When there was but one mind in England, Chaucer wrote his *Troilus and Cressida*, and thought he had written to be read, or to be read out—for our time was coming on apace—he was sung by minstrels for a while.

Rabindranath Tagore, like Chaucer's forerunners, writes music for his words, and one understands at every moment that he is so abundant, so spontaneous, so daring in his passion, so full of surprise, because he is doing something which has never seemed strange, unnatural, or in need of defence. These verses will not lie in little well-printed books upon ladies' tables, who turn the pages with indolent hands that they may sigh over a life without meaning, which is yet all they can know of life, or be carried by students at the university to be laid aside when the work of life begins, but, as the generations pass, travellers will hum them on the highway and men rowing upon the rivers. Lovers, while they await one another, shall find, in murmuring them, this love of God a magic gulf wherein their own more bitter passion may bathe and renew its youth. At every moment the heart of this poet flows outward to these without derogation or condescension, for it has known that they will understand; and it has filled itself with the circumstance of their lives.

The traveller in the read-brown clothes that he wears that dust may not show upon him, the girl searching in her bed for the petals fallen from the wreath of her royal lover, the servant or the bride awaiting the master's home-coming in the empty house, are images of the heart turning to God. Flowers and rivers, the blowing of conch shells, the heavy rain of the Indian July, or the moods of that heart in union or in separation; and a man sitting in a boat upon a river playing lute, like one of those figures full of mysterious meaning in a Chinese picture, is God Himself. A whole people, a whole civilization, immeasurably strange to us, seems to have been taken up into this imagination; and yet we are not moved because of its strangeness, but because we have met our own image, as though we had walked in Rossetti's willow wood, or heard, perhaps for the first time in literature, our voice as in a dream.

Since the Renaissance the writing of European saints—however familiar their metaphor and the general structure of their thought—has ceased to hold our attention. We know that we must at last forsake the world, and we are accustomed in moments of weariness or exaltation to consider a voluntary forsaking; but how can we, who have read so much poetry, seen so many paintings, listened to so much music, where the cry of the flesh and the cry of the soul seems one, forsake it harshly and rudely? What have we in common with St. Bernard covering his eyes that they may not dwell upon the beauty of the lakes of Switzerland, or with the violent rhetoric of the Book of Revelations? We would, if we might, find, as in this book, words full of courtesy. "I have got my leave. Bid me farewell, my brothers! I bow to you all and take my departure. Here I give back the keys of my door—and I give up all claims to my house. I only ask for last kind words from you. We were neighbours for long, but I received more than I could give. Now the day has dawned and the lamp that lit my dark corner is out. A summons has come and I am ready for my journey."

And it is our own mood, when it is furthest from 'a Kempis or John of the Cross, that cries, 'And because I love this life, I know I shall love death as well.' Yet it is not only in our thoughts of the parting that this book fathoms all. We had not known that we loved God, hardly it may be that we believed in Him; yet looking backward upon our life we discover, in our exploration of the pathways of woods, in our delight in the lonely places of hills, in that mysterious claim that we have made, unavailingly on the woman that we have loved, the emotion that created this insidious sweetness. 'Entering my heart unbidden even as one of the common crowd, unknown to me, my king, thou didst press the signet of eternity upon many a fleeting moment.' This is no longer the sanctity of the cell and of the scourge; being but a lifting up, as it were, into a greater intensity of the mood of the painter, painting the dust and the sunlight, and we go for a like voice to St. Francis and to William Blake who have seemed so alien in our violent history.

We write long books where no page perhaps has any quality to make writing a pleasure, being confident in some general design, just as we fight and make money and fill our heads with politics—all dull things in the doing—while Mr. Tagore, like the Indian civilization itself, has been content to discover the soul and surrender himself to its spontaneity. He often seems to contrast life with that of those who have loved more after our fashion, and have more seeming weight in the world, and always humbly as though he were only sure his way is best for him: "Men going home glance at me and smile and fill me with shame. I sit like a beggar maid, drawing my skirt over my face, and when they ask me, what it is I want, I drop my eyes and answer them not."

At another time, remembering how his life had once a different shape, he will say, 'Many an hour I have spent in the strife of the good and the evil, but now it is the pleasure of my playmate of the empty days to draw my heart on to him; and I know not why this sudden call to what useless inconsequence.' An innocence, a simplicity that one does not find elsewhere in literature makes the birds and the leaves seem as near to him as they are near to children, and the changes of the seasons great events as before our thoughts had arisen between them and us. At times I wonder if he has it from the literature of Bengal or from religion, and at other times, remembering the birds alighting on his brother's hands, I find pleasure in thinking it hereditary, a mystery that was growing through the centuries like the courtesy of a Tristan or a Pelanore.

Indeed, when he is speaking of children, so much a part of himself this quality seems, one is not certain that he is not also speaking of the saints, "They build their houses with sand and they play with empty shells. With withered leaves they weave their boats and smilingly float them on the vast deep. Children have their play on the seashore of worlds. They know not how to swim, they know not how to cast nets. Pearl fishers dive for pearls, merchants sail in their ships, while children gather pebbles and scatter them again. They seek not for hidden treasures, they know not how to cast nets."

W.B. YEATS September 1912

GITANJALI

1

Thou hast made me endless, such is thy pleasure. This frail vessel thou emptiest again and again, and fillest it ever with fresh life.

This little flute of a reed thou hast carried over hills and dales, and hast breathed through it melodies eternally new.

At the immortal touch of thy hands my little heart loses its limits in joy and gives birth to utterance ineffable.

Thy infinite gifts come to me only on these very small hands of mine. Ages pass, and still thou pourest, and still there is room to fill.

2

When thou commandest me to sing it seems that my heart would break with pride; and I look to thy face, and tears come to my eyes.

All that is harsh and dissonant in my life melts into one sweet harmony—and my adoration spreads wings like a glad bird on its flight across the sea.

I know thou takest pleasure in my singing. I know that only as a singer I come before thy presence.

I touch by the edge of the far-spreading wing of my song thy feet which I could never aspire to reach.

Drunk with the joy of singing I forget myself and call thee friend who art my lord.

3

I know not how thou singest, my master! I ever listen in silent amazement.

The light of thy music illumines the world. The life breath of thy music runs from sky to sky. The holy stream of thy music breaks through all stony obstacles and rushes on.

My heart longs to join in thy song, but vainly struggles for a voice. I would speak, but speech breaks not into song, and I cry out baffled. Ah, thou hast made my heart captive in the endless meshes of thy music, my master!

4

Life of my life, I shall ever try to keep my body pure, knowing that thy living touch is upon all my limbs.

I shall ever try to keep all untruths out from my thoughts, knowing that thou art that truth which has kindled the light of reason in my mind.

I shall ever try to drive all evils away from my heart and keep my love in flower, knowing that thou hast thy seat in the inmost shrine of my heart.

And it shall be my endeavour to reveal thee in my actions, knowing it is thy power gives me strength to act.

5

I ask for a moment's indulgence to sit by thy side. The works that I have in hand I will finish afterwards.

Away from the sight of thy face my heart knows no rest nor respite, and my work becomes an endless toil in a shoreless sea of toil.

Today the summer has come at my window with its sighs and murmurs; and the bees are plying their minstrelsy at the court of the flowering grove.

Now it is time to sit quite, face to face with thee, and to sing dedication of life in this silent and overflowing leisure.

6

Pluck this little flower and take it, delay not! I fear lest it droop and drop into the dust.

I may not find a place in thy garland, but honour it with a touch of pain from thy hand and pluck it. I fear lest the day end before I am aware, and the time of offering go by.

Though its colour be not deep and its smell be faint, use this flower in thy service and pluck it while there is time.

7

My song has put off her adornments. She has no pride of dress and decoration. Ornaments would mar our union; they would come between thee and me; their jingling would drown thy whispers.

My poet's vanity dies in shame before thy sight. O master poet, I have sat down at thy feet. Only let me make my life simple and straight, like a flute of reed for thee to fill with music.

8

The child who is decked with prince's robes and who has jewelled chains round his neck loses all pleasure in his play; his dress hampers him at every step.

In fear that it may be frayed, or stained with dust he keeps himself from the world, and is afraid even to move.

Mother, it is no gain, thy bondage of finery, if it keep one shut off from the healthful dust of the earth, if it rob one of the right of entrance to the great fair of common human life.

9

O Fool, try to carry thyself upon thy own shoulders! O beggar, to come beg at thy own door!

Leave all thy burdens on his hands who can bear all, and never look behind in regret.

Thy desire at once puts out the light from the lamp it touches with its breath. It is unholy—take not thy gifts through its unclean hands. Accept only what is offered by sacred love.

10

Here is thy footstool and there rest thy feet where live the poorest, and lowliest, and lost.

When I try to bow to thee, my obeisance cannot reach down to the depth where thy feet rest among the poorest, and lowliest, and lost.

Pride can never approach to where thou walkest in the clothes of the humble among the poorest, and lowliest, and lost.

My heart can never find its way to where thou keepest company with the companionless among the poorest, the lowliest, and the lost.

11

Leave this chanting and singing and telling of beads! Whom dost thou worship in this lonely dark corner of a temple with doors all shut? Open thine eyes and see thy God is not before thee!

He is there where the tiller is tilling the hard ground and where the pathmaker is breaking stones. He is with them in sun and in shower, and his garment is covered with dust. Put of thy holy mantle and even like him come down on the dusty soil!

Deliverance? Where is this deliverance to be found? Our master himself has joyfully taken upon him the bonds of creation; he is bound with us all for ever.

Come out of thy meditations and leave aside thy flowers and incense! What harm is there if thy clothes become tattered and stained? Meet him and stand by him in toil and in sweat of thy brow.

12

The time that my journey takes is long and the way of it long.

I came out on the chariot of the first gleam of light, and pursued my voyage through the wildernesses of worlds leaving my track on many a star and planet.

It is the most distant course that comes nearest to thyself, and that training is the most intricate which leads to the utter simplicity of a tune.

The traveller has to knock at every alien door to come to his own, and one has to wander through all the outer worlds to reach the innermost shrine at the end.

My eyes strayed far and wide before I shut them and said 'Here art thou!'

The question and the cry 'Oh, where?' melt into tears of a thousand streams and deluge the world with the flood of the assurance 'I am!'

13

The song that I came to sing remains unsung to this day.

I have spent my days in stringing and in unstringing my instrument.

The time has not come true, the words have not been rightly set; only there is the agony of wishing in my heart.

The blossom has not opened; only the wind is sighing by.

I have not seen his face, nor have I listened to his voice; only I have heard his gentle footsteps from the road before my house.

The livelong day has passed in spreading his seat on the floor; but the lamp has not been lit and I cannot ask him into my house.

I live in the hope of meeting with him; but this meeting is not yet.

14

My desires are many and my cry is pitiful, but ever didst thou save me by hard refusals; and this strong mercy has been wrought into my life through and through.

Day by day thou art making me worthy of the simple, great gifts that thou gavest to me unasked—this sky and the light, this body and the life and the mind—saving me from perils of overmuch desire.

There are times when I languidly linger and times when I awaken and hurry in search of my goal; but cruelly thou hidest thyself from before me.

Day by day thou art making me worthy of thy full acceptance by refusing me ever and anon, saving me from perils of weak, uncertain desire.

15

I am here to sing thee songs. In this hall of thine I have a corner seat.

In thy world I have no work to do; my useless life can only break out in tunes without a purpose.

When the hour strikes for thy silent worship at the dark temple of midnight, command me, my master, to stand before thee to sing.

When in the morning air the golden harp is tuned, honour me, commanding my presence.

16

I have had my invitation to this world's festival, and thus my life has been blessed. My eyes have seen and my ears have heard.

It was my part at this feast to play upon my instrument, and I have done all I could.

Now, I ask, has the time come at last when I may go in and see thy face and offer thee my silent salutation?

17

I am only waiting for love to give myself up at last into his hands. That is why it is so late and why I have been guilty of such omissions.

They come with their laws and their codes to bind me fast; but I evade them ever, for I am only waiting for love to give myself up at last into his hands.

People blame me and call me heedless; I doubt not they are right in their blame.

The market day is over and work is all done for the busy. Those who came to call me in vain have gone back in anger. I am only waiting for love to give myself up at last into his hands.

18

Clouds heap upon clouds and it darkens. Ah, love, why dost thou let me wait outside at the door all alone?

In the busy moments of the noontide work I am with the crowd, but on this dark lonely day it is only for thee that I hope.

If thou showest me not thy face, if thou leavest me wholly aside, I know not how I am to pass these long, rainy hours.

I keep gazing on the far-away gloom of the sky, and my heart wanders wailing with the restless wind.

19

If thou speakest not I will fill my heart with thy silence and endure it. I will keep still and wait like the night with starry vigil and its head bent low with patience.

The morning will surely come, the darkness will vanish, and thy voice pour down in golden streams breaking through the sky.

Then thy words will take wing in songs from every one of my birds' nests, and thy melodies will break forth in flowers in all my forest groves.

20

On the day when the lotus bloomed, alas, my mind was straying, and I knew it not. My basket was empty and the flower remained unheeded.

Only now and again a sadness fell upon me, and I started up from my dream and felt a sweet trace of a strange fragrance in the south wind.

That vague sweetness made my heart ache with longing and it

21

I must launch out my boat. The languid hours pass by on the shore—Alas for me!

The spring has done its flowering and taken leave. And now with the burden of faded futile flowers I wait and linger.

The waves have become clamorous, and upon the bank in the shady lane the yellow leaves flutter and fall.

What emptiness do you gaze upon! Do you not feel a thrill passing through the air with the notes of the far-away song floating from the other shore?

22

In the deep shadows of the rainy July, with secret steps, thou walkest, silent as night, eluding all watchers.

Today the morning has closed its eyes, heedless of the insistent calls of the loud east wind, and a thick veil has been drawn over the ever-wakeful blue sky.

The woodlands have hushed their songs, and doors are all shut at every house. Thou art the solitary wayfarer in this deserted street. Oh my only friend, my best beloved, the gates are open in my house—do not pass by like a dream.

23

Art thou abroad on this stormy night on thy journey of love, my friend? The sky groans like one in despair.

I have no sleep tonight. Ever and again I open my door and look out on the darkness, my friend!

I can see nothing before me. I wonder where lies thy path!

By what dim shore of the ink-black river, by what far edge of the frowning forest, through what mazy depth of gloom art thou threading thy course to come to me, my friend?

24

If the day is done, if birds sing no more, if the wind has flagged tired, then draw the veil of darkness thick upon me, even as thou hast wrapt the earth with the coverlet of sleep and tenderly closed the petals of the drooping lotus at dusk.

From the traveller, whose sack of provisions is empty before the voyage is ended, whose garment is torn and dust - laden, whose strength is exhausted, remove shame and poverty, and renew his life like a flower under the cover of thy kindly night.

25

In the night of weariness let me give myself up to sleep without struggle, resting my trust upon thee.

Let me not force my flagging spirit into a poor preparation for thy worship.

It is thou who drawest the veil of night upon the tired eyes of the day to renew its sight in a fresher gladness of awakening.

26

He came and sat by my side but I woke not. What a cursed sleep it was, O miserable me!

He came when the night was still; he had his harp in his hands, and my dreams became resonant with its melodies.

Alas, why are my nights all thus lost? Ah, why do I ever miss his sight whose breath touches my sleep?

27

Light, oh where is the light? Kindle it with the burning fire of desire!

There is the lamp but never a flicker of a flame—is such thy fate, my heart? Ah, death were better by far for thee!

Misery knocks at thy door, and her message is that thy lord is wakeful, and he calls thee to the love-tryst through the darkness of night.

The sky is overcast with clouds and the rain is ceaseless. I know not what this is that stirs in me—I know not its meaning.

A moment's flash of lightning drags down a deeper gloom on my sight, and my heart gropes for the path to where the music of the night calls me.

Light, oh where is the light! Kindle it with the burning fire of desire! It thunders and the wind rushes screaming through the void. The night is black as a black stone. Let not the hours pass by in the dark. Kindle the lamp of love with thy life.

28

Obstinate are the trammels, but my heart aches when I try to break them.

Freedom is all I want, but to hope for it I feel ashamed.

I am certain that priceless wealth is in thee, and that thou art my best friend, but I have not the heart to sweep away the tinsel that fills my room.

The shroud that covers me is a shroud of dust and death; I hate it, yet hug it in love.

My debts are large, my failures great, my shame secret and heavy; yet when I come to ask for my good, I quake in fear lest my prayer be granted.

29

He whom I enclose with my name is weeping in this dungeon. I am ever busy building this wall all around; and as this wall goes up into the sky day by day I lose sight of my true being in its dark shadow.

I take pride in this great wall, and I plaster it with dust and sand lest a least hole should be left in this name; and for all the care I take I lose sight of my true being.

30

I came out alone on my way to my tryst. But who is this that follows me in the silent dark?

I move aside to avoid his presence but I escape him not.

He makes the dust rise from the earth with his swagger; he adds his loud voice to every word that I utter.

He is my own little self, my lord, he knows no shame; but I am ashamed to come to thy door in his company.

31

'Prisoner, tell me, who was it that bound you?'

'It was my master,' said the prisoner. 'I thought I could outdo everybody in the world in wealth and power, and I amassed in my own treasure-house the money due to my king. When sleep overcame me I lay upon the bed that was for my lord, and on waking up I found I was a prisoner in my own treasure-house.'

'Prisoner, tell me, who was it that wrought this unbreakable chain?'

'It was I,' said the prisoner, 'who forged this chain very carefully. I thought my invincible power would hold the world captive leaving me in a freedom undisturbed. Thus night and day I worked at the chain with huge fires and cruel hard strokes. When at last the work was done and the links were complete and unbreakable, I found that it held me in its grip.'

32

By all means they try to hold me secure who love me in this world. But it is otherwise with thy love which is greater than theirs, and thou keepest me free.

Lest I forget them they never venture to leave me alone. But day passes by after day and thou art not seen.

If I call not thee in my prayers, if I keep not thee in my heart, thy love for me still waits for my love.

33

When it was day they came into my house and said, "We shall only take the smallest room here."

They said, "We shall help you in the worship of your God and humbly accept only our own share in his grace"; and then they took their seat in a corner and they sat quiet and meek.

But in the darkness of night I find they break into my sacred shrine, strong and turbulent, and snatch with unholy greed the offerings from God's altar.

34

Let only that little be left of me whereby I may name thee my all.

Let only that little be left of my will whereby I may feel thee on every side, and come to thee in everything, and offer to thee my love every moment.

Let only that little be left of me whereby I may never hide thee.

Let only that little of my fetters be left whereby I am bound with thy will, and thy purpose is carried out in my life—and that is the fetter of thy love.

35

Where the mind is without fear and the head is held high;

Where knowledge is free;

Where the world has not been broken up into fragments by narrow domestic walls;

Where words come out from the depth of truth;

Where tireless striving stretches its arms towards perfection;

Where the clear stream of reason has not lost its way into the dreary desert sand of dead habit;

Where the mind is led forward by thee into ever-widening thought and action—

Into that heaven of freedom, my Father, let my country awake.

36

This is my prayer to thee, my lord—strike, strike at the root of penury in my heart.

Give me the strength lightly to bear my joys and sorrows.

Give me the strength to make my love fruitful in service.

Give me the strength never to disown the poor or bend my knees before insolent might.

Give me the strength to raise my mind high above daily trifles.

And give me the strength to surrender my strength to thy will with love.

37

I thought that my voyage had come to its end at the last limit of my power,—that the path before me was closed, that provisions were exhausted and the time come to take shelter in a silent obscurity.

But I find that thy will knows no end in me. And when old words die out on the tongue, new melodies break forth from the heart; and where the old tracks are lost, new country is revealed with its wonders.

38

That I want thee, only thee—let my heart repeat without end. All desires that distract me, day and night, are false and empty to the core.

As the night keeps hidden in its gloom the petition for light, even thus in the depth of my unconsciousness rings the cry—'I want thee, only thee'.

As the storm still seeks its end in peace when it strikes against peace with all its might, even thus my rebellion strikes against thy love and still its cry is—'I want thee, only thee'.

39

When the heart is hard and parched up, come upon me with a shower of mercy.

When grace is lost from life, come with a burst of song.

When tumultuous work raises its din on all sides shutting me out from beyond, come to me, my lord of silence, with thy peace and rest.

When my beggarly heart sits crouched, shut up in a corner, break open the door, my king, and come with the ceremony of a king.

When desire blinds the mind with delusion and dust, O thou holy one, thou wakeful, come with thy light and thy thunder.

40

The rain has held back for days and days, my God, in my arid heart. The horizon is fiercely naked—not the thinnest cover of a soft cloud, not the vaguest hint of a distant cool shower.

Send thy angry storm, dark with death, if it is thy wish, and with lashes of lightning startle the sky from end to end.

But call back, my lord, call back this pervading silent heat, still and keen and cruel, burning the heart with dire despair.

Let the cloud of grace bend low from above like the tearful look of the mother on the day of the father's wrath.

41

Where dost thou stand behind them all, my lover, hiding thyself in the shadows? They push thee and pass thee by on the dusty road, taking thee for naught. I wait here weary hours spreading my offerings for thee, while passers-by come and take my flowers, one by one, and my basket is nearly empty.

The morning time is past, and the noon. In the shade of evening my eyes are drowsy with sleep. Men going home glance at me and smile and fill me with shame. I sit like a beggar maid, drawing my skirt over my face, and when they ask me, what it is I want, I drop my eyes and answer them not.

Oh, how, indeed, could I tell them that for thee I wait, and that thou hast promised to come. How could I utter for shame that I keep for my dowry this poverty. Ah, I hug this pride in the secret of my heart.

I sit on the grass and gaze upon the sky and dream of the sudden splendour of thy coming—all the lights ablaze, golden pennons flying over thy car, and they at the roadside standing agape, when they see thee come down from thy seat to raise me from the dust, and set at thy side this ragged beggar girl a-tremble with shame and pride, like a creeper in a summer breeze.

But time glides on and still no sound of the wheels of thy chariot. Many a procession passes by with noise and shouts and glamour of glory. Is it only thou who wouldst stand in the shadow silent and behind them all? And only I who would wait and weep and wear out my heart in vain longing?

42

Early in the day it was whispered that we should sail in a boat, only thou and I, and never a soul in the world would know of this our pilgrimage to no country and to no end.

In that shoreless ocean, at thy silently listening smile my songs would swell in melodies, free as waves, free from all bondage of words.

Is the time not come yet? Are there works still to do? Lo, the evening has come down upon the shore and in the fading light the seabirds come flying to their nests.

Who knows when the chains will be off, and the boat, like the last glimmer of sunset, vanish into the night?

43

The day was when I did not keep myself in readiness for thee; and entering my heart unbidden even as one of the common crowd, unknown to me, my king, thou didst press the signet of eternity upon many a fleeting moment of my life.

And today when by chance I light upon them and see thy signature, I find they have lain scattered in the dust mixed with the memory of joys and sorrows of my trivial days forgotten.

Thou didst not turn in contempt from my childish play among dust, and the steps that I heard in my playroom are the same that are echoing from star to star.

44

This is my delight, thus to wait and watch at the wayside where shadow chases light and the rain comes in the wake of the summer.

Messengers, with tidings from unknown skies, greet me and speed along the road. My heart is glad within, and the breath of the passing breeze is sweet.

From dawn till dusk I sit here before my door, and I know that of a sudden the happy moment will arrive when I shall see.

In the meanwhile I smile and I sing all alone. In the meanwhile the air is filling with the perfume of promise.

45

Have you not heard his silent steps?

He comes, comes, ever comes.

Every moment and every age, every day and every night he comes, comes, ever comes.

Many a song have I sung in many a mood of mind, but all their notes have always proclaimed, 'He comes, comes, ever comes.'

In the fragrant days of sunny April through the forest path he comes, comes, ever comes.

In the rainy gloom of July nights on the thundering chariot of clouds he comes, comes, ever comes.

In sorrow after sorrow it is his steps that press upon my heart, and it is the golden touch of his feet that makes my joy to shine.

46

I know not from what distant time thou art ever coming nearer to meet me. Thy sun and stars can never keep thee hidden from me for aye.

In many a morning and eve thy footsteps have been heard and thy messenger has come within my heart and called me in secret.

I know not only why today my life is all astir, and a feeling of tremulous joy is passing through my heart.

It is as if the time were come to wind up my work, and I feel in the air a faint smell of thy sweet presence.

47

The night is nearly spent waiting for him in vain. I fear lest in the morning he suddenly come to my door when I have fallen asleep wearied out. Oh friends, leave the way open to him— forbid him not.

If the sounds of his steps does not wake me, do not try to rouse me, I pray. I wish not to be called from my sleep by the clamorous choir of birds, by the riot of wind at the festival of morning light. Let me sleep undisturbed even if my lord comes of a sudden to my door.

Ah, my sleep, precious sleep, which only waits for his touch to vanish. Ah, my closed eyes that would open their lids only to the light of his smile when he stands before me like a dream emerging from darkness of sleep.

Let him appear before my sight as the first of all lights and all forms. The first thrill of joy to my awakened soul let it come from his glance. And let my return to myself be immediate return to him.

48

The morning sea of silence broke into ripples of bird songs; and the flowers were all merry by the roadside; and the wealth of gold was scattered through the rift of the clouds while we busily went on our way and paid no heed.

We sang no glad songs nor played; we went not to the village for barter; we spoke not a word nor smiled; we lingered not on the way. We quickened our pace more and more as the time sped by.

The sun rose to the mid sky and doves cooed in the shade. Withered leaves danced and whirled in the hot air of noon. The shepherd boy drowsed and dreamed in the shadow of the banyan tree, and I laid myself down by the water and stretched my tired limbs on the grass.

My companions laughed at me in scorn; they held their heads high and hurried on; they never looked back nor rested; they vanished in the distant blue haze. They crossed many meadows and hills, and passed through strange, far-away countries. All honour to you, heroic host of the interminable path! Mockery and reproach pricked me to rise, but found no response in me. I gave myself up for lost in the depth of a glad humiliation—in the shadow of a dim delight.

The repose of the sun-embroidered green gloom slowly spread over my heart. I forgot for what I had travelled, and I surrendered my mind without struggle to the maze of shadows and songs.

At last, when I woke from my slumber and opened my eyes, I saw thee standing by me, flooding my sleep with thy smile. How I had feared that the path was long and wearisome, and the struggle to reach thee was hard!

49

You came down from your throne and stood at my cottage door.

I was singing all alone in a corner, and the melody caught your ear. You came down and stood at my cottage door.

Masters are many in your hall, and songs are sung there at all hours. But the simple carol of this novice struck at your love. One plaintive little strain mingled with the great music of the world, and with a flower for a prize you came down and stopped at my cottage door.

50

I had gone a - begging from door to door in the village path, when thy golden chariot appeared in the distance like a gorgeous dream and I wondered who was this King of all kings!

My hopes rose high and methought my evil days were at an end, and I stood waiting for alms to be given unasked and for wealth scattered on all sides in the dust.

The chariot stopped where I stood. Thy glance fell on me and thou camest down with a smile. I felt that the luck of my life had come at last. Then of a sudden thou didst hold out thy right hand and say 'What hast thou to give to me?'

Ah, what a kingly jest was it to open thy palm to a beggar to beg! I was confused and stood undecided, and then from my wallet I slowly took out the least little grain of corn and gave it to thee.

But how great my surprise when at the day's end I emptied my bag on the floor to find a least little gram of gold among the poor heap. I bitterly wept and wished that I had had the heart to give thee my all.

51

The night darkened. Our day's works had been done. We thought that the last guest had arrived for the night and the doors in the village were all shut. Only some said the king was to come. We laughed and said 'No, it cannot be!'

It seemed there were knocks at the door and we said it was nothing but the wind. We put out the lamps and lay down to sleep. Only some said, 'It is the messenger!' We laughed and said 'No, it must be the wind!'

There came a sound in the dead of the night. We sleepily thought it was the distant thunder. The earth shook, the walls rocked, and it troubled us in our sleep. Only some said it was the sound of wheels. We said in a drowsy murmur, 'No, it must be the rumbling of clouds!'

The night was still dark when the drum sounded. The voice came 'Wake up! delay not!' We pressed our hands on our hearts and shuddered with fear. Some said, 'Lo, there is the king's flag!' We stood up on our feet and cried 'There is no time for delay!'

The king has come—but where are lights, where are wreaths? Where is the throne to seat him? Oh, shame! Oh utter shame! Where is the hall, the decorations? Someone has said, 'Vain is this cry! Greet him with empty hands, lead him into thy rooms all bare!'

Open the doors, let the conch-shells be sounded! In the depth of the night has come the king of our dark, dreary house. The thunder roars in the sky. The darkness shudders with lightning. Bring out thy tattered piece of mat and spread it in the courtyard. With the storm has come of a sudden our king of the fearful night.

52

I thought I should ask of thee—but I dared not—the rose wreath thou hadst on thy neck. Thus I waited for the morning, when thou didst depart, to find a few fragments on the bed. And like a beggar I searched in the dawn only for a stray petal or two.

Ah me, what is it I find? What token left of thy love? It is no flower, no spices, no vase of perfumed water. It is thy mighty sword, flashing as a flame, heavy as a bolt of thunder. The young light of morning comes through the window and spreads itself upon thy bed. The morning bird twitters and asks, 'Woman, what hast thou got?' No, it is no flower, nor spices, nor vase of perfumed water—it is thy dreadful sword.

I sit and muse in wonder, what gift is this of thine. I can find no place to hide it. I am ashamed to wear it, frail as I am, and it hurts me when I press it to my bosom. Yet shall I bear in my heart this honour of the burden of pain, this gift of thine.

From now there shall be no fear left for me in this world, and thou shalt be victorious in all my strife. Thou hast left death for my companion and I shall crown him with my life. Thy sword is with me to cut asunder my bonds, and there shall be no fear left for me in the world.

From now I leave off all petty decorations. Lord of my heart, no more shall there be for me waiting and weeping in corners, no more coyness and sweetness of demeanour. Thou hast given me thy sword for adornment. No more doll's decorations for me!

53

Beautiful is thy wristlet, decked with stars and cunningly wrought in myriad-coloured jewels. But more beautiful to me thy sword with its curve of lightning like the outspread wings of the divine bird of Vishnu, perfectly poised in the angry red light of the sunset.

It quivers like the one last response of life in ecstasy of pain at the final stroke of death; it shines like the pure flame of being burning up earthly sense with one fierce flash.

Beautiful is thy wristlet, decked with starry gems; but thy sword, O lord of thunder, is wrought with uttermost beauty, terrible to behold or think of.

54

I asked nothing from thee; I uttered not my name to thine ear. When thou took'st thy leave I stood silent. I was alone by the well where the shadow of the tree fell aslant, and the women had gone home with their brown earthen pitchers full to the brim. They called me and shouted, 'Come with us, the morning is wearing on to noon.' But I languidly lingered awhile lost in the midst of vague musings.

I heard not thy steps as thou camest. Thine eyes were sad when they fell on me; thy voice was tired as thou spokest low—'Ah, I am a thirsty traveller.' I started up from my day-dreams and poured water from my jar on thy joined palms. The leaves rustled overhead; the cuckoo sang from the unseen dark, and perfume of *babla* flowers came from the bend of the road.

I stood speechless with shame when my name thou didst ask. Indeed, what had I done for thee to keep me in remembrance? But the memory that I could give water to thee to allay thy thirst will cling to my heart and enfold it in sweetness. The morning hour is late, the bird sings in weary notes, *neem* leaves rustle overhead and I sit and think and think.

55

Languor is upon your heart and the slumber is still on your eyes.

Has not the word come to you that the flower is reigning in splendour among thorns? Wake, oh awaken! let not the time pass in vain!

At the end of the stony path, in the country of virgin solitude, my friend is sitting all alone. Deceive him not. Wake, oh awaken!

What if the sky pants and trembles with the heat of the midday sun—what if the burning sand spreads its mantle of thirst—

Is there no joy in the deep of your heart? At every footfall of yours, will not the harp of the road break out in sweet music of pain?

56

Thus it is that thy joy in me is so full. Thus it is that thou hast come down to me. O thou lord of all heavens, where would be thy love if I were not?

Thou hast taken me as thy partner of all this wealth. In my heart is the endless play of thy delight. In my life thy will is ever taking shape.

And for this, thou who art the King of kings hast decked thyself in beauty to captivate my heart. And for this thy love loses itself in the love of thy lover, and there art thou seen in the perfect union of two.

57

Light, my light, the world-filling light, the eye-kissing light, heart-sweetening light!

Ah, the light dances, my darling, at the centre of my life; the light strikes, my darling, the chords of my love; the sky opens, the wind runs wild, laughter passes over the earth.

The butterflies spread their sails on the sea of light. Lilies and jasmines surge up on the crest of the waves of light.

The light is shattered into gold on every cloud, my darling, and it scatters gems in profusion.

Mirth spreads from leaf to leaf, my darling, and gladness without measure. The heaven's river has drowned its banks and the flood of joy is abroad.

58

Let all the strains of joy mingle in my last song—the joy that makes the earth flow over in the riotous excess of the grass, the joy that sets the twin brothers, life and death, dancing over the wide world, the joy that sweeps in with the tempest, shaking and waking all life with laughter, the joy that sits still with its tears on the open red lotus of pain, and the joy that throws everything it has upon the dust, and knows not a word.

59

Yes, I know, this is nothing but thy love, O beloved of my heart— this golden light that dances upon the leaves, these idle clouds sailing across the sky, this passing breeze leaving its coolness upon my forehead.

The morning light has flooded my eyes—this is thy message to my heart. Thy face is bent from above, thy eyes look down on my eyes, and my heart has touched thy feet.

60

On the seashore of endless worlds children meet. The infinite sky is motionless overhead and the restless water is boisterous. On the seashore of endless worlds the children meet with shouts and dances.

They build their houses with sand and they play with empty shells. With withered leaves they weave their boats and smilingly float them on the vast deep. Children have their play on the seashore of worlds.

They know not how to swim, they know not how to cast nets. Pearl fishers dive for pearls, merchants sail in their ships, while children gather pebbles and scatter them again. They seek not for hidden treasures, they know not how to cast nets.

The sea surges up with laughter and pale gleams the smile of the sea beach. Death-dealing waves sing meaningless ballads to the children, even like a mother while rocking her baby's cradle. The sea plays with children, and pale gleams the smile of the sea beach.

On the seashore of endless worlds children meet. Tempest roams in the pathless sky, ships get wrecked in the trackless water, death is abroad and children play. On the seashore of endless worlds is the great meeting of children.

61

The sleep that flits on baby's eyes—does anybody know from where it comes? Yes, there is a rumour that it has its dwelling there, in the fairy village among shadows of the forest dimly lit with glow-worms, there hang two timid buds of enchantment. From there it comes to kiss baby's eyes.

The smile that flickers on baby's lips when he sleeps—does anybody know where it was born? Yes, there is a rumour that a young pale beam of a crescent moon touched the edge of a vanishing autumn cloud, and there the smile was first born in the dream of a dew-washed morning—the smile that flickers on baby's lips when he sleeps.

The sweet, soft freshness that blooms on baby's limbs—does anybody know where it was hidden so long? Yes, when the mother was a young girl it lay pervading her heart in tender and silent mystery of love—the sweet, soft freshness that has bloomed on baby's limbs.

62

When I bring to you coloured toys, my child, I understand why there is such a play of colours on clouds, on water, and why flowers are painted in tints—when I give coloured toys to you, my child.

When I sing to make you dance I truly now why there is music in leaves, and why waves send their chorus of voices to the heart of the listening earth—when I sing to make you dance.

When I bring sweet things to your greedy hands I know why there is honey in the cup of the flowers and why fruits are secretly filled with sweet juice—when I bring sweet things to your greedy hands.

When I kiss your face to make you smile, my darling, I surely understand what pleasure streams from the sky in morning light, and what delight that is that is which the summer breeze brings to my body—when I kiss you to make you smile.

63

Thou hast made me known to friends whom I knew not. Thou hast given me seats in homes not my own. Thou hast brought the distant near and made a brother of the stranger.

I am uneasy at heart when I have to leave my accustomed shelter; I forget that there abides the old in the new, and that there also thou abidest.

Through birth and death, in this world or in others, wherever thou leadest me it is thou, the same, the one companion of my endless life who ever linkest my heart with bonds of joy to the unfamiliar.

When one knows thee, then alien there is none, then no door is shut. Oh, grant me my prayer that I may never lose the bliss of the touch of the one in the play of many.

64

On the slope of the desolate river among tall grasses I asked her, 'Maiden, where do you go shading your lamp with your mantle? My house is all dark and lonesome—lend me your light!' she raised her dark eyes for a moment and looked at my face through the dusk. 'I have come to the river,' she said, 'to float my lamp on the stream when the daylight wanes in the west.' I stood alone among tall grasses and watched the timid flame of her lamp uselessly drifting in the tide.

In the silence of gathering night I asked her, 'Maiden, your lights are all lit—then where do you go with your lamp? My house is all dark and lonesome—lend me your light.' She raised her dark eyes on my face and stood for a moment doubtful. 'I have come,' she said at last, 'to dedicate my lamp to the sky.' I stood and watched her light uselessly burning in the void.

In the moonless gloom of midnight I ask her, 'Maiden, what is your quest, holding the lamp near your heart? My house is all dark and lonesome—lend me your light.' She stopped for a minute and thought and gazed at my face in the dark. 'I have brought my light,' she said, 'to join the carnival of lamps.' I stood and watched her little lamp uselessly lost among lights.

65

What divine drink wouldst thou have, my God, from this overflowing cup of my life?

My poet, is it thy delight to see thy creation through my eyes and to stand at the portals of my ears silently to listen to thine own eternal harmony?

Thy world is weaving words in my mind and thy joy is adding music to them. Thou givest thyself to me in love and then feelest thine own entire sweetness in me.

66

She who ever had remained in the depth of my being, in the twilight of gleams and of glimpses; she who never opened her veils in the morning light, will be my last gift to thee, my God, folded in my final song.

Words have wooed yet failed to win her; persuasion has stretched to her its eager arms in vain.

I have roamed from country to country keeping her in the core of my heart, and around her have risen and fallen the growth and decay of my life.

Over my thoughts and actions, my slumbers and dreams, she reigned yet dwelled alone and apart.

Many a man knocked at my door and asked for her and turned away in despair.

There was none in the world who ever saw her face to face, and she remained in her loneliness waiting for thy recognition.

67

Thou art the sky and thou art the nest as well.

O thou beautiful, there in the nest is thy love that encloses the soul with colours and sounds and odours.

There comes the morning with the golden basket in her right hand bearing the wreath of beauty, silently to crown the earth.

And there comes the evening over the lonely meadows deserted by herds, through trackless paths, carrying cool draughts of peace in her golden pitcher from the western ocean of rest.

But there, where spreads the infinite sky for the soul to take her flight in, reigns the stainless white radiance. There is no day nor night, nor form nor colour, and never, never a word.

68

Thy sunbeam comes upon this earth of mine with arms outstretched and stands at my door the livelong day to carry back to thy feet clouds made of my tears and sighs and songs.

With fond delight thou wrappest about thy starry breast that mantle of misty cloud, turning it into numberless shapes and folds and colouring it with hues ever changing.

It is so light and so fleeting, tender and tearful and dark, that is why thou lovest it, O thou spotless and serene. And that is why it may cover thy awful white light with its pathetic shadows.

69

The same stream of life that runs through my veins night and day runs through the world and dances in rhythmic measures.

It is the same life that shoots in joy through the dust of the earth in numberless blades of grass and breaks into tumultuous waves of leaves and flowers.

It is the same life that is rocked in the ocean-cradle of birth and of death, in ebb and in flow.

I feel my limbs are made glorious by the touch of this world of life. And my pride is from the life-throb of ages dancing in my blood this moment.

70

Is it beyond thee to be glad with the gladness of this rhythm? to be tossed and lost and broken in the whirl of this fearful joy?

All things rush on, they stop not, they look not behind, no power can hold them back, they rush on.

Keeping steps with that restless, rapid music, seasons come dancing and pass away—colours, tunes, and perfumes pour in endless cascades in the abounding joy that scatters and gives up and dies every moment.

71

That I should make much of myself and turn it on all sides, thus casting coloured shadows on thy radiance—such is thy maya.

Thou settest a barrier in thine own being and then callest thy severed self in myriad notes. This thy self-separation has taken body in me.

The poignant song is echoed through all the sky in many-coloured tears and smiles, alarms and hopes; waves rise up and sink again, dreams break and form. In me is thy own defeat of self.

This screen that thou hast raised is painted with innumerable figures with the brush of the night and the day. Behind it thy seat is woven in wondrous mysteries of curves, casting away all barren lines of straightness.

The great pageant of thee and me has overspread the sky. With the tune of thee and me all the air is vibrant, and all ages pass with the hiding and seeking of thee and me.

72

He it is, the innermost one, who awakens my being with his deep hidden touches.

He it is who puts his enchantment upon these eyes and joyfully plays on the chords of my heart in varied cadence of pleasure and pain.

He it is who weaves the web of this *maya* in evanescent hues of gold and silver, blue and green, and lets peep out through the folds his feet, at whose touch I forget myself.

Days come and ages pass, and it is ever he who moves my heart in many a name, in many a guise, in many a rapture of joy and of sorrow.

73

Deliverance is not for me in renunciation. I feel the embrace of freedom in a thousand bonds of delight.

Thou ever pourest for me the fresh draught of thy wine of various colours and fragrance, filling this earthen vessel to the brim.

My world will light its hundred different lamps with thy flame and place them before the altar of thy temple.

No, I will never shut the doors of my senses. The delights of sight and hearing and touch will bear thy delight.

Yes, all my illusions will burn into illumination of joy, and all my desires ripen into fruits of love.

74

The day is no more, the shadow is upon the earth. It is time that I go to the stream to fill my pitcher.

The evening air is eager with the sad music of the water. Ah, it calls me out into the dusk. In the lonely lane there is no passer-by, the wind is up, the ripples are rampant in the river.

I know not if I shall come back home. I know not whom I shall chance to meet. There at the fording in the little boat the unknown man plays upon his lute.

75

Thy gifts to us mortals fulfil all our needs and yet run back to thee undiminished.

The river has its everyday work to do and hastens through fields and hamlets; yet its incessant stream winds towards the washing of thy feet.

The flower sweetens the air with its perfume; yet its last service is to offer itself to thee.

Thy worship does not impoverish the world.

From the words of the poet men take what meanings please them; yet their last meaning points to thee.

76

Day after day, O lord of my life, shall I stand before thee face to face. With folded hands, O lord of all worlds, shall I stand before thee face to face.

Under thy great sky in solitude and silence, with humble heart shall I stand before thee face to face.

In this laborious world of thine, tumultuous with toil and with struggle, among hurrying crowds shall I stand before thee face to face.

And when my work shall be done in this world, O King of kings, alone and speechless shall I stand before thee face to face.

77

I know thee as my God and stand apart—I do not know thee as my own and come closer. I know thee as my father and bow before thy feet—I do not grasp thy hand as my friend's.

I stand not where thou comest down and ownest thyself as mine, there to clasp thee to my heart and take thee as my comrade.

Thou art the Brother amongst my brothers, but I heed them not, I divide not my earnings with them, thus sharing my all with thee.

In pleasure and in pain I stand not by the side of men, and thus stand by thee. I shrink to give up my life, and thus do not plunge into the great waters of life.

78

When the creation was new and all the stars shone in their first splendour, the gods held their assembly in the sky and sang 'Oh, the picture of perfection! The joy unalloyed!'

But one cried of a sudden—'It seems that somewhere there is a break in the chain of light and one of the stars has been lost.'

The golden string of their harp snapped, their song stopped, and they cried in dismay—'Yes, that lost star was the best, she was the glory of all heavens!'

From that day the search is unceasing for her, and the cry goes on from one to the other that in her the world has lost its one joy!

Only in the deepest silence of night the stars smile and whisper among themselves—'Vain is this seeking! Unbroken perfection is over all!'

79

If it is not my portion to meet thee in this life then let me ever feel that I have missed thy sight—let me not forget for a moment, let me carry the pangs of this sorrow in my dreams and in my wakeful hours.

As my days pass in the crowded market of this world and my hands grow full with the daily profits, let me ever feel that I have gained nothing—let me not forget for a moment, let me carry the pangs of this sorrow in my dreams and in my wakeful hours.

When I sit by the roadside, tired and panting, when I spread my bed low in the dust, let me ever feel that the long journey is still before me—let me not forget a moment, let me carry the pangs of this sorrow in my dreams and in my wakeful hours.

When my rooms have been decked out and the flutes sound and the laughter there is loud, let me ever feel that I have not invited thee to my house—let me not forget for a moment, let me carry the pangs of this sorrow in my dreams and in my wakeful hours.

80

I am like a remnant of a cloud of autumn uselessly roaming in the sky, O my sun ever-glorious! Thy touch has not yet melted my vapour, making me one with thy light, and thus I count months and years separated from thee.

If this be thy wish and if this be thy play, then take this fleeting emptiness of mine, paint it with colours, gild it with gold, float it on the wanton wind and spread it in varied wonders.

And again when it shall be thy wish to end this play at night, I shall melt and vanish away in the dark, or it may be in a smile of the white morning, in a coolness of purity transparent.

81

On many an idle day have I grieved over lost time. But it is never lost, my lord. Thou hast taken every moment of my life in thine own hands.

Hidden in the heart of things thou art nourishing seeds into sprouts, buds into blossoms, and ripening flowers into fruitfulness.

I was tired and sleeping on my idle bed and imagined all work had ceased. In the morning I woke up and found my garden full with wonders of flowers.

82

Time is endless in thy hands, my lord. There is none to count thy minutes.

Days and nights pass and ages bloom and fade like flowers. Thou knowest how to wait.

Thy centuries follow each other perfecting a small wild flower.

We have no time to lose, and having no time we must scramble for a chances. We are too poor to be late.

And thus it is that time goes by while I give it to every querulous man who claims it, and thine altar is empty of all offerings to the last.

At the end of the day I hasten in fear lest thy gate to be shut; but I find that yet there is time.

83

Mother, I shall weave a chain of pearls for thy neck with my tears of sorrow.

The stars have wrought their anklets of light to deck thy feet, but mine will hang upon thy breast.

Wealth and fame come from thee and it is for thee to give or to withhold them. But this my sorrow is absolutely mine own, and when I bring it to thee as my offering thou rewardest me with thy grace.

84

It is the pang of separation that spreads throughout the world and gives birth to shapes innumerable in the infinite sky.

It is this sorrow of separation that gazes in silence all nights from star to star and becomes lyric among rustling leaves in rainy darkness of July.

It is this overspreading pain that deepens into loves and desires, into sufferings and joy in human homes; and this it is that ever melts and flows in songs through my poet's heart.

85

When the warriors came out first from their master's hall, where had they hid their power? Where were their armour and their arms?

They looked poor and helpless, and the arrows were showered upon them on the day they came out from their master's hall.

When the warriors marched back again to their master's hall where did they hide their power?

They had dropped the sword and dropped the bow and the arrow; peace was on their foreheads, and they had left the fruits of their life behind them on the day they marched back again to their master's hall.

86

Death, thy servant, is at my door. He has crossed the unknown sea and brought thy call to my home.

The night is dark and my heart is fearful—yet I will take up the lamp, open my gates and bow to him my welcome. It is thy messenger who stands at my door.

I will worship him placing at his feet the treasure of my heart.

He will go back with his errand done, leaving a dark shadow on my morning; and in my desolate home only my forlorn self will remain as my last offering to thee.

87

In desperate hope I go and search for her in all the corners of my room; I find her not.

My house is small and what once has gone from it can never be regained.

But infinite is thy mansion, my lord, and seeking her I have to come to thy door.

I stand under the golden canopy of thine evening sky and I lift my eager eyes to thy face.

I have come to the brink of eternity from which nothing can vanish—no hope, no happiness, no vision of a face seen through tears.

Oh, dip my emptied life into that ocean, plunge it into the deepest fullness. Let me for once feel that lost sweet touch in the allness of the universe.

88

Deity of the ruined temple! The broken strings of Vina sing no more your praise. The bells in the evening proclaim not your time of worship. The air is still and silent about you.

In your desolate dwelling comes the vagrant spring breeze. It brings the tidings of flowers—the flowers that for your worship are offered no more.

Your worshipper of old wanders ever longing for favour still refused. In the eventide, when fires and shadows mingle with the gloom of dust, he wearily comes back to the ruined temple with hunger in his heart.

Many a festival day comes to you in silence, deity of the ruined temple. Many a night of worship goes away with lamp unlit.

Many new images are built by masters of cunning art and carried to the holy stream of oblivion when their time is come.

Only the deity of the ruined temple remains unworshipped in deathless neglect.

89

No more noisy, loud words from me—such is my master's will. Henceforth I deal in whispers. The speech of my heart will be carried on in murmurings of a song.

Men hasten to the King's market. All the buyers and sellers are there. But I have my untimely leave in the middle of the day, in the thick of work.

Let then the flowers come out in my garden, though it is not their time; and let the midday bees strike up their lazy hum.

Full many an hour have I spent in the strife of the good and the evil, but now it is the pleasure of my playmate of the empty days to draw my heart on to him; and I know not why is this sudden call to what useless inconsequence!

90

On the day when death will knock at thy door what wilt thou offer to him?

Oh, I will set before my guest the full vessel of my life—I will never let him go with empty hands.

All the sweet vintage of all my autumn days and summer nights, all the earnings and gleanings of my busy life will I place before him at the close of my days when death will knock at my door.

91

O thou the last fulfilment of life, Death, my death, come and whisper to me!

Day after day I have kept watch for thee; for thee have I borne the joys and pangs of life.

All that I am, that I have, that I hope and all my love have ever flowed towards thee in depth of secrecy. One final glance from thine eyes and my life will be ever thine own.

The flowers have been woven and the garland is ready for the bridegroom. After the wedding the bride shall leave her home and meet her lord alone in the solitude of night.

92

I know that the day will come when my sight of this earth shall be lost, and life will take its leave in silence, drawing the last curtain over my eyes.

Yet stars will watch at night, and morning rise as before, and hours heave like sea waves casting up pleasures and pains.

When I think of this end of my moments, the barrier of the moments breaks and I see by the light of death thy world with its careless treasures. Rare is its lowliest seat, rare is its meanest of lives.

Things that I longed for in vain and things that I got—let them pass. Let me but truly possess the things that I ever spurned and overlooked.

93

I have got my leave. Bid me farewell, my brothers! I bow to you all and take my departure.

Here I give back the keys of my door—and I give up all claims to my house. I only ask for last kind words from you.

We were neighbours for long, but I received more than I could give. Now the day has dawned and the lamp that lit my dark corner is out. A summons has come and I am ready for my journey.

94

At this time of my parting, wish me good luck, my friends! The sky is flushed with the dawn and my path lies beautiful.

Ask not what I have with me to take there. I start on my journey with empty hands and expectant heart.

I shall put on my wedding garland. Mine is not the red-brown dress of the traveller, and though there are dangers on the way I have no fear in mind.

The evening star will come out when my voyage is done and the plaintive notes of the twilight melodies be struck up from the King's gateway.

95

I was not aware of the moment when I first crossed the threshold of this life.

What was the power that made me open out into this vast mystery like a bud in the forest at midnight!

When in the morning I looked upon the light I felt in a moment that I was no stranger in this world, that the inscrutable without name and form had taken me in its arms in the form of my own mother.

Even so, in death the same unknown will appear as ever known to me. And because I love this life, I know I shall love death as well.

The child cries out when from the right breast the mother takes it away, in the very next moment to find in the left one its consolation.

96

When I go from hence let this be my parting word, that what I have seen is unsurpassable.

I have tasted of the hidden honey of this lotus that expands on the ocean of light, and thus am I blessed—let this be my parting word.

In this playhouse of infinite forms I have had my play and here have I caught sight of him that is formless.

My whole body and my limbs have thrilled with his touch who is beyond touch; and if the end comes here, let it come—let this be my parting word.

97

When my play was with thee I never questioned who thou wert. I knew nor shyness nor fear, my life was boisterous.

In the early morning thou wouldst call me from my sleep like my own comrade and lead me running from glade to glade.

On those days I never cared to know the meaning of songs thou sangest to me. Only my voice took up the tunes, and my heart danced in their cadence.

Now, when the playtime is over, what is this sudden sight that is come upon me? The world with eyes bent upon thy feet stands in awe with all its silent stars.

98

I will deck thee with trophies, garlands of my defeat. It is never in my power to escape unconquered.

I surely know my pride will go to the wall, my life will burst its bonds in exceeding pain, and my empty heart will sob out in music like a hollow reed, and the stone will melt in tears.

I surely know the hundred petals of a lotus will not remain closed for ever and the secret recess of its honey will be bared.

From the blue sky an eye shall gaze upon me and summon me in silence. Nothing will be left for me, nothing whatever, and utter death shall I receive at thy feet.

99

When I give up the helm I know that the time has come for thee to take it. What there is to do will be instantly done. Vain is this struggle.

Then take away your hands and silently put up with your defeat, my heart, and think it your good fortune to sit perfectly still where you are placed.

These my lamps are blown out at every little puff of wind, and trying to light them I forget all else again and again.

But I shall be wise this time and wait in the dark, spreading my mat on the floor; and whenever it is thy pleasure, my lord, come silently and take thy seat here.

100

I dive down into the depth of the ocean of forms, hoping to gain the perfect pearl of the formless.

No more sailing from harbour to harbour with this my weather-beaten boat. The days are long passed when my sport was to be tossed on waves.

And now I am eager to die into the deathless.

Into the audience hall by the fathomless abyss where swells up the music of toneless strings I shall take this harp of my life.

I shall tune it to the notes of forever, and when it has sobbed out its last utterance, lay down my silent harp at the feet of the silent.

101

Ever in my life have I sought thee with my songs. It was they who led me from door to door, and with them have I felt about me, searching and touching my world.

It was my songs that taught me all the lessons I ever learnt; they showed me secret paths, they brought before my sight many a star on the horizon of my heart.

They guided me all the day long to the mysteries of the country of pleasure and pain, and, at last, to what palace gate have the brought me in the evening at the end of my journey?

102

I boasted among men that I had known you. They see your pictures in all works of mine. They come and ask me, 'Who is he?' I know not how to answer them. I say, 'Indeed, I cannot tell.' They blame me and they go away in scorn. And you sit there smiling.

I put my tales of you into lasting songs. The secret gushes out from my heart. They come and ask me, 'Tell me all your meanings.' I know not how to answer them. I say, 'Ah, who knows what they mean!' They smile and go away in utter scorn. And you sit there smiling.

103

In one salutation to thee, my God, let all my senses spread out and touch this world at thy feet.

Like a rain-cloud of July hung low with its burden of unshed showers let all my mind bend down at thy door in one salutation to thee.

Let all my songs gather together their diverse strains into a single current and flow to a sea of silence in one salutation to thee.

Like a flock of homesick cranes flying night and day back to their mountain nests let all my life take its voyage to its eternal home in one salutation to thee.

THE HUNGRY STONES

My kinsman and myself were returning to Calcutta from our Puja trip when we met the man in a train. From his dress and bearing we took him at first for an up-country Mahomedan, but we were puzzled as we heard him talk. He discoursed upon all subjects so confidently that you might think the Disposer of All Things consulted him at all times in all that He did. Hitherto we had been perfectly happy, as we did not know that secret and unheard-of forces were at work, that the Russians had advanced close to us, that the English had deep and secret policies, that confusion among the native chiefs had come to a head. But our newly-acquired friend said with a sly smile: "There happen more things in heaven and earth, Horatio, than are reported in your newspapers." As we had never stirred out of our homes before, the demeanour of the man struck us dumb with wonder. Be the topic ever so trivial, he would quote science, or comment on the Vedas, or repeat quatrains from some Persian poet; and as we had no pretence to a knowledge of science or the Vedas or Persian, our admiration for him went on increasing, and my kinsman, a theosophist, was firmly convinced that our fellow-passenger must have been supernaturally inspired by some strange "magnetism" or "occult power," by an "astral body" or something of that kind. He listened to the tritest saying that fell from the lips of our extraordinary companion with devotional rapture, and secretly took down notes of his conversation. I fancy that the extraordinary man saw this, and was a little pleased with it.

When the train reached the junction, we assembled in the waiting room for the connection. It was then 10 P.M., and as the train, we heard, was likely to be very late, owing to something wrong in the lines, I spread my bed on the table and was about to lie down for a comfortable doze, when the extraordinary person deliberately set about spinning the following yarn. Of course, I could get no sleep that night.

When, owing to a disagreement about some questions of administrative policy, I threw up my post at Junagarh, and entered the service of the Nizam of Hydria, they appointed me at once, as a strong young man, collector of cotton duties at Barich.

Barich is a lovely place. The Susta "chatters over stony ways and babbles on the pebbles," tripping, like a skilful dancing girl, in through the woods below the lonely hills. A flight of 150 steps rises from the river, and above that flight, on the river's brim and at the foot of the hills, there stands a solitary marble palace. Around it there is no habitation of man--the village and the cotton mart of Barich being far off.

About 250 years ago the Emperor Mahmud Shah II. had built this lonely palace for his pleasure and luxury. In his days jets of rose-water spurted from its fountains, and on the cold marble floors of its spray-cooled rooms young Persian damsels would sit, their hair dishevelled before bathing, and, splashing their soft naked feet in the clear water of the reservoirs, would sing, to the tune of the guitar, the ghazals of their vineyards.

The fountains play no longer; the songs have ceased; no longer do snow-white feet step gracefully on the snowy marble. It is but the vast and solitary quarters of cess-collectors like us, men oppressed with solitude and deprived of the society of women. Now, Karim Khan, the old clerk of my office, warned me repeatedly not to take up my abode there. "Pass the day there, if you like," said he, "but never stay the night." I passed it off with a light laugh. The servants said that they would work till dark and go away at night. I gave my ready assent. The house had such a bad name that even thieves would not venture near it after dark.

At first the solitude of the deserted palace weighed upon me like a nightmare. I would stay out, and work hard as long as possible, then return home at night jaded and tired, go to bed and fall asleep.

Before a week had passed, the place began to exert a weird fascination upon me. It is difficult to describe or to induce people to believe; but I felt as if the whole house was like a living organism slowly and imperceptibly digesting me by the action of some stupefying gastric juice.

Perhaps the process had begun as soon as I set my foot in the house, but I distinctly remember the day on which I first was conscious of it.

It was the beginning of summer, and the market being dull I had no work to do. A little before sunset I was sitting in an arm-chair near the water's edge below the steps. The Susta had shrunk and sunk low; a broad patch of sand on the other side glowed with the hues of evening; on this side the pebbles at the bottom of the clear shallow waters were glistening. There was not a breath of wind anywhere, and the still air was laden with an oppressive scent from the spicy shrubs growing on the hills close by.

As the sun sank behind the hill-tops a long dark curtain fell upon the stage of day, and the intervening hills cut short the time in which light and shade mingle at sunset. I thought of going out for a ride, and was about to get up when I heard a footfall on the steps behind. I looked back, but there was no one.

As I sat down again, thinking it to be an illusion, I heard many footfalls, as if a large number of persons were rushing down the steps. A strange thrill of delight, slightly tinged with fear, passed through my frame, and though there was not a figure before my eyes, methought I saw a bevy of joyous maidens coming down the steps to bathe in the Susta in that summer evening. Not a sound was in the valley, in the river, or in the palace, to break the silence, but I distinctly heard the maidens' gay and mirthful laugh, like the gurgle of a spring gushing forth in a hundred cascades, as they ran past me, in quick playful pursuit of each other, towards the river, without noticing me at all. As they were invisible to me, so I was, as it were, invisible to them. The river was perfectly calm, but I felt that its still, shallow, and clear waters were stirred suddenly by the splash of many an arm jingling with bracelets, that the girls laughed and dashed and spattered water at one another, that the feet of the fair swimmers tossed the tiny waves up in showers of pearl.

I felt a thrill at my heart--I cannot say whether the excitement was due to fear or delight or curiosity. I had a strong desire to see them more clearly, but naught was visible before me; I thought I could catch all that they said if I only strained my ears; but however hard I strained them, I heard nothing but the chirping of the cicadas in the woods. It seemed as if a dark curtain of 250 years was hanging before me, and I would fain lift a corner of it tremblingly and peer through, though the assembly on the other side was completely enveloped in darkness.

The oppressive closeness of the evening was broken by a sudden gust of wind, and the still surface of the Suista rippled and curled like the hair of a nymph, and from the woods wrapt in the evening gloom there came forth a simultaneous murmur, as though they were awakening from a black dream. Call it reality or dream, the momentary glimpse of that invisible mirage reflected from a far-off world, 250 years old, vanished in a flash. The mystic forms that brushed past me with their quick unbodied steps, and loud, voiceless laughter, and threw themselves into the river, did not go back wringing their dripping robes as they went. Like fragrance wafted away by the wind they were dispersed by a single breath of the spring.

Then I was filled with a lively fear that it was the Muse that had taken advantage of my solitude and possessed me--the witch had evidently come to ruin a poor devil like myself making a living by collecting cotton duties. I decided to have a good dinner--it is the empty stomach that all sorts of incurable diseases find an easy prey. I sent for my cook and gave orders for a rich, sumptuous *moghlai* dinner, redolent of spices and *ghi*.

Next morning the whole affair appeared a queer fantasy. With a light heart I put on a sola hat like the sahebs, and drove out to my work. I was to have written my quarterly report that day, and expected to return late; but before it was dark I was strangely drawn to my house--by what I could not say--I felt they were all waiting, and that I should delay no longer. Leaving my report unfinished I rose, put on my sola hat, and startling the dark, shady, desolate path with the rattle of my carriage, I reached the vast silent palace standing on the gloomy skirts of the hills.

On the first floor the stairs led to a very spacious hall, its roof stretching wide over ornamental arches resting on three rows of massive pillars, and groaning day and night under the weight of its own intense solitude. The day had just closed, and the lamps had not yet been lighted. As I pushed the door open a great bustle seemed to follow within, as if a throng of people had broken up in confusion, and rushed out through the doors and windows and corridors and verandas and rooms, to make its hurried escape.

As I saw no one I stood bewildered, my hair on end in a kind of ecstatic delight, and a faint scent of attar and unguents almost effected by age lingered in my nostrils. Standing in the darkness of that vast desolate hall between the rows of those ancient pillars, I could hear the gurgle of fountains plashing on the marble floor, a strange tune on the guitar, the jingle of ornaments and the tinkle of anklets, the clang of bells tolling the hours, the distant note of nahabat, the din of the crystal pendants of chandeliers shaken by the breeze, the song of bulbuls from the cages in the corridors, the cackle of storks in the gardens, all creating round me a strange unearthly music.

Then I came under such a spell that this intangible, inaccessible, unearthly vision appeared to be the only reality in the world--and all else a mere dream. That I, that is to say, Srijut So-and-so, the eldest son of So-and-so of blessed memory, should be drawing a monthly salary of Rs. 450 by the discharge of my duties as collector of cotton duties, and driving in my dog-cart to my office every day in a short coat and soia hat, appeared to me to be such an astonishingly ludicrous illusion that I burst into a horse-laugh, as I stood in the gloom of that vast silent hall.

At that moment my servant entered with a lighted kerosene lamp in his hand. I do not know whether he thought me mad, but it came back to me at once that I was in very deed Srijut So-and-so, son of So-and-so of blessed memory, and that, while our poets, great and small, alone could say whether inside of or outside the earth there was a region where unseen fountains perpetually played and fairy guitars, struck by invisible fingers, sent forth an eternal harmony, this at any rate was certain, that I collected duties at the cotton market at Banch, and earned thereby Rs. 450 per mensem as my salary. I laughed in great glee at my curious illusion, as I sat over the newspaper at my camp-table, lighted by the kerosene lamp.

After I had finished my paper and eaten my moghlai dinner, I put out the lamp, and lay down on my bed in a small side-room. Through the open window a radiant star, high above the Avalli hills skirted by the darkness of their woods, was gazing intently from millions and millions of miles away in the sky at Mr. Collector lying on a humble camp-bedstead. I wondered and felt amused at the idea, and do not knew when I fell asleep or how long I slept; but I suddenly awoke with a start, though I heard no sound and saw no intruder--only the steady bright star on the hilltop had set, and the dim light of the new moon was stealthily entering the room through the open window, as if ashamed of its intrusion.

I saw nobody, but felt as if some one was gently pushing me. As I awoke she said not a word, but beckoned me with her five fingers bedecked with rings to follow her cautiously. I got up noiselessly, and, though not a soul save myself was there in the countless apartments of that deserted palace with its slumbering sounds and waiting echoes, I feared at every step lest any one should wake up. Most of the rooms of the palace were always kept closed, and I had never entered them.

I followed breathless and with silent steps my invisible guide - I cannot now say where. What endless dark and narrow passages, what long corridors, what silent and solemn audience-chambers and close secret cells I crossed!

Though I could not see my fair guide, her form was not invisible to my mind's eye,--an Arab girl, her arms, hard and smooth as marble, visible through her loose sleeves, a thin veil falling on her face from the fringe of her cap, and a curved dagger at her waist! Methought that one of the thousand and one Arabian Nights had been wafted to me from the world of romance, and that at the dead of night I was wending my way through the dark narrow alleys of slumbering Bagdad to a trysting - place fraught with peril.

At last my fair guide stopped abruptly before a deep blue screen, and seemed to point to something below. There was nothing there, but a sudden dread froze the blood in my heart-methought I saw there on the floor at the foot of the screen a terrible negro eunuch dressed in rich brocade, sitting and dozing with outstretched legs, with a naked sword on his lap. My fair guide lightly tripped over his legs and held up a fringe of the screen. I could catch a glimpse of a part of the room spread with a Persian carpet--some one was sitting inside on a bed--I could not see her, but only caught a glimpse of two exquisite feet in gold-embroidered slippers, hanging out from loose saffron-coloured *paijamas* and placed idly on the orange-coloured velvet carpet. On one side there was a bluish crystal tray on which a few apples, pears, oranges, and bunches of grapes in plenty, two small cups and a gold-tinted decanter were evidently waiting the guest. A fragrant intoxicating vapour, issuing from a strange sort of incense that burned within, almost overpowered my senses.

As with trembling heart I made an attempt to step across the outstretched legs of the eunuch, he woke up suddenly with a start, and the sword fell from his lap with a sharp clang on the marble floor. A terrific scream made me jump, and I saw I was sitting on that camp-bedstead of mine sweating heavily; and the crescent moon looked pale in the morning light like a weary sleepless patient at dawn; and our crazy Meher Ali was crying out, as is his daily custom, "Stand back! Stand back!!" while he went along the lonely road.

Such was the abrupt close of one of my Arabian Nights; but there were yet a thousand nights left.

Then followed a great discord between my days and nights. During the day I would go to my work worn and tired, cursing the bewitching night and her empty dreams, but as night came my daily life with its bonds and shackles of work would appear a petty, false, ludicrous vanity.

After nightfall I was caught and overwhelmed in the snare of a strange intoxication, I would then be transformed into some unknown personage of a bygone age, playing my part in unwritten history; and my short English coat and tight breeches did not suit me in the least. With a red velvet cap on my head, loose *paijamas*, an embroidered vest, a long flowing silk gown, and coloured handkerchiefs scented with attar,

I would complete my elaborate toilet, sit on a high-cushioned chair, and replace my cigarette with a many-coiled *narghileh* filled with rose-water, as if in eager expectation of a strange meeting with the beloved one.

I have no power to describe the marvellous incidents that unfolded themselves, as the gloom of the night deepened. I felt as if in the curious apartments of that vast edifice the fragments of a beautiful story, which I could follow for some distance, but of which I could never see the end, flew about in a sudden gust of the vernal breeze. And all the same I would wander from room to room in pursuit of them the whole night long.

Amid the eddy of these dream-fragments, amid the smell of henna and the twanging of the guitar, amid the waves of air charged with fragrant spray, I would catch like a flash of lightning the momentary glimpse of a fair damsel. She it was who had saffron-coloured paijamas, white ruddy soft feet in gold-embroidered slippers with curved toes, a close-fitting bodice wrought with gold, a red cap, from which a golden frill fell on her snowy brow and cheeks.

She had maddened me. In pursuit of her I wandered from room to room, from path to path among the bewildering maze of alleys in the enchanted dreamland of the nether world of sleep.

Sometimes in the evening, while arraying myself carefully as a prince of the blood-royal before a large mirror, with a candle burning on either side, I would see a sudden reflection of the Persian beauty by the side of my own. A swift turn of her neck, a quick eager glance of intense passion and pain glowing in her large dark eyes, just a suspicion of speech on her dainty red lips, her figure, fair and slim crowned with youth like a blossoming creeper, quickly uplifted in her graceful tilting gait, a dazzling flash of pain and craving and ecstasy, a smile and a glance and a blaze of jewels and silk, and she melted away. A wild glist of wind, laden with all the fragrance of hills and woods, would put out my light, and I would fling aside my dress and lie down on my bed, my eyes closed and my body thrilling with delight, and there around me in the breeze, amid all the perfume of the woods and hills, floated through the silent gloom many a caress and many a kiss and many a tender touch of hands, and gentle murmurs in my ears, and fragrant breaths on my brow; or a sweetly-perfumed kerchief was wafted again and again on my cheeks. Then slowly a mysterious serpent would twist her stupefying coils about me; and heaving a heavy sigh, I would lapse into insensibility, and then into a profound slumber.

One evening I decided to go out on my horse - I do not know who implored me to stay-but I would listen to no entreaties that day. My English hat and coat were resting on a rack, and I was about to take them down when a sudden whirlwind, crested with the sands of the Susta and the dead leaves of the Avalli hills, caught them up, and whirled them round and round, while a loud peal of merry laughter rose higher and higher, striking all the chords of mirth till it died away in the land of sunset.

I could not go out for my ride, and the next day I gave up my queer English coat and hat for good.

That day again at dead of night I heard the stifled heart-breaking sobs of some one--as if below the bed, below the floor, below the stony foundation of that gigantic palace, from the depths of a dark damp grave, a voice piteously cried and implored me: "Oh, rescue me! Break through these doors of hard illusion, deathlike slumber and fruitless dreams, place by your side on the saddle, press me to your heart, and, riding through hills and woods and across the river, take me to the warm radiance of your sunny rooms above!"

Who am I? Oh, how can I rescue thee? What drowning beauty, what incarnate passion shall I drag to the shore from this wild eddy of dreams? O lovely ethereal apparition! Where didst thou flourish and when? By what cool spring, under the shade of what date-groves, wast thou born--in the lap of what homeless wanderer in the desert? What Bedouin snatched thee from thy mother's arms, an opening bud plucked from a wild creeper, placed thee on a horse swift as lightning, crossed the burning sands, and took thee to the slave-market of what royal city? And there, what officer of the *Badshah*, seeing the glory of thy bashful blossoming youth, paid for thee in gold, placed thee in a golden palanquin, and offered thee as a present for the seraglio of his master? And O, the history of that place! The music of the *sareng*, the jingle of anklets, the occasional flash of daggers and the glowing wine of Shiraz poison, and the piercing flashing glance! What infinite grandeur, what endless servitude!

The slave-girls to thy right and left waved the *chamar* as diamonds flashed from their bracelets; the *Badshah*, the king of kings, fell on his knees at thy snowy feet in bejewelled shoes, and outside the terrible Abyssinian eunuch, looking like a messenger of death, but clothed like an angel, stood with a naked sword in his hand! Then, O, thou flower of the desert, swept away by the blood-stained dazzling ocean of grandeur, with its foam of jealousy, its rocks and shoals of intrigue, on what shore of cruel death wast thou cast, or in what other land more splendid and more cruel?

Suddenly at this moment that crazy Meher Ali screamed out: "Stand back! Stand back!! All is false! All is false!!" I opened my eyes and saw that it was already light. My *chaprasi* came and handed me my letters, and the cook waited with a *salam* for my orders.

I said; "No, I can stay here no longer." That very day I packed up, and moved to my office. Old Karim Khan smiled a little as he saw me. I felt nettled, but said nothing, and fell to my work.

As evening approached I grew absent-minded; I felt as if I had an appointment to keep; and the work of examining the cotton accounts seemed wholly useless; even the *Nizamat* of the *Nizam* did not appear to be of much worth. Whatever belonged to the present, whatever was moving and acting and working for bread seemed trivial, meaningless, and contemptible.

I threw my pen down, closed my ledgers, got into my dog-cart, and drove away. I noticed that it stopped of itself at the gate of the marble palace just at the hour of twilight. With quick steps I climbed the stairs, and entered the room.

A heavy silence was reigning within. The dark rooms were looking sullen as if they had taken offence. My heart was full of contrition, but there was no one to whom I could lay it bare, or of whom I could ask forgiveness. I wandered about the dark rooms with a vacant mind. I wished I had a guitar to which I could sing to the unknown: "O fire, the poor moth that made a vain effort to fly away has come back to thee! Forgive it but this once, burn its wings and consume it in thy flame!"

Suddenly two tear-drops fell from overhead on my brow. Dark masses of clouds overcast the top of the Avalli hills that day. The gloomy woods and the sooty waters of the Susta were waiting in terrible suspense and in an ominous calm. Suddenly land, water, and sky shivered, and a wild tempest-blast rushed howling through the distant pathless woods, showing its lightning-teeth like a raving maniac who had broken his chains. The desolate halls of the palace banged their doors, and moaned in the bitterness of anguish.

The servants were all in the office, and there was no one to light the lamps. The night was cloudy and moonless. In the dense gloom within I could distinctly feel that a woman was lying on her face on the carpet below the bed--clasping and tearing her long dishevelled hair with desperate fingers. Blood was tricking down her fair brow, and she was now laughing a hard, harsh, mirthless laugh, now bursting into violent wringing sobs, now rending her bodice and striking at her bare bosom, as the wind roared in through the open window, and the rain poured in torrents and soaked her through and through.

All night there was no cessation of the storm or of the passionate cry. I wandered from room to room in the dark, with unavailing sorrow. Whom could I console when no one was by? Whose was this intense agony of sorrow? Whence arose this inconsolable grief?

And the mad man cried out: "Stand back! Stand back!! All is false! All is false!!"

I saw that the day had dawned, and Meher Ali was going round and round the palace with his usual cry in that dreadful weather. Suddenly it came to me that perhaps he also had once lived in that house, and that, though he had gone mad, he came there every day, and went round and round, fascinated by the weird spell cast by the marble demon.

Despite the storm and rain I ran to him and asked: "Ho, Meher Ali, what is false?"

The man answered nothing, but pushing me aside went round and round with his frantic cry, like a bird flying fascinated about the jaws of a snake, and made a desperate effort to warn himself by repeating: "Stand back! Stand back!! All is false! All is false!!"

I ran like a mad man through the pelting rain to my office, and asked Karim Khan: "Tell me the meaning of all this!"

What I gathered from that old man was this: That at one time countless unrequited passions and unsatisfied longings and lurid flames of wild blazing pleasure raged within that palace, and that the curse of all the heart-aches and blasted hopes had made its every stone thirsty and hungry, eager to swallow up like a famished ogress any living man who might chance to approach. Not one of those who lived there for three consecutive nights could escape these cruel jaws, save Meher Ali, who had escaped at the cost of his reason.

I asked: "Is there no means whatever of my release?" The old man said: "There is only one means, and that is very difficult. I will tell you what it is, but first you must hear the history of a young Persian girl who once lived in that pleasure-dome. A stranger or a more bitterly heart-rending tragedy was never enacted on this earth."

Just at this moment the coolies announced that the train was coming. So soon? We hurriedly packed up our luggage, as the tram steamed in. An English gentleman, apparently just aroused from slumber, was looking out of a first-class carriage endeavouring to read the name of the station. As soon as he caught sight of our fellow-passenger, he cried, "Hallo," and took him into his own compartment. As we got into a second-class carriage, we had no chance of finding out who the man was nor what was the end of his story.

I said; "The man evidently took us for fools and imposed upon us out of fun. The story is pure fabrication from start to finish." The discussion that followed ended in a lifelong rupture between my theosophist kinsman and myself.

MY BOYHOOD DAYS

I

The Calcutta where I was born was an altogether old-world place. Hackney carriages lumbered about the city raising clouds of dust, and the whips fell on the backs of skinny horses whose bones showed plainly below their hide. There were no trams then, no buses, no motors. Business was not the breathless rush that it is now, and the days went by in leisurely fashion. Clerks would take a good pull at the hookah before starting for office, and chew their betel as they went along. Some rode in palanquins, others joined in groups of four or five to hire a carriage in common, which was known as a 'share-carriage'. Wealthy men had monograms painted on their carriages, and a leather hood over the rear portion, like a half-drawn veil. The coachman sat on the box with his turban stylishly tilted to one side, and two grooms rode behind, girdles of yaks' tails round their waists, startling the pedestrians from their path with their shouts of 'Hey-yo!'

Women used to go about in the stifling darkness of closed palanquins; they shrank from the idea of riding in carriages, and even to use an umbrella in sun or rain was considered unwomanly. Any woman who was so bold as to wear the new-fangled bodice, or shoes on her feet, was scornfully nicknamed 'mem-sahib', that is to say, one who had cast off all sense of propriety or shame. If any woman unexpectedly encountered a strange man, one outside her family circle, her veil would promptly descend to the very tip of her nose, and she would at once turn her back on him. The palanquins in which women went out were shut as closely as their apartments in the house. An additional covering, a kind of thick tilt, completely enveloped the palanquin of a rich man's daughters and daughters-in-law, so that it looked like a moving tomb. By its side went the durwan carrying his brass-bound stick. His work was to sit in the entrance and watch the house, to tend his beard, safely to conduct the money to the bank and the women to their relatives' houses, and on festival days to dip the lady of the house into the Ganges, closed palanquin and all. Hawkers who came to the door with their array of wares would grease Shivnandan's palm to gain admission, and the drivers of hired carriages were also a source of profit to him. Sometimes a man who was unwilling to fall in with this idea of going shares would create a great scene in front of the porch.

Our 'jamadar' Sobha Ram, who was a wrestler, used to spend a good deal of time in practising his preparatory feints and approaches, and in brandishing his heavy clubs. Sometimes he would sit and grind hemp for drink, and sometimes he would be quietly eating his raw radishes, tender leaves and all, when we boys would creep upon him and yell 'Radhakrishna!' in his ear. The more he waved his arms and protested the more we delighted in teasing him. And perhaps—who knows?—his protests were merely a cunning device for hearing repeated the name of his favourite god.

There was no gas then in the city, and no electric light. When the kerosene lamp was introduced, its brilliance amazed us. In the evening the house-servant lit castor-oil lamps in every room. The one in our study-room had two wicks in a glass bowl.

By this dim light my master taught me from Peary Sarkar's First Book. First I would begin to yawn, and then, growing more and more sleepy, rub my heavy eyes. At such times I heard over and over again of the virtues of my master's other pupil Satin, a paragon of a boy with a wonderful head for study, who would rub snuff in his eyes to keep himself awake, so earnest was he. But as for me—the less said about that the better! Even the awful thought that I should probably remain the only dunce in the family could not keep me awake. When nine o'clock struck I was released, my eyes dazed and my mind drugged with sleep.

There was a narrow passage, enclosed by latticed walls, leading from the outer apartments to the interior of the house. A dimly burning lantern swung from the ceiling. As I went along this passage, my mind would be haunted by the idea that something was creeping upon me from behind. Little shivers ran up and down my back. In those days devils and spirits lurked in the recesses of every man's mind, and the air was full of ghost stories. One day it would be some servant girl falling in a dead faint because she had heard the nasal whine of Shank-chunni. The female demon of that name was the most bad-tempered devil of all, and was said to be very greedy of fish. Another story was connected with the thick-leaved badam tree at the western corner of the house. A mysterious Shape was said to stand with one foot in its branches and the other on the third storey cornice of the house. Plenty of people declared that they had seen it, and there were not a few who believed them. A friend of my elder brother's laughingly made light of the story, and the servants looked upon him as lacking in all piety, and said that his neck would surely be wrung one day and his pretensions exposed. The very atmosphere was so enmeshed in ghostly terrors that I could not put my feet into the darkness under the table without them getting the creeps.

There were no water-pipes laid on in those days. In the spring months of Magh and Falgoon when the Ganges water was clear, our bearers would bring it up in brimming pots carried in a yoke across their shoulders. In the dark rooms of the ground floor stood rows of huge water jars filled with the whole year's supply of drinking water. All those musty, dingy, twilit rooms were the home of furtive "Things" – which of us did not know all about those "Things"? Great gaping mouths they had, eyes in their breasts, and ears like winnowing fans; and their feet turned backwards. Small wonder that my heart would pound in my breast and my knees tremble when I went into the inner garden, with the vision of those devilish shapes before me.

At high tide the water of the Ganges would flow along a masonry channel at the side of the road. Since my grandfather's time an allowance of this water had been discharged into our tank. When the sluices were opened the water rushed in, gurgling and foaming like a waterfall. I used to watch it fascinated, holding on by the railings of the south verandah. But the days of our tank were numbered, and finally there came a day when cartload after cartload of rubbish was tipped into it. When the tank no longer reflected the garden, the last lingering illusion of rural life left it. That badam tree is still standing near the third storey cornice, but though his footholds remain, the ghostly shape that once bestrode them has disappeared for ever.

II

The palanquin belonged to the days of my grandmother. It was of ample proportions and lordly appearance. It was big enough to have needed eight bearers for each pole. But when the former wealth and glory of the family had faded like the glowing clouds of sunset, the palanquin bearers, with their gold bracelets, their thick car-rings, and their sleeveless red tunics, had disappeared along with it. The body of the palanquin had been decorated with coloured line drawings, some of which were now defaced. Its surface was stained and discoloured, and the coir stuffing was coming out of the upholstery. It lay in a corner of the counting-house verandah as though it were a piece of commonplace lumber. I was seven or eight years old at that time.

I was not yet, therefore, of an age to put my hand to any serious work in the world, and the old palanquin on its part had been dismissed from all useful service. Perhaps it was this fellow-feeling that so much attracted me towards it. It was to me an island in the midst of the ocean, and I on my holidays became Robinson Crusoe. There I sat within its closed doors, completely lost to view, delightfully safe from prying eyes.

Outside my retreat, our house was full of people, innumerable relatives and other folk. From all parts of the house I could hear the shouts of the various servants at their work. Pari the maid is returning from the bazaar through the front courtyard with her vegetables in a basket on her hip. Dukhon the bearer is carrying in Ganges water in a yoke across his shoulder. The weaver woman has gone into the inner apartments to trade the newest style of saries. Dinu the goldsmith, who receives a monthly wage, usually sits in the room next to the lane, blowing his bellows and carrying out the orders of the family; now he is coming to the counting house to present his bill to Kailash Mukherjee, who has a quill pen stuck over his ear. The carder sits in the courtyard cleaning the cotton mattress stuffing on his twanging bow. Mukundalal the durwan is rolling on the ground outside with the one-eyed wrestler, trying out a new wrestling fall. He slaps his thighs loudly, and repeats his 'physical jerks' twenty or thirty times, dropping on all fours. There is a crowd of beggars sitting waiting for their regular dole.

The day wears on, the heat grows intense, the clock in the gate-house strikes the hour. But inside the palanquin the day does not acknowledge the authority of clocks. Our midday is that of former days, when the drum at the great door of the king's palace would be beaten for the breaking-up of the court, and the king would go to bathe in sandal-scented water. At midday on holidays those in charge of me have their meal and go to sleep. I sit on alone. My palanquin, outwardly at rest, travels on its imaginary journeys. My bearers, sprung from "airy nothing" at my bidding, eating the salt of my imagination, carry me whereever my fancy leads. We pass through far, strange lands, and I give each country a name from the books I have read. My imagination has cut a road through a deep forest. Tigers' eyes blaze from the thickets, my flesh creeps and tingles. With me is Biswanath the hunter; his gun speaks—Crack! Crack! —and there, all is still. Sometimes my palanquin becomes a peacock-boat, floating far out on the ocean till the shore is out of sight. The oars fall into the water with a gentle plash, the waves swing and swell around us. The sailors cry to us to beware, a storm is coming. By the tiller stands Abdul the sailor, with his pointed beard, shaven moustache and close-cropped head. I know him, he brings hilsa fish and turtle eggs from the Padma for my elder brother.

Abdul has a story for me. One day at the end of Chaitra he had gone out in a dinghy to catch fish when suddenly there arose a great Vaisakh gale. It was a tremendous typhoon and the boat sank lower and lower. Abdul seized the tow-rope in his teeth, and jumping into the water swam to the shore, where he pulled his dinghy up after him by the rope. But the story comes to an end far too quickly for my taste, and besides, the boat is not lost, everything is saved —that isn't what I call a story! Again and again I demand, "What next?" "Well," says Abdul at last, "after that there were great doings. What should I see next but a panther with enormous whiskers. During the storm he had climbed up a pakur tree on the village ghat on the other side of the river. In the violent wind the tree broke and fell into the Padma. Brother Panther came floating down on the current, rolled over and over in the crater and reached and climbed the bank on my side. As soon as I saw him I made a noose in my tow-rope. The wild beast drew near, his big eyes glaring. He had grown very hungry with swimming, and when he saw me saliva dribbled from his red, lolling tongue. But though he had known many other men, inside and out, he did not know Abdul. I shouted to him, 'Come on, old boy', and as soon as he raised his fore-feet for the attack I dropped my noose round his neck. The more he struggled to get free the tighter grew the noose, until his tongue began to loll out...." I am tremendously excited. "He didn't die, did he Abdul?" I ask. "Die?" says Abdul, "He couldn't die for the life of him! Well, the river was in spate, and I had to get back to Bahadurganj. I yoked my young panther to the dinghy and made him tow me fully forty miles. Oh, he might roar and snarl, but I goaded him on with my oar, and he carried me a ten or fifteen hours' journey in an hour and a half! Now, my little fellow, don't ask me what happened next, for you won't get an answer."

"All right," say I, "so much for the panther; now for the crocodile?" Says Abdul, "I have often seen the tip of his nose above the water. And how wickedly he smiles as he lies basking in the sun, stretched at full length on the shelving sandbanks of the river. If I'd had a gun I should have made his acquaintance. But my license has expired....

"Still, I can tell you one good yarn. One day Kanchi the gypsy woman was sitting on the bank of the river trimming bamboo with a bill-hook, with her young goat tethered near by. All at once the crocodile appeared on the surface, seized the billy-goat by the leg and dragged it into the water. With one jump the gypsy woman landed astride on its back, and began sawing with her sickle at the throat of the 'demon-lizard', over and over again. The beast let go of the goat and plunged into the water..."

"And then? And then?" comes my excited question. "Why," says Abdul, "the rest of the story went down to the bottom of the river with the crocodile. It will take some time to get it up again. Before I see you again I will send somebody to find out about it, and let you know." Abdul has never come again; perhaps he is still looking for news.

So much, then, for my travels in the palanquin. Outside the palanquin there were days when I assumed the role of teacher, and the railings of the verandah were my pupils. They were all afraid of me, and would cower before me in silence. Some of them were very naughty, and cared absolutely nothing for their books. I told them with dire threats that when they grew up they would be fit for nothing but casual labour. They bore the marks of my beatings from head to foot, yet they did not stop being naughty. For it would not have done for them to stop, it would have made an end of my game.

There was another game too, with my wooden lion. I heard stories of poojah sacrifices and decided that a lion sacrifice would be a magnificent thing. I rained blows on his back—with a frail little stick. There had to be a 'mantra', of course, otherwise it would not have been a proper poojah:

'Liony, liony, off with your head,

Liony, liony, now you are dead.

Woofle the walnut goes clappety clap.

Snip, snop, SNAP!'

I had borrowed almost every word in this from other sources; only the word walnut was my own. I was very fond of walnuts. From the words 'clappety clap' you can see that my sacrificial knife was made of wood. And the word 'snap' shows that it was not a strong one.

III

The clouds have had no rest since yesterday evening. The rain is pouring incessantly. The trees stand huddled together in a seemingly foolish manner; the birds are silent. I call to mind the evenings of my boyhood.

We used then to spend our evening in the servants' quarters. At that time English spellings and meanings did not yet lie like a nightmare on my shoulders. My third brother used to say that I ought first to get a good foundation of Bengali and only afterwards to go on to the English superstructure. Consequently, while other school-boys of my age were glibly reciting "I am up", "He is down", I had not even started on B, A, D, bad and M, A, D, mad.

In the speech of the nabobs the servants' quarters were then called 'tosha-khana'. Even though our house had fallen far below its former aristocratic state, these old high-sounding names, 'tosha-khana', 'daftar-khana', 'baithak-khana', still clung to it.

On the southern side of this "tosha-khana", a castor oil lamp burned dimly on a glass stand in a big room; on the wall was a picture of Ganesh and a crude country painting of the goddess Kali, round which the wall lizards hunted their insect prey. There was no furniture in the room, merely a soiled mat spread on the floor.

You must understand that we lived like poor people, and were consequently saved the trouble of keeping a good stable. Away in a corner outside, in a thatched shed under a tamarind tree, were a shabby carriage and an old horse. We wore the very simplest and plainest clothes, and it was a long time before we even began to wear socks. It was luxury beyond our wildest dreams when our tiffin rations went beyond Brajeswar's inventory and included a loaf of bread, and butter wrapped in a banana leaf. We adapted ourselves easily to the broken wrecks of our former glory.

Brajeswar was the name of the servant who presided over our mat seat. His hair and beard were grizzled, the skin of his face dry and tight-drawn; he was a man of serious disposition, harsh voice, and deliberately mouthed speech. His former master had been a prosperous and well-known man, yet necessity had degraded him from that service to the work of looking after neglected children like us. I have heard that he used to be a master in a village school. To the end of his life he kept this school-masterly language and prim manner. Instead of saying "The gentlemen are waiting", he would say "They await you", and his masters smiled when they heard him. He was as finicky about caste matters as he was conceited. When bathing he would go down into the tank and push back the oily surface water five or six times with his hands before taking a plunge. When he came out of the tank after his bath Brajeswar would edge his way through the garden in so gingerly a way that one would think he could only keep caste by avoiding all contact with this unclean world that God has made. He would talk very emphatically about what was right and what was wrong in manners and behaviour. And besides, he held his head a little on one side, which made his words all the more impressive.

But with all this there was one flaw in his character as guru. He cherished secretly a suppressed greed for food. It was not his method to place a proper portion of food on our plates before the meal. Instead, when we sat down to eat he would take one luchi at a time, and dangling it at a little distance ask, "Do you want any more?" We knew by the tone of his voice what answer he desired, and I usually said that I didn't want any. After that he never gave us an opportunity to change our minds. The milk bowls also had an irresistible attraction for him—an attraction which I never felt at all. In his room was a small wired foodsafe with shelves in it. In it was a big brass bowl of milk, and luchis and vegetables on a wooden platter. Outside the wire-netting the cat prowled longingly to and fro sniffing the air.

From my childhood upwards these short commons suited me very well. Small rations cannot be said to have made me weak. I was, if anything, stronger, certainly not weaker, than boys who had unlimited food. My constitution was so abominably sound that even when the most urgent need arose for avoiding school, I could never make myself ill by fair means or foul. I would get wet through, shoes, stockings and all, but I could not catch cold. I would lie on the open roof in the heavy autumn dew; my hair and clothes would be soaked, but I never had the slightest suspicion of a cough. And as for that sign of bad digestion known as stomach-ache, my stomach was a complete stranger to it, though my tongue made use of its name with mother in time of need. Mother would smile to herself and not feel the least anxiety, she would merely call the servant and tell him to go and tell my master that he should not teach me that evening. Our old-fashioned mothers used to think it no great harm if the boys occasionally took a holiday from study. If we had fallen into the hands of these present-day mothers, we should certainly have been sent to the master, and had our cars tweaked into the bargain. Perhaps with a knowing smile they would have dosed us with castor oil, and our pains would have been permanently cured. If by chance I got a flight temperature no one ever called it fever, but "heated blood". I had never set eyes on a thermometer in those days. Dr. Nilmadhav would come and place his hand on my body, and then prescribe as the first day's treatment castor oil and fasting. I was allowed very little water to drink, and what I had was hot, with a few sugar-coated cardamoms for flavouring. After this fast, the mourala fish soup and soft-boiled rice which I got on the third day seemed a veritable food of the gods.

Serious fever I do not remember, and I never heard the name of malaria. I do not remember quinine—that castor oil was my most distasteful medicine. I never knew the slightest scratch of a surgeon's knife; and to this very day I do not know what measles and chicken-pox are. In short, my body remained obstinately healthy. If mothers want their children to be so healthy that they will be unable to escape from the school master, I recommend them to find a servant like Brajeswar. He would save not only food bills but doctor's bills also, especially in these days of mill flour and adulterated ghee and oil. You must remember that in those days chocolate was still unknown in the bazaar. There was a kind of rose lollipop to be had for a pice. I do not know whether modern boys' pockets are still made sticky by this sesamum-covered sugar-lump, with its faint scent of roses. It has certainly fled in shame from the houses of the respectable people of today. What has become of those cone-shaped packets of fried spices? And those cheap sesame sweetmeats? Do they still linger on? If not, it is no good trying to bring them back.

Day after day, in the evenings, I listened to Brajeswar reciting the seven cantos of Krittibas' Ramayana. Kishori Chatterjee used to drop in sometimes while the reading was going on. He had by heart Panchali versions of the whole Ramayana, tune and all. He took possession at once of the seat of authority, and superseding Krittibas, would begin to recite his simple folk-stanzas in great style:

"Lakshman O hear me

Greatly I fear me

Dangers are near me."

There was a smile on his lips, his bald head gleamed, the song poured from his throat in a torrent of sound, the rhymes jingled and rang verse after verse, like the music of pebbles in a brook. At the same time he would be using his hands and feet in acting out the thought. It was Kishori Chatterjee's greatest grief that Dadabhai, as he called me, could not join a troupe of strolling players and turn such a voice to account. If I did that, he said, I should certainly make my name.

By and by it would grow late and the assembly on the mat would break up. We would go into the house, to Mother's room, haunted and oppressed on our way by the terror of devils. Mother would be playing cards with her aunt, the inlaid parquet floor gleamed like ivory, and a coverlet was spread on the big divan. We would make such a disturbance that Mother would soon throw down her hand and say, "If they are going to be such a nuisance, auntie, you'd better go and tell them stories." We would wash our feet with water from the pot on the verandah outside, and climb on to the bed, pulling 'Didima' with us. Then it would begin—stories of the magical awakening of the princess and her rescue from the demon city. The princess might wake, but who could waken me?... In the early part of the night the jackals would begin to howl, for in those days they still haunted the basements of some of the old houses of Calcutta with their nightly wail.

IV

When I was a little boy Calcutta city was not so wakeful at night as it is now. Nowadays, as soon as the day of sunlight is over, the day of electric light begins. There is not much work done in it, but there, is no rest, for the fire continues, as it were, to smoulder in the charcoal after the blazing wood has burnt itself out. The oil mills are still, the steamer sirens are silent, the labourers have left the factories, the buffaloes which pull the carts of jute bales are stabled in the tin-roofed sheds. But the nerves of the city are throbbing still with the fever of thought which has burned all day in her brain. Buying and selling go on as by day in the shops that line the streets, though the fire is a little choked with ash. Motors continue to run in all directions, emitting all kinds of raucous grunts and groans, though they no longer run with the zest of the morning. But in those old times which we knew, when the day was over whatever business remained undone wrapped itself up in the black blanket of the night and went to sleep in the darkened ground-floor premises of the city. Outside the house the evening sky rose quiet and mysterious. It was so still that we could hear, even in our own street, the shouts of the grooms from the carriages of those people of fashion who were returning from taking the air in Eden Gardens by the side of the Ganges.

In the hot season of Chaitra and Vaishakh the hawkers would go about the streets shouting "I-i-i-ce". In a big pot full of lumps of ice and salt water were little tin containers of what we called "kulpi" ice—nowadays ousted by the more fashionable ices or 'ice-cream'. No one but myself knows how my mind thrilled to that cry as I stood on the verandah facing the street. Then there was another cry, 'Bela flowers'. Nowadays for some reason one hears little of the gardeners baskets of spring flowers—I do not know why. But in those days the air was full of the scent of the thickly strung flowers, which the women and girls wore in their hair knots. Before they went to bathe the women would sit outside their rooms with a hand-mirror set up before them, and dress their hair. The knot would be skillfully bound with the black hair-braid into all sorts of different styles. They wore black-bordered Chandernagore saris, skillfully crinkled before use by pleating and twisting after the fashion of those days. The barber's wife would come to scrub their feet with pumice and paint them with red lac. She and her like were the gossipmongers of the women's courts.

The crowds returning from office or from college did not then, as they do now, rush to the football fields, clinging in swarms to the footboards of the trams. Nor did they crowd in front of cinema halls as they returned. There was some active interest shown in drama, but alas! I was only a child then.

Children of those times got no share in the pleasures of the grown-ups, even from a distance. If we were bold enough to go near, we should be told, "Off with you, go and play." But if we boys made the amount of noise appropriate for proper play, it would then be, "Be quiet, do." Not that the grownups themselves conducted their pleasures and conversation in silence, by any means; and now and again we would stand on the fringe of their far-flung jubilations, as though sprinkled by the spray of a waterfall. We would hang over the verandah on our side of the courtyard, staring across at the brilliantly lit reception-room on the other side. Big coaches would roll up to the portico one after another. Some of our elder brothers conducted the guests upstairs from the front door, sprinkling them with rose-water from the sprinkler, and giving each one a small buttonhole or nosegay of flowers. As the dramatic entertainment proceeded, we could hear the sobs of the "high caste kulin heroine", but we could make out nothing of their meaning, and our longing to know grew intense. We discovered later that though the sobber was certainly highcaste, 'she' was merely our own brother-in-law. But in those days grown-ups and children were kept apart as strictly as men and women with their separate apartments. The singing and dancing would go on in the blaze of the drawing-room chandeliers, the men would pull at the hookah, the women of the family would take their betel boxes and sit in the subdued light behind their screen, the visiting ladies would gather in these retired nooks, and there would be much whispering of intimate domestic gossip. But we children were in bed by this time, and lay listening as our maid-servants Piyari or Sankari told us stories—"In the moonlight, expanding like an opening flower...."

V

A little before our day it was the fashion among wealthy householders to run jatras or troupes of actors. There was a great demand for boys with shrill voices to join these troupes. One of my uncles was patron of such an amateur company. He had a gift for writing plays, and was very enthusiastic about training the boys. All over Bengal professional companies were the rage, just as the amateur companies were in aristocratic circles. Troupes of players sprang up like mushrooms on all sides, under the leadership of some well-known actor or other. Not that either patron or manager was necessarily of high family or good education. Their fame rested on their own merits. Jatra performances used to take place in our house from time to time. But we children had no part in them, and I managed to see only the preliminaries. The verandah would be full of members of the company, the air full of tobacco smoke. There were the boys, long-haired, with dark rings of weariness under their eyes, and, young as they were, with the faces of grown men. Their lips were stained black with constant betel chewing. Their costumes and other paraphernalia were in painted tin boxes. The entrance door was open, people swarmed like ants into the courtyard, which, filled to the brim with the seething, buzzing mass, spilled over into the lane and beyond into the Chitpore Road. Then nine o'clock would strike, and Shyam would swoop down on me like a hawk on a dove, grip my elbow with his rough, gnarled hand, and tell me that Mother was calling me to go to bed. I would hang my head in confusion at being thus publicly dragged away, but would bow to superior force and go to my bedroom. Outside all was tumult and shouting, outside flared the lighted chandeliers, but in my room there was not a sound and a brass lamp burned low on its stand. Even in sleep I was dimly conscious of the crash of the cymbals marking the rhythm of the dance.

The grown-ups usually forbade everything on principle, but on one occasion for some reason or other they decided to be indulgent, and the order went forth that the children also might come to the play. It was a drama about Nala and Damayanti. Before it began we were sent to bed till half-past eleven. We were assured again and again that when the time came we should be roused, but we knew the ways of the grown-ups, and we had no faith at all in these promises —they were adults, and we were children!

That night, however, I did drag my unwilling body to bed. For one thing, Mother promised that she herself would come and wake me. For another thing, I always had to pinch myself to keep myself awake after nine o'clock. When the time came I was awakened and brought outside, blinking and bewildered in the dazzling glare. Light streamed brightly from coloured chandeliers on the first and second storeys, and the white sheets spread in the courtyard made it seem much bigger than usual. On one side were seated the people of importance, senior members of the family, and their invited guests. The remaining space was filled with a motley crowd of all who cared to come. The performing company was led by a famous actor wearing a gold chain across his stomach, and old and young crowded together in the audience. The majority of the audience were what the respectable would call 'riff-raff'. The play itself had been written by men whose hands were trained only to the villager's reed pen, and who had never practiced on the letters of an English copy book. Tunes, dances, and story had all sprung from the very heart of rural Bengal, and no pundit had polished their style.

We went and sat by our elder brothers in the audience, and they tied up small sums of money in kerchiefs and gave them to us. It was the custom to throw this money on to the stage at the points where applause was most deserved. By this means the actors gained some extra profit and the family a good reputation.

The night came to an end, but the play would not. I never knew whose arms gathered up my limp body, or where they carried me. I was far too much ashamed to try to find out. I, a fellow who had beensitting like an equal among the grown-ups and doling out baksheesh, to be disgraced in this way before a whole courtyard full of people! When I woke up I was lying on the divan in my mother's room; it was very late, and already blazing hot. The sun had risen, but I had not risen! Such a thing had never happened before.

Nowadays the city's pleasures flow on in an unbroken stream. There is always a cinema show somewhere, and whoever pleases may see it for a trifling sum. But in those days entertainments were few and far between, like water holes dug in the sandy bed of a dried up river, three or four miles apart. Like these too they lasted only a few hours, and the wayfarers hastily gathered round, drinking from their cupped hands to quench their thirst.

The old days were like a king's son who, from time to time on festive occasions, or according to his whim, distributes rich and royal gifts to all within his jurisdiction. Modern days are like a merchant's son, sitting at the cross-roads on some great highway with many kinds of cheap and tawdry goods spread glittering before him, and drawing his customers by highway and byway from every side.

VI

Brajeswar was the head-servant, and his second-in-command was called Shyam. He came from Jessore, and he was a real countryman, speaking in a dialect strange to Calcutta. He would say "tenara" and "onara" for "tara" and "ora", "jati" and "khati" for "jete" and "khete". He used to call us affectionately "Domani". He had a dark skin, big eyes, long hair glistening with oil, and a strong, well-built body. He was really good at heart, and affectionate and kind to children. He used to tell us stories of dacoits. Dacoity stories filled men's houses then as universally as the fear of ghosts filled their minds. Even today dacoity is not uncommon; murder, assault and looting still take place, and the police still do not catch the right man. But nowadays, this is only a news-item; it has none of the fascination of romance. In those days dacoities were woven into stories, and passed from mouth to mouth for long periods. In my childhood men were still to be met with who in their prime had been members of dacoit gangs. They were all past-masters in the science of the lathi, and were surrounded by disciples eager to learn the art of single-stick. Men salaamed at the very mention of their names. Dacoity then was usually not a mere matter of rash, headstrong bloodshed. As bodily strength and skill played their part, so did a generous, gallant mind. Moreover, gentlemen's houses often contained an exercise-ground for the practice of lathi-fighting, and those who made a name on these grounds were acknowledged as masters even by dacoits, who gave them a wide berth. Many zemindars made a profession of dacoity. There was a story of a man of this class who had stationed his desperadoes at the mouth of a river. It was new moon, and poojah night, and when they returned, carrying a severed head to the temple in honour of Kali Kankali, the zemindar clapped his hands to his head and cried out, "What have you done? It's my son-in-law!"

We heard also about the exploits of the dacoits Raghu and Bishu. They used to give notice before they attacked, and there was nothing underhand in their dacoity. When their rallying-cry was heard in the distance, the blood of the villagers ran cold. But their code forbade them to lay hands on women. On one occasion, in fact, a woman even succeeded in 'robbing the robbers', by appearing to them dressed as Kali, brandishing the goddess's heavy curved blade, and claiming their devout offerings.

One day there was a display of dacoits' wresting feats in our house. They were all strong young fellows, big-made, dark-skinned, and long-haired. One man tied a cloth round a heavy grain-pounder, seized the cloth in his teeth, and then flung the pounder upwards and backwards over his shoulder. Another got a man to grasp him by his shaggy hair, and then whirled him round and round by a mere turn of his head. Using a long pole as support and lever, they leaped up to the second storey. Then one man stood with his hands clasped above his bent head, and others shot through the aperture like diving birds. They also showed how it was possible for them to manage a dacoity twenty or thirty miles away, and the same night be found sleeping peacefully in their beds like law-abiding citizens. They had a pair of very long poles with a piece of wood lashed cross-wise in the middle of each as a footrest. These poles were called rang-pa (stilts). When walking with the tops of the poles held in the hands, and the feet on these footholds, one stride had the value of ten ordinary steps, and a man could run faster than a horse. I used to encourage boys at Santiniketan to practise stilt-walking —though without any idea of committing dacoity! My imagination mingled such pictures of dacoity feats with Shyam's stories with gruesome effect, so that I have often spent the evening with my arms huddled against my pounding heart!

Sunday was a holiday. On the previous evening the crickets were chirping in the thickets outside in the south garden, and the story was about Raghu the highwayman. My heart went pit-a-pat in the dimlight and flickering shadows of the room. The next day in my holiday leisure I climbed into the palanquin. It began to move unbidden, its destination unknown, and my mind, enthralled still by the magic of the previous night's romance, and knew a thrill of delicious fear. In the silent darkness my pulses attuned themselves to the rhythmic shouts of the bearers, and my body grew numb with terrified anticipation.

On the boundless expanse of plain the air quivers in the heat, in the distance glistens the Kali tank; the sand sparkles, the wide-spreading pakur tree leans from the bank of the river over the cracked, ruined ghat. My romance-fed terrors are concentrated on that thick clump of reeds, and in the shade of the tree on that unknown plain. Nearer and nearer we approach, quicker and quicker beats my heart. Above the reeds can be seen the tips of one or two stout bamboo staves. The bearers will stop there to change shoulders. They will drink, and wind wet towels round their heads. And then?...

Then with a blood-curdling shout, the dacoits are upon us....

VII

From morning till night the mills of learning went on grinding. To wind up this creaking machinery was the work of Shejadada, Hemendranath. He was a stern taskmaster, but it is useless now to try to hide the fact that the greater part of the cargo with which he sought to load our minds tipped out of the boat and sent to the bottom. My learning at any rate was a profitless cargo. If one seeks to key an instrument to too high a pitch, the strings will snap beneath the strain.

Shejadada made all arrangements for the education of his eldest daughter. When the time came he got her admitted into the Loreto Convent School, but even before that she had been given a foundation in Bengali. He also gave Protibha a thorough training in western music, which, however, did not cause her to lose her skill in Indian music. Among the gentlemen's families of that time she had no equal in Hindustani songs.

It is one merit of western music that its scales and exercises demand diligent practice, that it makes for a sensitive ear, and that the discipline of the piano allows of no slackness in the matter of rhythm.

Meanwhile she had learnt Indian music from her earliest years from our teacher Vishnu. In this school of music I also had to be entered. No present-day musician, whether famous or obscure, would have consented to touch the kind of songs with which Vishnu initiated us. They were the very commonest kind of Bengali folk songs. Let me give you a few examples:

'A gypsy lass is come to town
To paint tattoos, my sister.
The painting's nothing, so they tell,
Yet she on me has cast a spell,
And makes me weep and mocks me well,
By her tattoos, my sister.'

I remember also a few fragmentary lines, such as:

'The sun and moon have owned defeat,
the firefly's lamp lights up the stage;

the Moghul and the Pathan flag,
the weaver reads the Persian page.'
and;
"Your daughter-in-law is the plantain tree.
Mother of Ganesh, let her be.
For if but one flower should blossom and grow
She will have so many children you won't
know what to do."

Lines too come back to me in which one can catch a glimpse of old forgotten histories:

"There was a jungle of thorn and burr,
Fit for the dogs alone;
There did he cut for himself a throne…"

The modern custom is first to practice scales— sa-re-ga-ma etc., on the harmonium, and then to teach some simple Hindi songs. But the wise supervisor who was then in charge of our studies understood that boyhood has its own childish needs, and that these simple Bengali words would come much more easily to Bengali children than Hindi speech. Besides this, the rhythm of this folk music defied all accompaniments by tabla. It danced itself into our very pulses. The experiment thus made showed that just as a child learns his first enjoyment of literature from his mother's nursery rhymes, he learns his first enjoyment of music also from the same source.

The harmonium, that bane of Indian music, was not then in vogue, I practiced my songs with my tambura resting on my shoulder, I did not subject myself to the slavery of the keyboard.

It was no one's fault but my own, that nothing could keep me for many days together in the beaten track of learning. I strayed at will, filling my wallet with whatever gleanings of knowledge I chanced upon. If I had been disposed to give my mind to my studies, the musicians of these days would have had no cause to slight my work. For I had plenty of opportunity. As long as my brother was in charge of my education,

I repeated Brahmo songs with Vishnu in an absent-minded fashion. When I felt so inclined I would sometimes hang about the doorway while Shejadada was practising, and pick up the song that was going on. Once he was singing to the Behag air, "O thou of slow and stately tread". Unobserved I listened and fixed the tune in my mind, and astounded my mother -an easy task—by singing it to her that evening. Our family friend Srikantha Babu was absorbed in music day and night. He would sit on the verandah, rubbing chameli oil on his body before his bath, his hookah in his hand, and the fragrance of amber-scented tobacco rising into the air. He was always humming tunes, which attracted us boys around him. He never taught us songs, he simply sang them to us, and we picked them up almost without knowing it. When he could no longer restrain his enthusiasm, he would stand up and dance, accompanying himself on the sitar. His big expressive eyes shone with enjoyment, he burst into the song, Mai chhoro brajaki basari, and would not rest content till I joined in too.

In matters of hospitality, people kept open house in those days. There was no need for a man to be intimately known before he was received. There was a bed to be had at any time, and a plate of rice at the regular meal times for any who chanced to come. One day, for example, one such stranger guest, who carried his tambura wrapped in a quilt on his shoulder, opened his bundle, sat down, and stretched his legs at case on one side of our reception room, and Kanai the hookah-tender offered him the customary courtesy of the hookah.

Pan, like tobacco, played a great part in the reception of guests. In those days the morning occupation of the women in the inner apartments consisted in preparing piles of pan for the use of those who visited the outer reception room. Deftly they placed the lime on the leaf, smeared catechu on it with a small stick, and putting in the appropriate amount of spice folded and secured it with a clove. This prepared pan was then piled into a brass container, and a moist piece of cloth, stained with catechu, acted as cover. Meanwhile, in the room under the staircase outside, the stir and bustle of preparing tobacco would be going on. In a big earthenware tub were balls of charcoal covered with ash, the pipes of the hookahs hung down like snakes of Nagaloka, with the scent of rosewater in their veins. This amber scent of tobacco was the first welcome extended by the household to those who climbed the steps to visit the house. Such was the invariable custom then prescribed for the fitting reception of guests. That overflowing bowl of pan has long since been discarded, and the caste of hookah-tenders have thrown off their liveries and taken to the sweetmeat shops, where they knead up three-day-old sandesh and refashion it for sale.

That unknown musician stayed for a few days, just as he chose. No one asked him any questions. At dawn I used to drag him from his mosquito curtains and make him sing to me. (Those who have no fancy for regular study revel in study that is irregular). The morning melody of *Bansi hamari re...* would rise on the air.

After this, when I was a little older, a very great musician called Jadu Bhatta came and stayed in the house. He made one big mistake in being determined to teach me music, and consequently no teaching took place. Nevertheless, I did casually pick up from him a certain amount of stolen knowledge. I was very fond of the song *Ruma jhuma barakha ajubadaraa...* which was set to a Kafi tune, and which remains to this day in my store of rainy season songs. But unfortunately just at this time another guest arrived without warning, who had a name as a tiger-killer. A Bengali tiger-killer was a real marvel in those days, and it followed that I remained captivated in his room for the greater part of the time. I realise clearly now what I never dreamed of then, that the tiger whose fell clutches he so thrillingly described could never have bitten him at all; perhaps he got the idea from the snarling jaws of the stuffed Museum tigers. But in those days I busied myself eagerly in the liberal provision of pan and tobacco for this hero, while the distant strains of kanara music fell faintly on my indifferent ears.

So much for music. In other studies the foundation provided by Shejadada was equally generously laid. It was the fault of my own nature that no great matter came of it. It was with people like me in view that Ramprosad Sen wrote, "O Mind, you do not understand the art of cultivation." With me, the work of cultivation never took place.

But let me tell you of a few fields where the ploughing at least was done.

I got up while it was still dark and practiced wrestling—on cold days I shivered and trembled with cold. In the city was a celebrated one-eyed wrestler, who gave me practice. On the north side of the outer room was an open space known as the 'granary'. The name clearly had survived from a time when the city had not yet completely crushed out all rural life, and a few open spaces still remained. When the life of the city was still young our granary had been filled with the whole year's store of grain, and the ryots who held their land on lease from us brought to it their appointed portion. It was here that the lean-to shed for wrestling was built against the compound wall. The ground had been prepared by digging and loosening the earth to a depth of about a cubit and pouring over it a maund of mustard oil. It was mere child's play for the wrestler to try a fall with me there, but I would manage to get well smeared with dust by the end of the lesson, when I put on my shirt and went indoors.

Mother did not like to see me come in every morning so covered with dust—she feared that the colour of her son's skin would be darkened and spoiled. As a result, she occupied herself on holidays in scrubbing me. (Fashionable housewives of today buy their toilet preparations in boxes from western shops; but then they used to make their unguent with their own hands. It contained almond paste, thickened cream, the rind of oranges and many other things which I forget. If only I had learnt and remembered the receipt, I might have set up a shop and sold it as 'Begum Bilash' unguent, and made at least as much money as the sandesh-wallahs.) On Sunday mornings there was a great rubbing and scrubbing on the verandah, and I would begin to grow restless to get away. Incidentally a story used to go about among our school fellows that in our house babies were bathed in wine as soon as they were born, and that was the reason for our fair European complexions.

When I came in from the wrestling ground I saw a Medical College student waiting to teach me the lore of bones. A whole skeleton hung on the wall. It used to hang at night on the wall of our bedroom, and the bones swayed in the wind and rattled together. But the fear I might otherwise have felt had been overcome by constantly handling it, and by learning by heart the long, difficult names of the bones.

The clock in the porch struck seven. Master Nilkamal was a stickler for punctuality, there was no chance of a moment's variation. He had a thin, shrunken body, but his health was as good as his pupil's, and never once, unluckily for us, was he afflicted even by a headache. Taking my book and slate I sat down before the table, and he began to write figures on the blackboard in chalk. Everything was in Bengali, arithmetic, algebra and geometry. In literature I jumped at one bound from Sitar Banabas to Meghnadbadh Kabya. Along with this there was natural science. From time to time Sitanath Datta would come, and we acquired some superficial knowledge of science by experiments with familiar things. Once Heramba Tattvaratna, the Sanskrit scholar, came; and I began to learn the Mugdhabodh Sanskrit grammar by heart, though without understanding a word of it.

In this way, all through the morning, studies of all kinds were heaped upon me, but as the burden grew greater, my mind contrived to get rid of fragments of it; making a hole in the enveloping net, my parrot-learning slipped through its meshes and escaped—and the opinion that Master Nilkamal expressed of his pupil's intelligence was not of the kind to be made public.

In another part of the verandah is the old tailor, his thick-lensed spectacles on his nose, sitting bent over his sewing, and ever and anon, at the prescribed hours, going through the ritual of his Namaz. I watch him and think what a lucky fellow Niamat is. Then, with my head in a whirl from doing sums, I shade my eyes with my slate, and looking down see in front of the entrance porch Chandrabhan the durwan combing his long beard with a wooden comb, dividing it in two and looping it round each ear. The assistant durwan, a slender boy, is sitting near by, a bracelet on his arm, and cutting tobacco. Over there the horse has already finished his morning allowance of gram, and the crows are hopping round pecking at the scattered grains. Our dog Johnny's sense of duty is aroused and he drives them away barking.

I had planted a custard-apple seed in the dust which continual sweeping had collected in one corner of the verandah. All agog with excitement, I watched for the sprouting of the new leaves. As soon as Master Nilkamal had gone, I had to run and examine it, and water it. In the end my hopes went unfulfilled —the same broom that had gathered the dust together dispersed it again to the four winds.

Now the sun climbs higher, and the slanting shadows cover only half the courtyard. The clock strikes nine. Govinda, short and dark, with a dirty yellow towel slung over his shoulder, takes me off to bathe me. Promptly at half past nine comes our monotonous, unvarying meal—the daily ration of rice, dal and fish curry—it was not much to my taste.

The clock strikes ten. From the main street isheard the hawker's cry of "Green Mangoes"—what wistful dreams it awakens! From further and further away resounds the clanging of the receding brass-peddler, striking his wares till they ring again. The lady of the neighbouring house in the lane is drying her hair on the roof, and her two little girls are playing with shells. They have plenty of leisure, for in those days girls were not obliged to go to school, and I used to think how fine it would have been to be born a girl. But as it is, the old horse draws me in the rickety carriage to my Andamans, in which from ten to four I am doomed to exile.

At half past four I return from school. The gymnastic master has come, and for about an hour I exercise my body on the parallel bars. He has no sooner gone than the drawing master arrives.

Gradually the rusty light of day fades away. The many blurred noises of the evening are heard as a dreamy hum resounding over the demon city of brick and mortar. In the study room an oil lamp is burning. Master Aghor has come and the English lesson begins. The black-covered reader is lying in wait for me on the table. The cover is loose; the pages are stained and a little torn; I have tried my hand at writing my name in English in it, in the wrong places, and all in capital letters. As I read I nod, then jerk myself awake again with a start, but miss far more than I read. When finally I tumble into bed I have at last a little time to call my own.And there I listen to endless stories of the king's son travelling over an endless, trackless plain.

VIII

When I see the roofs of modern houses, uninhabited by either men or ghosts, I realise vividly the change that has taken place between those times and these. I have already mentioned how the brahma-daitya of the badam tree has fled, unable to endure the modern atmosphere of excessive learning. On the cornice where rumour had it that he had rested his foot, the crows snatch and squabble over our discarded mango stones. And men too restrict themselves nowadays to the confined, boxed-in rooms of the lower storeys, and pass their time within four walls.

My mind goes back to the parapet-surrounded roof of the inner apartments. It is evening, and Mother has spread her mat and seated herself, with her friends gossiping round her. Their talk has no need of authentic information; it is only a means of passing the time. There was then no regular supply of valuable and varied ingredients to fill the day, which was not, as now, a closely woven mesh, but like a net of loose texture, full of holes. And therefore, stories and rumours, laughter and jokes, all in the lightest vein, filled both the social gatherings of the men and the women's assemblies. Among Mother's friends the first in importance was Braja Acharji's lister, who was called 'Acharjini'. She was the daily purveyor of news to the company. Almost every day she picked up, (or made up) and brought with her, every item of fantastic, ominous news in the country. By this means expenditure on all ceremonies calculated to avert impending calamity or the evil eye, was greatly increased.

Into this assembly I imported from time to time my recently acquired book-learning. I informed them that the sun is nine crores of miles distant from the earth. From the second part of my Rju-Path I recited a portion of Valmiki's Ramayana in the original complete with Sanskrit terminations. Mother was no judge of the accuracy of her son's pronunciation, but the range of his learning filled her with awe, and seemed to her far to outrun the nine-crore mile journey of light. Who would have thought that any except Naradmuni himself could recite all these slokas?

This inner apartment roof was entirely the women's domain, and had a close connection with the store room. The sun's rays fell full upon it, so it was used for preparing lemons for pickle. The women used to sit there with brass vessels full of kalai paste, and while their hair was drying they made pulse-balls with their deft, quick fingers. The maid-servants who had washed the soiled linen came here to spread it in the sun, for the dhoby had little work in those days. Green mangoes were cut in slices and dried into amsi. The mango juice was poured layer after layer into black stone moulds of all sizes and all patterns. A pickle of young jack-fruit stood there to season in sun-warmed mustard oil. Catechu, scented with the fragrant screw-pine, would be prepared with great care.

I had a special reason for remembering this item. When my schoolmaster informed me that he had heard the fame of my family's screw-pine catechu, it was not difficult to understand his meaning. What he had heard of, he wished to become acquainted with. So to preserve the good name of my family, I occasionally climbed secretly to the roof containing the screw-pine catechu, and—what shall I say? 'Appropriated' a piece or two sounds better than 'stole'. For even kings and emperors may make 'appropriations' when need arises, or indeed even if it does not, but vulgar 'stealing' is punished by prison or impaling.

In the pleasant sunlight of the cold weather it was the family tradition for the women to sit on the roof gossiping, driving off crows and passing the time of day. I was the only younger brother-in-law in the house, the guardian of my sister-in-law's 'amsatta', and her friend and ally in many other trivial pursuits. I used to read to them from Bangadhipa Parajaya. From time to time the duty of cutting up betel-nut would devolve on me. I could cut betel very finely. My sister-in-law would never admit that I had any other good quality, so much so that she even made me angry with God for giving me such a faulty appearance. But she found no difficulty in speaking in exaggerated fashion of my skill in cutting betel. Therefore the work of betel-cutting used to go on at a fine pace. But for a long time now, for want of anyone to encourage me, the hand that was so skilled in fine betel-cutting has perforce busied itself in other fine work.

Around all this women's work spread on the roof there lingered the aroma of village life. These occupations belonged to the days when there was a pounding-room in the house, when confectionery balls were made, when the maid-servants sat in the evening rolling on their thighs the cotton wicks for the oil lamps, when invitations came from neighbours' houses to the ceremonies of the eighth day after birth. Modern children do not hear fairy stories from their mothers' lips; they read them for themselves in printed books. Pickles and chutney are bought from the Newmarket by the bottleful, each bottle corked and scaled with wax.

Another relic of a bygone village life was the chandimandap, the outer verandah where the school was held. Not only the boys of the house, but those of the neighbourhood, also, made there their first attempt to search letters on palm-leaves. I suppose that I too must have traced out my first laborious letters on that verandah, but I have no clear memory of the child I then was, who seems as far removed as the farthest planet of the solar system, and I possess no telescope which can bring him into view.

The first thing I remember about reading after this is the terrible story of Sanamarka Muni's school, and of the avatar Narasimha tearing the bowels of Hiranyakasipu; I think also that there was a lead-plate engraving of it in the same book—and I remember also reading a few slokas of Chanakya.

My chief holiday resort was the unfenced roof of the outer apartments. From my earliest childhood till I was grown up, many varied days were spent on that roof in many moods and thoughts. When my father was at home his room was on the second floor. How often I watched him at a distance, from my hiding place at the head of the staircase. The sun had not yet risen, and he sat on the roof silent as an image of white stone, his hands folded in his lap. From time to time he would leave home for long periods in the mountains, and then the journey to the roof held for me the joy of a voyage through the seven seas. Sitting on the familiar first floor verandah I had daily watched through the railings the people going about the street. But to climb to that roof was to be raised beyond the swarming habitations of men. When I went on to the roof my mind strode proudly over prostrate Calcutta to where the last blue of the sky mingled with the last green of the earth ; my eye fell on the roofs of countless houses, of all shapes and sizes, high and low, with the shaggy tops of trees between.

I would go up secretly to this roof, usually at midday. The midday hours have always held a fascination for me. They are like the night of the daytime, the time when the Sannyasi spirit in every boy makes him long to quit his familiar surroundings. I put my hand through the shutter and drew the bolt of the door. Right opposite the door was a sofa, and I sat there in perfect bliss of solitude. The servants who acted as my warders had eaten their fill and become drowsy, and yawning and stretching had betaken themselves to sleep on their mats. The afternoon sunlight deepened into gold, and the kite rose screaming into the sky. The bangle-seller went crying his wares down the opposite lane. His sudden cry would penetrate to where the housewife lay with her loosened hair falling over her pillow, a maidservant would bring him in, and the old bangle-seller dexterously kneaded the tender fingers as he fitted on the glass bangles that took her fancy. The hushed pause of that old-world midday is now no more, and the hawkers of the silent time are heard no longer. The girl who in those days had married status, nowadays has still not attained it, she is learning her lessons in the second class. Perhaps the bangle-seller runs, pulling a rickshaw, down that very lane.

The roof was like what I imagined the deserts of my books to be, a sheer expanse of quivering haze. A hot wind ran panting across it, whirling up the dust, the blue of the sky paled above it. Moreover, in this roof desert there appeared an oasis. Nowadays the pipe water does not reach the upper floors, but then it ran even up to the second floor rooms. Like some young Livingstone of Bengal, alone and unaided, I secretly sought and found a new Niagara, the private bathroom. I would turn on the tap, and the water would run all over my body. I then took a sheet from the bed and dried myself, looking the picture of innocence.

Gradually the holiday drew towards its close, and four struck on the gateway clock. The face of the sky on Sunday evenings was always very ill-favoured. There fell across it the shadow of the coming Monday's gaping jaws, already swallowing it in dark eclipse. Below at last a search had been instituted for the boy who had given his guards the slip, for now it was tiffin time. This part of the day was a red-letter time for Brajeswar. He was in charge of buying the tiffin. In those days the shopkeepers did not make thirty or forty per cent, profit on the price of ghee, and in odour and flavour the tiffin was still unpoisoned. When we were lucky enough to get them, we lost no time in eating up our kochuri, singard, or even alur dom. But when the time came round and Brajeswar, with his neck still further twisted, called to us, "Look babu, what I have brought you today", what was usually to be found in his cone of paper was merely a handful of fried groundnuts. It was not that I did not like this, but its attractiveness lay in its price. I never made the least objection, not even on the days when only sesamum goja came out of the palm-leaf wrapper.

The light of day begins to grow murky. Once more with a gloomy spirit, I make the round of the roof. I gaze down at the scene below, where a procession of geese has climbed out of the tank. People have begun to come and go again on the steps of the ghat, the shadow of the banyan tree lengthens across half the tank, the driver of a carriage and pair is yelling at the pedestrians in the street.

IX

In this way the days passed monotonously on. School grabbed the best part of the day, and only fragments of time in the morning and evening slipped through its clutching fingers. As soon as I entered the classroom, the benches and tables forced themselves rudely on my attention, elbowing and jostling their way into my mind. They were always the same—stiff, cramping, and dead. In the evening I went home, and the oil lamp in our study-room, like a stern signal, summoned me to the preparation of the next day's lessons. There is a kind of grass-hopper which takes die colour of the withered leaves among which it lurks unobserved. In like manner my spirit also shrank and faded among those faded, drab-coloured days.

Now and again there came to our courtyard a man with a dancing bear, or a snake-charmer playing with his snakes. Now and again the visit of a juggler provided some little novelty. Today the drums of the juggler and snake-charmer no longer beat in our Chitpore Road. From afar they have salaamed to the cinema, and fled before it from the city. Games were few and of very ordinary kinds. We had marbles, we had what is called 'bat-ball' a very poor distant relation of cricket, and there were also top-spinning and kite-flying. All the games of the city childrenwere of this same lazy kind. Football, with all its running and jumping about on a big field, was still in its overseas home. And so I was fenced in by the deadly sameness of the days, as though by an imprisoning hedge of lifeless, withered twigs.

In the midst of this monotony there played one day the flutes of festivity. A new bride came to the house, slender gold bracelets on her delicate brown hands. In the twinkling of an eye the cramping fence was broken, and a new being came into view from the magic land beyond the bounds of the familiar. I circled around her at a safe distance, but I did not dare to go near. She was enthroned at the centre of affection, and I was only a neglected, insignificant child.

The house was then divided into two suites of rooms. The men lived in the outer, and the women in the inner apartments. The ways of the nabobs obtained there still. I remember how my elder sister was walking on the roof with the new bride at her side, and they were exchanging intimacies freely. As soon as I tried to go near, however, I brought reprimand on my head, for these quarters were outside the boundaries laid down for boys. I saw myself obliged to go back crestfallen to my shabby retreat of former days.

The monsoon rain, rushing down suddenly from the distant mountains, undermines the ancient banks in a moment, and that is what happened now. The new mistress brought a new regime into the house. The quarters of the bride were in the room adjoining the roof of the inner suite. That roof was under her complete control. It was there that the leaf-plates were spread for the dolls' weddings. On such feast days, boy as I was, I became the guest of honour. My new sister-in-law could cook well, and enjoyed feeding people, and I was always ready to satisfy this craving for playing the hostess. As soon as I returned from school some delicacy made with her own hands stood ready for me. One day she gave me shrimp curry with yesterday's soaked rice, and a dash of chillies for flavouring, and I felt that I had nothing left to wish for. Sometimes when she went to stay with relatives and I did not see her slippers outside the door of her room, I would go in a temper and steal some valuable object from her room, and lay the foundation of a quarrel. When she returned and missed it, I had only to make such a remark as 'Do you expect me to keep an eye on your room when you go away? Am I a watchman?' She would pretend to be angry and say, 'You have no need to keep an eye on the room. Watch your own hands.' Modern women will smile at the nad'vete of their predecessors who knew how to entertain only their own brothers-in-law, and I daresay they are right. People today are much more grown-up in every way than they were then. Then we were all children alike, both young and old.

X

And so began a new chapter of my lonely Bedouin life on the roof, and human company and friendship entered it. Across the roof kingdom a new wind blew, and a new season began there. My brother Jyotidada played a large part in this change. At that time my father finally left our home at Jorasanko. Jyotidada settled himself into that outside second-floor room, and I claimed a little corner of it for my own.

No purdah was observed in my sister-in-law's apartments. That will strike no one as strange today, but it then sounded an unimaginable depth of novelty. A long time even before that, when I was a baby, my second brother had returned from England to enter the Civil Service. When he went to Bombay to take up his first post he astonished the neighbourhood by taking off his wife with him before their very eyes. And as if it was not enough to take her away to a distant province, instead of leaving her in the family home, he made no provision for proper privacy on the journey. That was a terrible breach of propriety. Even the relatives felt as if the sky had fallen on their heads.

A style of dress suitable for going out was still not in vogue among women. It was this sister-in-law who first introduced the manner of wearing the sari and blouse which is now customary. Little girls had not then begun to wear frocks or let their hair hang in plaits—at least not in our family. The little ones used to wear the tight Rajput pyjamas instead of the traditional sari. When the Bethune School was first opened my eldest sister was quite young. She was one of the pioneers who made the road to education easy for girls. She was very fair, uniquely so for this country. I have heard that once when she was going to school in her palanquin the police detained her, thinking her in her Rajput dress to be an English girl who had been kidnapped.

I said before that in those days there was no bridge of intimacy between adults and children. Into the tangle of these old customs Jyotidada brought a vigorously original mind. I was twelve years younger than he, and that I should come to his notice in spite of such a difference in age is in itself surprising. What was more surprising is that in my talks with him he never called me impudent or snubbed me. Thanks to this, I never lacked courage to think for myself. Today I live with children, I try all kinds of subjects of conversation, but I find them dumb. They hesitate to ask questions. They seem to me to belong to those old times when the grown-ups talked and the children remained silent. The self-confidence that doubts and questions is the mark of the children of the new age; those of the former age are known by a meek and docile acceptance of what they are told.

A piano appeared in the terrace room. There came also modern varnished furniture from Bow-bazar. My breast swelled with pride, as the cheap grandeur of modern times was displayed before eyes inured to poverty. At this time the fountain of my song was unloosed. Jyotidada's hands would stray about the piano as he composed and rattled off tunes in various new styles, and he would keep me by his side as he did so. It was my work to fix the tunes which he composed so rapidly by setting words to them then and there.

At the end of the day a mat and pillow were spread on the terrace. Nearby was a thick garland of bel flowers on a silver plate, in a wet handkerchief, a glass of iced water on a saucer, and some chhanchi pan in a bowl. My sister-in-law would bathe, dress her hair and come and sit with us. Jyotidada would come out with a silk chaddar thrown over his shoulders, and draw the bow across his violin, and I would sing in my clear treble voice. For providence had not yet taken away the gift of voice it had given me, and under the sunset sky my song rang out across the house-tops. The south wind came in great gusts from the distant sea, the sky filled with stars.

My sister-in-law turned the whole roof into a garden. She arranged rows of tall palms in barrels and beside and around them chameli, gandharaj, rajanigandha, karabi and dolan-champa. She considered not at all the possible damage to the roof— we were all alike unpractical visionaries.

Akshay Chaudhuri used to come almost every day. He himself knew that he had no voice; other people knew it even better. In spite of that nothing could stop the flow of his song. His special favourite was the Behag mode. He sang with his eyes shut, so he did not see the expression on the faces of his hearers. As soon as anything capable of making a noise came to hand, he took it and turned it into a drum, beating it in happy absorption, biting his lips with his teeth in his earnestness. Even a book with a stiff binding would do very well. He was by nature a dreamy kind of man; one could see no difference between his working days and his holidays.

The evening party broke up, but I was a boy of nocturnal habits. All went to lie down; I alone would wander about all night with the Brahma-daitya. The whole district was steeped in silence. On moonlight nights the shadows of the lines of palm-trees on the terrace lay in dream-patterns on the floor. Beyond the terrace the top of the sishu tree swayed and tossed in the breeze, and its leaves gleamed as they caught the light. But for some reason, what caught my eye more than anything was a squat room with a sloping roof built over the staircase of the sleeping house on the opposite side of the lane. It stood like a finger pointing forever towards I knew not what.

It may have been one or two in the morning, when in the main street in front a wailing chant arose- Bolo-Hari Hari-bol

XI

It was the fashion then in every house to keep caged birds. I hated this, and the worst thing of all to me was the call of a koel imprisoned in a cage in some house in the neighbourhood. Bouthakrun had acquired a Chinese shyama. From under its covering of cloth its sweet whistling rose continuously, a fountain of song. Besides this there were other birds of all kinds, and their cages hung in the west verandah. Every morning a bird-seed and insect hawker provided the birds food. Grass-hoppers came from his basket, and gram-flour for the grain-eating birds.

Jyotidada gave me proper answers in my difficulties, but as much could not be expected from the women. Once Bouthakrun took a fancy for keeping pet squirrels in cages. I said it wasn't right, and she told me not to set myself up to be her teacher. That could hardly be called a reasoned reply, and consequently, instead of wasting time in bickering, I privately set two of the little creatures free. After that too I had to listen to a certain amount of scolding, but I made no retort.

There was a permanent quarrel between us which was never made up, which was as follows.

There was a smart fellow called Umesh. He used to go the rounds of the English tailoring shops and buy up for an old song all their scraps, remnants and strips of many coloured silk, and make up women's garments from them with the addition of a bit of net and cheap lace. He would open his paper parcel and spread them carefully out before the eyes of the women, extolling them as "the very latest fashion". The women could not resist the attraction of such a mantra, but I disliked it all intensely. Again and again, unable to contain myself, I made known my objections, but all the answer I got was "Don't be cheeky". I used to tell Bouthakrun that the old-fashioned black-bordered white saries, and the Dacca ones, were far better and more tasteful than these. I sometimes wonder, do modern brothers-in-law never open their mouths when they see their Boudidis robed in these modern georgette saris, with their faces painted like dolls? Even Bouthakrun decked out in Umesh's handiwork was not as bad as they are. Ladies then were at least not so guilty of forgery in dress or complexion.

I was however always beaten by Bouthakrun in argument, because she would never deign to give a logical answer; and I was beaten too in chess, in which she was an expert.

As I have referred to Jyotidada I ought to give a little more information about him, to make him better known. To do that I must go back to rather earlier days.

He had to go very often to Shelidah to see after the business of the zemindari. Once when he was travelling for this purpose he took me also with him. This was quite contrary to custom in those days; in fact it was what people would have called 'altogether too much'. He certainly considered that this travelling away from home was a kind of peripatetic schooling. He realized that my nature was attuned to ramblings in the open air, that in such surroundings it nourished itself spontaneously. A little later, when I was more mature, it was in Shelidah that my nature developed.

The old indigo factory was still standing, with the river Padma in the distance. The zemindari office was on the ground floor, and our living quarters on the upper floor. In front of them was a very large terrace. Beyond were tall casuarina trees, which had grown in stature with the growing prosperity of the indigo-trading sahebs. Today the blustering shouts of the sahebs are completely silent. Where is now the indigo factory's steward, that 'messenger of death'? Where the troop of bailiffs, loins girded up and lathis on shoulder? Where is the dining hall with its long tables, where the sahebs rode back from their business in the town and turned night into day? The feasting reached its height, the dancing couples whirled round the room, the blood coursed madly through the veins in the swelling intoxication of champagne—and the authorities never heard the appealing cries of the wretched ryots, whose weary journey took them only to the District Jail. All traces of those days have vanished, save one record alone—the two graves of two of the sahebs. The high casuarina trees bend and sway in the wind, and sometimes at midnight the grandsons and grand-daughters of the former ryots see the ghosts of the sahebs wandering in the deserted waste of garden.

Here I revelled in my solitude, I had a little corner room, and my days of ample leisure were spacious as the wide-spreading terrace. It was the leisure of a strange and unknown region, unfathomable as the dark waters of some ancient tank. The bou-katha-kao calls incessantly, my fancy unweariedly takes wing. Meantime my note-book is gradually filled with verses. They were like the blossoms of the mango-tree's first flowering in the month of Magh, destined like them to wither forgotten.

In those days if a young boy, or still more a young gild, laboriously counted out the fourteen syllables and wrote two lines of verse, the wise critics of the country used to hail it as a unique and unparalleled achievement.

I saw in the papers and magazines the names of these girl-poets, and their verses also were published. Nowadays these carefully constructed metres and crude rhyming platitudes have vanished along with the names of their authors, and the names of countless modern girls have appeared in their stead.

Boys are less bold and far more self-conscious than girls. I do not remember any young boy-poet writing verse in those days, except myself. My sister's son, who was older than I, explained to me one day that if one poured words into a fourteen-syllable mould, they would condense into verse. I soon tried this magic formula for myself. The lotus of poetry blossomed in no time in this fourteen-syllabled form and even the bees found a foot-hold on it. The gulf between me and the poets was bridged, and from that time on I have struggled to overtake them.

I remember how, when I was in the lowest class of the chhatra britti our superintendent Govinda Babu heard a rumour that I l wrote poetry. He thereupon ordered me to write, thinking that it would redound to the credit of the Normal School. There was nothing for it but to write, to read my work before my class-mates, and to hear the verdict—"this verse is assuredly stolen goods". The cynics of that day did not know that when I increased in worldly wisdom I should grow shrewd in stealing, not words but thoughts. Yet it is these stolen goods which are valuable.

I remember once composing a poem in the Payar and Tripadi metres, in which I lamented that as one swims to pluck the lotus it floats further and further away on the waves raised by one's own arms, and remains always out of reach. Akshay Babu took me round to the houses of his relatives and made me recite it to them. "The boy has certainly a gift for writing," they said.

Bouthakrun's attitude was just the opposite. She would never admit that I should ever make a success of writing. She would say mockingly that I should never be able to write like Bihari Chakravarti. I used to think despondently that even if I were placed in a far lower class than he, she would then be prevented from so disregarding her little poet-brother-in-law's disapprobation of women's fashions.

Jyotidada was very fond of riding. He actually took even Bouthakrun riding along Chitpore Road to the Eden Gardens. In Shelidah he gave me a pony, a beast that was no mean runner. He sent me to give the pony a run on the open rath-tala field. I did as I was bidden, in continual imminent danger of a fall on that uneven ground. That I did not fall was solely because he was so determined that I should not do so. Shortly afterwards Jyotidada sent me out riding on the roads of Calcutta also. Not on the pony, but on a high-spirited thorough bred. One day it galloped straight in through the porch, with me on its back, to the courtyard where it was accustomed to be fed. From that day on I had nothing more to do with it.

I have referred elsewhere to the fact that Jyotidada was a practiced shot. He was always eager for a tiger-hunt. One day the shikari Biswanath brought news that a tiger was living in the Shelidah jungle, and Jyotidada at once furbished up his gun and prepared for sport. Surprising to say, he took me with him. It never seemed to occur to him that there could be any danger.

Biswanath was indeed an expert shikari. He knew that there was nothing manly about hunting from a machan. He would call the tiger out and shoot face to face, and he never missed his aim.

The jungle was dense, and in its lights and shadows the tiger refused to show himself. A rough kind of ladder was made by cutting footholds in a stout bamboo, and Jyotidada climbed up with his gun ready to hand. As for me, I was not even wearing slippers, I had not even that poor instrument with which to beat and humiliate the tiger. Biswanath signed to us to be on the alert, but for some time Jyotidada could not even see the tiger. After long straining of his bespectacled eyes he at last caught a glimpse of one of its markings in the thicket. He fired. By a lucky fluke the shot pierced the animal's backbone, and it was unable to rise. It roared furiously, biting at all the sticks and twigs within reach, and lashing its tail. Thinking it over, I know that it is not in the nature of tigers to wait so long and patiently to be killed. I wonder if some one had had the forethought to mix a little opium with its feed on the previous night? Otherwise, why such sound sleep?

There was another occasion when a tiger came to the jungles of Shelidah. My brother and I set out on elephants to look for him. My elephant lurched majestically on, uprooting cane from the sugar-cane fields and munching as he went, so that it was like riding on an earthquake. The jungle lay ahead of us. He crushed the trees with his knees, pulled them up with his trunk and cast them to the ground. I had previously heard tales of terrible possibilities from Biswanath's brother

Chamru, how sometimes the tiger leaps on to the elephant's back and clings there, digging in his claws. Then the elephant, trumpeting with pain, rushes madly through the forest, and whoever is on his back is dashed against the trees till arms, legs and head are crushed out of all recognition. That day, as I sat my elephant, the image of myself thus being pounded to a jelly filled my imagination from first to last. For very shame I concealed my fear, and glanced from side to side in nonchalant fashion, as though to say "Let me but catch a glimpse of the tiger, and then!..." The elephant entered the densest part of the jungle, and coming to a certain place, suddenly stood stock-still. The mahout made no attempt to urge it forward. Hehad clearly more respect for the tiger's powers as a shikari than for my brother's. His great anxiety was undoubtedly that Jyotidada should so wound the tiger as to drive it to desperation. Suddenly the tiger leaped from the jungle, swift as the thunder-charged storm from the cloud. We are accustomed to the sight of a cat, dog, or jackal, but here were shoulders of terrific bulk and power, yet no sense of heaviness in that perfectly proportioned strength. It crossed the open fields at a canter in the full blaze of the midday sun. What loveliness, ease and speed of motion! The land was empty of crops; here indeed was a setting in which to feast one's eyes on the running tiger, this wide stretch of golden stubble drenched in the noonday sunlight.

There is one more story that may prove amusing. In Shelidah the gardener used to pluck flowers and arrange them in the vases. I took a fancy to write poetry with a pen dipped in the coloured essences of flowers. But the moisture that I could obtain by squeezing was not sufficient to wet the tip of my pen. I decided that it must be done by machinery. It would do, I thought, if I had a cup-shaped wooden sieve and a pestle revolving in it. It could be turned by an arrangement of ropes and pulleys. I made known my wants to Jyotidada. It may be that he smiled to himself, but he gave no outward sign. He issued instructions, and the carpenter brought wood. The machine was ready. I filled the wooden cup with flowers, but turn the ropes of the pestle as I would, the flowers merely turned to mud and not a drop of essence ran out. Jyotidada had seen that the essence of flowers was incompatible with the grinding of machinery, yet he never laughed at me.

This was the only occasion in my life on which I tried my hand at engineering. It is said in the sastras that there is a god who compasses the humiliation of those who ignore their limitations. That god cast a mocking glance that day upon my engineering, and from that time I have not so much as laid hands on any kind of instrument, not even on a sitar or an esraj.

I described in my Reminiscences how Jyotidada went bankrupt in his attempt to run a swadeshi steamer company on the rivers of Bengal in competition with the Flotilla Company. Bouthakrun's death had taken place before then. Jyotidada gave up his rooms on the third storey and finally built himself a house on a hill at Ranchi.

XII

A new chapter in the life of the third storey room now opened, as I took up my abode there. Up to that time it had been merely one of my gypsy haunts, like the palanquin and the granary, and I roamed from one to another. But when Bouthakrun came a garden appeared on the roof, and in the room a piano was established. Its flow of new tunes symbolised the changed tenor of my life.

Jyotidada used to arrange to have his coffee in the mornings in the shade of the staircase room on the eastern side of the terrace. At such times he would read to us the first draft of some new play of his. From time to time I also would be called upon to add a few lines with my unpracticed hand. The sun's rays gradually invaded the shade, the crows cried hoarsely to each other as they sat on the roof keeping an eye upon the bread-crumbs. By ten o'clock the patch of shade had dwindled away and the terrace grew hot.

At midday Jyotidada used to go down to the office on the ground-floor. Bouthakrun peeled and cut fruit and arranged it carefully on a silver plate, along with a few sweetmeats made with her own hands, and strewed a few rose petals over it. In a tumbler was coconut milk or fruit-juice or tal shans (fresh palmyra kernels) cooled in ice. Then she covered it with a silk kerchief embroidered with flowers, put it on a Moradabad tray and dispatched it to the office at tiffin time, about one or two o'clock.

Just then Bangadarsan was at the height of its fame, and Suryamukhi and Kundanandini were familiar figures in every house. The whole country thought of nothing else but what had happened and what was going to happen to the heroines.

When Bangadarsan came there was no midday nap for anyone in the neighbourhood. It was my good fortune not to have to snatch for it, for I had the gift of being an acceptable reader. Bouthakrun would rather listen to my reading aloud than read for herself. There were no electric fens then, but as I read I shared the benefits of Bouthakrun's hand fen.

XIII

Now and again Jyotidada used to go for change of air to a garden house on the bank of the Ganges. The Ganges shores had then not yet lost caste at the defiling touch of English commerce. Both shores alike were still the undisturbed haunt of birds, and the mechanised dragons of industry did not darken the light of heaven with the black breath of their up reared snouts.

My earliest memory of our life by the Ganges is of a small two-storey house. The first rains had just fallen. Cloud shadows danced on the ripples of the stream, cloud shadows lay dark upon the jungles of the further shore. I had often composed songs of my own on such days, but that day I did not do so. The lines of Vidyapati came to my mind, e bhara badara maha bhadara sunya mandira mor. Moulding them to my own melody and stamping them with my own musical mood, I made them my own. The memory of that monsoon day jeweled with that music on the Ganges shore, is still preserved in my treasury of rainy season songs. I see in memory the tree-tops struck ever and again by great gusts of wind, till their boughs and branches were tangled together in an ecstasy of play. The boats and dinghies raised their white sails, and scudded before the gale, the waves leaped against the ghat with sharp, slapping sounds. Bouthakrun came back and I sang my song to her. She listened in silence and said no word of praise. I must then have been sixteen or seventeen years old. We used to have arguments even then about various matters, but no longer in the old spirit of childish wrangling.

A little while after we removed to Moran's Garden. That was a regular palace. The rooms, of varying heights, had coloured glass in their windows, the floors were of marble, and steps led down from the long verandah to the very edge of the Ganges. Here a fit of wakefulness by night came upon me, and I used to pace to and fro, as I did later on the banks of the Sabarmati. That Garden is no longer in existence, the iron jaws of the Dundee Mills have crushed and swallowed it.

At the mention of Moran's Garden there comes back the memory of our occasional picnics under the bakul tree. The food owed its flavour not to spices but to the hands that prepared it. How I remember our sacred-thread ceremony, when we two boys were fed by Bouthakrun with the ceremonial rice and fresh ghee! For those three days we had our fill of tasty and savory dishes.

It was a great annoyance to me that it was so difficult for me to fall ill. All the other boys in the house could manage it, and then they would enjoy Bouthakrun's personal care. Not only did they enjoy her care, but also they took up all her time, and my own share of it was correspondingly diminished.

So came to an end that page of the history of tile third storey, and with it Bouthakrun also passed away. After that the second floor became my own domain, but it was no longer as in the old days.

I have wandered in my story up to the very gateway of my young manhood. I must return to the territory of my boyhood once more.

Now I must give some account of my sixteenth year. At its very entrance stands Bharati. Nowadays the whole country seethes with the excitement of bringing out papers, and I can well understand the strength of that passion when I look back on my own madcap escapades. That a boy like me, with, neither learning nor talents, should succeed in establishing himself in that salon, or at least in escaping reprimand there, shows what a youthful spirit was abroad everywhere. Bangadarsan was then the only magazine in the country controlled by a mature hand. As for ours, it was a medley of the mature and the crude. Badadada's contributions were as difficult to understand as they were to write; and side by side with them stood astory of mine, the raw verbosity of whose style I was too young to appraise, nor did others apparently possess the critical judgment to do so.

The time has come to say something of Badadada. Jyotidada held court in that third storey room, and Badadada in our south verandah. At one time he plunged into the deepest problems of metaphysics, far outside the range of our comprehension. There were few to listen to what he wrote and thought, and he would not lightly let any man go who showed himself willing to be audience. Nor would the man himself soon relinquish Badadada, but what he claimed from him was not alone the privilege of listening to metaphysics. One such man attached himself whose name I do not remember, but everyone called him "The Philosopher". My other brothers made great fun of him, not only about his love for mutton chops, but about his endless stream of varied and urgent necessities. Besides philosophy, Badadada then began to take great interest in the construction of mathematical problems. The verandah would be full of papers, covered with figures, flying about in the south wind. Badadada could not sing, but he used to play an English flute, not for the sake of the music, but in order to measure mathematically the notes of each scale. After that he occupied himself for a time in writing Svapm-Prayana. To start with, he began to experiment in verse-making, weighing the sound values of Sanskrit words in the scales ofBengali rhythm, and so creating new forms. Many of these attempts he retained, but many he threw away, and torn pages were scattered everywhere. After that he started to write his book of poems, but he rejected far more than he kept, for he was not easily satisfied with his work. We had not the sense to pick up and keep all these discarded lines. As he wrote he would read his work, and people would gather round him to listen. Our whole household was intoxicated with this wine of poetry. Sometimes in the midst of his reading he would burst into a great shout of laughter. His laughter was ample and generous as the skies, but woe betide the man who sat within reach when the fit took him; he received slaps on the back to shake his very soul. The south verandah was the living fountain of the life of Jorasanko, but the fountain dried up when Badadada went to live at the Santiniketan asrama, I remember, however, times spent in the garden opposite that south verandah, when with mind made listless by the touch of the autumn sun I composed and sang a new song: "Today in the autumn sun, in my dreams of dawn, a nameless yearning fills my soul." I remember also a song made in the quivering heat of one blazing noon: "In this listless abandon of spirit, I know not what games I keep on playing with my own self."

Another striking thing about Badadada was his swimming. He would swim backwards and forwards across our tank at least fifty times. When he lived at Panihati Garden he used to swim far out into the Ganges. With his example before us we also learned to swim as boys. We started to learn by ourselves. We would wet our pyjamas and then pull them up tight so as to fill them with air. In the water they swelled out round our waists like balloons, and we could not possibly sink. When I was older and stayed on the river-lands of Shelidah, I once swam across the Padma. This was not as wonderful an achievement as it sounds. The Padma was full of alluvial islands which broke the force of its current, so that the feat was not worthy of any great respect. Still, it was certainly a story with which to impress others, and I have used it so many times. When I went as a boy to Dalhousie, my father never forbade me to 'wander about by myself. With an alpenstock in my hand I traversed the footpaths, climbing one hill after another. It was most amusing to scare myself with my own make-believe. Once while going steeply downhill I stepped on a heap of withered leaves at the foot of a tree. My foot slipped a little and I saved myself with my stick. But perhaps I might not have been able to stop myself! I wondered how long it would have taken to roll down the steep slope and fall into the waterfall far below. I described to Mother with picturesque inventiveness all that might have happened. Then, wandering in the deep pinewoods, I might suddenly have come upon a bear that also was certainly something worth talking about. As nothing ever really happened I stored up all these imaginary adventures in my mind. The story of swimming across the Padma was much of a piece with to this class of romances.

When I was seventeen I had to leave the editorial board of Bharati, for it was then decided that I should go to England. Further it was considered that before sailing I should live with Mejadada for a time to get some grounding in English manners. He was then a judge in Ahmedabad, and Meja-Bouthakrun and her children were in England, waiting for Mejadada to get a furlough and join them.

I was torn up by the roots and transplanted from one soil to another, and had to get acclimatised to a new mental atmosphere. At first my shyness was a stumbling-block at every turn. I wondered how I should keep my self-respect among all these new acquaintances. It was not easy to habituate myself to strange surroundings, yet there was no means of escape from them; in such a situation a boy of my temperament was bound to find his path a rough one.

My fancy, free to wander, conjured up pictures of the history of Ahmedabad in the Moghul period. The judge's quarters were in Shahibag, the formergrounds of the Muslim kings. During the daytime Mejadada was away at his work, the vast house seemed one cavernous emptiness, and I wandered about all day like one possessed. In front was a wide race, which commanded a view of the Sabarmati river, whose knee-deep waters meandered along through the sands. I felt as though the stone-built tanks scattered here and there along the terrace, held locked in their masonry wonderful secrets of the luxurious bathing-halls of the Begums.

We are Calcutta people, and history nowhere gives us any evidence of its past grandeur there. Our vision had been confined to the narrow boundaries of these stunted times. In Ahmedabad I felt for the first time that history had paused, and was standing with her face turned towards the aristocratic past. Her former days were buried in the earth like the treasure of the yakshas. My mind received the first suggestion for the story of Hungry Stones.

How many hundred years have passed since those times! Then, in the Nahabat-khana, the minstrel's gallery, an orchestra played day and night, choosing tunes appropriate to the eight periods of the day. The rhythmic beat of horses' hoofs echoed on the streets, and great parades were held of the mounted Turkish cavalry, the sun glittering on the points of their spears. In the court of the Padshah whispered conspiracies were ominously rife. Abyssinian eunuchs, with drawn swords, kept guard in the inner apartments. Rose-water fountains played in the hamams of the Begums, the bangles tinkled on their arms. Today Shahibag stands silent, like a forgotten tale; all its colour has faded, and its varied sounds have died away; the splendours of the day are withered and the nights have lost their savour.

Only the bare skeleton of those old days remained, its head a naked skull whose crown was gone. It was like a mummy in a museum, but it would be too much to say that my mind was able fully to re-clothe those dry bones with flesh and blood and restore the original form. Both the first rough model, and the background against which it stood, were largely a creation of the fancy. Such patch-work is easy when little is known and the rest has been forgotten. After these eighty years even the picture of myself that comes before me does not correspond line for line with the reality, but is largely a product of the imagination.

After I had stayed there for some time Mejadada decided that perhaps 1 should be less homesick if I could mix with women who could familiarise me with conditions abroad. It would also be an easy way to learn English. So for a while I lived with a Bombay family. One of the daughters of the house was a modern educated girl who had just returned with all the polish of a visit to England. My own attainments were only ordinary, and she could not have beenblamed if she had ignored me. But she did not do so. Not having any store of book-learning to offer her, I took the first opportunity to tell her that I could write poetry. This was the only capital I had with which to gain attention. When I told her of my poetical gift, she did not receive it in any carping or dubious spirit, but accepted it without question. She asked the poet to give her a special name, and I chose one for her which she thought very beautiful. I wanted that name to be entwined with the music of my verse, and I enshrined it in a poem which I made for her. She listened as I sang it in the Bhairavi mode of early dawn, and then said, "Poet, I think that even if I were on my death-bed your songs would call me back to life." There is an example of how well girls know how to show their appreciation by some pleasant exaggeration. They simply do it for the pleasure of pleasing. I remember that it was from her that I first heard praise of my personal appearance, —praise that was often very delicately given.

For example, she asked me once very particularly to remember one thing: "You must never wear a beard. Don't let anything hide the outline of your face." Everyone knows that I have not followed that advice. But she herself did not live to see my disobedience proclaimed upon my face.

In some years, birds strange to Calcutta used to come and build in that banyan tree of ours. They would be off again almost before I had learnt torecognize the dance of their wings, but they brought with them a strangely lovely music from their distant jungle homes. So, in the course of our life's journey, some angel from a strange and unexpected quarter may cross our path, speaking the language of our own soul, and enlarging the boundaries of the heart's possessions. She comes unbidden, and when at last we call for her she is no longer there. But as she goes, she leaves on the drab web of our lives a border of embroidered flowers, and for ever and ever the night and day are for us enriched.

XIV

The Master-Workman, who made me, fashioned his first model from the native clay of Bengal. I have described this first model, which is what I call my boyhood, and in it there is little admixture of other elements. Most of its ingredients were gathered from within, though the atmosphere of the home and the home people counted for something too. Very often the work of moulding goes no further than this stage. Some people get hammered into shape in the book-learning factories, and these are considered in the market to be goods of a superior stamp.

It was my fortune to escape almost entirely the impress of these mills of learning. The masters and pundits who were charged with my education soon abandoned the thankless task. There was Jnanachandra Bhattacharya, the son of Anandachandra Vedantabagish, who was a B.A. He realized that this boy could never be driven along the beaten tract of learning. The teachers of those days, alas! were note so strongly convinced that boys should all be poured into the mould of degree-holding respectability. There was then no demand that rich and poor alike should all be confined within the fenced-off regions of college studies. Our family had no wealth then, but it had a reputation, so the old traditions held good, and they were indifferent to conventional academic success. From the lower classed of the Normal School we were transferred to De Cruz's Bengal Academy. It was the hope of my guardians that even if I got nothing else, I should get enough mastery of spoken English to save my face. In the Latin class I was deaf and dumb, and my exercise books of all kinds kept from beginning to end the relieved whiteness of a widow's cloth. Confronted by such unprecedented determination not to study, my class-teacher complained to Mr. De Cruz, who explained that we were not born for study, but for the purpose of paying our monthly fees. Jnana Babu was of a similar opinion, but found means of keeping me occupied nevertheless. He gave me the whole of Kumarasambhava to learn by heart. He shut me in a room and gave me Macbeth to translate. Then Pundit Ramsarbaswa read Sakuntala with me. By setting me free in this way from the fixed curriculum, they reaped some reward for their labours. These then were the materials that formed my boyish mind, together with what other Bengali books I picked up a random.

I landed in England, and foreign workmanship began to play a part in the fashioning of my life. The result is what is known in chemistry as a compound. How capricious is Fortune! – I went to England for a regular course of study, and a desultory start was made, but it came to nothing. Meja-Bouthan was there, and her children, and my own family circle absorbed nearly all my interest. I hung about around the school-room, a master taught me at the house, but I did not give my mind to it.

However, gradually the atmosphere of England made its impression on my mind, and what little I brought back from that country was from the people I came in contact with. Mr. Palit finally succeeded in getting me away from my own family. I went to live with a doctor's family, where they made me forget that I was in a foreign land. Mrs. Scott lavished on me a genuine affection, and cared for me like a mother. I had then been admitted to London University, and Henry Morley was teaching English literature. His teaching was no dry-as-dust exposition of dead books. Literature came to life in his mind and in the sound of his voice, it reached to our inner being where the soul seeks its nourishment, and nothing of its essential nature was lost. With his guidance, I found the study of the Clarendon Press books at home to be an easy matter and I took upon myself to be my own teacher. For no reason at all Mrs. Scott would sometimes fancy that I did not look well, and would become very worried about me. She did not know that the portals of sickness had been barred against me from childhood. I used to bathe every morning in ice-cold water—in fact, in the opinion of the doctors; it was almost a sacrilege that I should survive such flagrant disregard of the accepted rules!

I was able to study in the University for three months only, but I obtained almost all my understanding of English culture from personal contacts. The Artist who fashions us takes every opportunity to mingle new elements in his creation. Three months of close intimacy with English hearts sufficed for this development. Mrs. Scott made it my duty each evening till eleven o'clock to read aloud from poetic drama and history by turn. In this way I did a great deal of reading in a short space of lime. It was not prescribed class study, and my understanding of human nature developed side by side with my knowledge of literature. I went to England but I did not become a barrister. I received no shock calculated to shatter the original framework of my life—rather East and West met in friendship in my own person. Thus it has been given me to realise in my own life the meaning of my name.

www.ingramcontent.com/pod-product-compliance
Ingram Content Group UK Ltd.
Pitfield, Milton Keynes, MK11 3LW, UK
UKHW041415180426
11947UKWH00007B/146